THE POWER OF TWO

Leigh Vining

Supposed Crimes LLC • Matthews, North Carolina

This book is a work of fiction. Names, characters, places, and incidents are products of the author's imagination or are used fictitiously. Any resemblance to actual events or locales or persons, living or dead, is entirely coincidental.

Published in the United States.

ISBN: 978-1-944591-49-6

www.supposedcrimes.com

This book is typeset in Goudy Old Style.

This book is dedicated to my imaginary friends who have been with me from the beginning.

CHAPTER ONE

DESPITE A storm blowing in, a steady flow of traffic had come and gone all day at the New U Fitness Center in Redding, California. Business had been booming since Corey Preston had bought the gym on Main Street two years ago. It had taken some serious money for the up-to-date equipment—and for the state-of-the-art security features required for a gym to run twenty-four hours a day, seven days a week, and 365 days a year and to be unstaffed outside of normal business hours. So far, the investment had been worth it.

Moving away from his mid-west hometown and from his narrow-minded parents after graduating from college with a business degree had been the best decision he'd ever made. Life had opened up for him when he'd made the move to Northern California to live close to his uncle Ed and cousin Katie.

Ed had gone out on a limb, loaning him most of the money for the gym and had told him that, with his fancy degree and his way with people, he'd have folks standing in line to join. His cousin Katie had added with a laugh, that 'his dashing goods looks wouldn't hurt either.'

Having lost his train of thought while doing payroll, Corey looked up from his computer and sent his gaze through the foyer and out the front window and watched the cars coming and going in the parking lot. Between the beat of the music coming from the satellite radio, and the clang of heavy weights falling from the weight lifter's grip, it sometimes got a little too loud to concentrate. He'd also been covering Katie's duties for the past few hours while she was out on errands. It never ceased to amaze him how fast the trash cans filled up with disinfectant wipes, paper towels, and plastic bottles, and how often something needed to be mopped up, or the free weights put back into place. In addition, he'd signed up five new members in those hours, and had sold six T-shirts.

Checking the clock, and hoping she'd be back soon, he was relieved to hear her laughter from the weight room mixed in with the gym sounds. Peering out the partially opened office door, he was just in time to see her plant a big smooch on Alan, her muscle head boyfriend. *Shit, what does she see in him?* he thought, trying not to become overly annoyed at the sight of them together. He didn't want to stare but did anyway, as the kiss turned into something much too passionate for the time and place. The sight of those muscular full-sleeved tattooed arms wrapping around Katie caused his stomach to clench in revulsion. He'd seen what some of those tats were, and he'd found them quite distasteful, especially the one of the half-naked woman.

He instantly regretted gawking at them when Alan caught him and gave him an icy glare. Those deep, brown eyes always put Corey in mind of a storm brewing. Embarrassed at being caught staring, he looked away quickly.

Finally, Katie came breezing in, a dreamy smile on her face. "Hi, Cuz."

Corey sighed, and instead of saying what he was tempted to say, he asked instead, "How'd you do shopping? Get everything you wanted?"

"I did," she answered, flopping down in the chair across from him. "Even got a great pair of lime green and purple running shoes."

"You're planning to hit the treadmill?"

"Yeah, Alan keeps saying—"

"Alan keeps saying what?" he asked, not even trying to hide his disapproval.

"Alan thinks, uh, certain parts of me could use some sculpting. And don't be that way, Corey. It's obvious I could stand to lose a few pounds."

"Tell me you're kidding."

"Come on, I'm the manager of New U. I should look at least as good as the women who exercise here."

"And you do."

"Come on, Cuz. Cut me some slack. I know you're not a fan of Alan, but–"

"He's not the right guy for you."

"I think I'm the best judge of that, don't you think?"

He and Uncle Ed could see heartbreak ahead for Katie. They had discussed the relationship at length and it concerned them both very much, but the more they said against Alan, the more it seemed to push Katie in his direction, not to mention those arms of his.

Corey leaned back in the chair and cleared his throat, needing a change of subject.

"Wes will be in tomorrow to do repairs and adjustments on some of the equipment."

"That's nice," Katie said, obviously irritated. She reached into her purse and found her hairbrush, stood up and began giving her long brown hair a good brushing.

Corey lowered his gaze back to the computer and said softly, "Just thought you might want to say hi to him."

"I'm not interested in Wes anymore. We broke up. I'm dating Alan now," she snapped.

"You mean *you* broke up with him. I thought you were still friends."

"If you want to talk boyfriends, how 'bout we talk about *your* ex, shall we?" Katie said, roughly placing her brush on the desk.

"Keep your voice down, will you," he cautioned.

"Why, is he out there today?" Katie turned her attention to the video surveillance monitor above the desk.

"He's doing personal training with a new member."

"I really never understood why you decided to call it quits with him. I always thought you two made a great looking couple, both of you tall, dark, and handsome. By the way, while I'm on the subject of your good looks, isn't it about time for a haircut? I've never seen you this shaggy before."

Corey ran his hand through his chestnut brown hair and shrugged, ignoring the question about his hair.

"Your idea of a great couple wasn't mine. Can we drop it, please?"

"Let's make a deal. I'll stop talking about Dean if you get off my case about Alan."

Corey had to smile at the satisfied smirk on her face. "Okay, you win."

"By the way, plan to be home the day after tomorrow between eight and ten in the morning," Katie said.

"Why?"

"Part of my shopping involved getting you a housewarming gift. It's being delivered."

"You shouldn't have done that."

"I wanted to. It's not every day my favorite cousin buys a house. I'm real happy for you."

"Are you happy about my house, or the fact it freed up the garage apartment for you?" Corey smiled and giggled under his breath, knowing full well it was the latter.

Katie shot him a look. "I'm happy you bought a house—I'm not denying that it's nice to be out of Dad's, though, and have a little more freedom. Maybe even have friends over without feeling like I'm bothering him, you know?"

Corey wondered which friends she meant since all the free time she had was spent with Alan, but he just smiled at her and kept his mouth shut.

"Do you want me to take over in here now?" Katie asked, moving toward the chair Corey occupied.

"No, I'm fine for now. How 'bout you go run the dust mop around downstairs before the kickboxing class starts."

"If that's what you want me to do. Be back soon." She left the office leaving him to finish payroll.

It wasn't his normal routine to spend this much time behind the desk, but with Patty on vacation and Rhonda out sick, he was stuck for the time being. He preferred being out on the floor checking equipment or spotting someone or making sure the members were happy and the staff keeping them that way.

Once he finished on the computer, he grabbed a bottle of water and went downstairs to the lower level to oversee the new kickboxing instructor he'd hired. The guy was sexy as hell, and had a wife, but that didn't stop Corey from wondering what it would feel like to pull the band off the ponytail he wore and to run his fingers through that long, wavy hair. He watched the class too and was happy to see they were into what Mike was leading them through.

When it was time to close the office at seven o'clock, Corey watched as Katie began gathering her things to leave.

"What about you? You're not leaving too?" Katie asked, looking at Corey sitting behind the desk.

"We've got the new cleaning service starting tonight, and I want to be here to make sure they understand what's expected. I'd also like to run a few miles on the treadmill while I'm waiting."

"Oh, the cleaning service, I forgot. Okay, then. I'll see you tomorrow," she said, walking into the foyer toward the front door. Corey followed behind, stopping at the office doorway, glancing out the window.

"Drive safely. It looks like the rain's started again." He watched the parking lot video monitor as Katie got into her car. Not many people came to the gym at this time. *Probably home with their families having supper*, he thought, feeling lonely, as he visualized the stack of frozen dinners for one in his freezer.

After closing up the office and grabbing a bottle of water and his gym towel, Corey headed to the cardio room. He stepped on to his favorite treadmill in the front row, facing the Members' door. Almost on cue, the door opened.

"Hey, hey, hey, it's your lucky night," Dean said, plowing through the door, his words dripping with sarcasm.

"Why are you back?" Corey asked, irritated at seeing him twice in one day, but trying not to let it show.

"Is that any way to talk to your number one personal trainer?" Dean pulled off his hooded sweatshirt and stuffed it into a cubicle in the cabinet just inside the door.

Ignoring Dean for a moment, Corey programed his info into the treadmill and began a slow walk.

"I just thought you'd have done your workout when you were in earlier today."

"That's all, huh? It kind of sounded like you were disappointed that I came back."

Corey didn't answer the baited statement, choosing not to get into any kind of negative discussion with his ex. Dean wasted no time getting on the treadmill next to him and entered in his own routine.

Not able to help himself, Corey focused on the barbed-wire tattoo on Dean's bicep. He'd always thought it accentuated the well-defined muscle underneath perfectly. He shook his head and shifted his attention back to the small TV mounted on the front of the treadmill, trying to concentrate on the closed captioning that scrolled past, wishing he'd brought his earbuds with him. It would be a matter of moments before Dean started yapping at him, not caring at all that Corey was not in the mood for him.

"How'd Mike's class go?" Dean asked him, breaking into a jog.

Corey huffed in a lungful of air and raised his speed too, going straight to running, his eyes focused straight ahead.

"Mike's one sexy man. I'm sure you've noticed," Dean added, looking Corey's way teasingly.

Corey stared at the TV as he ran, trying his best to ignore the guy. He knew the chance was slim to none that the two gray-haired ladies riding the stationary bikes in the row behind them had heard Dean, since the rhythmic beat from their feet nearly drowned out his words, but it made him uncomfortable anyway.

After a few minutes of silence between them, Corey chanced another glance at Dean and saw amusement sparkling in his eyes, a look he'd seen often while they'd been together. He finally slowed to a jog, feeling the sweat on his forehead and on his neck, preferring to think it was the humidity in the gym getting to him, not Dean. It hadn't been that long since he broke it off with Dean, and he was still trying to find a way to coexist with him on a daily basis.

"I wonder if the two of us together could manage to convert Mike and have a threesome," Dean said, snickering, finishing that statement with a suggestive lick to his lips.

Corey almost tripped and closed his eyes for a few seconds, wishing Dean would shut up, or better yet, leave. But since that wasn't going to happen, Corey hit the cool-down button and walked for a few moments before stopping altogether. It was just like Dean to suggest something like that, and he sure didn't want any of the members to hear that kind of talk. He quickly wiped his face with his towel, took a swig of water, and slapped Dean on the shoulder, motioning with his head toward the office.

Once they were inside, Corey shut the door and set his water on the desk. Turning to Dean, he was caught off-guard by the seductive look in those all too familiar brown eyes. Before he had time to say a thing, Dean grabbed him in a tight embrace, planting a deep wet kiss on his mouth, pushing his tongue past his lips. Corey almost let himself respond to Dean's heat, especially when Dean pressed them so tightly together—there was no denying that his dick had missed this for sure, and the thin material of their gym shorts left no question that Dean felt the same. While Corey let the kiss happen, the only thought that popped into his mind was, *I need to get someone else in my life or I'm gonna end up back with this asshole.*

He used all the willpower he had to push Dean away; after all, he'd made the decision—Dean Powell was not the guy for him. He was his ex-boyfriend, and he couldn't let the wrong head do his thinking for him. It was true his dick had been happy during the six months they'd been a couple, but it hadn't taken long to realize that a successful relationship required more than sex. He was thankful that the head on his shoulders was doing his thinking now. In the things that really mattered—a quiet home life with one special person, not the lifestyle Dean was into—they just didn't have much in common at all. He wasn't into the party scene like Dean was— preferring to stay home and watch a movie rather than closing down the dance club every Saturday night.

"Come on, baby, relax," Dean murmured in that seductive tone that got him every time, trying to pull Corey back into his arms. "Your bedroom eyes are so dilated I can barely see any brown," Dean purred, but Corey stepped back.

"Knock it off," he said, as he stepped farther away, bumping into his desk chair, wiping at his mouth.

"Come on, babe, we can lock the door—"

"We are *not* doing anything like that, *babe*, for a lot of reasons."

"But you know you want it, I can see you do." Dean waggled his eyebrows and shot a pointed look at Corey's hard-on. "Well... if not here, then let's head back to my place, or better yet, how about you invite me over to your new house?"

"Not going to happen, either way. I'm moving on, and you need to forget about me."

Dean's sly smile indicated that he hadn't gotten through to him. "You may have moved on, but it's pretty obvious your dick still wants to be in the game. Maybe you should stop kidding yourself. We could sneak into the tanning bed. No one uses it this late."

"Are you out of your mind? This is where we work! This is my gym. I'm not doing *that* here and neither is anybody else!"

"Don't be a prude, man. I'll bet you haven't gotten any since we broke up, have you?" Dean stepped in close once again and tried to get another kiss started, running his hands over Corey's chest, tweaking a nipple.

Corey couldn't take it. He pushed Dean hard, sending him staggering back a few steps toward the door. "And how many one-night stands have you had in the last month, huh?" Corey snapped with anger.

"I'm not a monk—sure I've been out a couple of times, but that doesn't mean—"

"That's what I thought, and that's why it will never work between us. I'm just not interested in what you have to offer anymore. Now back off, will you?"

Dean gave him a pissed-off and disgusted look. It hurt Corey to see that, but he had to remind himself that he'd made the right decision all around.

"Look, I've got a new cleaning crew coming in soon and I've got to—"

"Yeah, yeah. Fine." Dean threw up his hands. "I'm outta here. Sounds like an exciting night for you." Dean had made air-quotes with the word exciting. Then he turned, yanked the door open, and stalked out of the office.

Corey dragged his eyes from the spot where Dean had been a moment ago and turned his gaze to the surveillance monitor. He watched Dean pull on his sweatshirt, stick his keys in his pocket, and then leave through the Members Only door.

Letting out a long haggard sigh as he checked the time, he realized the cleaning people were due any second. He adjusted his shirt and shorts, smoothed a hand over his face, glad that his dick was no longer a problem. He took in a deep breath and blew it out as he walked out of the office, through the foyer, and opened the front door to the damp night air. He stood there trying to regain some calmness, stretching slowly, wondering how he'd come so close to giving in to Dean's advances, and wishing he'd never see the guy again.

A definite chill had settled in with the light mist falling. He sure wasn't dressed for being outside and felt a bit foolish. The aroma of crisp baked crust, hot pizza sauce, and melted cheese from the pizzeria a few doors down, wafted toward him through the air. Normally it would have his mouth watering, especially considering he hadn't eaten since lunchtime, but he just wasn't interested tonight.

As he lingered a few more moments outside the door, he felt melancholy. He made a nice living from the gym, he loved the work and the people he worked with, and he'd just bought his first home. All that was missing was the right guy to share it with.

Was he a fool to have let Dean go?

Suddenly he felt much older than his twenty-six years. In the distance, he heard the long, lonely whistle of a train, and that added to the gloom settling around him, inside and out.

CHAPTER TWO

MEANWHILE IN *Northern Oregon...*

His breath came out in ragged gasps as he ran faster down the alley, but no amount of distance could erase the misery that had come crashing down on him on this chilly November afternoon.

Life as Nick Sanders knew it had changed in the blink of an eye. It wasn't as if he hadn't expected this to have happened. In some ways, he was ready for this change, but in others, he wasn't. Ready or not, there was no turning back now.

At the end of the alley he veered off into a field, trampling down the tall weeds while a horde of grasshoppers leapt in all directions around him, his heart pounding ever harder in his chest. He had to stop soon to catch his breath and think, because what he was about to do required a level head, not running off half-cocked like he was doing now.

Quickly heading up a hill to a crooked old tree, he rested against the rough bark and sucked in air as he glanced around him, sweat dripping down the side of his face. From this vantage point, he had a pretty good view of the rail yard below him, the tops of the freight cars pulling his attention. He set his pack on the ground at his feet, using the bottom of his hoodie to wipe his face and push strands of his sandy blond hair from his forehead.

He had stood here many times before, fascinated by the trains and what they represented to him. A freight train to *freedom*, just pack it all in and go. Yeah, he'd thought about stealing away for more years than he could remember, wondering if—or maybe, when—he'd ever be driven to this point. Now here he was. This time, not just imagining what it would be like, but carrying out his plan to disappear without a trace.

Crouching down to his pack, he pulled out a pair of compact binoculars. While he scanned the yard, he also listened for any indication that someone was nearby. Satisfied that he was still alone, he crept to the edge of the slope where he could get a better view of what was happening below him. Lying flat on his belly, he lifted his head and trained the binoculars on a few rail workers walking along the track, not seeing any sign of the railroad cops, but that didn't mean they weren't around there someplace.

The sun wouldn't be setting for a while yet, so, for now, he'd bide his time and wait for darkness and then, if luck was on his side, he'd be tucked away in a train car and not in a jail cell... or a hospital bed.

He rested his head on his pack and rubbed his eyes, the image of a teenager coming to mind, maybe sixteen, in dirty, ragged clothes jogging away from a train. He himself had been all of eleven, but he could still see the guy as plain as day. He'd watched the scruffy teen hop from the train then struggle up the hill holding his pack, breathing heavily, and he'd not been able to take his eyes off him. He could still hear the words the kid had said to him as he'd passed by—*it's the greatest thing I've ever done*—and then he had headed toward the field and disappeared. That had been his first up-close and personal glimpse of a real hobo, and it had left a strong impression.

A few years later, when he'd turned fourteen, he'd gotten hold of a documentary about train-hopping told through the eyes of several modern-day travelers. He'd watched that DVD over and over, memorizing the stories about hitching rides on the rails. Remembering, he closed his eyes and thought of his favorite part of the DVD. A dark-haired guy with curly hair telling what train-hopping meant to him—hitching a ride on a train represented the pursuit of freedom from the constrictions of society.

Feeling stiff, he sat up and glanced around, recalling a couple of vagabonds he'd crossed paths with a couple years ago. They had shared their experiences with him, and he'd tucked what they'd said away, just in case he ever needed it. 'It's safe, *if* you know what you're doing,' one had chuckled.

The other man had left him with these words. 'The world is there for you, just go and discover it.'

By sundown, he had a plan for his get-away. He'd picked out a few open boxcars that seemed like good choices, hoping he wouldn't have to change things up once he made his descent to the tracks. He knew full well he'd be risking his life hopping a train, but what *was* left of his life anyway? Crushing guilt threatened to overwhelm him, but he shook it off, clutching his pack close to his body. All he had left in this world was inside that small black bag, the rest of his things he'd left for his family. After what he'd done they deserved to have it. He didn't. He'd make new beginnings, make new memories, he didn't need much to live on.

As it got darker, the more nervous he became. He knew there'd be just a small window of opportunity to make his escape, and his success would depend on what he'd read from books, the internet, and the folks he'd spoken to who knew firsthand what it was like to sneak on to a freight train. There was an art to getting on and off a moving train. It required timely focus, but more importantly, going undetected. That was why he'd thrown on all black clothing before leaving the house. The rest of this plan would have to depend on skill, but mostly pure luck.

As the minutes ticked by, he felt a sense of loss—his life as he knew it was coming to an end. He had no idea where he'd even end up once he hopped the train, but he hoped he'd be a long ways from *here*. His plan just had to work, because there was no going back, that just wasn't an option for him any more.

He pulled his hood tightly around his face and sprang to his feet, hauling up the backpack and settling it on his back in one smooth motion. It was now that he needed to make his move. Crouching, he slid down the embankment and then quickly darted forward, not stopping until he reached a rail maintenance truck. He hunched down, his back against the side, catching his breath and wits, trying to stay calm. Luckily, in this low volume train yard, security was rail cops, not cameras or dogs.

He closed his eyes briefly and then peeked around the back of the truck. He didn't hear anyone, but that didn't mean they weren't nearby because it would be impossible to detect voices over the train horns and the clack of movement from the rail cars. The noise worked in his favor, masking any sound he might make in his approach, and this helped give him the confidence he needed to continue with his plan. He moved along to the front of the truck, ready to make a dash toward the boxcar he had in mind, grateful for the deep shadows that were cast from the rail yard lights. But he suddenly froze, squeezing his eyes closed tight. Two railroad guards appeared out of nowhere and passed within twenty feet of him. He mentally prepared himself for what would come next, but to his extreme relief the men walked on by, not missing a beat in their conversation. From the few words he caught it was obvious their minds weren't on their nightly patrol. If he were truly a religious man, he would have thrown up a prayer of thanks.

As the train whistle blared its final departure he snapped to attention. With adrenalin pumping through him, he sprinted as fast as he could toward an open car, but as he reached it the train was really starting to move. At first, he kept up with a brisk jog, but the train was speeding up. It was now or never, or his chance for escape would be blown, because he knew that if the train was moving faster than he could run it was way too dangerous to try. With such dim light, he couldn't judge distance properly. He kept losing his footing on the loose gravel, and he'd tripped himself several times jumping over the ties. Frantically, he raced beside the train chanting to himself, *"I can do this! I can do this!"*

Realizing he'd reached the point of no return—there were three cars left—he grabbed for the ladder that was attached to a refrigerated boxcar with an opening by the cooling unit that he hoped would fit him. As he hauled himself up his foot slid on the rung and he whacked his ankle good. Wincing, he squeezed inside the tiny space, his heart beating right out of his chest. As he tried to get comfortable his ankle gave a throb of protest, and he hoped like hell he hadn't broken it.

The deafening sound of the wheels on the track and the refrigeration unit cycling on and off made for a noisy ride, but that didn't bother him at all. He felt like shouting and pumping his fist in the air, and he would have if he hadn't been so cramped or scared to death of any chance of detection.

At first, he felt giddy having accomplished something so difficult and dangerous—stowing away on a rail car—but after about an hour of listening to the incessant drone of the compressor and dealing with a sore back and ankle, not to mention the wind sandblasting his face, he settled in for a long, miserable ride. He had no idea how long he'd have to stay in the confines of this tiny space, or if he'd be able to get some sleep, let alone eat. He didn't know if it would still be dark by the time the train prepared to stop, or if it would slow down enough for him to jump off before it pulled into another station. He counted on his ankle feeling better by then. So far this wasn't anything like what he'd read or what he'd dreamed. Maybe if he had more room it wouldn't seem so bad.

His stomach growled, and he thought about trying to root in his pack for a granola bar and some water, but he decided to wait. He might need to save what food he had, because who knew where he'd end up. His stomach rumbled again, making him think of his mother, her great cooking, and Thanksgiving, which was coming up later in the month. This would be the first Thanksgiving in his twenty-five years not spent with her or the rest of his family. This year, his brother would get his piece of pie. He could almost hear Richard teasing him in years past while reaching for his plate. *You're too full to eat your pie, aren't you, Nick?* He fought against the tears that flowed every time he thought about *them,* knowing crying wouldn't help anything, so he wiped at his eyes with his sleeve and took some deep breaths. After what he'd done, he wouldn't ever be welcome at his family's Thanksgiving table.

As he tried to shift into a better position, he wondered where he'd be for the holiday. Where would the train leave him after all was said and done?

One day at a time, he told himself, or maybe it would have to be one hour at a time. Shivering and desperately needing his jacket he carefully fished it out of his pack, keeping a tight hold on it as the wind tried to rip it away. He used it for a blanket, the pack for a pillow, and wedged against the cooler he hunkered down, waiting for his new life to begin.

CHAPTER THREE

EARLY THE next morning Corey headed to the gym, his windshield wipers on high since the rain was coming down hard. He made a left into the strip mall parking lot and drove his black Kia Soul toward the gym. Not one space was vacant in front of the main entrance, but luckily there was one about thirty feet to the left by the Members Only door. Once parked, he stared at the building wondering what he was doing there at five forty-five in the morning on such a cold and rainy day. It wasn't like he *had* to be there at the break of dawn, but since he hadn't slept well that night he'd decided to get up and do something useful, the gym being the obvious choice. Katie would certainly thank him for having most of the menial tasks taken care of by the time she arrived.

Snuggling deep into his coat he pulled up the hood, climbed from the car and hurried for the entrance, not surprised to see his breath in the chilly morning air. Once inside, he stopped to say good morning to a couple of regulars and then headed straight for the office. He had to admire those who didn't let the early hour, or the bad weather, stand in their way to a healthy life.

He hung his damp coat on a chair, and after booting up the computer and starting a fresh pot of coffee he checked the waste paper cans on the gym floor. He wasn't surprised to find them nearly overflowing and that the bathroom floors needed some touching up, despite the cleaning crew having been there the night before. They'd done a good job, but it was obvious there had been a steady stream of members through the gym since then. He pulled the trash bags out and tied the tops, taking them to the front door.

When fresh bags lined every can, he looked outside and was happy to see that it wasn't as gloomy as when he'd first arrived and that the heavy rain was fizzling into a light sprinkle. He headed back to the office and put his coat on, then grabbed the trash bags.

A blast of cold air hit him in the face as he stepped out the door. He trudged past several of the other businesses—standing quiet and dark—and headed toward the corner of the parking lot and the enclosed garbage bins. When he passed the smoke shop he had the same thought as always, that such a shop by a gym, vitamin store, and sporting goods store seemed out of place, but then again, so did the pizza place out near the street next to the hair salon.

As he approached the enclosure, a gust of wind rattled the large front metal doors used by the trash truck operator. When he entered through the small side walk-in entrance, he stopped in his tracks and sharply drew in a breath. He dropped the bags, not expecting to see a man slumped in the corner clutching a black backpack tightly to his chest.

"Jesus," Corey said out loud, his heart pounding, wondering if the guy was ill or the victim of a crime, or if he'd have to perform CPR in the next ten seconds. Taking a step forward, he was relieved that he didn't see any blood or visible injuries. He bent down for a closer look, and all indications pointed to the fact that the man was either asleep or passed out.

The hood that covered the man's head was wet, as well as the legs of his jeans, but the clothing covering his neck, shoulders, and back appeared fairly dry because of the small amount of shelter the tin overhang offered. His shoes were also most likely dry because of the plastic bags tied around them.

From what he could tell, it appeared this guy was close to his own age. He cautiously looked to either side of the man and didn't see or smell any liquor and wondered if what he was seeing was simply a homeless person seeking shelter from the cold and rain. He wanted to believe that anyway, and he didn't want to call the police if that were the case.

Hesitantly, he reached out and touched the man's arm, and then gave it a gentle shake saying softly, "Hey, are you okay?" When he didn't get any response, he shook him again, wondering once again if this guy was truly unconscious or was sleeping deeply.

It took several more hard shakes before he got any reaction, but finally, the man lifted his head and looked blearily at him. Corey was shocked at how beautiful this guy's eyes were—a beautiful piercing blue—and for a moment he forgot to breathe. He hadn't expected this guy to be so handsome—after all, he was just some vagrant sleeping next to a dumpster, right?

How did a guy like this ever get into such a state?

He didn't have long to think on that because the stranger suddenly jerked back with a strangled gasp, clutching his bag even closer to his chest and then began struggling to his feet.

"I was just trying to find a place to get out of the rain and must have fallen asleep. I'll get out of here," he stammered. Once on his feet, he hefted the backpack on to his shoulder, hanging on to the strap with both of his gloved hands. But instead of pushing Corey out of the way and hightailing it out of there, he just stood there, still looking dazed.

Corey wasn't sure what to say or do, he was so caught up in the whole bizarre encounter. Just a few moments ago he wasn't even sure if this guy was alive or not, but now here they stood, face to face, and there didn't seem to be anything wrong with him at all.

Looking directly into the stranger's face, Corey noticed that complementing those piercing blue eyes was a head of blond waves sticking out from the guy's hood, giving him a boyish, innocent look. He didn't look like any of the homeless people Corey had ever seen before. The clothes that fit this stranger so well weren't tattered and faded. Other than a stubbled face and rumpled wet clothes, this guy looked like he belonged at the gym or rushing off to a high-end job. Corey realized he was staring and, not only that, he was blocking the path out of the garbage enclosure.

He tried to step aside, but the space was too narrow to go far, so he picked up the trash bags that he'd dropped and hoisted them into the bin, giving them room to move back outside. Once they were a few feet away, Corey noticed the guy had a slight limp.

"Are you hurt?"

The guy looked down toward his foot. "Uh, I guess I must've sprained my ankle. It'll be okay."

"Are you from around here?" Corey blurted out.

"No... I'm just passing through," he said, stepping from foot to foot as if testing his ankle.

"You been hitchhiking?" Corey wondered if he was going to get any information other than just short answers to his questions.

A wry smile slowly spread across the guy's lips. "Yeah, you could say that."

Corey wondered about *that* answer. Either he had hitchhiked, or he hadn't. Why be so cryptic about it? Shaking his head, Corey realized he had been so distracted by the whole situation that he hadn't noticed that the rain had completely stopped, and the sun was trying to peek out.

"Corey Preston," he said, sticking out his hand because it just seemed the thing to do right then.

"Nick," was all the stranger said, as he pulled off his glove to shake Corey's hand.

Nick's hand was very warm considering the conditions, and Corey didn't want to let it go. He held on longer than he should have, because Nick broke contact, quickly replacing the glove back on to his hand.

"How long were you in there? You must be freezing in those wet jeans," Corey said because Nick did look uncomfortable—miserable—in fact.

Nick pushed up his sleeve and checked his watch. "A couple hours, maybe."

"Uh, can I give you a lift somewhere?" Corey asked before thinking the offer through.

Nick gave a slanted smile. "I've no place *to* go. Like I said, I'm just passing through and stopped to rest and get out of the rain for a bit." Nick smiled wider this time and it seemed friendly and sincere. "Thanks just the same, though." He pulled the collar of his jacket around his neck, aiming for the sidewalk, the plastic bags still tied around his feet.

Corey caught up with him in a few long strides. "You'll freeze to death walking. Let me drive you to the mission."

"You don't have to do that. I'll just find a bench where I can sit and think awhile 'till I decide where I go from here."

"You can get a hot meal there, change into some dry clothes, stay the night and rest up."

For a moment Nick stared at the traffic going by on Main Street as if deep in thought. He finally said, "Just point me in the right direction and I'll find it."

"But your ankle!" Corey protested. "And besides, the mission isn't within walking distance from here." He couldn't believe the way he was acting—begging Nick for permission to give him a lift. He'd lost his mind, that had to be it, because he was offering to take this guy, who he'd just found sleeping next to the garbage bin, across town to the mission. And that pack—the way Nick was clutching it made it seem as if he was trying to keep the contents safe. Corey hoped it was just something of sentimental value and not something sinister. He gave a slight shake of his head because his imagination was getting the better of him.

"Well, if you're sure." Nick finally relented, readjusting the pack on his shoulder, the slightest hint of a real smile curving his lips. "That would be nice of you."

Nick did look genuinely appreciative, which reassured Corey that he'd done the right thing by offering the ride. He took a deep breath and smiled back.

"Okay then. Follow me." When they reached his Kia, he said, "I'll be just a second, so wait right here."

He rushed into his office, frantically looking for the travel mug he kept. He yanked open a few drawers and finally found it, filling it with the coffee he'd made earlier and snapped the lid on securely. He then locked both doors to the office as he left with the mug in hand.

Once he made it back to his car, he was relieved to see that Nick was still standing there, but he had removed the plastic bags from his shoes.

"I thought you could use this," Corey said, noticing that his shoes looked to be in good shape. He handed Nick the mug and then unlocked the car door. "I wasn't sure how you took it, so it's just black. Hope that's okay."

Nick nodded, carefully taking the mug in his gloved hands. The longer Corey stood there, the more nervous and awkward he felt, so he automatically reached for the backpack. "Let me put that in the back."

Nick handed it over and Corey placed it in the hatchback and then got in, Nick following into the passenger seat as Corey started the car.

"Ready?" Corey asked, cranking up the heat. When Nick nodded, Corey pulled out of the lot and made a right on to Main Street heading to Warren Avenue. He was cold to the bone, despite the heat blasting out of the vents, so he knew Nick had to be a block of ice too, and that was proven by the way he was guzzling down the coffee.

"They'll give you something to eat at the mission," Corey said into the silence. "They're some really nice folks there. I volunteered to help with the Thanksgiving meal last year, and I've helped out some during their food drives too. You tell them Corey sent you and they'll treat you good."

Nick turned toward him and gave him a shy, lopsided smile, pulling off his gloves once more and pushing the hood off his head. "Okay, I'll be sure to do that."

As they crawled down Main—traffic was getting heavy now this time of the morning—Corey glanced at Nick and the world outside all but disappeared. The only two things he could see or think about for a few brief seconds were Nick's blue eyes and that mop of blond hair. Nick fit Corey's idea of the boy next door to a T—wholesome and unassuming—and his attention was definitely caught. Cutting his gaze back to the street and then once more to Nick, he again wondered what circumstances had brought Nick here, to this city he lived in, inside his black Kia on their way to the mission.

He supposed that after Nick got something to eat, changed into dry clothes, and got some rest that he'd be on his way again, because that was the way of transients, right?

He turned onto Warren Avenue, and all too soon they were parking in front of the old brick building of the mission also known as the homeless shelter. "This is it," he said, putting the car in park.

Nick had put the empty travel mug into the cup holder and had his hand on the door handle, pushing it open and stepping out.

"I'll need my bag," he said, looking toward the back of the car.

Instead of just unlocking the hatchback, Corey jumped out of the driver's side.

"Sure, I'll get it for you." He quickly opened the back, but before he could reach for the bag Nick got it himself and arranged it on his shoulder, smiling and sticking out his hand.

Corey took it and smiled back, liking the feel of that ungloved hand on his. This time when they shook, Nick held on a little longer than necessary, and Corey felt flushed when those beautiful blue eyes found his, holding his gaze for many long seconds.

"It was nice meeting you, and thanks for helping me out," Nick said, finally letting go.

"Nice meeting you too. Uhm. Good luck." He wanted to say more, but really, what else was there to say, standing out on the sidewalk with the car running, so he turned and got back in and drove off, leaving Nick standing at the curb.

Thirty minutes later, Corey was back at the gym keeping

himself busy at the computer, and when Katie arrived he was none too pleased that she was over a half hour late, and even less pleased with who had come in with her—Alan—who kissed her cheek before heading into the weight room.

"Sorry I'm late, Cuz," was the first thing she said when she breezed into the office. "I couldn't even tell if it was morning when I woke up it was so dark and dreary out," she added.

"Oh, is that your excuse?" Corey looked disapprovingly into the weight room where Alan was adjusting the Lat Pulldown machine. He didn't want to sound like a nag and pull rank on her but knowing full well that Alan was the reason she'd come in late he couldn't stop himself. "Well, it's not dark now," he continued sarcastically. "It's after eight thirty."

Katie just stared at him. "Well, I'm glad to see you're in such a good mood," she replied with equal sarcasm as she opened a cabinet and started folding T-shirts for members to purchase.

Corey didn't say any more. He just stared at the wall calendar where Wes's name was written in red on today's date. He was looking forward to seeing Katie's ex, not only because of getting the out-of-order equipment fixed but because he hoped Wes might be able to help him with the 'situation' between Katie and Alan.

Wes would be in at any minute, as he liked to get an early start, and it wasn't long before Corey saw the familiar white pick-up truck pull into the parking lot. He watched Wes park, get out of the truck, grab his toolbox, and head straight to one of the treadmills marked for repair, not bothering to check-in at the office. Corey figured he was trying to avoid Katie, which sure wouldn't help the cause, but there was no harm in asking.

Corey glanced at Katie, who was intent on opening a carton of protein bars not paying attention to who had just walked in. He frowned at her and headed to the cardio room.

"Hey, Wes," he said, patting the man in the red and black plaid flannel shirt on the back.

Wes looked up from the walk belt he was working on and removed his cowboy hat. "Hey, how's it goin'?"

"Real well. As you can see, business is so good the equipment is wearing out."

"Yeah. Definitely being put through the ringer," Wes said, examining the belt.

"You got that right," Corey answered.

"Keeps me in business, so I have no complaints."

"Yeah, uh, before you get too far into this, I was wondering..." Corey paused, noticing Wes wasn't paying attention to him or his work; his gaze had traveled across the gym to the weight benches. There was no way for Wes to miss Alan doing bench presses, his tattooed arms lifting enough weight to cause loud grunting to come their way. It sounded obscene, and Corey noticed frown-lines creasing Wes's forehead.

"I can't understand how Katie could go for someone like that when she had you—"

Wes stood then. "Hey, I really don't wanna talk about this," he said, turning his attention back to Corey.

"Well, I'm sorry to hear that, because I was hoping—well, I was hoping we could figure something out here."

"Figure out something about what?" Wes asked, tossing his wrench into his toolbox.

"Making Katie see what she had with you. Look. Uncle Ed and I think she's just rebelling. She just turned twenty-two—"

Wes interrupted again. "She's made her choice. She as much as told me I was boring. There's nothing you, or I, can do. I am what I am."

"But you'd take her back if she changed her mind, right?"

"In a heartbeat," Wes said, looking serious. "But it's just not gonna happen."

One look into Wes's eyes told Corey everything he needed to know. Wes was still in love with his cousin. He sighed and patted Wes on the shoulder.

"It wouldn't hurt if you poked your head into the office and said hi to her before you leave," Corey said.

"You expect too much, my friend. I'm not a glutton for punishment," Wes said, sounding more sad than mad, as he toed his toolbox.

"Well.... Ok, but if you brought your lunch, come on in to the office and eat it in there, and we can talk some more."

Corey felt guilty. He had no right to ask Wes to hang around after what Katie had done to the relationship, but he felt he had to try for Katie's sake, and for her dad too. Uncle Ed had worked himself into an awful state over Katie's new choice in a boyfriend.

With another pat on Wes's back, Corey left the man to his work. On the way through the weight room back to the office he came face to face with Alan—and if looks could kill. Evidently, he'd been seen talking to Wes and knowing Alan, he probably figured their conversation was about him and Katie and not just the repair work. He stepped around Alan thinking he *should* stay completely out of it and not meddle with the way things were.

After that, Corey hung around the office helping Katie with inventory until Rhonda came in at one thirty p.m., and then he decided to cut his workday short. Wes hadn't come in to talk, and Corey felt he should butt out—for now. Besides, Nick hadn't been far from his thoughts since he'd first set eyes on him early that morning, and he was having trouble concentrating. He wondered if Nick was still at the mission, how his ankle was doing, and if that injury was enough to keep him around for a while.

Corey had every intention to head straight for home, but he decided to take a side trip to the mission instead. He had no plans of going in, just to drive by and hopefully see Nick somewhere outside.

To his utter surprise, Nick *was* out in front of the old building, sweeping, and he must have recognized the car right away because he stopped, leaned on the broom and smiled. Corey had no choice now but to stop, not having any idea what he would say—it was like his body had become detached from his brain and he had no control. He parked at the curb and lowered the passenger side window when Nick started walking toward the car.

"Hey, stranger. Did they put you to work?" he finally asked when Nick stood close enough to hear.

"I volunteered. It's turned into such a nice day, I felt like being outside," Nick said into the open window.

"Your ankle's better?"

"Yeah, it feels pretty good right now. They gave me an ice pack earlier and I elevated it for a while. I'll do it again when I go back inside."

Nick looked a lot different from their first meeting—even better now that he'd shaven and had on dry, clean clothes.

"I hope they served you something you liked after I recommended the place and all," Corey said.

Nick's smile widened. "Everything was good. Everyone is real nice, like you said. Considering how my day started... well, it's ending up better than I expected, and I owe that to you."

"No problem." Corey nervously toyed with the sun visor, looked out the windshield, down at the steering wheel and then at Nick. "Uh... are you planning on sticking around awhile then, or are you ready to take off?"

"Not sure yet," Nick said, leaning on the broom again. His strong, steady eye contact made Corey wonder if Nick would like to get to know him better, just as he would like to get to know more about Nick.

Nick went on. "It seems like a pretty nice town from the few hours I've been here, friendly people so far." Nick switched the broom to his other hand. "I suppose it depends on what opportunities open up. If I can find work... sure, I could stay awhile."

Corey's heart skipped a beat at the possibility Nick might want to stick around. He sure was good to look at, but he didn't want to come across as trying to force anything, because what would be the chance? So, he tried to sound matter-of-fact. "Okay, I hope things go well for you. Maybe I'll see you around here or... town maybe."

"Could be," Nick answered, pushing his tousled hair away from his face and going back to sweeping.

As he pulled away from the curb, Corey glanced at Nick one last time and gave him a small wave. He tried to figure out what it was about this Nick guy that affected him so strongly. Sure, he was good-looking, and he did feel compassion for the man and his circumstances, but he knew absolutely nothing about him at all. Well, maybe one thing—unless his gaydar was totally off, and it seldom was—Nick *had* to be gay, if the looks he'd been getting were any indication. Or maybe that hand thing he did when he passed the broom to his other hand while they'd been talking.

He turned on the radio and headed for home.

CHAPTER FOUR

WAKING UP on the sagging cot, Nick was too tired to move more than his arm, so he lifted his wrist to check the time on his watch. Through heavy eyelids he made out the time, eight fifteen. He yawned and propped himself up on his elbow to check out his surroundings—a small, drab room at the mission. So, the train and ending up here hadn't been a dream. He'd had some pretty vivid dreams during the night though—things he'd rather forget.

He sat up on the edge of his temporary bed and rubbed his eyes. The old man who'd slept in the next cot was up and gone. He knew he should get up too, but he couldn't find the gumption to do so. Not having plans for the day was new to him. His work had been such a big part of his life, but he'd left all that, so what was he going to do now? He had no choice but to be optimistic, adapt, and start making plans.

Suddenly the idea of going back to the strip mall where he'd been the day before popped into his head. Besides the few people he'd encountered at the mission, he'd met Corey at the strip mall. Corey said maybe they'd run into one another again, and for some reason the thought of that lifted his spirits a little bit. He stood up, testing his ankle and it felt pretty good. His mother always used to say to count your blessings, and arriving here in one piece was a miracle, and for that, he was thankful. There were so many things he wished he could stop thinking about, and his mother was one of them. He stretched and reached for his pack to dig out some clothes and start the day, whatever it held.

Corey looked out his living room window to see if there was any sign of the delivery truck. Katie had told him they'd be there between eight and ten, and it was now going on nine-thirty. He was getting impatient, so instead of waiting in the house, he decided to head outside and walk around the front yard to pass some time. He had plans to landscape once spring came around, but until then, there was plenty of work inside the house to keep him busy for the rest of the winter.

Standing under the big fruitless mulberry tree in the middle of the lawn, he thought about how it had looked in the early fall when he'd moved in. The flaming color of its leaves had been a sight to behold, but its beauty had faded once the last leaf had fallen, making the tree look sad and lonely now. He looked forward to seeing it come back to life in the spring when nature made everything flourish once again.

The sound of a truck coming down the street brought his attention back to the present, only to find that it was Uncle Ed and not the delivery truck he'd been waiting on. He watched Ed park at the curb and then get out.

"Morning," they both said at almost the same time while walking toward each other.

Ed laughed. He had always been a morning person, so he was always extra cheerful then, and he loved his work and showed no signs of slowing down at sixty years old.

"You headed for a job?" Corey asked.

"Yeah, three streets over. I saw you out here, so I thought I'd stop a minute. So, your present hasn't come yet?"

"You know about that, huh?"

"Yep. Katie told me all about it. Was nice hearing her excited over something besides that new beau of hers." Ed rolled his eyes and pursed his lips with that statement.

Corey wished his uncle wouldn't dwell on Katie's involvement with Alan so much, but he'd always been very protective of her, especially after they had lost Katie's mother when she was just eleven years old.

"Well, I'm anxious to see what Katie got me. I'm thinking whatever's coming must be big if it's being delivered in a truck."

"You'll see soon," Ed said. "This isn't the best time of year for what she picked out, but you'll get some use out of it sooner or later."

"Well, go on, you've said that much—What is it?"

Ed laughed, held up his hands and took a few steps backward toward his truck. "I'm late. People are expecting me, gotta go!"

And, with that, Ed opened the door to his truck, but before getting in he took a step back toward Corey. "If you plan to help at the mission with the Thanksgiving dinner this year put my name down, if you don't mind. And if we do go, we may as well plan on spending the whole day there."

"The whole day?" Corey asked.

"Yeah, Katie made other plans—she's having her Thanksgiving with the muscle head."

"I thought he didn't have family here."

"He doesn't, it'll be him and some friends... and her."

Corey didn't miss the tone Ed used and the connotation he put on the word *friends*. "Sure, we can spend the day at the mission. It'll be nice," Corey said, suppressing a smile when the mention of the mission brought back thoughts of Nick.

Ed gave a half-wave and got in his truck and pulled away. Corey waved and then watched until the purple lettering that spelled out *Done Right Plumbing* became too small to read.

Less than a minute later the delivery truck from one of the local home improvement stores pulled up and two guys hopped out of the cab. They seemed to be in a hurry because they quickly made sure they had the correct address and then shoved paperwork toward Corey.

While Corey looked in surprise at what he had in his hand, the two workers rushed to the back of the truck and hauled out an antique bronze cast iron garden bench. It looked like it would seat two people easily, and it came with a cushion that looked very soft.

"Where should we put it?" one of the men asked.

"Uh, how about up on the porch," Corey said.

The conversation he and Katie'd had right after he'd bought the house was fresh in his mind. She'd looked at the porch and told him that he needed a bench where he could sit with a "special friend" once he got settled. Well, he didn't know if anyone would be sitting on it with him, but it was a sweet gesture, and he appreciated it.

Once the two men had put the bench where Corey instructed, they were gone as fast as they came. He took out his phone and snapped a picture of his new present and, knowing Katie would ask him if he'd tried the bench out, he sat down and patted the cushion on either side of him. It *was* actually quite comfortable, and he was impressed with her gift. He stretched his legs out and leaned back, trying to picture Nick sitting there next to him. He liked that idea, and that got him wondering if Nick would still be around on Thanksgiving Day, which was nearly three weeks away. Well, Nick or no Nick, he'd better make time today to swing by the mission to volunteer his and Uncle Ed's services for the holiday.

Between arriving at the gym later than usual, and the million little things that needed his attention, the day had flown by. He was anxious to leave, so he gathered up his jacket and keys, thanked and hugged Katie again for her generous gift, and all but ran out the door. But before he could get in his car, Dean-the-ex appeared from around the side of the Kia.

"Hey, babe, how 'bout we grab some coffee to unwind after a long day?"

"Why would we go and drink coffee together?" Corey answered, irritated, fumbling with his keys.

"Why not? I know you still want me. I'm still remembering our kiss from the other night and your reaction to it." Dean gave him a seductive smile.

"In your dreams," Corey said, keying the driver door open.

"I don't hold grudges. Unlike you. The past is past," Dean said.

Corey stared briefly at Dean and then sent his gaze to the sky. "You're right—the past is past." Bringing his eyes back to Dean, he said, "And to remind you, again—we have a past, not a future."

"Okay, suit yourself. If you get lonely, give me a call," Dean said abruptly.

Corey watched him strut his stuff to his jeep. Dean seemed far from heartbroken, and Corey figured his ex wouldn't be alone for long.

Driving toward the mission, Corey felt more and more apprehensive the closer he got. He wasn't sure what was making him so nervous—that Nick might have already left town, that Nick was *still* in town, or that he could possibly be seeing that handsome face and sexy smile again any moment. He didn't like admitting he was infatuated, how could he be? He'd spent maybe all of twenty minutes with the guy, but he couldn't deny that he was getting there fast.

Nick had said he had a mind to stay, so Corey tried not to worry that he wouldn't find him there. He slowed down as he came up the street, wishing Nick would be out in front like the day before, but instead of Nick there were just two old men sitting on the steps. Sighing in disappointment, or relief—he really didn't know which one—he parked the car, got out, and locked it.

"Hey, how's it going?" he said to the twosome when he made it to the steps.

He was eyed suspiciously, and neither one of them spoke. Corey shrugged and ran up the steps to the heavy, weather-beaten door, and pulled it open.

He scanned the great hall, hoping to see Nick among the people gathered there, but no such luck. The mission was a big place though and had many rooms, so Nick could still be around somewhere.

Taking another glance around, Corey looked for the shelter supervisor—or someone else he recognized—and wondered why no one was at the front desk. It seemed he'd caught them at a busy time, maybe because the dinner hour was near. Finally, he saw Mrs. Franklin, the program director, coming from a door at the back of the hall. She seemed to know him immediately and hurried over, holding out her hand and smiling warmly at him.

"Corey Preston, please tell me you're here to volunteer to help serve the Thanksgiving meal this year."

He shook her hand. "Yes ma'am, I'd like to put my name down, and my uncle's too, Ed Knight."

"Well, that's great, just great," she said enthusiastically. "Thank you so much. You were a big help last year, and this year you've recruited your uncle. How nice." She moved to the desk and rummaged around for a clipboard, handing it to Corey. "Just write both your names and phone numbers on the form, if you would."

He did as she asked and handed it back to her.

"You can't know how much we appreciate this." She placed the clipboard back where she'd found it and looked at him thoughtfully. "My daughter is a member at your gym. She keeps trying to get me to sign up."

"Well, whenever you're ready, come on over. I'll sign you up and get you started."

"I just might do that. Now, is there anything else I can help you with today, Corey?"

"Uh, I was wondering if... Nick was still here? I brought him around yesterday."

"Oh, you know Nick?" Before he could answer she went on. "He and a couple of others are painting at the Living Way church down the street. One of their pastors came looking for workers, saying they'd be paid. It was a good opportunity apparently, as they jumped at the offer."

A wave of relief washed over Corey at that piece of news, but his relief shifted to unease when one of the unfriendly old men he'd seen outside appeared next to Mrs. Franklin, scowling. "I don't like that Nick fella. Can't get a wink of sleep with him in the cot beside me."

Mrs. Franklin gave the man a concerned look. "What do you mean, Bob?"

"Nightmares. He had nightmares all night long."

"Did he?" she said quietly, almost to herself. "Hmm. We'll have to see if we can move him, so you can rest better tonight." She patted the old man on the arm and then turned to Corey. "Well, if that's all, I need to see to this."

"Of course. See you later," Corey said, doing his best to smile, but what the old man had said bothered him. Were Nick's dreams really that loud? What was he dreaming about?

Pushing those thoughts out of his mind, he drove toward the church, deciding on inviting Nick out for supper. He had no idea if he'd accept, but he was hopeful that he would because he sure wanted to get to know this mysterious stranger.

Parked in the church's parking lot and wondering if he should go in or wait, the decision was made for him when Nick and two other men came out of a side door and were headed across the parking lot. All three looked like they were leaving, probably headed back to the mission. Corey sat and watched, noticing that Nick was dressed in carpenter jeans, a white T-shirt, and a blue cap, and as he walked he was pulling on his black hoodie. Nick had a sexy physique, which Corey had seen a lot of in his line of work, but there was something special about this guy, the way he carried himself. He wasn't flaunting his good looks—he probably didn't even realize how hot he was—and Corey wondered how Nick stayed in such good shape.

Corey hadn't thought how he was going to invite Nick with those other guys around, so he decided to roll down the window and call out to him.

Nick turned and looked around, and when he was spotted, waved, then said something to the others, who continued on without him. He strode over to the open driver's side window.

"How you doing?" Corey greeted. "You're not limping at all."

"Yeah, it's close to normal. What are you doing here?" Corey could tell that Nick was glad to see him, judging from his tone of voice and his smile when he spoke.

"I was in the neighborhood and I decided to look you up," Corey said, feeling heat in his cheeks and hoping he didn't sound like he was coming on too strong.

Nick shoved his hands in his pockets and looked at the ground. All of a sudden he seemed ill at ease, or maybe even shy. Maybe Nick was self-conscious because of how they'd met. Damn, he didn't want that.

Corey smiled, and in his best attempt to break the awkward silence said, "I stopped by the mission to put me and my uncle's names down to help out for Thanksgiving and thought while I was there, I'd ask you if you wanted to grab a bite to eat."

"But I wasn't there," Nick said, lowering his gaze to the ground again and kicking at a pebble.

"Right... so I asked Mrs. Franklin where you were, and she sent me here. Uh... I hope you're okay with that. Look, if you'd rather I buzz off, I can do that too."

Nick made eye contact then, and that slow, easy smile Corey had seen before spread across his face. "No, I was just surprised to see you here, that's all."

"So, what do you say? You want to get something to eat? My treat."

"I guess that would be okay."

"Do you like sub sandwiches?"

"Sure."

"Well, get in and we'll go."

Corey put the car in gear and felt like he was on his first date, not just his first date with Nick, but his *first* date ever. He wondered if Nick considered this a date? More than ever now, his intuition told him that he and Nick batted for the same team.

"Shit, I hope I don't have paint in my hair," Nick said from the passenger seat. He removed his cap and ran his hand through his hair. "I might even have some on my clothes," he said, looking himself over. He sounded genuinely worried, like a little kid who might have gotten something on his Sunday best.

"I don't see any," Corey said, glancing over. "What color were you using?"

"Sahara Sands."

"Sahara Sands? What color is that?"

"It's Sahara Sands," Nick said, grinning. When Corey didn't say anything else, Nick added, "You might call it tan."

"What do you mean, *I* might call it tan?"

"Oh, I don't know, you just don't strike me as someone who goes for fancy color names."

There was that smile again. Corey couldn't help but smile back. "You're right about that, I guess. Tan is tan. Seems the simple way to go."

"Well, I'm a painter by trade, so I use the official color names for whatever paint I'm using. Depends on the brand I'm using. Tan can be Sahara Sands or Whispering Oats, or a number of other names."

"No kidding. So, you what? Paint houses and stuff?"

"Yeah, houses and stuff. I do murals too, personalized—whatever customers want."

"Wow, so you're an *artist*."

"Yeah."

Corey witnessed another toe-curling, shy smile, but he could tell that Nick wasn't willing to give any more on the subject. He had turned his head to stare out the window as they rode.

"There's a few days' worth of work at the church, so it looks like I'll be doing that for now," Nick said.

There was so much Corey wanted to know about this guy, but one thing he knew for certain was that Nick hadn't been homeless for long. His teeth were white and straight, and his blond curls had a healthy shine to them. His skin was smooth without blemishes, and his fingernails weren't ragged looking or broken down.

Corey made a right turn into the *Subway* and pulled into a space near the front of the building.

"We can go Dutch," Nick said before getting out. "I'm not completely penniless, and I'm being paid for the work at the church."

"No, I invited you, so it's on me." Corey opened his door and got out.

"Okay then, whatever you say," Nick said, joining Corey outside the car.

Nick hurried ahead a couple steps and opened the door for

Corey and then held it open for a couple with two young kids. They let the family order first while looking over the menu, and Corey found that their taste in food was the same when they both ordered the oven roasted chicken sub, baked chips, and Coke. Nick's enthusiasm while watching his sandwich being assembled made Corey smile. He wondered if being in a restaurant was a treat for Nick compared to having his meals at the mission.

Looking around the small seating area with the tray in his hand, Corey asked, "Where shall we sit?"

"How 'bout over there," Nick said, leading the way to a table next to a far wall. Corey gladly followed, and Nick taking the lead gave him more of a chance to check out the view from behind.

Once seated, Nick got comfortable, pulling off his hoodie and relaxing in his chair with his long legs extended and crossed at the ankles. Corey hoped he looked half as calm as Nick because he sure didn't feel like it. He wanted to impress this guy and show him a nice time so that maybe this would be just the first of many dates for them. At least he felt like he'd chosen the right place to eat judging from the way Nick was wolfing down his sandwich, so he didn't think Nick was just being polite when he'd copied his order.

"Good Italian bread, don't you think?" Nick asked after a few bites. Before Corey could answer, Nick commented on the Ranch sauce too.

A middle-aged couple passed their table, and when Nick jumped from his seat and went after them Corey didn't know what to think until he saw Nick reach for something on the floor.

"Ma'am," Nick called, and when he caught up to her, he handed over what looked like a bill and received a huge "Thank you."

Nick returned to their table, smiling ear-to-ear.

"What did she drop?" Corey asked.

"A dollar bill."

Corey smiled. "Nice of you to help her out that way." He took a sip from his straw. "Have you eaten in a *Subway* before?"

"Yeah, a few times," Nick answered, and then he let out a huff of laughter as if something funny came to mind.

Corey waited for him to say more, and after a few more seconds Nick chuckled and leaned a little closer as if trying to make sure no one but Corey would hear. Seeing Nick's grin made him fight to suppress a giggle.

"One time I was in this sandwich shop—not a *Subway*—and after

I ordered, and the waitress turned around, I saw this—"

It was obvious Nick was trying hard not to burst out laughing before he could finish the story, but whatever was coming had him on the brink of a full-out laugh.

"There was this—" He swallowed, then glanced around like he was making sure no one would overhear. "It was a huge—no, more like ginormous—*cockroach* hanging on her apron!" Nick went into a deep belly laugh, and Corey let out one of his own. Through his laughter, Nick said, "I wondered if it was her pet or something, the way it was clinging to her."

Another round of laughter burst from both of them. When Corey's laugh had died to a giggle he asked, "Was it wearing a collar and leash?"

That brought on more uncontrollable laughter, and Corey noticed a few people looking their way. He hadn't laughed that hard in ages, and it felt damn good. Being with Nick was *damn* good. He could hardly keep his eyes off Nick while they finished their food. He'd enjoyed himself so much he felt like he'd fallen under some kind of spell.

Corey wished they could stay longer, but he noticed other customers looking around for an open table, so it was time to go. Even though the conversation had been superficial, Cory felt like he'd gotten to know more about Nick—he had a good sense of humor, he was well mannered and easygoing, and he was someone Corey wanted to spend more time with.

It was eight thirty when Corey and Nick pulled up next to the curb near the lone streetlight that lit the mission. The porch lights on either side of the mission door gave off a welcoming glow, much more welcoming than the two old men had been earlier.

"Too bad you don't have your jacket. It's damn cold out tonight," Corey said.

"I don't have far to go," Nick answered, his hand on the door handle. "Thanks a lot for dinner." He turned toward Corey and seemed to study his face for a few seconds.

Even in the dim light, those blue eyes sparkled, and Corey had the urge to lean over and kiss Nick on his hot and inviting lips, but he thought better of it. Instead, he reached into the glove compartment, and when his arm brushed Nick's leg he felt his temperature rise a notch and wondered if Nick felt the same, since it seemed Nick pressed slightly against his forearm.

"Give me a call if you want to get together again," Corey said, handing Nick one of his business cards, feeling another spark as Nick's fingers grazed his.

Nick shoved it into the pocket of his hoodie and paused for a few breaths and then opened the car door. "Okay, thanks. I'd better go check in," he said, stepping out into the cold November night.

Corey watched him until he disappeared into the mission and hoped he wouldn't have long to wait for that call.

Nick eased the door open and stepped into the silence of the great hall. The warmth of the room was all that greeted him. He expected to see someone to check-in with, but no one was in sight. Standing in the middle of the room with his hands in his pockets, he realized that the fingers of his right hand were wrapped around the business card Corey had given him. He brought it out and slowly read each word printed on the card.

He'd had a good day all things considered, and he'd felt at least semi-useful while painting at the church. Then seeing Corey waiting for him outside had cheered him up. The evening at the sandwich shop had let him push his problems aside awhile longer. Corey was great company and talking and laughing with him had sure felt good. Something else had felt good too—sitting in the dark car next to him. The thought occurred to him that he might have stared at Corey's lips too long, but it had been all he could do to pull his eyes away. He sensed that Corey might have felt the same way too, but he wasn't sure. Corey had given him his card though, so he must want to see him again.

He remembered how it felt to kiss a man. Immediately he pushed that thought out of his mind—nothing good had come from that, in fact, it had been a disaster... but what about Corey? Different place, new life. Studying the card once more, he placed it into his T-shirt pocket for safekeeping.

He quietly headed down the long corridor toward the bedrooms just as his roommate was leaving the bathroom.

"You ain't in the room you slept in last night," the old man said gruffly.

"Why's that?" Nick asked.

"Mrs. Franklin moved your bag across the hall. There's another fella in with me now."

The old man didn't stick around to answer any more questions, so Nick went into the room that he'd indicated, and sure enough, there was his bag waiting for him. No one else was there, so he picked the cot he wanted, not that one was any better than the other. With a sigh, he sat down, a little confused, but maybe that was how they did things around there. He appreciated the roof over his head, but this just wasn't going to work out for him long term. He needed to make plans—first off, decide if it was worth staying in this town or if moving on was best for him.

CHAPTER FIVE

AFTER SITTING for most of the morning, Corey got up from the desk to stretch his legs. He walked out of the office to the front window to watch Patty show the woman they'd just signed up how to use her key fob to open the Members Only door. When Patty seemed satisfied that the new member was all set, she turned back toward the main entry while the member walked toward a little Fiat. He always wondered why new members seldom worked out right after they signed up. Maybe they needed to psych themselves up first, or maybe get their brains wrapped around the idea of exercising. Maybe he expected too much out of people.

He sighed as he stared out the window at nothing in particular. He tried to convince himself he was thinking about the woman who'd just left, but he had to admit it, his thoughts were constantly about Nick, and why he hadn't heard from the guy. It'd been three days since he gave Nick his card with the phone number on it.

He'd felt plenty disappointed at the end of each day after not receiving a call. They'd gotten on well at *Subway* the other night, and he'd been optimistic they'd soon get together again. Maybe he shouldn't have given Nick his card and left the ball in his court, because now if he were to look Nick up, he'd surely come across as pushy if he hadn't already. That was probably it—he'd come on too strong.

Had he been wrong after all about Nick being gay? He still didn't think so, but gay or not, their tentative relationship, or whatever it was happening between them, wasn't an ordinary situation, and he had to keep reminding himself of that. The way they'd met wasn't very conventional, to say the least. But even if Nick wasn't interested in a dating relationship, having just gotten to town, wouldn't he need a friend? Corey would be happy to be Nick's friend if that's all he wanted.

All these thoughts had him wondering if he was being selfish. Nick had to have a lot more on his mind right now than calling someone he just met, because after all, less than a week ago he was sitting next to a trash bin in the rain. He was homeless, and Corey had no idea why or how he got to be that way. Something bad must have happened to cause him to leave where he'd come from. He hoped he'd find out what that might be sooner rather than later.

One of the reasons the situation was really bugging him was because he'd been tossing around an idea in his head that might help Nick, and him both. But, if Nick never called, how could he proceed? More than ever, he had the feeling that he'd really blown it somehow.

He closed his eyes and rubbed his temples. Maybe he hadn't considered the situation from all angles. Maybe Nick didn't have his own phone or have access to a phone at the mission. Or maybe he was uncomfortable talking on a public phone with so many people around. Maybe the reason was as simple as that.

He snapped out of his thoughts and realized that Katie had finally arrived for work and was talking and laughing with Patty outside the front entrance. They both looked like they'd been caught with their hands in the cookie jar when they noticed he was looking at them. They hurried inside just as the phone rang, so Patty rushed into the office and picked it up on the second ring.

"Morning, Katieeee. Or is it afternoon?" he said with a bit of teasing snark to his tone, making a big production of looking up at the clock on the wall.

"Fifteen minutes left to go, so good morning to you too. And thanks for letting me come in late today," she answered. Her smile lit up the whole foyer.

Patty stuck her head out of the office door. "I'll take my lunch now if that's okay." She winked at Katie.

Corey looked from Patty to Katie. "Go on ahead," he told Patty, feeling that something was up with Katie. The sooner he could get her alone, the sooner he could find out what was causing those *looks* between the two of them. Patty grabbed her purse from the office and left so fast Corey wondered if the office had caught on fire while he'd had his back turned.

"If you've got a few minutes, uh... there's something I wanna show you," Katie said in a near whisper, trying not to giggle.

"Uh, is it good or bad?" Corey asked as he followed her into the office.

Katie closed the door that looked out into the weight room. "You've gotta promise me you won't freak out, and the main thing you've gotta promise—" And here she paused, Corey waiting for the bomb she was about to drop. "—Is that you won't tell my dad."

She had her big bright smile going again as she asked for these promises, so he figured it couldn't be anything *that* bad, although he did wonder why she told him not to freak out. Maybe it was some sort of surprise for Uncle Ed.

He rubbed the back of his neck, staring down at the floor for a moment then looking back up at her, wondering how women could manage to be so perplexing. "I hope I'm not going to be sorry, but yeah, I promise."

Katie craned her neck toward the front window, obviously checking to make sure no one was coming in and then she even went to the doorway leading to the foyer, giving a quick glance around there. She gave a nod of satisfaction, and without another word, she turned to face Corey with her hands clasped in the middle of her chest, looking like an excited child. She took a step toward him, turned her back, and pulled her long hair to one side.

He stood there stunned at what he saw between his cousin's neck and shoulder. His mouth hung open, and he blinked a few times in utter surprise at what he was seeing. "Oh. My. God."

Katie turned back to face him, letting her hair fall back into place. "Is that all you have to say?" she asked in a teasing innocent tone.

Corey drew in a deep breath and let it out slowly. "Uh... what do you want me to say?"

"Do you like it? Isn't it beautiful?"

The butterfly tattoo she now sported was very pretty, he couldn't deny that, but it was large. The colors were a bit bright for his taste, mostly greens and reds, with gold dotted in as accents. "It's... nice," he finally said.

"I love it," she exclaimed. "I had it put where I can hide it from you-know-who. He'd have a total cow about this, you know that."

"Then why did you do it, knowing how your dad would feel?"

"Cuz. I can't live my life for Dad. I have to live it for myself. You of all people should understand that."

Corey caught a hint of shininess in her eyes. He walked over and hugged her. "Alan put you up to this, didn't he?"

She squirmed out of the hug and huffed. "There you go again, talking down about Alan. I don't want to hear it, Corey."

"I didn't mean anything by it. I was just saying—"

"You think the only reason I wanted a tattoo is because Alan likes them. Well, I have news for you."

Corey placed his hands on her shoulders to try to calm her down. "It's okay—I'm glad you showed it to me. It looks really nice."

He actually wasn't sure how he felt about the thing, but if she liked it, that was what counted. He sure had a bad feeling, though, about Uncle Ed seeing it.

"Okay, so you promised not to say anything to Dad about the tattoo," she said, looking him straight in the eye, all traces of unshed tears gone.

He grinned. "What tattoo?"

Corey closed up the office and locked the main door after Katie and Patty left at seven o'clock. He wanted to stay and put in a hard thirty minutes on the treadmill, and once he had a good run going, he relaxed because Dean hadn't shown up to interrupt him. He lifted weights after that, stalling because he wasn't anxious to go home to a cold empty house. While doing his last set of bicep curls he wondered if he should get a dog for a companion, but quickly pushed that idea out of his mind. He didn't need a pet. What he needed was someone to share his life with, someone to talk to and eat meals with, someone to make him a better person, someone to come home to every night, someone to love and be loved back.

He took his time in the shower, and then he talked to a few people who were working out, but he was careful not to get in their space and slow them down. So, after several minutes, he decided to call it a night. He said good night to the members, surprised that it was almost nine. Resettling his gym bag strap on his shoulder, he went out into the breezy, chilly night.

As he stepped off the sidewalk bordering the parking lot, a gust of wind swirled dirt and debris around his legs. He pulled his jacket tight around himself and continued toward his car when he heard his name. He looked around and didn't see anyone, so he kept on walking, but then he heard his name again. The familiarity of the voice caused some serious fluttering in his stomach, and he knew it had to be Nick.

He stopped a few paces from his car and stood still trying to locate the source of the voice when suddenly a form dressed in black emerged from between a dark gray van and a big, black pick-up truck. Corey took a step back, somewhat spooked, but seeing Nick's easygoing smile had him letting out a long breath, a rush of foolishness slamming through him.

"Hey, Nick, it's been awhile," he said, trying to shake off a flow of emotions.

"Yeah. I've been waiting for you to come out," Nick answered, giving a nod toward the gym's main door.

"If I'd have seen you, I'd have let you in."

"The posted hours say you close at seven. I tried the door, but it was locked, so I wasn't sure how to get in." Nick laughed softly, looking toward the door marked 'Members Only'. "I saw people going in this other door, though."

"Oh, yeah. Well, if you come by during business hours, you can come in the main door. After that, only members with a key fob can come in the Members' door, but like I said, I'd have let you in if I'd known you were here."

"That's okay, I didn't mind waiting. I saw your car, so I knew you'd be coming out eventually."

"How have you been?" Corey asked.

"Good. I've been good. Finished the job at the church and been looking for another, but so far, no luck. Got enough cash to keep me afloat for a while though, in fact, that's why I stopped by. I thought if you're free, I'd buy you a pizza." Nick looked toward the nearby pizzeria.

Corey's butterflies started flapping their wings again. "Uh.... That would be great. I'm starving, actually." He caught himself grinning, rocking back a bit on his heels, but he didn't try to rein it in. After all, this is what he'd been hoping for since he'd given Nick his card, and now it was happening.

They walked side-by-side the sixty some feet to the pizza restaurant, and when they got to the lighted doorway, Corey opened the door to let Nick enter first.

"Thanks," Nick said, as he pushed his hood off, his mop of unruly hair making Corey feel weak in the knees. He really liked those curls.

Corey followed Nick up to the counter. "What's your preference?" Nick asked.

"I usually have Canadian bacon, mushrooms, and olives," Corey said, looking up at the menu mounted above the counter behind the cash register.

"Sounds good to me." Nick smiled at the young man who was waiting on them and gave him the order. "And drinks—Coke okay?" he asked Corey.

"Fine with me."

They chose a table and sat, sipping on their drinks while waiting for the pizza. Nick reached into his pocket and pulled out the business card that Corey had given him. He held it up like this was the first time he'd read it.

"It says here that you're the owner of that fancy gym next door."

Corey smiled, finding it hard not to feel proud. "That's right. I'm a businessman." He felt good to emphasize that word and felt even better to see Nick smile.

"How long have you owned the gym?" Nick asked.

"A couple years now."

"Seems like you're pretty successful. While I was standing around outside, I saw a lot of people going in and out."

"Yeah. The gym does all right." Corey felt shy and wanted to say more about his successes, but he didn't want to sound like he was bragging, since Nick had no job, let alone a permanent place to stay.

"Hard work though?"

"I do put in a lot of hours, but I like what I do."

"That's what counts." Nick leaned back in his chair and looked up at the ceiling. "It's like this huge two-story house I was painting a few months ago, putting in ten hours a day...."

Corey noticed a sad tone to Nick's voice and saw a faraway look flash in his eyes, but their pizza came, and the mood changed. Nick dove into his share like he hadn't eaten all day and didn't speak while he stuffed his face. Corey even let him have more than half of the pie.

When Nick finished the last bite, he wiped his mouth and leaned back in his chair. "I've never had that combination of toppings before. It's something I'd have again. Totally delicious."

Corey smiled and sniggered, looking at the empty pan and all the napkins littering the table. "No kidding. I'd never have guessed you liked it."

Nick let out a deep laugh like he was being thoroughly entertained. "I figured a man like you, you know, a man like you who wants to set a good example to all your members, wouldn't want to overdo it on the pizza, so I thought I'd help you out by eating more than my share."

Corey loved how Nick's eyes danced with mischief. Just looking at the guy made him hard. He couldn't imagine what it would be like to touch him. Well, actually he could, and he wanted that with every fiber of his being.

"If you're like this drinking Coke, I'd hate to see what you'd be like on beer."

"You're allowed to drink beer?" Nick asked, brows arched, obviously trying to look serious.

"I don't look of age?" Corey shot back, playfully.

That brought another hearty laugh from Nick. "I'm robbing the cradle," he said after his laughter had died down.

Corey let that statement sink in for a moment. It seemed they were on date number two, or at least he was seeing this as their second date. "I'll have you know, I'm way, way past twenty-one."

Nick sat quietly, his eyes glued to Corey's, and a slight smile lifted the corners of his lips. "Well, I'm twenty-five, old enough to know better and too young to care."

Jesus. Corey felt his pants threaten to cut off his circulation. "Uh, I'm twenty-six." He wondered if he was blushing. It sure felt hot in there.

"So, you're an old man then, huh?"

Corey rolled his eyes and couldn't help but laugh with Nick. When they were joking around, like right at that moment, it seemed like they'd known each other longer than just a week.

But then, Nick looked serious all of a sudden, as if all his problems had come into focus again. Corey's spirits fell as well. He'd been having such a good time, and it seemed like Nick had too, but now the reality of the situation was staring them straight in the face. They weren't simply two guys who had just met and were becoming friends—Nick was a man carrying some kind of burden—Corey could see it in his eyes, could see the pain that lurked there. That made his heart ache.

"Sometimes I feel like an old man," Corey said, stirring what was left of his Coke with his straw.

He realized Nick was looking at him, waiting for him to say something else so he went on. "Uh, I can't really complain. Like I said earlier, I enjoy my work, but work isn't everything." Corey felt uncomfortable getting into that topic, so he stopped before he said something awkward.

"I hear you," Nick said, his eyes still carrying that haunted look. "Have faith, I have a feeling you'll get everything you want in time. Every day's a second chance." After a few seconds of silence, he went on. "I guess it's about time to go before they throw us outta here. It is pretty late." He stood up and put his jacket on, and Corey did as well.

When they both were out on the sidewalk, Corey said, "I can give you a ride back to the mission, if you want."

Nick stuffed his hands in his pockets and kicked at the ground. "I've moved out of the mission."

"Oh? Where are you living, then?" He hadn't expected to hear that and was quite surprised about it.

Nick clenched his jaw ever so slightly, but Corey noticed it and read that as discomfort. He regretted having asked, but hell, what kind of relationship could he hope to have with the guy if he couldn't even ask a simple question? He studied Nick's face and waited for an answer.

"I didn't want to keep imposing at the mission, and if I'm being honest, it was hard being there with so many people, you know? So, yeah, I decided even though I can't afford much I needed to leave there."

Corey could hear the sincerity in Nick's voice and appreciated that. Seemed Nick wanted to stand on his own two feet and not be a freeloader. "Well, I can give you a lift to wherever it is you're staying," he offered.

He waited patiently while Nick made up his mind on what to do. He hoped Nick trusted him enough to share his new address with him.

Finally, Nick said, "I'm renting a room by the week, over on Crown Street. You know the area?"

Corey knew the area and it wasn't the best part of town by a long shot, but he tried to act as if it didn't faze him. "Okay, I'll drive you over there, not a problem."

"Thanks. It's a roof over my head and that's about it," Nick said. "I won't even be able to afford that for long if I don't find work. I pounded the pavement all damn day today and even checked the want ads in the paper, but I haven't found anything that I'm qualified to do."

"You know," Corey said excitedly, as he waited until Nick gave him his attention. "I have something to run by you. Something that will help us both out. You game?"

"I'm all ears," Nick said, smiling slightly.

"Come with me and tell me what you think." Corey pulled on Nick's jacket sleeve to get him walking in the right direction. Nick followed behind him and they stopped at the door leading into the gym.

"I've been thinking of having some painting done," Corey said matter-of-factly. "Let me show you around and you can tell me your opinion on what I have in mind."

As Corey unlocked the door, Nick looked skeptical, like he might have something to say or to argue against Corey's suggestion, but Nick stayed quiet and gave a slight nod of his head. Corey held the door open and Nick walked in, stopping short inside the doorway. Corey was glad there wasn't much of a crowd, just seven people he could see scattered among the weight machines and two on the bikes.

"Nice place," Nick said, glancing around, and the way he was looking at what he saw, Corey knew Nick really meant it. "Looks like it would be easy to stay in shape here—that is, if a person can figure out what all this stuff does." Nick rubbed the back of his neck, and the look of confusion, made Corey wonder if he'd ever seen the inside of a gym before.

"Check out the lower areas of most of the walls," Corey said, walking over to the closest wall and stooping down to run his hand over some black smudge marks on the green surface. "This is from the members leaning weights against the wall. As you can see, I have signs up asking them not to do it, that we have weight racks, but—"

"Maybe you need a security guard more than a painter." Nick grinned.

"I don't think that would go over too well," Corey said, smiling back.

"Yeah, you don't wanna push your luck there. You've got a good thing going here." Nick glanced around again, seeming to focus on the larger pieces of equipment.

"Another idea I've had is over here." Corey led Nick to a smaller wall between the cardio room and weight room. "I've been wondering if I should have a mural or our logo painted on this wall.

Do you think that would look good? Could you do something like that?"

Nick seemed deep in thought, looking at the wall from different angles. "Yeah, I'm sure I can do something here. I could make a few sketches for you, then you could take your pick.... uh, if you decide to hire me, that is."

"If you want the job, it's yours."

Nick gave him a half-smile and nod. "You really don't have to offer me a job. I'm sure something'll turn up. And besides, you don't know I'm that good."

"Like I said, I've been wanting to do something to spruce the place up. It's a win-win. I get what I want, and you get a paying job, and I'm pretty sure you're that good."

Corey sensed that Nick wasn't totally comfortable about the arrangement, but at least he'd agreed, and Corey was anxious to see where it could take them.

"Let me show you the rest of the place and then we'll go into the office to work out the details—uh, you know," Corey paused a moment. "I don't think you've ever told me your last name."

Nick swallowed hard and looked off to the side toward the wall they'd been discussing. Corey waited, and in a mumbled whisper, Nick said, "Stewart."

Corey didn't say anything, but for the first time since they'd met, he wondered if Nick was being truthful. He had sure gotten tense at the mention of his last name. But Corey had no intention of calling him out on it, so without missing a beat, he headed to the office, pointing out the bathrooms, vending machine, and janitor closet on the way. He unlocked the office door, flipped on a light, and invited Nick inside.

"Have a seat." Corey motioned to the chair in front of the desk and then he sat down across from Nick. He reached to the left of the desk and opened the drawer in the copier and took out a piece of paper and slid it to Nick. "Take this with you so you'll have the logo to work with."

Nick took the paper and studied it briefly. "I'm sure I can do something creative with it. Are you thinking of keeping the walls the same colors or would you be open to a change?"

"I'm open to change, but I'd like to keep it bright and bold."

"Sure. Pastels don't fit in a place like this."

Corey wasn't quite sure if Nick had just winked at him. He blinked, and the moment passed as fast as it had come, but it did seem the awkwardness Nick had displayed earlier had gone, and Corey's gut feeling told him not to mention Nick's last name any time soon.

"I think the simplest thing for both of us is for me to just pay you under the table."

"Fine with me," Nick was quick to reply. "I'd prefer it that way."

They then discussed fees and other details, and when Corey felt they'd covered everything they could, Nick stood. Corey did as well, and he came around the front of the desk and stood a few feet from Nick. He stuck out his hand for a shake, and Nick took it to seal the deal. Corey inhaled deeply, once again feeling flutters deep in his belly at the warmth stealing up his arm. He resisted the urge to keep hanging on to Nick's hand because Nick now had that scared rabbit look about him, ready to run for the hills.

Reluctantly, Corey let go. "Since that's a wrap, let me drive you to your new place. My offer still stands."

Nick was shaking his head 'no.' "I can walk, I don't want to put you out."

"I don't mind. I'm leaving anyway, and besides, you might not want to walk around that area this late. It's a pretty rough neighborhood."

"No. It's better this way." Nick seemed adamant. "I need to walk off all that pizza I ate and being in here... makes me feel like I need to like... exercise."

Nick lifted a shoulder and smiled shyly then, and Corey's heart melted. It was a lame excuse, but Corey let it go. Nick had pride, and he sure didn't want to trample on that. He just hoped, once again, that whatever had happened to bring Nick here couldn't have been all that bad. Corey needed to believe he was doing the right thing offering Nick a job, hoping to make things a little easier for him, and hopefully in the process try to get to know him better.

"I'll activate a member's key fob for you. Come by sometime tomorrow and I'll have it ready. That way, you can come in and work whenever you want, even during unstaffed hours."

Nick nodded, zipping up his coat. "Sounds good. Uh... I'll see you tomorrow."

Corey walked with him to the main door and unlocked it, watching from the window as Nick headed out into the parking lot, until the dusk-to-dawn lights in the parking lot didn't do a good enough job keeping him illuminated.

Nick faded into the night.

CHAPTER SIX

THE NEXT morning after a quick trip to the store, Nick set about doing the sketches for the mural. His concentration was broken by the sound of children squealing outside his window. He leaned back from his sketch pad and looked up at the cracks in the ceiling. At least the kids sounded happy—too young and innocent to realize they were living in a dump. As depressing as this place was, he felt better here than he had at the mission. But this place, as bad as it was, wasn't free as the mission had been; he needed to make money in order to stay, and these sketches were important. He glanced at the one he'd been working on. What if Corey didn't like them? What if he took back the job offer? He closed the sketch pad and took a drink from his water bottle.

He started second-guessing himself, thinking he should have bought the set of colored pencils and a larger pad, but he needed to keep his costs down and this sketch pad along with a couple of standard sketching pencils were about all he could afford.

He'd been so excited and anxious to get his ideas down on paper that he'd hardly slept all night. Was he so inspired because of the job, or was it more because of who he'd be working for? This must be fate, he thought—what were the odds of ending up here and meeting a guy like Corey?

You mean a gay guy, don't you?

Well, whatever, it sure felt good last night actually flirting with someone and having him flirt right back without having to pay the consequences. He tapped his pencil on the cover of the sketch pad. He really needed to put the past out of his mind.

He checked the time and focused on his drawings again, not wanting to keep Corey waiting too long.

"I'm surprised at how many people are signing up this time of year, aren't you?" Katie asked while finishing the paperwork for the new member who'd just left. "You'd think people would be too busy with the holidays right around the corner, but maybe they're thinking of all the food they'll be stuffing in their faces, so that must be what's bringing them in. In January, with all the New Year's resolutions being made, there should be even more." She looked up from her work. "Corey? Earth to Corey," she said.

"Huh? Sorry, what'd you say?" Corey shut the file cabinet drawer he'd been digging in and turned toward her, giving her what little attention he had. His thoughts were still all about Nick.

"Never mind, it's not important. You're waiting for the new couple who need instruction on the equipment, right?"

"Yeah, their appointment's at ten." Corey took a drink from his coffee cup he had sitting on top of the cabinet, wondering if and when Nick would show up.

"You've seemed antsy all morning, Cuz. What's up?"

"Nothing," Corey said, sitting down in the chair across the desk from Katie.

Katie placed her elbow on the desktop and rested her chin in her hand. "You're acting very strange. Come on, tell Cousin Katie what's wrong." She reached for his wrist. "Let me take your pulse." She giggled.

Corey pulled away feigning annoyance. "I'm fine. It's just that I'm not really in the mood for this lesson."

Katie sat up straight. "Why? You've always enjoyed showing people around."

"I know, but... " Corey sighed and looked at the clock hanging on the wall.

Katie's eyes were on him, obviously waiting for him to finish his sentence, but before he had to, something drew her attention away from him. He followed her line of sight through the foyer and out the front window where his new members were walking across the parking lot toward the entrance.

Corey stood and straightened his T-shirt. "Look, I'll be tied up with these people for a while, so if anyone else comes in looking for me, tell them to have a seat and I'll be with them as soon as I can."

"Are you expecting someone?"

"Maybe. I'm not sure," he mumbled as he headed out, leaving Katie looking confused.

He hurried toward the Members Only entrance to greet the couple. On his way, he saw Dean giving private instruction to a client. He tried to look away without catching Dean's eye, but failed, watching as Dean's tongue darted out of his mouth suggestively, his hand slipping slightly under the waistband of his gym shorts. Corey jerked his gaze away, trying not to let his irritation show at the mere sight of him, and tried to wipe the sight from his mind so he could concentrate on the business at hand.

Once he began his instruction though, Corey really got into his job of introducing each cardio machine and demonstrating posture and position, so they could get maximum benefit from their workout, and after thirty minutes he'd covered all he could there. He paused to answer one last question regarding the cardio equipment, and while doing so, he saw Nick come through the main door.

Corey proceeded to the weight room with the pair following behind and tried not to let on that his attention had been diverted by Nick being in the gym, *right this very second*, looking all windblown, his jacket zipped up to his chin, his cheeks ruddy from the cool morning air. He hoped Katie had seen Nick standing in the foyer and that she'd do as he'd asked and tell him to sit down to wait.

He stopped at the leg press and proceeded to demonstrate how that worked, all the while glancing to where Nick stood in the foyer. The gym was crowded, and it didn't seem like Nick, who was fidgeting with a notebook and stepping from foot to foot, had seen him. Finally, Katie came out of the office and spoke to him for a few seconds. When she left, Nick unzipped his jacket and sat down by the window. Corey wished he'd have thought to tell her to offer him some coffee while he waited, hoping she might think of it on her own. He really wanted to break away to say "hi," but with a whole row of strength-training machines, as well as the free weights still to go, he knew he had to stick with it.

When they reached the shoulder press machine, about thirty feet from where Nick sat, Corey saw him look his way. Corey positioned himself on the seat and gripped the handles to perform the exercise. While doing the repetitions for his new members, he felt Nick's eyes on him and couldn't help but tighten his abs and sit up straighter. He kind of wished he'd worn a muscle shirt instead of the T-shirt he had on, because Nick was intently staring at him, his gaze darting from his arms to his middle to his chest and then a slow slide down his torso, spending a few seconds *there*, before quickly turning away, his cheeks high in color, to stare out the window again.

Then from his peripheral vision, Corey noticed Dean had zoned in on him like an eagle to a mouse. Between Dean and his antics, and Nick sitting in the foyer looking cute and flustered at the same time, Corey was definitely having one heck of a time concentrating on what he needed to do.

With supreme effort, he stood and focused on the couple before him and had one, then the other, practice the moves he'd just shown them. When every piece of equipment had finally been covered, and the couple had run out of questions, Corey shook their hands and reminded them not to hesitate to ask if they couldn't remember something.

As he approached the small sitting area he tried to act calm and cool, but in reality, he was anything but. His heart was beating hard, and he felt somewhat breathless. Nick had taken off his jacket at some point and sat with his leg crossed, ankle over his opposite knee, looking friendly and casual, no trace of those flushed cheeks from earlier. Corey felt relieved that it didn't appear Nick minded having to wait, although it also didn't appear that Katie had offered him anything to drink, but why would she have? She had no way of knowing who Nick was and that Corey wanted him to feel welcome and to be treated right.

"Hey, good to see you. Thanks for coming," Corey said, sticking his hand out for a shake.

Nick stood and took the offered hand, giving it a firm shake. "Hi there," he said in a soft tone of voice.

Compared to Dean he was a breath of fresh air, and man did he look great in camouflage cargo pants and a plain white T-shirt. Even his worn boots looked good on him. He held up the sketch pad as a lopsided smile appeared across his face, which made him look extremely shy.

"Sorry to make you wait all that time," Corey said. "I maybe should have told you I had clients, or... but... Anyway."

"I didn't mind, I knew coming in here that I might have to

wait, that you had work to do, but...." Nick trailed off this time.

"But what?" Corey prompted, his hands sweaty all of a sudden. Nick really was a shy guy and Corey found that quite endearing, but at the same time he wanted to pounce on him and kiss that shyness away.

"Uh," Nick started. He turned his head as if trying not to let anyone else hear. "The receptionist keeps staring."

Corey snorted out a laugh and glanced into the open office door. "Yes, she is."

"Is this a private joke?" Nick asked with a small chuckle, glancing over his shoulder to the office and then back again.

"She's my cousin—my manager—and, uh, we both kind of get into each other's business a lot more than we should."

"Your cousin—no kidding?"

"Yeah, she does an awesome job around here."

"If she's the manager, well, it doesn't seem like you told her about the work I'm gonna be doing—or, have you? She didn't seem to know why I was here."

"That's my fault. I should have found the time to fill her in. I was going to tell her, but I had to take care of some paperwork and then my new members came, and I had to get started with them."

Nick gave Corey a sideways look, and Corey could tell he was confused. Hell, *he* was confused. He'd invited this handsome new friend here—hired him—and hadn't bothered to tell Katie or any of the others working there what he was up to. He was all kinds of upside down when it came to Nick. He guessed that part of him wanted to keep Nick a secret, someone just for him. He took in a breath and straightened his shoulders.

"Follow me. I'll introduce you." Corey took a few steps toward the office, looked over his shoulder to make sure Nick was behind him and led the way to the desk where Katie sat.

"Katie, I want you to meet Nick. Nick, my cousin Katie," Corey said in a rush. He purposely used only first names, because he didn't believe for a minute that Stewart was Nick's last name. No matter—he'd learn his real last name all in good time.

"Nick's going to be doing some painting for us. He brought me some ideas to look over."

Katie got to her feet and shook Nick's hand, although she looked hesitant.

"Can I get you some coffee, or maybe something from the vending machine?" Corey asked Nick.

"Anything cold would be nice," Nick answered.

"Katie, we'll be downstairs going over the plans Nick drew up."

Before Corey could take two steps, Katie had sat back down, her elbows on the desk again, her expression telling him she knew he was up to something.

"Sure. Uh, nice meeting you," she said as Corey hustled Nick out of the office.

On the way to the vending machine in the cardio room, Corey caught Dean watching their every move, no doubt wanting to know who Nick was and why he was there. He wanted to pretend Dean wasn't an issue, but he knew that before long, Dean would be all up in Nick's business, not to mention in the office at the first opportunity trying to get the scoop. Well, the painting project was none of Dean's business, he'd just have to butt out.

Corey stopped in front of the drink machine. "See anything you like?"

Nick took a few moments studying the labels on some of the bottles. "I'll have the lemon-lime *Gatorade*," he said, reaching into his pants pocket.

"Nope. It's on me." Corey put some money in and got two bottles, handing one to Nick. "I'm anxious to talk about the painting." Corey led Nick to the stairs and paused at the top step. "After you," he said with a sweep of his hand.

"I thought it was age before beauty," Nick joked but went on ahead anyway.

Corey enjoyed the view from behind. Nick definitely had a great body—especially a great ass—but more than that, he didn't act full of himself like Dean, or most of the other guys who came in to the gym. Nick didn't act like he even realized he was freaking hot.

Luckily, only two men were downstairs in the far corner using the punching bags, not paying attention to anything else but beating the bags senseless. Corey set up two folding chairs that were leaning against the back wall, and after they sat down, he reached for Nick's drawing pad.

"May I see what you've done?" His fingertips brushed against Nick's knee when he took the pad, sending sparks through his body. If that small bit of contact could do that to him, he could hardly imagine what would happen if he ever got the opportunity to kiss those lips.

Corey flipped open the cover and stared intently at the pad. He couldn't take his eyes off the pencil drawings on the pages before him.

"Where'd you learn to draw like this?" Each page was to scale, subtle shading giving depth. Nick's idea for the mural was way beyond his expectations. He felt like he could walk in to each page, they were so lifelike.

Nick grinned like a Cheshire cat. "I'm self-taught."

"Wow, you've got talent."

"So, you like them then?"

Nick's modesty was becoming. "They're amazing," Corey said. He looked into Nick's eyes and saw the sensitivity of an artist and the pride and passion for his work.

Corey studied the drawings some more, turning each page as if it were some ancient parchment, trying to decide which one he liked the best.

"Sorry they're not in color," Nick said, leaning in closer to the sketch pad on Corey's lap, the first drawing showing. "I'd do the logo in the colors on the sample you gave me, of course. I wasn't sure if you'd like simple, or something more elaborate."

Nick flipped the page to the second drawing and ran his fingers over the design as he spoke. "This one is more detailed with the shading around the logo." He flipped to the final design. "The third one is even more intricate, with the shadowing really making it come alive."

They looked into each other's eyes for several heartbeats and then Corey had to look away. Damn. He could get lost in those blue eyes for days.

"Wow, it's hard to choose," Corey said, looking at all three drawings again, exhilarated, not only because of imagining how great the gym was going to look with one of these murals painted on the wall, but Nick sitting so close was turning him on beyond belief.

He wondered if he should get Katie's opinion, but decided it would be far simpler to do this on his own, and he knew which one he wanted to choose—the most detailed one that would leap off the page to the wall and really pop. In the back of his mind, he knew he had another reason for picking the most difficult—it would keep Nick there longer, after all.

"I'd like this one," Corey said, pointing to the third drawing.

"Awesome," Nick said, grinning from ear-to-ear again. "You won't regret it. I'll make it look fantastic."

"I know you will," Corey answered, secretly pleased with how this was turning out.

"Now let me show you these paint swatches." Nick handed Corey several samples. "I thought it would be best to go with what's on the walls now, only a shade or two lighter to brighten it up."

Corey smiled and nodded and then gave Nick a sideways glance. "I guess you could tell I was a little concerned about any major changes, huh?"

"Hey, that's cool—the mural you picked shows me you've got an adventurous side, so no problem." Nick patted Corey's arm.

After they sat for a good half hour discussing all the details, they went back upstairs to look at the walls. Nick looked closer than he had the night before, running his hands over some of the areas, paying particular attention to the wall where the mural would be.

"We're lucky there aren't any cracks, or mildew, or anything else that would need attention before we... I start," he said. "I'll need to give all the walls a good scrubbing though, including a good rinse. I'd like to sand the wall where the mural goes. It'll help it adhere and last forever."

Corey felt like he could listen to Nick talk all day long. He was very articulate and had a pleasant tone to his voice. His attention to detail was amazing, and so were a lot of other things about him. Corey hoped that he'd made as good of an impression on Nick.

Nick seemed focused on the task at hand, so easily having slipped into work mode—definitely separating business and pleasure, but that was good—Corey wanted this job done right. But still—all work and no play. He was hoping there'd be some time after they finished discussing the work to go out and relax a bit. Having Nick there talking about his painting was great but having a little more privacy away from the gym would be too.

Nick looked down at his drawing and the swatches and made some more notes. "I'll catch the bus to the hardware store and get the paint. How should I pay for it?"

Corey shook his head 'no.' "I'll drive you and we'll put it on my card. No way can you carry paint and whatever else you need on a crowded bus."

"Uhm okay. That'd be great. I guess it would be awkward juggling all that. My luck, I'd probably drop a can of Sultry Sand or Bayou Blue on some poor old lady's head."

They both laughed at that and then Corey squeezed Nick's bicep. "You do have some pretty good guns, but I can't picture you doing a juggling act with paint cans."

Nick flexed his muscles and smiled. "Do you have time to grab a bite for lunch after we shop?"

Now that was encouraging, and there was that dazzling smile again. *He wants to spend more time with me away from all these prying eyes.*

"Lunch sounds great," Corey answered.

By the time they left the hardware store loaded down with all the supplies they'd need, Corey could honestly say that was the best shopping experience he'd ever been a part of. Nick knew exactly how to find what they needed, and without being rude or pushy to the salespeople, he knew how to get noticed and how to receive service with a smile. Feeling satisfied, Corey pushed the large shopping cart to the car and Nick helped him unload everything into the hatchback.

Once they were buckled in and heading out of the parking lot, Corey asked, "What are you in the mood for?"

Nick's lips twitched like he was trying not to smile and then he opened his mouth as if to speak, but nothing came out. Suddenly Corey felt himself blush and realized the way he'd worded the question could totally be taken the wrong way.

Finally, Nick answered with a slight chuckle, and Corey was relieved. "You know what's around here better than me, so whatever you feel like eating is fine by me."

"Yeah," Corey said, sure that his face was still red.

Nick reached toward Corey and touched his cheek. "Uh, you look hot... you don't have a fever, do you?" Nick laughed full-out then. It was contagious, and within seconds, Corey broke into a fit of laughter too.

"Keep your eyes on the road, friend." Nick cautioned, clearly trying to get his laughter under control.

Corey didn't know how he'd managed to get them to *Sonic* without hitting anything, but he pulled the car under the canopy and shut off the engine.

"*Sonic*, the place with the retro carhops on roller skates," Nick said.

"If we're lucky, our server will actually know how to skate."

"And if they don't, does that mean we'll see our food scattered all over the parking lot?" Nick snickered.

"That definitely would be a sight! I can just see the girl coming out, the tray wobbling in her hands, trying to stay upright, her hair crazy all over the place, and just when she gets to the car—BAM!

Food flying everywhere."

Another round of laughter ensued and then they finally pulled themselves together. Corey couldn't remember the last time he'd laughed so freely. Not even with Katie, who was always cracking some joke or other.

It was time to eat, Corey's stomach growled loudly and that set Nick off again, Corey joining in the laughter when Nick's stomach answered in return. Nick leaned into Corey's right shoulder—a pleasant and warm weight Corey could get used to—and read the menu board in the bay where they'd parked the car. When they'd decided what they wanted, Corey pushed the button for service and soon an order-taker came on the intercom.

As Corey finished giving their order, Nick hollered, "Send someone who knows how to skate," and then under his breath, so only Corey could hear. "Preferably a cute guy."

Corey raised his eyebrows in Nick's direction, and playfully slapped Nick on the wrist, and the smile he got made him glad to be alive. Besides being nice to look at, Nick was coming off as someone who was a lot of fun to be with. Corey sure didn't want to do anything that would ruin it, but if he planned to get to know this guy better he needed to ask some questions, and when he did, he hoped he'd get some honest answers.

But instead of asking those questions, Corey stalled, preferring to watch the servers bring out orders to the people in other cars. He'd keep an ear open though, for when it might be a good time to try. Nick sat quietly beside him, and when their food arrived, it was delivered to Corey's window by a young girl on skates.

"Hi, I'm Sarah," she said, smiling wide. "I have your order, sir." When she leaned in to hook the tray on the door, she noticed Nick and changed it to "Sirs," giving Nick a friendly smile too.

"Thank you," Corey said, holding out the money.

"You'd better take the food before you give her the money," Nick groused. "She'll drop the whole works and we don't want that."

"No chance of that. As you can see, I made it without a mishap." She smirked at Nick, taking the money from Corey.

"Did you know how to skate before you started working here, or did they teach you?" Nick asked, sounding more curious than teasing.

She laughed. "Oh, I've been skating since I was in kindergarten."

"Is it a prerequisite that you need to know how to skate before they'll hire you?" Nick asked.

"Why, do you plan to apply?" Corey joked before their waitress could reply, trying to act serious when he looked at Nick.

"Well, you never know, I might need something to fall back on if my mural doesn't meet employer expectations." He gave Corey a smile and wink.

"No, you don't have to skate at all," Sarah said. "Some of our servers just walk out to deliver orders."

"Well, that's no fun. I'm glad we got you," Nick said, giving her a sweet smile, the one Corey *loved* seeing.

"Have you ever fallen down with an order?" Corey asked.

"No, but I've seen a couple of others fall," she said, giggling.

"That must have been funny to see," Nick said.

"Yeah, get your entertainment from someone else's misfortune," Corey said, shaking his head.

"You two enjoy your lunch. Come back soon," she said, turning and skating away.

Corey put both their drinks in the cup holders in the center console and passed Nick his cheeseburger and fries.

"I don't want to spill anything in your car," Nick said, trying to neatly arrange his meal on his lap. "It's gotten nice enough outside that we could sit at a table, if you want."

"Don't worry, I eat in here all the time," Corey answered. "Uh, unless you'd rather sit outside?"

"No, it's good in here, if you don't mind a greasy fingerprint or two."

"Here, take some extra napkins, she brought plenty."

They went about eating their lunch, and when all they had left was the last of their limeades, Corey turned toward Nick and came right to the point.

"I've been wondering where you're from." The way he'd just blurted that out surprised him, but after it set on the tip of his tongue all through lunch, he just couldn't hold it in any longer.

Nick tensed up immediately. The silence seemed to drag on and on, making it obvious that Nick didn't want to answer the question. But after a long delay, Nick sighed.

"I'd rather not talk about where I come from if it's all the same to you." He paused before taking a deep breath and going on. "Nothing was working for me there. I had problems—I need... needed to start over. I'm never going back there, so I want to look forward and not back."

"Well, I can understand that—I mean, about needing to get away and make a new start."

"Can you?" Nick asked, sounding defeated and slightly angry as he slumped down into the seat.

"Sure." Corey thought maybe if he revealed a little about himself, it would help Nick feel more at ease, maybe enough to let his guard down a little, so he took a sip of his drink and continued. "Things for me were pretty bad with my folks, especially after I came out of the closet, so, uh, as soon as I could, I moved here to be near the only family who has ever understood and accepted me."

"Your cousin who works at the gym?" Nick asked.

"Yeah, and her dad, my uncle Ed."

"Your folks couldn't accept that you're gay?"

"No way." Corey forged ahead, trying to draw Nick out. "Is that how it was with your family?"

Nick looked like a lost little boy, like he might cry if he tried to talk, and Corey hated to see him that way, so different from earlier when they were laughing and at ease with each other.

Finally, in a soft voice cracking with emotion, Nick said, "My family—I honestly don't know how they feel, but I could guess, and it wouldn't be good." He pinched the bridge of his nose and closed his eyes.

"I don't understand," Corey said softly.

Nick sat up straighter and turned toward Corey, cutting him off. "There's nothing for you to understand."

"I thought we were friends, Nick. You can confide in me. I can keep secrets," he said, feeling hurt by Nick's curt words.

When Nick turned fully toward him, it was obvious he was holding back tears. "I'm glad you think of me as a friend. You really don't know how much I need one right now."

Corey reached for Nick's hand and Nick let him have it. Holding that hand felt natural, trying to soothe and give comfort.

Nick squeezed Corey's hand tighter and then said in a tone so low Corey could barely hear.

"I didn't tell you my real last name. I'm not so certain that I want to right now. But... If we're to be friends... then I need to take that chance and trust you." At that point, Nick drew in a shaky breath and blew it out. "It's not Stewart, it's Sanders." After a few beats he went on. "I can't let anyone else know my real last name because I don't want there to be any way for my family to find me. I'm trusting you to say it's Stewart if anyone asks."

Corey rubbed his thumb in a circle on the top of Nick's hand, pleased and a bit sad at the same time.

"But if they wanted to find you, wouldn't that be a good thing? Wouldn't it show they accept you and really care about you?"

Nick was shaking his head 'no.' "No more questions, ok? Please?"

Corey wanted so much to know who or what had hurt Nick so deeply—to understand why he couldn't talk about what was bothering him. But, yeah, this wasn't the time. Nick had been honest, took that chance to open up some and had taken Corey into his confidence, and that was enough, at least for now.

When they got back to the gym and began unloading the paint and supplies, the Members Only door opened and out walked Dean.

"Hey, looks like you guys could use some help," he said, eyeing the paint cans already on the ground and coming to the hatchback to peer inside.

"We've got it, Dean," Corey said, letting out a sigh.

Dean looked Nick over as if he was assessing one of his clients. Corey hoped Nick didn't notice because Corey saw it as rude, and he knew why Dean did it. He also knew he had no choice but to introduce them.

"Nick Stewart, meet Dean Powell. Dean, Nick." While they shook hands, Corey said, "Dean's one of our personal trainers. Nick's going to do some painting inside."

Dean didn't say anything at first, but then he finally spoke.

"Hum," he began. Narrowing his eyes, he went on. "Yeah, I saw you two talking earlier, seemed pretty intense."

Corey ignored that remark and said instead, "Well, we can handle this. Are you *just* now leaving?"

"Yeah, I had two more clients after *you* left."

"Well then, you must be tired and more than ready to take off. Have a nice afternoon," Corey said, picking up as much as he could carry. Nick must have gotten the hint that Corey didn't want Dean's help because he struggled to pick up the rest, and they walked unsteadily toward the main door. Corey was relieved when someone opened it for them, but that was short-lived when he saw Alan's scowling face.

"Should have used a dolly," Alan said gruffly, making himself comfortable leaning against the door frame.

"Why didn't I think of that," Corey snapped, the weight straining his voice. He hobbled the few steps to the office door and set his load down just outside with Nick doing the same. "Let's put everything here and we can make a couple trips downstairs, so we won't kill our backs," he said to Nick.

Nick nodded and picked up two paint cans, one in each hand, groaning for effect.

Corey rolled his eyes and chuckled, but then focused his gaze on Alan for a second before turning back to Nick.

"We can store everything downstairs since it'll be out of the way of the exercise equipment."

"I'd be glad to help," Alan butted in, "but I'm leaving for a late *lunch* with Katie." He smirked. "She might be delayed getting back. I have plans for her." He smirked again, raising his eyebrows up and down.

Corey groaned inwardly and tried to ignore him, but it was hard to do when Alan walked right up to him and got in his face. "The cable cross-over is still hanging up. Maybe the cowboy forgot to check it the other day."

Annoyed, Corey said, "Wes did adjust it. I'll tell him to look at it again the next time he's in."

"Good, you do that. And, if he can't do better work than that, maybe you should consider hiring somebody else."

Corey noticed Nick's stunned expression as they watched Alan stalk into the office. "Who was that?" Nick asked, putting emphasis on the last word.

"Sorry to say, he's my cousin's current boyfriend, although I have no idea what she sees in him. He's nothing but an arrogant meathead who can't help himself showing off his 'guns' and tats." Corey scratched at his neck. "And, you heard him mention Wes, uh, the cowboy.... he's her ex-boyfriend, super shy, but all around nice guy—a million times different from Alan, like night and day."

"Yeah, that Alan guy seems to be a little rough around the edges. Dean seemed okay though."

Corey wondered if he should mention that he used to date Dean, but before he could slip it in, Patty came in the front door looking disheveled and carrying her two-year-old son.

"Sorry I'm late, you can go now, Katie," she called toward the open office door. She turned to Corey and rearranged the toddler in her arms. "I'm so sorry. My husband will be in to get him soon. Our schedules got messed up and I had to bring him with me."

"That's all right. Just make sure he doesn't get into any mischief."

"He'll be good. It'll only be for a little while."

Corey sighed and turned to Nick. "Let's get this stuff downstairs before someone stumbles on it."

It did take a couple trips, but finally the paint cans, drop cloths, and the other items that Nick would need were stored away.

"The stuff should be fine here in the corner," Corey said, pushing some of the paint cans closer to the wall with his foot. "There's a ladder and some buckets upstairs in the janitor closet, where I showed you last night," Corey said.

"Yeah, I remember." Nick shoved his hands in his pockets. "Well, I guess I should go and get some shuteye, so I can come on back and get started tonight when it thins out in here. After eleven okay?"

"Whatever works for you." Corey steered Nick in the direction of the stairs, feeling good that Nick seemed so enthusiastic about the job. "Yeah, you'll have more peace and quiet then, although any time's okay. Whenever you can fit it in, we'll all work around each other. I'll get you a key fob and show you how it works so you can get in."

When they reached the top of the stairs, Corey asked, "You want a ride back to your room?"

"I'll walk. It's good exercise."

"Yeah, well. It is. But remember, you can use the equipment here whenever you want. I'll explain how everything works if you have questions."

"Thanks, I just might do that," Nick said.

Before they parted ways, Corey introduced Nick to Patty and got him squared away with the key. He didn't like seeing Nick walk away and wished Nick would've taken him up on the ride so they could have spent more time together.

Corey had plans though, and they involved getting in very early the next morning, hoping Nick would still be there.

Shivering, Nick grabbed the blanket on his bed and yanked it up to his chin. He vaguely remembered throwing off the ragged cover when he'd woken up with a start from a terrible nightmare. The more he tried to recall something about the dream, the more it drifted away until all he could remember for certain, was the light had still been shining through the old curtains at the time, and now pitch black filled the room.

The blanket was better than nothing, but he was cold. He realized his fingers were cramping up from gripping the unraveling band, trying to find comfort. The multicolored afghan on his bed at home, handmade by his mother, came to mind. For a long time, the smell of her perfume had lingered in the yarn, in fact, even after washing it numerous times he had still been able to smell the fragrance. More than likely he'd just remembered the scent in his mind, just like now.

He ran his hand over his face and then covered both his ears trying to shake the memory of a woman crying. Was that from his dream? Was the sobbing a real memory from the nightmare, or maybe like his mother's perfume, the sound was seared into his brain?

Reaching for the bedside lamp he clicked on the light to check the time on his watch. Late enough to get up and get dressed and head over to the gym to start working.

"Thank God for this job," he said aloud as he pushed the blanket and sheet aside and swung his legs over the edge of the bed.

The bathroom mirror was such a mess it was hard to shave—definitely an antique, but not a collectible treasure like his mom had in the house back home, just a piece of junk. The lighting wasn't the best in the tiny room, which added to the difficulty. He did the best he could to finish and then decided to check the lightbulb. He stretched up to see inside the cracked light fixture and found the bulb was covered in grime. Well, at least it could be cleaned and that would help to solve one problem.

When he was dressed and ready to leave, he picked up his room key from the nightstand and reached into the pocket of his camo pants for the special key that would get him into the gym. He clipped it onto the old piece of string attached to his room key. Next time he went to the thrift shop he could probably find a key chain, or maybe he'd splurge and get one in the convenience store now that he was a working man. Maybe one that said California—that would be perfect.

CHAPTER SEVEN

COREY FELT like he should have his head examined leaving his warm house in the pitch dark, with rain coming down in a steady pour and no guarantee that Nick would even still be at the gym. He put the windshield wipers on high and backed out of the driveway, then pointed his Kia toward Main Street, but he planned on a side trip to the donut shop before showing up at the New U Fitness Center. With any luck, Nick would still be there hard at work, and he'd get to spend some time with the object of his desire before the morning rush began at about five a.m.

The chilly morning, if one could call three thirty a.m. morning, reminded him of a week and a half ago, when he'd gone in early and found Nick sound asleep by the dumpster. After their talk the day before, he had more questions than ever about the handsome, complex guy he'd met.

Corey had barely slept that night, he'd been so keyed up—anxious about getting back to the gym early enough, and because he'd been plagued by sexual tension. Jacking off with the image of Nick's full lips and kind, gentle, bright blue eyes hadn't helped at all to relax him enough to sleep well. He'd tossed and turned for hours in the darkness of his lonely bedroom with visions of Nick on the way to *Subway* worried about having paint in his hair and on his clothes—as if he'd be scolded if he did.

He wondered how Nick was sleeping in that rundown, fleabag motel. At least on the nights when he'd be working the graveyard shift at the gym he wouldn't be subjected to whatever went on around a place like that after dark. Hopefully, for Nick's sake, daytime wasn't as bad.

With these thoughts of Nick distracting him, and the fact he hadn't been to the donut shop that often, he nearly missed the turn into the small complex where it was located. At this early hour, he figured there'd be a variety of donuts, muffins, and bagels to choose from, but he realized he didn't have a clue what Nick liked to eat besides pizza, sub sandwiches, hamburgers, and soft drinks. From the looks of him, he must know something about good nutrition.

Corey parked close to the shop, opened his door, and made a mad dash to the entrance. The cheerful little ring of the shopkeeper's bell jingled when he yanked the door open, causing the man on duty to spin around, his mouth in a perfect O.

Corey grinned apologetically and cleared his throat. "Uh, the rain is sure coming down out there."

"And you have braved the storm to shop for pastries," the man said in a thick Filipino accent, wiping his hands on his apron. "What can I get for you?"

Corey stared into the case, bending at the waist to get a closer look. "I'm not exactly sure yet."

"Take your time, no hurry."

The longer Corey carefully considered each variety of donut, the more amused the man looked, standing with his arms crossed, a small smile playing on his lips.

"Well, I think you'll need to put them in a box," Corey finally said. "I'm going to get quite a few."

"Are you the one chosen to serve your office today?" the man asked, picking up his tongs and opening a large box, standing poised to begin filling it.

"Uh, something like that."

After choosing plain, fancy, glazed, and cake donuts, the muffins drew Corey's attention. "I think I need to add a few muffins too," he said. He focused in on the healthy sounding names. "I'll take zucchini, carrot, and sweet potato."

"Good choices," the man said, cheerfully adding them to the box. "Are you in need of any coffee, sir?"

"No, not today, this will do nicely."

After paying the bill, Corey slipped a few dollars into the tip jar, gave the shop owner a big smile and then dashed out to his car, shielding the sweet goodies under his jacket.

With the box sitting on the passenger seat, he headed toward the gym. He'd start a pot of coffee as soon as he opened the office, that is if he ever got there—he seemed to be hitting every red light along the way. It would really be disappointing if Nick had already left by the time he got there, although he couldn't see Nick heading out with the rain coming down like it was.

The only business open in the complex at four a.m. was the gym, and with only two vehicles in front, the parking lot looked like a ghost town.

Unlocking the main door and stepping inside he glanced into the weight room and saw two guys working out. He craned his neck to look into the cardio section to see the most important person he'd been looking for—Nick.

He remembered the first day he'd seen Nick at the church wearing carpenter jeans, and how good he'd looked in them. The laid-back cut of those jeans—fuller from the thigh to the hem, that didn't scream "look at me"—was actually quite appealing. Corey imagined what the sweet curve of his glutes would look like under those jeans. Nick looked serious in his work, having already cleaned the walls. He was up on the ladder, looking so focused as he held the paintbrush at just the right angle to make a clean stroke across the trim to get a smooth finish.

Corey shook himself out of his trance and quickly unlocked the office door and deposited the box of goodies on the desk. He then hastily measured coffee into the filter in the coffee maker and headed—with the water pitcher—to the water cooler that sat in an alcove about ten feet from where Nick was deep in concentration, oblivious to his arrival.

He stood and took another few breaths to admire Nick's backside, but began to feel like a voyeur, even though he was out in plain sight, so he cleared his throat to make his presence known. The sound obviously startled Nick, because the hand that held his paintbrush jerked enough to mess up the straight line he'd been painting. At least he was sure-footed enough not to fall off the ladder.

"Damn," Nick cursed, looking down and over his shoulder. His irritation was short-lived, because at seeing Corey he at once offered up his easygoing smile. "Hey, is it that late already?" he asked, looking toward the clock on the far wall.

"Are you implying I come to work late?" Corey asked, smiling himself, still holding the empty water jug.

"Uh, no—I just meant—"

"I'm only kidding," Corey said. "I actually don't usually come in so early, but today I made an exception."

Nick put his paintbrush down on the ladder tray and wiped his hands on a wet rag. "Any particular reason?" His crooked smile made him look shy once again.

All of a sudden Corey felt shy too, so he changed the subject. "It looks like you got a lot done on your first night. Did you have any problems?"

"No, it was quiet for the most part."

"Good—well, if you're ready to quit, I'll help you pick up your stuff after I start a pot of coffee. I brought us some donuts and muffins if you're hungry."

"That's the best offer I've had all day," Nick said, as he climbed down the ladder.

Corey was momentarily distracted by Nick's cloth covered, muscular thighs, but he pulled it together and turned to fill up the canister. Once finished, he took another glance at Nick, who was now putting the lid on the paint can, giving Corey a slightly more awesome view of what lay hidden under the denim of his pants. He spun on his heel and just about ran back to the office to start the coffee, and by the time he got back Nick had folded up the ladder and was leaning it up against the wall.

"How 'bout giving me a hand with the drop cloth," Nick suggested. "And then I can wash out my paintbrush."

"Sure." Corey reached down and grabbed one end of the tarp while Nick took up the other.

"I like to fold each side to the middle," Nick said. "Like this." He then proceeded to fold his side to the middle and then came around and helped Corey fold his side the same way. "This keeps it nice and neat," he said. "Keep doing it just like this."

Corey was impressed. "Usually I'd just bunch it up and throw it into a corner."

Nick chuckled. "Well, I guess that's another reason you need me around."

"Sure is," Corey said quietly.

When the drop cloth was folded small enough to drape over the ladder, Nick did so and picked up his brush.

"I'll get this rinsed out real quick."

He went into the closest men's bathroom and turned on the faucet in the sink. Corey followed and stepped inside, leaning against the wall watching intently.

After several seconds, Nick looked in the mirror and locked eyes with him. "What? Am I covered in paint that I can't see?" he said, glancing behind him, trying to see.

Corey realized how blatantly he must have been staring and felt the heat of embarrassment wash over him.

"Uh, no, I don't see any," he quickly said, looking down at the floor tiles and then back up again to Nick's face, hoping he wasn't red as a tomato.

Nick just smiled coyly back at him and pushed his hair out of his face with the back of his arm. "Well, if I do ever get covered in paint specks, it's okay to use the shower, isn't it?" Now it was Nick's turn to blush.

Before Corey had a chance to answer about the shower, Nick cleared his throat and turned off the water. "We better stick all the painting stuff away, so the place is nice and neat again." Nick grabbed a handful of paper towels to dry the brush, the silence between them heavy.

"Use the shower anytime you like. It's... private." Corey didn't know why he added that.

Nick brought his eyes up to meet Corey's, a startled look there, which disappeared just as quickly.

"Uhm, cool. Thank you." He then placed the handle end of the brush into a loop at his back pocket and threw the towels into the garbage can. "If you take the ladder to the closet, I'll take the rest downstairs, then we'll go eat our breakfast?"

Corey sighed in relief, having something to do, the awkward moment passing. "Sounds like a plan. I'll wait for you in the office then."

A few moments later, Corey looked up from his desk to see Nick lurking at the doorway. "Come on in and make yourself comfortable," he said standing, pointing to a chair next to the desk. The aroma of fresh donuts and coffee made the office feel warm and welcoming.

"It was raining cats and dogs when I came in," Corey said, as he closed both office doors and then sat, turning on the computer.

"Really?" Nick said, pulling out the chair. "I've been so lost in painting that I hadn't noticed what it was doing out there." Nick then sat down, stretching his legs out. "I did hear a couple guys say something about rain when they came in—oh, about two, I think it was. One of them was your cousin's boyfriend."

"Alan came in at that hour?" Corey asked surprised as he reached for the coffee pot, pouring out two cups.

"Yeah, I recognized him right away, but I just kept on working and didn't say anything to him."

Corey passed Nick a cup. "Help yourself to cream and sugar in the drawer there," he said, pointing at the drawer, then he slid the goodie box toward Nick, lifting the lid. "I hope something strikes your fancy in here. I got donuts, or if you'd rather have something made with healthy veggies, there's muffins too."

Nick smiled at him and let out a rush of breath. "You think of everything. I think I'll like working here." Nick took two sugars and picked out a glazed donut while Corey brought up the data management program on the computer and turned his attention to the record of incoming members.

"Aren't you eating?" Nick asked, taking another big bite and then washing it down with a swallow of coffee.

"In a minute," Corey said, looking intently at the list of names on the screen.

"Is something wrong?" Nick asked between chewing. "What are you looking at?"

"This is kind of weird." Corey leaned closer to the monitor, tapping his finger against the screen.

"What is?"

"I don't see Alan's name on this list."

"Is he supposed to be?"

Nick got up and came around the desk to look over Corey's shoulder. "How does this work? Hey, I see my name there. Uh, by the way, thanks for introducing me as Stewart yesterday and using it in the members list too."

"You're welcome," Corey said, looking him in the eye, grinning for a second before looking back at the screen. "Yeah, it recorded your name when you used your key fob to check in."

"Cool. Then where's Alan's name?"

"Evidently, he piggy-backed on the guy he was with. Sometimes that happens, but we try to discourage it because we like to know who's in here at any given time. It has to do with liability."

"Who was he with?" Nick asked, leaning in closer toward the computer.

"A fairly new guy who I haven't talked to yet. His name's Ted.

Says he checked in at two fifteen."

"You don't think anything's wrong, do you?" Nick leaned even closer, resting his forearms on the back of Corey's chair.

Nick's face was so close to his ear he could feel his warm breath there, and a strong, sudden feeling of excitement gave Corey goosebumps.

"Uh, no, not really—just being nosey I guess, because of Katie. Did Alan and this Ted guy work out?"

"They were in the weight room, but I didn't pay much attention to them or what they were doing." Nick sat back down in the chair and took a cake donut covered with chocolate and nuts, winking at Corey. "I guess I'll be healthy another day."

Corey took his attention away from the monitor and smiled at Nick's comment. He wasn't coming up with any real reason to worry or be suspicious about Alan, so he reached for a donut, placing it on a napkin in front of him, not paying attention to what he grabbed. Then he got up and poured more coffee, thinking he sure could make a habit of this breakfast thing with Nick. It felt good having someone other than Katie to talk to over coffee.

"You tired?" Corey asked, sitting down again.

"A little, but I feel good. I enjoyed working." Nick stretched like a cat and yawned. "Sorry—guess I *am* tired."

There was that smile again, the one that made Corey's heart race, and he could hardly resist staring. "More coffee? Hope it doesn't keep you awake—uh, I guess you'll be going back to the motel to get some sleep."

"Yeah—these hours we're keeping," Nick started, but then trailed off.

"What were you going to say?" Corey asked, leaning forward, almost reaching out a hand to place on Nick's arm.

"Oh, nothing, just that us not being on the same schedule, we probably won't have a chance to go out together much."

It pleased Corey that it bothered Nick about their schedules. More and more, it seemed like they were on the same page, and that maybe it was time to take their budding friendship a step further.

Nick got up again and poured himself more coffee. "The monitoring screen is pretty cool," he said, looking up intently at the six views on the thirty-six-inch screen mounted on the wall.

Corey looked up too, the views were like still pictures except for the one showing the two guys lifting weights out in the weight room. As Nick and Corey watched the monitors, a man and woman entered through the Members Only door. Nick seemed transfixed watching their every move as they shook rainwater from their jackets, deposited their gear in the storage shelf and then moved to the treadmills.

"It even shows the parking lot?" Nick asked.

"Yeah, part of it," Corey answered.

"So, if you were inclined to review what the cameras picked up during the time you weren't here, you'd see everyone who came in and everything they did?" Nick asked.

"Yeah, sure would. Of course, there aren't cameras in the bathrooms, and there's a few spots they don't reach, but it catches most of what's going on. So, between that and the computer here keeping track of who comes in, it's a pretty secure place."

"I can see that. I'm impressed."

"Thanks," Corey said, pleased that Nick was interested enough to comment about it.

Nick set his half-full coffee cup down on the desk and crumpled up his napkin. "Well, I sure do appreciate the donuts and coffee, but it looks like I should go now." He gestured toward the monitors again which were catching a wave of activity from the five a.m. crowd beginning to arrive.

"Let's see if the rain has stopped," Corey said, opening the office door and taking a few steps to the main door to look out. "Can't really tell from the monitors how heavy the rain is, it still being so dark out there."

Nick followed and stood shoulder to shoulder with him at the door. "Damn, it sure is coming down."

"Bet you won't refuse a ride today," Corey said, hopeful that Nick would take him up on the offer, giving them more time to spend together.

"You got that right," Nick answered.

"Get your stuff then, and I'll drive you over."

By the time they arrived at the motel, the sky had really opened up.

"Pull around behind, my room's in the back corner," Nick said.

Corey did as he was told, the windshield wipers whipping back and forth, and the beam from the headlights showed him a grungy old door with peeling paint. There was a dimly lit porch light above Nick's doorway, but it didn't seem that anyone else had bothered with theirs, or more likely, most of them didn't work. Out of consideration to whoever might be behind the various doorways, and even though he hadn't planned to, he killed the lights and shut off the engine. Barely daybreak, with next to no lighting on the premises, and with the chilly rain adding to the eeriness Corey had to try hard not to shiver.

Nick put his hand on the door handle, but Corey didn't hear it click. Instead, Nick looked slowly his way. In the gloomy darkness it was hard to make out Nick's features, but Corey was sure he could find that delectable mouth without even trying. His fingers ached to touch Nick's face, framed by hair which glistened from the faint light that hit it. All he could hear was the rain pelting the car, and he wondered if Nick was hesitating because of the downpour, if he was lingering for another reason, or was he waiting for him to make the first move?

He didn't think Nick ever wore aftershave—he'd never detected any—but it didn't matter, his own unique scent affected him like some kind of magic potion.

An undercurrent of desire hung in the air between them, and Corey couldn't resist the temptation for one second longer. He leaned in, wanting to be as close as he could get, his eyelids fluttering shut as he took in a deep breath.

He moved his left hand around to the back of Nick's neck and pulled him in close, thrilled and scared half to death when he didn't get any resistance. He was met halfway, their lips coming together in a soft, yet intimate kiss. Nick's right arm came around to grasp him tight at the shoulder and held him close, like this was what he craved. Nick intensified the kiss, his tongue probing Corey's mouth, their tongues wildly dancing around each other. Soon their making-out became far too steamy for the front seat of a car. Way overdressed in his jacket, Corey was quickly overheating, and his leg bumping the steering wheel with every movement was quite awkward, not to mention the center console restricting contact. Despite all that, Corey felt like they'd definitely crossed the threshold of just friends to a whole lot more. His heart was pumping hard, way harder than when he used any of the equipment in the gym.

When they finally parted, he thought he heard a faint sigh from Nick, and a whispered, "Daaaamn," but he couldn't be sure. Nick still had a grip on him though, so that had to mean something. All he knew for sure was that he was soaring. Beyond any doubt, Nick was definitely under his skin.

Nick's resourcefulness at getting his life on track since getting to town was inspiring and a huge turn on. He'd been through something—something really bad—but to look at him now and that winning smile, he hid it well. He seemed like he was happy just to be.

"Come to my room with me," Nick whispered into his ear, his fingers now gripping the front of Corey's jacket.

Already hard as a rock, Corey hoped he could walk because he certainly wasn't going to refuse that offer.

"What are we waiting for?" He yanked the key out of the ignition and stuffed it into his jacket pocket, snugging up in his jacket in preparation for braving the torrential rain.

Nick pulled his hood over his head and opened the car door. "Last one there is a rotten egg."

Corey dove out of his door, slammed it shut, and sprinted after Nick, who by then was at the door fumbling with the key. With no eaves above to shelter them, he and Nick were getting a soaking. He couldn't help giggling and grabbed for the key in Nick's hand.

"Let me do it, you're too slow."

Nick jerked his hand back, laughing. "It's my door, I can open it."

Folding his arms around himself, Corey shifted his weight from foot to foot, when finally, Nick got the key to work and pushed the door wide open. "Age before beauty," he said.

Corey wasted no time getting himself in out of the rain. Once inside the cramped, stale smelling room lit only by a small table lamp, the first thing he noticed was a trash can near the foot of the bed—the plink-plink-plink of the water drops hitting the overflowing can.

"Oh shit, help me carry this to the tub," Nick said.

Corey picked up one side of the can while Nick took the other. They moved toward the bathroom as slowly and as carefully as they could, but their effort was nearly sabotaged by a loose piece of floor tile that tripped Nick up, causing them to spill some of the water on the bathroom floor.

"Damn," Nick cursed.

"Look at it this way, it's lighter now," Corey said, trying to be helpful.

"I knew there was a reason I liked you. You see the bright side of things."

They dumped what was left into the gray-stained bathtub. With

Corey following behind, Nick carried the can back into the bedroom and put it down under the drip again.

"Sorry about that," Nick said, gesturing to the roof.

"Got a slight leak, huh?"

That caused Nick to go into a laughing fit. Corey couldn't help but join in because this was too much like a Lucy and Ricky moment. What started out as the best kiss Corey had in a long time, was turning into, literally, a cold shower.

Patting Corey on the arm, Nick said, "These walls are paper-thin, so we gotta quiet down."

Corey tried to get serious. "Okay, sorry," he said through his smile.

Despite the dank, seedy room, he felt all kinds of happy and excited. Nick had invited him to his place, where he slept, ate, and was trying to start a new life. Here he was with someone he hoped would soon be his new boyfriend—and if he was right about the vibes he'd been getting from Nick, then he was sure it would happen. He hoped Nick was still in the same mood as he was out in the car, and that the trash can incident hadn't put a damper on it. He realized Nick's hand was still on his arm and there was a dreamy, wanting, look in his vibrant blue eyes.

"You aim to lead me astray—I can tell," Corey murmured softly, leaning in toward Nick's neck.

Instead of answering, Nick gave him access, and when Corey licked and lightly sucked, Nick groaned and wrapped his arms around him and pulled him into a deep kiss that was enough to curl Corey's toes. God, the guy could kiss. Even the sounds Nick made were erotic as hell. Corey had gone without for a couple months now, and he got the feeling it had been even longer for Nick. The bottled-up passion inside him seemed about to explode if the iron grip he found himself in, and the noises coming out of Nick were any indication.

Corey experienced a shiver of apprehension, but that was only fleeting because this was what he'd wanted almost from the first moment he'd laid eyes on this man. He didn't know Nick well, but in the short time he had, he'd found him to be sweet and charming, and today Nick was most likely going to charm the pants right off him. He instantly relaxed when Nick softly took his hand.

"I promise the roof doesn't leak over the bed. I'll show you."

Corey let himself be tugged toward the bed and watched as Nick stripped off his hoodie and then his shirt. Nick stopped then, eyeing him with a frown, and Corey realized Nick was waiting for him to do the same, so he threw off his jacket and his shirt while Nick pulled the faded old bedspread off the bed and tossed it on the floor.

"That thing is gross, but the sheets are clean." He climbed on the bed resting on his knees, and Corey wanted to just stop and fill his senses at the sight, but he needed to be up-close and personal. When he dove onto the bed, it bounced under his weight, nearly causing Nick to lose his balance, the two of them sharing a nervous, but playful laugh.

When Nick pulled them close together, bare chest to bare chest, and dug his fingernails into Corey's back, Corey sucked in a breath at the suddenness of Nick's unleashed need, but he sure wasn't going to complain. So what if he sported red scratches? They'd be a welcome reminder of this day.

After several long moments of wet kisses, Nick's touches became less rushed. Corey wasn't sure what was giving him the biggest high, Nick's hands roaming over his naked back and chest, or the feel of Nick's skin under his hands as he did his own exploration.

Corey pushed his fingers into Nick's waistband, but that didn't give him near enough of what he wanted. He was the first to pull back and began undoing his own belt and unbuttoning his jeans. His hands were shaking so much, his heart pounding so hard, and his breath coming so fast, he wondered if he'd hyperventilate and faint. Nick was right with him, undoing his belt and jeans, ready to show everything he had inside his pants. He was ready to see and to show as well. Nick's pants and shorts flew onto the floor in a heap, and Corey's landed someplace else, though he wasn't quite sure where.

When they were both naked, Corey pushed Nick back on the bed and he went readily. Spread out before him, Nick's body was a vision. No big muscles bulging out everywhere, just nicely toned with the right amount of muscle definition, wide shoulders, and a slight sprinkling of chest hair—sensuous and manly. And his legs— nothing like some of those guys who only work their upper body and have chicken legs. Since it seemed Nick liked to walk, Corey wondered if he was also a runner. From the looks of his strong, well-defined legs and calves, he wondered if maybe he'd played soccer sometime in his life.

"How did you get such fantastic legs?"

Nick snorted softly. "Since I graduated from high school, all I've been doing is climbing up and down ladders."

Corey liked that answer and kissed his way down Nick's chest while using his fingers to rub and tweak Nick's nipples. The groan he got told him Nick approved of what he was getting so far, so Corey took it further. He ran his tongue down Nick's treasure trail, which was soft, and darker blond than the hair on his head. He had Nick squirming by the time he reached his dick. He hesitated for a few seconds, taking time to savor the moment, staring down at the rigid shaft, there for the taking.

"What the hell are you waiting for?" Nick gasped, raising his head up slightly to see what the holdup was.

Corey snickered. He'd accomplished what he wanted—to drive Nick up the wall in want. He ran his fingers over the tops of Nick's sturdy thighs and then the prize waiting for him jutting out at the juncture, fondling it, making his own eager cock plump up to match.

Seeing Nick grasp the edge of the mattress and buck up turned Corey on beyond belief. He went down and devoured Nick's cock all at once, no licking or teasing, just swallowed it right down and sucked. Nick was totally and completely into what he was getting from Corey, his head thrashing from side-to-side, and the sexy moans he was making—pure ecstasy.

As this was his first time with Nick, it was damn hard to take it slow. He knew he'd be next, so he sucked and lapped and teased for all he was worth, wondering if Nick had forgotten his warning about the paper-thin walls because he was anything but quiet. It didn't take long before Nick arched up from the bed, the sheets wadded up in his fists, as he erupted in Corey's mouth, a hoarse cry filling the air. Corey moaned deeply, not backing off Nick's cock while he rode his orgasm. Only when Nick sighed and went limp did he let go, burying his face in Nick's groin, as Nick trembled against him.

When Nick stilled, Corey scooted alongside him and reached out to touch his face. Nick turned his head toward Corey and gave him a lazy, blissed-out smile. He looked young and so innocent.

"Your turn," Nick said in a sex-drenched voice that sounded anything but innocent.

Corey ran his hand through Nick's long hair before lying down on his back beside his new lover. He raised his hands over his head, closed his eyes, and waited in anticipation. When he felt a hand wrap around his hardness, it took him by surprise. He nearly jumped because of the jolt it gave him, Nick's fingers cool against the heat of his shaft, but he quickly relaxed and focused on the lightning bolts zinging through his body, and more importantly, through his brain, because this wasn't just about the physical, this was about forging a bond between him and the guy he was crazy about.

"You're beautiful," Nick said, his voice sounding far away, and his touch uncertain. After a few more seconds, he felt Nick's left hand wrap gently around his balls while the right hand continued toying with him. Corey needed more caressing and a lot more contact. Like now.

"I want your mouth," he whispered urgently, trying to encourage Nick to move faster, but all he got was Nick's tongue circling the head of his dick, light as a feather. Nick moved on to light nibbles and sucks as a low moan escaped from him into the quiet room. Nick was obviously enjoying his exploration.

Corey felt like moaning too, but for a different reason than Nick. "You're driving me insane, baby," he said, an edge to his voice.

Finally, after what seemed like an eternity, Nick's warm, wet mouth took him. In little time, Nick had him pounding the mattress with his fists, thrusting erratically, trying to fuck Nick's mouth—anything to create some rhythm so he could get off. He finally raked his fingers through Nick's hair to hold him in place, and within ten seconds, he unloaded with a strangled cry.

When his dick had gone soft, Nick gave it a small tug and then moved up and kissed the corner of his lips. Corey smelled himself on Nick's breath, not at all put off by that, his semi-coherent thoughts telling him that a deep connection was forming between them. He felt it right down into the depths of his soul.

"Are you okay?" Corey asked.

"I'm great," Nick said, grinning and running a finger across Corey's bottom lip. "Are you all right?"

"Better than all right."

After a few seconds of silence, Nick's expression became serious, his brows drawn tightly together. "Was it okay?" Nick asked, his eyes darting away.

Corey reached out, gently moving Nick's chin to make eye contact and looked into Nick's hopeful but skittish eyes.

"It was the best I've ever had," he said sincerely. Being with someone he truly cared about far outweighed the clumsiness and lack of technique Nick had displayed.

Nick's smile returned, and the scared look in eyes disappeared. He snuggled up next to Corey with his head in the hollow of Corey's neck and shoulder and his arm over Corey's chest.

Corey realized the rain must have stopped because he didn't hear it hitting the roof or dripping in the trash can. For a span of minutes, all he heard was the sound of their shared breathing. He wondered if Nick had fallen asleep, after all, he'd worked through the night, but then Nick repositioned himself, so his head rested on his hand looking down at Corey.

"What is it?" Corey asked.

"I... I, uh, haven't done that much, so I'm not too good at it, but I'll get better, I promise."

Corey frowned in confusion. "Uh, you're gay, you've been gay all your life—"

"That's true," Nick said, dropping his gaze. "But—"

"You've had boyfriends before, haven't you?"

"Back in high school, but you couldn't really call them that. Just friends, really," Nick said softly, a slight tremor to his voice.

With those words, Corey noticed a bleak, pained look cross Nick's face, as if he were remembering something, or maybe it was someone, who had been important to him at some point.

"There was one guy not too long back..." Nick said, but he didn't finish.

Corey wanted to hear more, but he didn't want to push. He felt bad for his friend and wanted to be supportive, but there wasn't much he could do when he knew so little. He wanted to lighten the mood instead of worrying about what Nick wouldn't or couldn't tell him.

"I'd think a good-looking guy like you would have had a lot of boyfriends."

Finally, Nick made eye contact. "Have you? Uh, had a lot of boyfriends?"

"Not that many," Corey answered. "Just a few." He knew he should mention Dean, but he didn't think now was the right time. They really didn't need more people in bed with them just then.

Nick looked tired and beat down, and his eyes suddenly filled with tears. Corey reached up and wiped a few away with the tip of his finger, his own heart breaking at what he saw on Nicks' face. He was trying to think of something to say when Nick said softly, "I've been married since I was twenty-one."

CHAPTER EIGHT

ALL COREY could do was blink and try to breathe. He resisted the urge to get out of the bed and move around—do anything that would force his mind to think of something else. It wasn't that he was mad—upset maybe—but certainly surprised as all get-out. Lying there in the semi-darkness, he couldn't be mad looking at Nick in the state he was in—mourning the end of life as he'd known it, reduced to living in a dirty hole-in-the-wall motel room. What right did he have to be mad or hurt anyway? Or even to judge for that matter, because he didn't know the exact circumstances that had brought Nick here. Would it have changed anything if he'd known about Nick's situation from the start?

All the signs that Corey had seen pointed to the fact that Nick wasn't a man living in the closet, but wherever he'd come from, he sure must have been. Because what else could the reason have been to make Nick leave like he had? Any fleeting suspicions of wrongdoing he may have had when they'd first met were now replaced with realizing Nick had been running from who he was.

It was just such a shock to hear that he was married, and he even wondered if he'd heard right, but from the look on Nick's face, he knew it to be true. As the seconds ticked by, the awkwardness that hung between them made Corey feel more and more uncomfortable, and he knew it must be even worse for Nick. But that was his burden, something he had to work out in his own time.

Nick raised his arms and covered his eyes, but Corey could still see the tears that stood out on his face. He felt he had to say *something*, he just didn't know what that would be. His heart went out to Nick—he'd taken the plunge and opened up about something so personal and painful, he deserved some kind of reaction from the person he'd shared such intimacy with, other than just lying there, mute.

Corey sat up, gently pulling Nick against him, as they leaned against the rickety headboard. He reached behind them, making a cushion of the pillows.

"Damn, Nick," he finally said, once they had settled in. "You sure know how to shock the shit out of someone."

"I'm sorry," Nick said softly, wiping at his eyes.

"Don't be sorry, that's not what I meant—Jesus, I hardly know what I meant." Nick remained silent, staring out into space. With his right arm around Nick, Corey gave him a little squeeze. "I'm just surprised at what you said. I'm glad you told me."

Nick took a deep breath but didn't speak.

Corey wondered if Nick regretted having told him because he sure didn't seem to want to discuss it, but Corey had to know more, so he braced himself for what he might hear.

"Do you have any kids?"

"No," Nick said simply, his voice trembling. He sat up straighter, crossing his arms over his chest. Corey sensed Nick wanted to put some distance between them, so he took his arm away from Nick's shoulder.

"Are you going to get a divorce?"

Nick squeezed the bridge of his nose. "We both want that," he choked out.

Corey was becoming discouraged at trying to get any more information. Nick had clammed up and was pulling into himself. He'd crossed his arms more tightly over his chest as if to shield himself. Corey was reminded of the day they'd first met when Nick had done the same thing and had been evasive in his answers. He wanted Nick to explain more, but it was clear that wasn't going to happen at this point. It was all Nick could do to hold it together, he was so tense.

"Are you okay?" Corey asked.

Nick's lack of eye contact made Corey wonder if he should get lost or take a flying leap somewhere, but he wanted to convey to Nick—in some way—that he was with him one hundred percent, and that what Nick had revealed wasn't going to send him running. He took in a long breath and blew it out. Communicating with someone who had just shut down was hard.

Corey tried to pry Nick's hands apart and got resistance. "Please?" After a few more tries, Nick finally relented, and Corey took that hand in his and squeezed. "Thank you for telling me. This doesn't change anything between us as far as I'm concerned. I need you to know that."

Nick finally looked at him, and Corey gave him a soft kiss on the lips, letting out a heavy sigh of relief when Nick kissed him back.

Corey tapped his fingers on the steering wheel while waiting for the light to turn green. He just could *not* get out of his head what Nick had told him.

Nick is married.

He sure didn't see that one coming. Not once in all the times he'd been trying to figure out what made Nick leave his home had he ever thought it would have anything to do with a wife.

He pressed his foot down on the gas pedal and continued toward the gym, still deep in thought. *Okay, so he comes with baggage, big deal. Who doesn't? We can... we will work it out.*

Corey lowered the visor to block a ray of sun breaking through the clouds. The rain had stopped, the sky had brightened, and soon it would match the color of Nick's eyes again. If only the storm that followed Nick could pass over too.

Shit, he should be walking on air after what had gone down between them. He'd loved kissing Nick. It was electrifying and then to be invited into Nick's room, their lovemaking. God, it was all so perfect—until.

But why should what he'd learned make any difference? In his mind, the marriage should never have happened, because not being true to yourself ends up hurting everyone involved. Nick had said it was over, so he'd have to take him at his word.

But how, he wondered, could Nick get a divorce if he didn't want anyone to find him? That didn't make sense, so there had to be more to the situation. Maybe Nick couldn't bear to face anyone because of the sorrow and regret of marrying a woman when he knew he was gay? To a sensitive man like Nick, the guilt was probably eating greedily away at him.

Lots of gay men marry. That doesn't make it right, but hell,

Nick had been twenty-one years old, and from the little Corey knew about him there was some kind of problem with his family, not just the wife.

Corey considered himself lucky he'd never fallen into that trap. No, he'd never pretended to be something he wasn't, even if it meant losing most of his family, he just couldn't live a lie.

When he slowed down for a yellow light near the bus stop closest to the gym, two guys standing by the bench caught his eye— Alan and some other dude who looked about Alan's age, someone Corey didn't think he'd seen before, at least not in the gym. It didn't appear that Alan had noticed his car in the midst of the morning traffic. While he waited for the light to turn green, glad that he was in the middle lane, he watched the pair and it seemed like they were having a heated discussion if their facial expressions and hand gestures were any indication. He didn't have any idea what Alan's work schedule as a groundskeeper at the cemetery was, but it seemed odd that he'd been in the gym at two a.m. and was now standing around at the bus stop at this time of the morning.

When the light changed Corey turned into the gym parking lot, which by now was half full, and damned if Katie wasn't already there. It was just his luck that she'd be early on a day he wished she'd be late. He had hoped for enough time to clean the coffee pot and pick up the left-over donuts before she arrived.

After locking his car, Corey rushed into the office to find Katie with a donut in her hand. The coffee smelled fresh and he noticed the pot was full.

"You made more coffee, good." He grabbed his cup and filled it.

"Where did the donuts come from? And where have you been?" Katie asked, chewing away merrily.

"I bought the donuts at Donuts Galore. Glad to see you like them."

"You're sabotaging my diet, I hope you know."

"Good, because you don't need a diet."

"Why were you in so early?" Katie looked at him intently. "And where did you just now come from?"

Corey tried to look innocent, but he knew he wasn't doing a good job of it. "Uh, did you notice the painter has started?"

"The painter? You mean Nick? Yes, I noticed." She sounded a bit stern like she was scolding him. He didn't much care for her tone.

"Yeah, yeah, I mean Nick."

"I was surprised about the painting project. We hadn't even talked about needing the walls done. Who is this Nick guy anyway? Where'd you find him? Is he doing the work by himself?"

"You're sure full of questions this morning, aren't you?"

"I was full of questions yesterday when you introduced me to him, but I never got a chance to ask until now."

"Well, I hired him to spruce up the place. He's also going to paint a design of our logo on the wall between the cardio and weight rooms." Corey looked at her expectantly. "Won't that look cool?"

"Cool?" She gave him a sour look.

"Uh, maybe I should have asked for your input, but this just... sort of snowballed."

"Oh really. Where does he work?"

"Uh, he's freelance."

"Have you seen his work?" Where has he painted before?"

"In answer to your first question, yes, I have seen his sketches." He didn't want to tell her that the sketches of their logo were the only ones he had seen—he wanted to ward off her protective nature. "And to answer your other question, he's new in town."

"I don't get it, Cuz. You hired a stranger to paint in here?"

"He's not exactly a stranger. I met him awhile back." He coughed into his coffee mug. Not but a couple hours ago did he truly get to meet the real Nick.

"How long ago?"

Corey felt heat in his cheeks and saw from Katie's face that she'd had a light bulb moment. Her eyes widened, and a slight smile played on her lips.

"He's gay, isn't he, and you're dating?"

Corey couldn't help but smile too. "We may have been out a few times."

"Where'd you meet?" She pushed the donut box to the other side of the desk and leaned her elbows on the desktop, making herself comfy, giving him her whole undivided attention.

Corey sighed. He had no intention of answering that question, but he didn't want to lie to her either, although standing there, mute, wasn't going to cut it at all. He thought he was off the hook when he heard a sound at the office door, but that was temporary when he realized it was Dean. He cringed when it became obvious that Dean had been eavesdropping.

"Yeah, tell us where you met," Dean taunted, stepping into the office, his hands on his hips.

"What can we do for you, Dean?" Corey asked.

"You can answer the question," Dean said.

"To be honest, it's none of your business."

Neither Dean nor Katie said anything for a few beats, but it seemed that Dean wouldn't keep his mouth shut.

"Seems like a simple enough question. Is there some reason you don't want to tell us where you met?"

Corey headed for the door, pushing past Dean. "We've all got work to do, so I suggest we get on with it."

After a rocky start, the rest of the morning had gone smoother, with Dean being too busy with clients to bother harassing him further and Katie keeping busy in the office. Corey had gone about his routine as usual, but by the time he broke for lunch he felt beat.

He decided to take a long lunch at home, but once there he wondered why because all he could do was wander from room to room thinking about Nick and what would become of them. He even entertained the thought that Nick might skip out on him—just up and leave town like he'd done to the people who'd been in his prior life. He tried to calm himself down about that happening, telling himself that Nick wasn't the kind of person who'd up and leave in the middle of a job. And, he also told himself, that what they'd started that morning meant something, not only to him but to Nick too, that it wasn't just about getting off.

After finally sitting down at the kitchen table to eat a sandwich, he arrived back at the gym in time to see Wes heading through the main entrance, but no sign of Katie. He'd been looking forward to seeing Wes again, because it didn't matter how many times the equipment was repaired around there, or how good of a job Wes did, something always needed attention, and this week wasn't any exception. Besides needing his services, Corey still held out hope that Katie and Wes would get back together, so having him there as much as possible could help make things move in that direction.

Corey caught up to Wes at the far wall of the cardio room. He came up behind him and patted him on the shoulder. "Good to see you, Wes."

Wes turned to look at him and gave him a friendly smile. "Hey, Corey. How are you today?"

"Hanging in there."

"Looks like you're dressing the place up," Wes said, indicating the wall where Nick had begun painting.

"Yeah, wait until you see what we have planned for the small wall between the two rooms."

"Oh, yeah? Tell me about it."

"It'll be a mural with our logo incorporated into it."

"Well, I'm impressed. Can't wait to see it. Who's doing the work?"

"Uh, a guy I met who's an artist. I found out he's a painter and one thing led to another, so I hired him."

"That's great. Well, I'd better get started on the list you gave me," Wes said, removing his cowboy hat.

Before Wes could take a step, Corey looked toward the office and said, "I wonder if Katie's back from lunch."

"I wouldn't know—or much care," Wes said with a loud sigh. "I wish you'd let that go. It's a done deal."

"Keep the faith, buddy. You never know." Corey patted Wes on the back and headed to the office leaving him to do his thing.

A few moments later, he found Rhonda sitting behind the desk. "How was your vacation?"

"Wonderful, but it's nice to get back into my old routine."

"It's good to have you back. Is Katie still on lunch break? I haven't seen her for a while."

Rhonda looked down and timidly said, "I guess she didn't really want to be here when Wes came, so she said she had to run some errands and wouldn't be back until later."

Corey must have had a look on his face that had Rhonda catching on to what he was thinking.

"I wish she'd have stayed too. I'd much rather see her with Wes than that Alan." She made a disgusted face when she said Alan's name. "He's bad news in my book."

Corey smiled in agreement. "Did I say that I'm glad you're back?" He winked at her and she smiled back.

Corey took the five o'clock Active Aging class for the instructor who couldn't make it, and that was fine with him because it helped give him something to focus on besides Nick.

When class let out, he stuck around answering questions and talking with some of the group before heading back upstairs, and when he got to the top of the stairs, the sight that greeted him took a big load off his mind. Nick had set up the ladder and had one of the mop buckets out on the floor. Corey stopped in his tracks and admired the view of Nick bent over, squeezing out a wet rag in the bucket.

He looked at the clock and decided not to interrupt, mainly because Katie and Rhonda weren't gone yet and he didn't need them gawking when he talked to Nick. Waiting another half hour for them to check out would be better, and once they were gone he and Nick could have some breathing room. Looking around, he saw that Wes had gone and, thank God, Dean wasn't there either.

Just then, Rhonda came out of the women's bathroom with a trash bag in her hand and stopped to change the one near the Member-of-the-Month wall. Corey walked toward the office and could see Katie at the desk talking on the phone; he hoped the call would last long enough that she wouldn't have time to talk to him before she'd leave at seven o'clock. He smiled at her when he entered the office and took a look at the computer screen to see if she'd left anything partly done that he could help tie up for the day, but everything looked finished.

When Katie ended the call, she didn't waste any time picking up where she'd left off that morning.

"Okay, now that we're alone, are you going to tell me where you met your painter?"

Corey smiled in defeat. "I guess you know he's here."

"Yes, I saw him come in. I assumed he'd be working late at night though. Aren't you concerned the smell of the paint might bother the members?"

"I told him he could do it whenever he has the time. Besides, Nick said this paint is low odor, and with all the fans going it smells fine to me."

"Okay then, whatever you say," Katie said, looking at him expectantly. She let a few seconds of silence pass. "Aren't you going to answer my question about where you met him?"

"Uh, I first saw him outside the gym," Corey answered, trying to sound calm and matter-of-fact.

"Oh, that was convenient," Katie said, glancing at the clock, preoccupied all of a sudden. She got up and started gathering her things and seemed ready to leave, most likely to meet Alan considering the way she was hurrying, so Corey figured that saved him from further questions, at least for the time being.

After the girls had left, Corey headed to the wall where Nick was working. He stopped a couple of feet behind him and cleared his throat. Nick paused in mid-stroke and turned to look over his shoulder, down to where Corey was standing. A weight lifted off Corey's shoulders when Nick broke into a wide, friendly smile. He couldn't help but to smile back. That smile let him know that everything between them was still good.

"Well, if it isn't the owner of this fine gym, finally getting time to stop by and say hello," Nick said in that easygoing way of his. "I was beginning to wonder if you were giving me the cold shoulder."

"You must have come in when I was downstairs teaching a class. I was surprised to see you in this early."

"I finally fell asleep about eleven, and when I woke up, I felt like getting out of that place, so I decided to come on over. That's all right, isn't it? I'm not in the way?"

"No! Not at all. Sure, it's fine. There's room where people can still use the bikes." He glanced at the row of bikes that were a good ten feet away from the wall, two of which were in use at the far end.

"I'll just go ahead working, not 'cause I'm rude, but I wanna get this paint on. I can still talk though," Nick said.

"No problem." Corey had no objection to the view. He folded his arms across his chest and leaned against one of the bikes to watch the most attractive painter he'd ever seen in action.

"I couldn't imagine how much this new orange color would change the room when we talked about it in the store and we looked on those little swatches, but seeing the new color up against the old one I can tell it's going to look a lot lighter and brighter in here. I'm impressed."

"So, you do like the Mango Tango better than the original color." Nick tapped his lips with a finger. "I think it was probably Spanish Orange before. Not one of my favorites."

Corey wrinkled his nose. "I'm not ever going to remember the names of the colors you so conveniently have tucked in your brain. What's up there just looks orange to me."

"Keep hanging around with me, friend, and we'll have you spouting out colors in no time, just like the pros."

Corey got a warm feeling in his middle hearing Nick call him *friend*. That meant the world to him. After a minute of silence, all except the noise of the gym equipment, fans, and the radio, Nick turned and looked down from the ladder again.

"I was thinking there might not be many people in here because of the holiday coming up. Maybe I should come in on Thanksgiving Day. I could probably get a lot done then."

Corey moved a couple of steps closer and said adamantly. "No, no, no—I'm not having you spend the holiday alone, and certainly not working."

"I don't mind, and I've got nowhere else to be," Nick answered, a shadow of remorse crossing over his face.

"How about you plan on coming with me and my uncle to the mission and help serve dinners that day?"

Nick was silent for a moment, considering the invitation, but then he said, "If I worked here, I'd get a lot done."

"Everyone needs time off, especially on a holiday. Please. What do you say?" Corey walked up to the ladder, his shoulder brushing against Nick's thigh and looked up at him. "Pretty please?"

Nick didn't look convinced, so Corey went on. "Come on, I'd like you to meet my uncle Ed. Katie is going off with Alan someplace, so it's just me and him this year. I'd love for you to be there. You'll know a few people, and Mrs. Franklin is one of the women in charge."

"You're sure?"

"Yes, I am."

"I guess that would be okay. I could help them out, just like they helped me."

Corey nodded. "If that's how you want to look at it."

"Well, all right, if you think it's okay, I'll go. Who all is invited for the meal? I mean—well, I've met a few people at the motel—some nice families who probably won't get a Thanksgiving dinner."

"Sure, let them know they're welcome to come to the mission for dinner."

Nick gave a half-smile as if he still wasn't totally sure he wanted to go, but he said, "Okay, sounds good."

Nick looked around from his vantage point on the ladder as if making sure no one was within earshot. "Uh, me and you—we're okay, you know, after what I told you this morning?"

Corey dropped his voice to a near whisper, hoping no one was listening from around corners like Dean had been earlier that day. "Yeah, Nick, we're okay. I'd like to talk more about that when you're ready, but like I told you this morning it doesn't change how I feel about you."

Nick nodded. "I'm glad. I wasn't sure."

Corey then checked the time. "Damn, I've got to close up the office and get out of here. I promised my uncle I'd be over to watch TV with him tonight. He gets kind of lonesome now that Katie and

I moved out. I'd been living in his garage apartment, and when I moved a couple months ago Katie took it over, but she's tied up with Alan now and not home that much."

"It's okay, I understand. No problem," Nick said, looking at the wall where he'd been painting and then to the brush still in his hand.

"I know, shut up and leave so you can work, right?" Corey said teasingly.

Nick laughed. "Don't put words in my mouth."

"I'll be back in a minute, I just thought of something," Corey said.

He hurried to the office, and after shutting the computer down, he grabbed two T-shirts in size large, one in gray and the other in blue, both with New U Fitness Center printed across the front. He locked the office and hustled over to Nick's bag on the floor across from where he was working and laid them on top.

"I think these will look good on you. Hope they fit," he said.

Nick looked toward his bag. "Well, thanks. I appreciate that."

"Guess I'll see you sometime tomorrow?"

"Yeah. At some point. Have fun watching TV."

"Have fun painting."

Corey walked slowly toward the main door, wishing he didn't have to leave. He stepped out into the chilly night, glad that at least it wasn't raining. He wished he could have gotten a goodnight kiss, but doing that in the middle of the gym wasn't exactly the right place.

Lost in thought as he walked slowly to his car, he got in and thought about seeing Uncle Ed. He wondered if he should tell him someone special had come into his life. He knew he should, because if he didn't, now that Katie knew he was dating, she'd beat him to it. Ed would be happy for him, but probably not if he knew how they'd met.

Just like he'd done when Katie had asked, he'd need to be vague because if his uncle knew Nick had just drifted into town and had been sleeping next to a trash bin, not to mention him being married, he'd have plenty to say and it wouldn't be good. Ed was almost as protective of him as he was with Katie.

If Ed got to know Nick before hearing any details that would be better, otherwise he knew his uncle well enough to know he'd say that Nick wasn't right for him, and he might even think he was an opportunist. But he didn't want to out-and-out lie, so what had he been thinking asking Nick to the mission on Thanksgiving when Ed would be there too? Would Ed ask Nick any uncomfortable questions, like where he was from, anything about his family? And what if Mrs. Franklin or someone else at the mission were to mention Nick having stayed there? That would be a bad way for Ed to get clued in. The more he thought about it, the more nervous he felt, so he tried to put it out of his mind, so he could try to enjoy his evening with his uncle. He turned onto Main Street and headed to Uncle Ed's place, wishing that it was Nick he was spending the evening with instead.

Nick tried to keep his mind on his work, but his thoughts were scattered. He wondered if he'd made a mistake agreeing to Corey's Thanksgiving plans. Meeting Corey's uncle was a big deal, him being the most important member of Corey's family.

It's like meeting the parents.

He couldn't help but think back to when he'd met his in-laws for the first time. Sitting at their dinner table he'd been afraid of spilling something because his hands had been so sweaty. He'd felt so out of place he couldn't wait for the evening to end. He'd actually wished they'd hate him and forbid their daughter to marry him. So many lives could have been spared the pain he'd caused... if only.

But there was no use thinking about all that now. This was a new place, new people, a new life. Everything would be okay. And, he'd have a place to be this Thanksgiving. That was a heck of a lot more than he'd ever thought he'd have a couple weeks ago when he'd been huddled on that cold train hurtling through the darkness to the unknown.

He moved the ladder a few feet and continued painting. So far, things had worked out pretty darned good in this new town. He loved being with Corey. That morning in his room—man, he could hardly believe what happened between them. Not just the sex part, but him actually saying out loud that he was married. He felt so close to Corey that telling him had just seemed right. This connection, relationship, or whatever, was moving fast, but maybe after keeping his true self locked up for so long, it was bound to happen this way once he met the right man. He felt that Corey Preston was the right man.

Focusing on his brush strokes, he determined they all looked even and smooth. He was satisfied with his work so far, and with what he'd found here.

CHAPTER NINE

SINCE NICK had started painting early the evening before, Corey knew he'd be long gone by sun up, so Corey's usual arrival time of eight-ish would do. Actually, it would be closer to eight thirty when he reached the gym since he'd spent some time cleaning up the house before he'd left, just in case it worked out that he could invite Nick over for lunch. Lunch and some get-to-know-you-better time.

He'd also taken the time to call Mrs. Franklin at the mission, informing her that Nick would be there to help serve Thanksgiving dinner. He couldn't help smiling at how pleased she'd sounded to hear this.

As he drove toward Main Street, he thought about his uncle. Last night's conversation with him had gone well—seemed like his decision to tell Ed that he was dating someone new and that he would get to meet him on Thanksgiving, had been the right thing to do. His uncle had acted happy about that prospect, and Corey hoped it would give him something to look forward to, considering how unhappy he was that Katie preferred to spend the holiday with Alan rather than her family. He just hoped his uncle would like Nick, and if he found out about Nick's circumstances that he wouldn't overreact.

At a red light, Corey started calculating when Nick might be back to the gym. He'd begun painting at seven the evening before, and if he worked eight hours and then went back to the motel to sleep, he'd maybe be up around lunchtime. With Nick's reluctance to sit around doing nothing, he was counting on him showing up to paint midday. He smiled at his theory and turned up the radio—it sure felt good having someone to spend time with.

His good mood quickly evaporated when he turned into the parking lot and noticed three police cars parked across the lot from the gym, right in front of the smoke shop, which was closed this time of the morning.

He pulled into a parking space in front of the gym and felt even more alarmed when he got out of his car and saw through the glass door and windows of the main entrance that an officer was standing in the foyer. He quickly approached the door with a tense feeling in his gut, and before he could reach for the door handle, Katie suddenly appeared and flung it open, which only added to his uneasiness.

"I thought you'd never get here," she said, almost breathlessly. "Why didn't you pick up your phone?"

"Sorry, I didn't hear it ring, and I had a few things to do this morning. What's going on?"

"Come in, and you'll find out."

"Good morning," an officer said as Corey stepped inside.

Katie spoke over Corey's "Good Morning," introducing him to Officer Kelly.

"Nice to meet you," Corey said, offering his hand for a shake.

"Same here," Officer Kelly said, ignoring the offer. Instead, he took out a small notepad and pen from his pocket.

Corey let his hand drop, noting the policeman was a no-nonsense kind of person and seemed in a hurry to get on with his job. Corey figured he'd probably been waiting awhile for him to arrive.

"What do you need from us?" Corey asked. "What's happened?"

"Someone broke into the smoke shop during the early hours of the morning."

"Damn, I don't think we've had any trouble like that since I've had the gym," Corey said.

"We haven't that I'm aware of," Katie added.

"How long have you been in business?" Officer Kelly asked, turning his attention back to Corey.

"A couple years."

"I understand you're open twenty-four hours, and that you

have an extensive monitoring system in place."

"That's right," Corey said.

"Well, at 3:10 a.m., the alarm in the smoke shop was tripped. Officers arrived within five minutes, but the thieves got away with ten cases of cigarettes. Mr. Chun is still taking inventory, but he's pretty sure that's all he's missing. Officers have dusted for fingerprints, and it looks like the suspect, or suspects, entered through the back door." Officer Kelly gestured toward Katie. "Miss Knight has stated that your outdoor surveillance cameras don't reach far enough across the parking lot to have captured anything in front of the smoke shop."

"That's right, that'd be out of range," Corey said.

"Then what might help is if you have a list of who was in the gym at that time, so we can question them. The shop is lit inside, although rather dimly, but enough that someone might have detected movement if they happened to be looking in that direction. I noticed from the treadmill area that it's quite possible to see across the lot to the smoke shop windows. Miss Knight indicated that the blinds were open when she arrived this morning."

"Sometimes we forget to close them before we leave," she said.

"Also, the robbers might have cased the shop earlier, so I'm interested in finding out if any of your patrons might have seen anything suspicious, or maybe someone milling around more than usual. And of course, someone in here could have heard the alarm sounding. Are there many members who use the gym at that hour?"

Katie interjected. "We had a painter in here last night doing some work for us."

Corey tensed, but he ignored her comment and directed a response to Officer Kelly. "I'll check the computer to see who was here at that time. Normally it's not very busy." Corey looked to Katie and said, "I don't know if Nick would have stayed that late since he came in early in the evening."

"Well, we can ask him," she said.

"Why don't you come into the office with me, Officer," Corey said, stepping to the door.

"I'll go check on supplies," Katie said, hurrying in the direction of the janitor closet.

Corey walked to the desk, the officer right on his heels. "Have a seat. Can I get you some coffee?"

"I'm good," Officer Kelly said, sitting. "I'll just jot down the names you've got and be on my way. Looks like you're getting pretty busy in here."

While Corey scanned the computer, the officer looked out in to the gym, tapping his pen on his thigh. It didn't take but a moment to see who had been in during the hours in question. There were the four EMTs who usually came into the gym at that hour, and the other was an older man he didn't know. Again, he wondered what time Nick had left, but figured he could wait and ask him when he came in, rather than check the monitor.

"Seems there were just five here at the time," Corey said, looking up.

"Thank you," Officer Kelly said, standing so he could see the screen, writing down the names on his notepad. "What about the painter Miss Knight mentioned?"

"I'll ask him what time he left when he comes in later today. He's currently without a phone."

"All right, that's fine," the officer replied. "If anything comes up, I'd appreciate a call."

Corey took the card the officer handed him and walked him out. When he came back inside he saw Katie across the gym talking to Dean, more than likely telling him about the break-in. He'd just as soon not have that news spread around to the members and have them worrying about their safety, but there was no way to stop the other gym members from talking. As far as he was concerned it was just a petty theft, probably carried out by some teen punks with nothing else better to do.

By the time noon rolled around, the police having left around nine, Corey couldn't help himself from looking out the windows for Nick. Not having any way to call him was a real pain in the backside, and he wondered if Nick had ever had a cell phone—probably one of the things he'd left behind since that would be a good way for his family to trace him.

Damn, there were so many negatives with trying to get something going with Nick, but his heart wouldn't let him turn Nick away.

The farther the hands moved on the clock, the more Corey's heart sank. By twelve forty-five, he started thinking that maybe he hadn't guessed right about what time Nick would be in. Maybe he wasn't coming in until evening again like he had been, but each time Nick walked through the door, it was earlier than his previous arrival. Just as he was about to give up hope, he caught sight of his gorgeous, hardworking guy striding across the parking lot.

Corey couldn't help but grin as he stood up from the desk, and then walked to the main door to open it. "Hey, over here," he called out as Nick headed toward the Members' door with his key fob in his hand. "You can come in this door during business hours if you want."

Nick flashed him a broad smile. "Is that 'cause I'm tight with the boss?" he asked as he got closer.

Corey snickered. "The fringe benefits are endless, just you wait and see."

Once inside, Nick gestured toward the side wall in the cardio room. "After I finished the wall I was working on before you left, I painted the Gamma Green wall. How do you like it?"

"It looks great, especially next to the orange one."

"That would be Mango Tango," Nick corrected, winking, as he removed his black hoodie to reveal his new blue fitness center T-shirt underneath.

Corey snorted out a laugh and could hardly take his eyes off him. The blue of the shirt brought out Nick's eyes just like Corey knew it would, and he half wondered if Nick had some fancy name for that kind of blue.

"You got a lot done. What time did you leave?"

"Must have been a few minutes before three."

"You didn't happen to see or hear anything out of the ordinary when you walked through the parking lot, did you?"

The question seemed to take Nick by surprise if the expression on his face was any indication. "What do you mean?"

"The cops were here this morning because someone broke into the smoke shop early this morning. They said the alarm went off not long after three."

Nick brought a finger to his chin. "I didn't see anyone when I went out the door, but I wasn't really paying attention either. The wind was blowing right in my face, so I had to duck my head as I hurried to leave. Did they catch whoever it was?"

"No, not as of nine this morning. When I got in one of the officers was here asking questions."

"What kind of questions?" Nick asked as he turned to look out the window.

Corey frowned as he joined Nick at the window. "Like, if our security cameras would show the parking lot over that way, and who was in here at that time."

"Was anything taken?"

"Just some cases of cigarettes. Guess they didn't have a lot of time once the alarm started ringing."

"Do your cameras show that area?" Nick glanced at Corey then looked out the window again.

"No, they don't go that far out."

"Well, I hope they catch whoever it was. That's not something you want to happen while you have people here."

Corey nodded. "Me too. I don't want the members here to get nervous, especially at night."

Nick gave him another quick glance and turned from the window to look at what he'd done the night before. They walked toward the wall that had been freshly painted.

"Listen, I thought I'd work on the small wall next because I'm kinda anxious to start the artwork. I'll get back to the other walls after I finish. Is that okay?"

"Sure, whatever you want. But, I had an idea."

"What's that?"

"How about before you start working today, we take a drive over to my place. Have you had lunch?"

"Yeah, I had something on my way over."

"Shoot, I thought we could eat at the house."

"Sorry."

"That's okay, but how about coming over anyway? Uh, maybe we could have a snack after I show you around."

Nick's smile lit up his eyes as if he could read between the lines of Corey's invitation.

"I like the sound of that," he said and then shyly looked down at the floor, still smiling.

"Well then, let's go."

On the way back to the office, they couldn't avoid Dean standing at the reverse fly machine that was closest to the door.

"Hey, boys," he said in the abrasive way he sometimes had.

"Hey, Dean," Corey said. "We're kind of in a hurry, so I can't really stop and chat."

"Need to go put out a fire?" he asked, giving up a big, fake smile.

Ignoring him, Corey quickened his stride. "Talk to you later." He didn't think Nick had acknowledged Dean, which was the best thing for all of them.

After a quick wave into the office letting Rhonda know he was leaving, Corey opened the door for Nick, and they were on their way.

They'd driven a short distance down Main Street when Corey said, "I'll take you on a little side-trip before we go to my house. That is... if you don't mind?"

"Do you need to get something for your lunch?" Nick asked.

"No," Corey said, giving Nick what he hoped was a seductive sideways glance. "I thought I'd have *you* for lunch today." He looked back at the road but couldn't resist taking another quick peek at Nick, and from the way Nick met his gaze, Corey could tell he was on board.

He turned off Main and made a second turn on to a quiet tree-lined lane. "Halfway up this street is where my uncle and Katie live."

Nick was quiet while looking intently at the houses and yards they passed. Corey wondered if Nick had lived in a similar house on a street like this, or in a neighborhood such as this that might be bringing back memories of where he had come from. They were both still quiet when he approached Uncle Ed's home. He didn't come to a complete stop, just slowed down enough to give Nick a quick look.

"See there?" he pointed. "Above the garage doors? That's the apartment I used to stay in before I bought my house."

Nick ducked his head to take a look from the side window and finally spoke. "So, that's where you lived, huh?"

"Sure was. It was a little small, but modern and comfortable."

"I'm glad you've got your own house now," Nick said. With sparkling eyes and a playful smile, there was no mistaking what he had on his mind. His breathing had quickened and there was now a slight flush to his cheeks. The squirming Nick was doing in the seat to get comfortable was a straight call to Corey's own dick.

God, how he wanted to jump that man right then and there. "Good thing I don't live very far," Corey said as he stepped on the gas. In less than two minutes he made the turn on to his street and had pulled into the driveway.

"Nice house," Nick said, getting out before Corey had even killed the engine.

Corey quickly joined him in the driveway, tugging on the front of his jeans.

"The house needs quite a bit of work. I haven't had much of a chance to get started on it. I've put most of my time and attention into running the gym. The house is just somewhere I sleep. At least for the time being."

"Looks nice from outside," Nick said, but Corey could tell he was just being polite.

"Let's go see the inside."

Once they passed through the front door, Corey kicked it shut, tore off his jacket, and closed the distance between them in about two seconds flat. He couldn't wait to get his arms around Nick, that was all there was to it. For now, finding out more about Nick's past would be put on hold because he had to feel this man in his arms. Nick wrapped his strong arms around him and it felt so damn good. And those amazing kisses Nick was planting on his lips turned Corey on so fast it was mind-boggling. God, how he craved this alone time with Nick. He needed to find a way for them to spend more time together—private time—as much as possible.

Corey closed his eyes, feeling lost in Nick's kisses. He ran his hands over Nick's back and then grabbed his ass, pressing their hips tightly together. Nick let that happen for a few long seconds, but then he pulled back to get his hoodie off, tossing it aside.

Finally, this empty house seemed alive, and he hoped that soon it wouldn't just be a place to sleep. Corey grasped the wild strands of Nick's hair and pulled back, exposing his neck. After a few heavy moments of licking, sucking, and kissing, the sounds of Nick's moans coming from deep in his throat helped to further ignite Corey's desire. He didn't want to break contact, but the sooner he got Nick into the bedroom and onto the bed, the quicker he could continue to explore. Stepping back, he tugged on Nick's hand and whispered in his ear.

"The bedroom's this way."

As he led Nick down the hallway, Nick seemed just as anxious to get into the room as he was. They stumbled, hit the wall, and then were racing to see who could get to the bed first. In their haste, the weight of them together made the mattress dip, knocking Corey off balance into Nick, causing him to land flat on his back right where Corey wanted him.

He then dove for Nick's neck again and heard him whisper, "I've never felt this way before."

Corey was so turned on he was afraid he'd come in his pants. He grabbed the hem of Nick's T-shirt, and with Nick's help, yanked it off. Nick's hair looked even wilder than it had in the living room, and his laughter—clear and rich—made Corey feel alive as Nick reached to pull Corey's shirt off.

Corey was in a hurry to get them both completely undressed. He quickly unbuckled his belt and undid his jeans and then fumbled with his shoes, nearly falling off the bed in the process. Nick had begun getting out of his clothes too, and when they were finally undressed, Nick flopped down, flat on his back again breathing hard.

"I'm already worn out," he said panting and laughing at the same time.

"I'll give you ten seconds to get your second wind. I have plans for you," Corey smirked, inches from Nicks face.

He didn't wait the ten seconds before planting a big kiss on Nick's lips and moving his leg so that it rested over one of Nick's. It wasn't that he thought Nick might get away, but that he wanted to feel as much skin as he could. He could tell Nick felt the same by the way his hands roamed over Corey's shoulders and back and then down to his ass. When Nick's fingers reached into his ass crack, Corey couldn't help but jerk and a strangled yelp escaped.

"I wasn't expecting that, but that doesn't mean I didn't like it," Corey gasped.

Nick chuckled, and to Corey it sounded quite evil. He could be evil as well, and laughing manically, he adjusted them to fit more comfortably while reaching between them to grab hold of Nick's balls, giving them a slight squeeze.

"Watch out, buddy, I've got you right where I want you."

"No place I'd rather be," Nick answered breathlessly.

Corey inched his way further up Nick's body until their dicks were side by side. Nick gasped this time, and Corey closed his eyes and tried to breathe deeply, not wanting to get to the finish line before they even got started. With Nick nibbling at his ear, Corey surged upward, biting his lip hard, the pain of it helping him not to totally lose it.

When he felt able to go on, he wrapped his right hand around Nick's dick and then slid his own into his grasp and rubbed them together, sending shockwaves through him. Nick showed how he was feeling with his eyes squeezed tightly shut, his mouth opened in a soft O. The noises that came from him were nothing but pure pleasure. Corey used his left hand to retrieve the tube he had strategically hidden under his pillow and squeezed out a glob on to his palm. He spread the lube along their lengths helping in his mission to bring them both to climax.

"Damn, damn, damn," Nick chanted.

Corey felt Nick's fingers digging into his side and a split second later, he felt Nick's release coat his fingers. Looking down, he could see the evidence puddling on the hair on Nick's belly. The sight of that, and Nick's coming, pushed Corey over the edge, his hips stuttering, his fingers clumsy as his own cum blended together with Nick's. Taking in a deep breath, Corey collapsed next to Nick.

Not sure how much time had passed since the last wave had hit him, Corey slowly opened one eye and then the other. The last thing he remembered was Nick gasping and shuddering and then himself, but he could tell they had been in each other's arms for a time. He felt cool, and they were both sticky where they touched. His head rested on Nick's shoulder and his ear felt numb, but he liked where he was and didn't want to move. He knew he should be polite and get Nick a washcloth to clean up with, but he just didn't have it in him yet to do that.

When he started to doze again, Nick stirred and groaned, and Corey rose up to an elbow, afraid that he was too heavy. Looking down at Nick's sleepy but blissed-out face—he could stare all damn day long—Corey knew he'd fallen hard for this guy. He leaned down and gave Nick a light kiss on the lips—they were the softest lips he'd ever kissed.

"Be right back," Corey said. Even though he hated getting off the bed, he did anyway and headed to the bathroom for a cloth. When he returned and began the cleanup, the look Nick gave him melted his heart.

"No one's ever been this nice to me before," Nick said.

"That's hard to believe. I find it very easy to be nice to you." Corey took his time doing the cleanup. As long as he had Nick in his bed, he was going to keep him there as long as possible. Only when Nick started to giggle and get twitchy did Corey finish the job. He quickly wiped himself down and then tossed the washcloth over the side of the bed.

Nick sat up when Corey rested against the headboard and propped himself up with the pillows. Although Corey wasn't speaking, thoughts whirled around in his mind concerning the questions he had for Nick. He didn't want to ruin what they'd just shared, but he had to get answers, and now was the time. He wasn't sure how or where to begin and wondered if they'd be more comfortable dressed and sitting in the kitchen, but he knew he was procrastinating, something he hated doing.

"How will you and your wife get divorced if she doesn't know where you are?"

Nick blinked in surprise at that direct question and then frowned at the change in mood. His eyes showed the sadness he felt, and a faraway look settled on his face.

Corey was prepared to wait it out, but after several minutes, the silence stretched out to the point where he was totally uncomfortable. He scooted a little closer to Nick, pushing one of the pillows behind his back and pulling the sheet up to their waists.

"You know, I don't even know where you come from. How'd you come to be where I found you that day?" Corey asked quietly.

Nick still stared straight ahead. "I guess there's no way of *not* having this conversation, is there." It wasn't a question, rather a statement said resignedly.

Corey took Nick's hand and laced their fingers together. He looked at Nick. "I want to know all there is to know about you."

Nick didn't turn his head but spoke slowly. "I hopped a train—wasn't even sure where I was when I jumped off, when it finally slowed down enough."

"Jesus, Nick. That sounds dangerous."

"I made it okay—banging my ankle when I got on was actually the worst that happened."

"You were limping when I first met you."

"Yeah, I wondered how I'd be able to jump off with it hurt like that, but I had no choice, so I just had to grit my teeth and go for it." After a pause, Nick went on. "It wasn't raining when I got off, but it started pretty quick like when I was wandering around, not knowing where the heck I ended up."

"So, you found shelter under that tin roof."

"Lucky me that the track is close to here. I stumbled in on my sore ankle and kind of crashed. I was exhausted... being wedged into such a tight place on the train sure didn't make for a comfortable place to sleep."

"How far did you come on the train?"

"From Northern Oregon."

"Not too far then."

"Easy for you to say," Nick snorted. "You weren't crammed in that little cubby hole."

"Whatever possessed you to leave town on a train?"

"It's been a dream I've had ever since I was a kid. It sure wasn't what I imagined it was going to be like, though." Nick's smile looked sad and forced. After a few moments of silence, he went on. "But, I thought it was the best way to disappear without a trace. No way to track me since there was no paper trail, so to speak. Credit cards, ATM withdrawals, those leave evidence where you've been, or where you've ended up."

"Cell phones too?"

Nick nodded.

"Why did you feel you had to do that, leave your home? Why don't you want anyone to know where you are?"

Nick looked briefly his way and then went back to staring at the wall in front of him. "It was a bad, bad scene between me and Melissa—my wife. I blew it, Corey. She was hysterical and there was no way of calming her down. The things she said—I knew I had to get out of there, and that I'd never be able to face her, her parents, my parents, or anyone else in that small, overly religious town again."

"But you said you two were married for a while—years. What happened to bring it to that point?"

The look on Nick's face made Corey feel like he'd asked one too many questions because Nick looked so angry. He wasn't sure he'd get any more answers, so he gently gave Nick's hand another squeeze, trying to encourage him. "You can talk to me, Nick."

Nick took a deep breath and let it out. "I don't like to think about that day. I have nightmares about it."

Corey heard the heaviness in Nick's words and wished he didn't have to push, but if there was a way for him to help, he needed to hear the whole story.

Nick groaned as he looked up at the ceiling, and his words were barely a whisper. "We—me and Melissa—had volunteered to help at a garage sale fundraiser for her school. She's a preschool teacher at a Christian school, and the sale was at another teacher's house." After a long pause, he went on. "Well, someone else was there to help out—this guy I'd met, David. He was new in town and we'd talked a few times and gone out for a beer once."

Corey waited, giving Nick time to gather his thoughts. Nick let go of Corey's hand and rubbed his eyes. "I went inside to get some iced tea and David was in the kitchen, so we started talking. One thing led to another—it was the stupidest thing I could have done, but I let him kiss me right there in the kitchen."

"Oh, boy," Corey muttered.

"Yeah, well, Melissa walked in on us. There was absolutely no way she didn't know what was happening. She ran out screaming and left in the car."

"Shit," was all Corey was able to say.

"By the time I got back to our place, she'd thrown a bunch of my stuff out in the yard and was ranting and raving, threatening to call the police if I didn't leave—saying she hated me, wanted a divorce, and that I disgusted her more than she could ever imagine, and that she was going to tell my folks and my whole family, our friends, and that everyone in town would know what I was."

Now it was Corey's turn to rub his eyes. Nick was on a roll and the words just tumbled out of his mouth in a rush. The pangs of sympathy he felt for Nick almost overwhelmed him.

"My parents love Melissa. Everyone does. She's cute and sweet and everything a man should want in a woman. Everyone expected us to start a family. I tried to love her, but I was never any good at it—I couldn't be the husband she deserved." Nick looked up at the ceiling and sighed. "And it's really too bad, because I actually liked being married, a lot." Nick let out a humorless chuckle. "I know it probably sounds weird, but the idea of being married—having one person in your life to make a home with, to share everything with—to provide for. That part of the whole set up I really liked. She just wasn't my type, to put it politely." Nick drew in a shaky breath and his eyes filled with unshed tears. "I felt like scum that day and there was nothing I could do but what I did. She would have called the police on me if I hadn't left, and I couldn't let that happen." After another pause, he went on. "My hometown is really small—everyone knows everyone else. I'd never have gotten another job—I'd have been the laughing stock, and worse. We all would have suffered if I'd stayed. And that's why I can't let anyone find me. I want them to think I died. It's best for everyone."

"How can it be best for your folks to think you're dead?"

"You don't know them, Corey," Nick said in a slightly raised voice. "If they were the kind of parents I could have opened up to, none of this would have ever happened—living a damn lie my entire life, marrying Melissa." Nick lowered his voice. "My dad especially—he'd wish I had died, believe me, so what I did spares him of having to look at me—the son who brought down a pile of pain and humiliation on the family."

"What about your mom?" Corey asked, his voice barely a whisper.

"She always goes along with what he says, so my guess is she's glad I'm gone too." Nick turned his head toward Corey. "Your parents are glad you left, aren't they?"

"This isn't the same as your situation. It's true we never got along that well, and sure, they were uncomfortable with me around after I came out—didn't know how to relate to me at all, but they know I'm safe and living near my mom's brother."

"Well, I did what I felt I had to do," Nick said firmly.

Corey gathered a somewhat stiff and resisting Nick into his arms. He didn't think what Nick was doing was right, not by a mile, but this wasn't the time to try to talk him out of it.

Instead, he whispered into Nick's ear, "I love you."

CHAPTER TEN

THE SATURDAY before Thanksgiving, Nick stepped outside his room carrying a pillowcase of dirty laundry and his backpack. Once he made sure the door was locked, he set out on a nice brisk walk toward Main Street. He was looking forward to being at the gym again because he felt comfortable and more at home there than in his room.

Thoughts of the night before were at the forefront of his mind. He'd made good progress on the mural even with Corey breathing down his neck and looking at him with those big brown eyes of his. Corey always seemed to bring out the best in him, and maybe he'd been showing off a bit with his paintbrush, because he'd done some of his best work to date.

He decided to grab a cup of coffee at the convenience store, a habit he'd gotten into on his walks to and from the gym. He filled the cup, paid, and sat down at a tiny table. After taking a few sips of the scalding hot coffee, he looked up to see Mrs. Geiego, the owner, heading his way with a sandwich in each hand.

"Are you hungry for breakfast or lunch?" she asked with a big smile.

"You don't have to feed me. I've got coffee, I'm good."

She set the sandwiches down in front of him. "Nick, you're too thin, eat... eat!"

He reached for his wallet, but she slapped his hand. "No, no, no, I brought them for you—on the house."

"You've gotta stop this, you'll go broke feeding me."

"Nonsense," she said, pinching his cheek. Just then her husband called out needing her help, so she was off as quickly as she'd come.

Nick unwrapped the breakfast sandwich and took a bite. He'd only been in town two weeks, but he felt much more at home here than he had in the town he'd lived in his whole life.

He thought about the last breakfast he and Melissa had eaten together—scrambled eggs and toast. She'd always gone out of her way to do special things for him. All the times she'd told him she loved him, not one time had he ever felt even one-tenth how he'd felt a couple nights ago when Corey had said those words to him. What an ass he was. Why couldn't he have been honest with her—with everyone?

He finished his breakfast and stuck the other sandwich into his pack and headed out. He didn't see Mr. and Mrs. Griego around, but he'd see them again soon.

Corey arrived at work at eight fifteen in a great mood. He'd invited Nick to his house for the weekend, and he definitely had plans for his boyfriend. The gym wasn't staffed on Sundays, so they could stay up late and then sleep in. Corey had been to the store bright and early that morning and bought what he needed for his weekend guest—food, and condoms and lube, things he couldn't wait to use. Thinking about those items, and what they'd get up to under the sheets, made his dick stir.

Since two days before, when they'd had the heart-to-heart in his bed, he felt so much closer to Nick and that made him over the moon happy.

As he parked the car he couldn't help smiling to himself, and he couldn't help thinking about the evening before when they'd flirted right there in the gym while Nick worked on his creation. Every time he was with Nick, he fell more in love with him.

He got out of the car, anxious to begin the day. With the holiday looming, classes were canceled and there were no personal training appointments scheduled. The gym was less crowded than usual, so Corey and the girls were able to take it a little easier. Nick, on the other hand, sure hadn't slowed down and had gotten a lot done on the mural. Corey was more than impressed with what Nick had accomplished, and so was everyone else who'd seen and commented on it.

He barely got through the front door before Dean was on him like an annoying fly. Corey sighed as Dean came out of the office.

"Got plans for Thanksgiving?" Dean asked.

"I'm serving dinners at the mission, why?"

"Just making friendly conversation." After a brief pause, Dean went on. "Aren't you going to ask me what *I'm* doing?"

Corey figured he'd humor the guy and maybe he'd shut up quicker. "Okay, I'll bite. What are you doing for the holiday?"

"I'm going to my sister's place. She said I could bring someone." Dean waggled his eyebrows. "Don't suppose you'd change your plans and come?"

Corey could tell by the way Dean said that, and by the ridiculous look on his face, he wasn't serious about the offer. "You're full of hot air, Dean."

"Well, if you don't want to come, I wonder if Nick would if I invited him?"

Corey kept his mouth shut and tried not to show his irritation. He knew Dean was just trying to push his buttons, and he certainly wasn't going to volunteer the information that Nick would be with him at the mission.

Dean laughed like he'd told a hilarious joke. "Don't worry, man, I know Nick's taken." He slapped Corey on the arm. "It's so damn obvious that the two of you have been in each other's pants."

Corey quickly glanced around to see if anyone was within earshot. Luckily, no one was. He gave Dean a hostile stare—he seemed to take the hint and backed down.

Looking across the gym toward the mural wall, Dean sounded sincere when he said, "Your artist sure knows his way around a paintbrush. It's really looking good."

"Thanks, I like it too," Corey said gruffly and walked into the office, wondering if he'd ever be able to talk to Dean without becoming so irritated. He took in a deep breath and then blew it out, wondering where Katie was. Looking to the weight room, he caught sight of her coming out of the janitor closet carrying a broom. He gave a slight wave, so she'd know he'd arrived.

Not long after, he noticed Dean leaving, so that got rid of one annoyance, but unfortunately, Alan had come in to lift weights and Katie had joined him. Lately, she'd been letting Alan show her how to tone her arms, and Corey had to admit that she looked pretty good.

Anxious to get on with the weekend, he hoped it wouldn't be long before Nick came in to paint. The night before, Nick had said he wanted to work some on the mural before they left for Corey's house. Obviously slacking off was not part of Nick's nature.

He'd been so deep in thought, sitting behind the computer, that he'd missed seeing Nick out the front window, but when the main door opened and in Nick stepped, he was surprised but pleased that Nick was carrying his backpack and a stuffed full pillowcase.

Corey smiled and got up from his chair and met Nick at the office door. He thought better of giving him a hug, and instead, settled for a fist bump as Nick entered the office.

"Hey, I see you brought your laundry after all," Corey said, gesturing at the pillowcase.

"Yeah," Nick sighed. "I appreciate you letting me take care of it at your place. It'll save me a few bucks, but I'd rather be doing... other things than watching my clothes go around and around in the washer and then the dryer."

Corey smiled at that part, 'doing other things,' because he was aiming for exactly just that. "Good. Glad you reconsidered. You're going to be there anyway."

"Yeah, you're right. It's just that I hate having to do laundry during our weekend together."

"It won't interfere, I promise."

"Shall I leave my stuff in here or out in a cubicle?"

"You can put it in the corner. Nobody'll bother it there."

"Okay, I'll get started working so I can at least get a little done." Nick had started to turn toward the door but stopped. "Oh, and guess what?" he said beaming.

"What?"

"I've lined up another painting job."

"Great—where?"

"It's not too glamorous... a gas station bathroom, but hey! Money's money, right?"

Corey joined Nick in a hearty laugh, but he couldn't help but have mixed feelings about what it was going to be like when Nick was finished at the gym and started going off to new jobs. With no painting for Nick to do at the gym, Corey wondered how much he'd be seeing his man in the future. Nick leaned against the doorframe and Corey focused his attention back to what Nick was saying.

"Yeah, it's that big gas station and mini-mart about half way between here and the motel. I stop there for a bite to eat sometimes and I've gotten to know the husband and wife who manage it. Really nice people—married forty years. They even tried to set me up with their niece, and I had to tell them if they had a nephew that'd be more my speed." Nick laughed. "Don't worry, only kidding about going out with their nephew." His expression turned thoughtful. "It's sure nice to start fresh in a new place and not have to try to be something, or someone, I'm not." He smiled then. "Shoot, how'd I get so serious? Anyway, when they found out I paint, one thing led to another. And don't worry, this won't interfere with my work here. I can do both jobs."

"You don't want to spread yourself too thin," Corey said.

"Back home, I'd have two or three jobs going at the same time, in a good month."

Corey loved Nick's enthusiasm. "All right then. Sounds like a plan—let's see," he said seriously. "I'll bet you'll be using a color like... oh, I don't know, Fresh Lime, or Peppermint Leaf?"

Nick snorted out a laugh. "How'd you know the bathroom will be green?"

"Green? Now who needs to learn the proper name of the colors?" Corey bumped his shoulder against Nick's. "I don't know why I thought of green. I guess a lot of gas station bathrooms I've been in have been green."

"Well, for your information, I was thinking of something like 'Sound of Nature' for the shade of green." Nick chuckled and headed out into the gym.

Corey hadn't noticed until then that Nick had on the gray T-shirt he'd given him, and he couldn't take his eyes off Nick's backside as he walked toward the wall where he'd been working. With some effort, he tore his gaze away and went back to sit behind the desk.

Just then, Katie came in looking like she had something on her mind if her pursed lips were any indication. Before she spoke, she glanced at Nick's stuff in the corner.

"What's this?"

"Nick left his things in here," Corey said, trying to sound like it was no big deal so she wouldn't start interrogating him.

"Is he going someplace?"

"The backpack? I guess so."

Katie smiled knowingly, and he knew she'd figured out what was up. Luckily for him, she seemed preoccupied, so she didn't give him a bad time.

She pulled the band off her ponytail letting her hair fall loosely. "Um, I wanted to see if it was okay for me to take an extra-long lunch break today."

"Again? You going somewhere with Alan?"

"Yeah, he invited me out."

"How long do you plan to be?"

"Is a couple hours too long?"

"I... guess not, but don't make it any longer than that, okay? I want to leave early."

"Thanks, Cuz. You're the best." She came around the desk and gave him a quick hug. "I'm going to go change." She then started for the door but stopped and looked back. "When you get to know Alan better, you'll like him. You and Dad both will."

Corey saw the hope in her eyes like she expected him to say something reassuring, and he wanted to, but the nagging feeling that Alan would end up hurting her hadn't gone away. If anything, as each day passed, he felt even more strongly that Alan was *not* the man for her.

"How well do you really know Alan?" he asked.

Her brown eyes flashed with anger. "I know him a lot better than you know that painter out there," she said with a defiant toss of her head toward the door. She turned her back and left without another word.

Corey sat still for a moment thinking that he'd really blown it. He and Uncle Ed had to be careful, because anything unfavorable said about Alan, pushed Katie toward him even more.

He sat for a good ten minutes not doing anything but fretting about Katie. On the monitor he saw her and Alan get into the car and leave. Sighing, he stood and headed to the cardio room to the drink machine, but detoured to where Nick crouched at the wall, working on the lower section of the mural.

"I'm getting a bottle of water from the machine. You want something?"

"I'll have what you're having," Nick said, giving Corey a quick glance over his shoulder. Corey wondered how Nick could make such a simple sentence sound so damn provocative.

After getting their drinks, he handed one to Nick, admiring the work he'd done. Nick was in the zone, so Corey headed back to the office. On his way, he stopped to chat with a couple of diehard members who hadn't let the holiday week stop them from their workouts.

Once back at the desk, he couldn't get Katie off his mind. He didn't want to jeopardize his relationship with her, so that was why he hadn't mentioned anything about the morning he'd seen her boyfriend by the bus stop arguing with some guy. But the uncomfortable feeling of doom wouldn't let him go. He slapped his hands on the desk in frustration and thought about the computer that stored the names of the members who came in each day and then he looked up at the monitors. He took a deep breath and let it out, got up and closed the office door on the gym side and sat back down, entering the codes he needed to review the video feed from a few days before.

A red flag had gone up for him on the morning when Nick had said that Alan was there in the middle of the night. He'd been tempted to check up on it then, but he'd been too preoccupied with Nick. He'd also tried to give Alan the benefit of the doubt, but he was going to have to review the video, as he should have done at the time.

The first order of business was finding the date stamp for the night when Nick had begun painting. That was about three and a half days back. Before he could really get anywhere in his investigation, the unwelcome ring of the phone interrupted him. He took the call, dealing with it as fast as he could and went right back to his search, quickly locating the date.

He glanced at the menu for that twenty-four-hour period and figured it would take some time to locate the exact spot he needed to see. Instead of wishing that Nick would finish his painting quickly, he now hoped Nick would take his time—but Nick wasn't the problem—it was Katie. If she came back before he finished his search, he wasn't sure what he would say to her—if she were still speaking to him—should she catch on to what he was doing.

He sat immersed in the video for a good hour, stopping only twice for members who'd tapped on the door to ask a question. His eyes were getting blurry and his butt was getting sore, so he stood for a moment, willing some blood flow back there, rubbing his glutes. A sore butt wasn't something he needed before the night got started. If he was lucky, he'd have that before the night was over.

Sitting back down, he had to be close to finding what he was looking for. Scrolling through a few more frames... Ah, there was Nick that first night washing the walls—and man, he looked hot. He had a well-toned back, and his arms—Corey took a swig of water, which so far was all he'd had for lunch, and focused on the screen again. As tempted as he was to watch Nick on the video, he went to the next menu box and continued there. Soon he saw Ted and Alan enter the gym; thanking God that he was finally at the right spot in the video feed. He looked to the clock and tried to stay calm because he figured he didn't have much time left before Katie would be back.

He watched intently while the pair bypassed the cubicles and headed for the weight room, still fully clothed, including jackets. That got his attention right off the bat. Obviously, they weren't there to work out if they kept their jackets on. He went to another frame—Alan leaning back against the lateral raise machine, while Ted stood a couple feet away. It looked like they were just having a casual conversation, so maybe they'd just come in to get out of the cold. He started to wonder if anything worth looking at would happen when he noticed Alan crane his neck as if he were looking into the cardio room. Then he stood up straight and quickly headed over to the stairs with Ted hot on his heels.

Corey advanced to the next frames to see what might take place downstairs. He'd bet money they hadn't gone down there to use the punching bags. Seemingly they wanted privacy and wanted to make sure Nick, or anyone else, wouldn't hear their conversation.

Katie's looming return made him so jittery he felt like he'd surely jump out of his skin. *Please no interruptions right now, and maybe I can get to the bottom of this before she walks in on me.*

Alan and Ted moved toward the far wall until they were partly out of range. Corey held his breath, waiting to see if they'd take one more step and be totally off camera. They stopped, but there was no guarantee they wouldn't at some point end up beyond the camera, which added to his tension. He needed to see what was going on.

Come on guys, give me something I can use.

He kept watching and it soon became clear that they were having an intense discussion. He couldn't see Alan's face, but the angle of the camera showed Ted's quite well. The image wasn't crystal clear, but it was enough to tell him that Ted was angry by the way his face scrunched up when he spoke and by the way he waved his hands around. What came next was jaw-dropping and eye-opening. Alan reached into his pants pocket and then held something out to Ted. All of a sudden, bills flew into the air when Ted struck Alan's hand away.

If Corey thought Ted had looked pissed off before, it was

nothing compared to how he appeared at this point. Ted drew his clenched fist back and looked as if he might smash Alan in the face, but he backed off, said a few more words and then left Alan to pick up the money on the floor. After that, Alan scrambled to follow Ted, who'd stomped toward the stairs.

What Corey had seen disgusted him. Having two jerks in the gym in such a volatile situation had his blood boiling, and one being the idiot his cousin was head-over-heels with, made it all the worse.

What the heck was going on? This was the second guy he'd seen Alan having an argument with. Alan was up to no good, that Corey was sure of. But there wasn't time to think any more about it. He hurriedly shut the video program down and opened the office door. Wiping his sweaty palms on his pants, he glanced around to see if Katie had snuck in without him seeing her, but to his relief, she wasn't in sight. He'd have to put the Alan-Ted problem on the back burner for now, because the rest of the weekend was for him and Nick, and nothing was going to ruin that.

"Take your bag to the bedroom and make yourself at home," Corey said when he and Nick finally stepped through the front door of Corey's house.

"Don't mind if I do," Nick hollered from halfway down the hall.

"I'm going to have something to drink, do you want anything? How about a snack?" Corey called back to him from the kitchen doorway.

"No thanks, I'm good."

Nick was in an awfully good mood, Corey mused. It was easy to recognize how much working on the mural meant to him. Art was obviously his passion, and every time Nick spoke of it his eyes lit up. Besides that, landing another job, even though it was strictly painting, had to boost his spirits and help take his mind off his troubles.

Corey also figured that avoiding going back to that rundown room might have something to do with his mood too. He took a drink of green tea from a bottle in the refrigerator, grabbed a handful of trail mix, and gave the dining room table the once-over, making sure he'd set out all the dishes they'd need for their dinner later that evening. He hoped there'd be a lot more opportunities for Nick to spend time at the house, possibly even make it a permanent arrangement—yes, the thought had crossed his mind on more than one occasion. Maybe come spring he'd have this man to share the porch bench with, the one that Katie had given him for a housewarming present.

Then there was what they'd planned for tonight, and Corey wasn't thinking about the dinner he'd prepared, although he hoped Nick liked lasagna. Well, maybe he didn't actually make it himself since he bought it frozen from the store and had it tucked away in the freezer, along with the mint gelato for dessert. The salad came in a package, the bread from a bag, and the wine from a bottle, but he'd put a lot of thought into it and had shopped his heart out.

He looked down the hall and saw no sign of Nick, so he wondered if he'd stopped to use the hall bathroom. He waited a minute longer, and seeing nothing more than the dim hallway, he went looking. The bathroom was empty when he peeked in, so he proceeded to his bedroom. When he opened the door, what he saw surprised the hell out of him. His bare-chested man was a vision to his eyes, the way he was sprawled in the bed, the sheet draped seductively over his lower half, a hint of his treasure trail just visible at the edge of the sheet. The slight tenting of said sheet sent Corey's dick into overdrive.

"Damn," he said, trying not to drool. He couldn't wait to stare at what lay hidden under there. His eyes stayed fixed on the folds and wrinkles across Nick's lap and then with difficulty, because damn! He raised his gaze to meet Nick's hooded eyes.

Nick snorted out a small laugh and drawled, "What are you waiting for?"

Corey threw off his shirt and nearly tripped getting his shoes off as he reached the bed. Nick stretched forward and yanked him by his belt on to the bed, then pulled him close. The kiss Nick laid on him—full of passion and hunger—took his breath away. When they pulled apart, Nick went for the belt buckle, and between the two of them, Corey's pants and boxers came off within seconds, despite the obstacle of his stiff cock.

"Glad we didn't break that off," Nick said, patting it lightly. He barely had the words out before devouring it to the root.

Corey moaned and fell back on the bed, Nick not losing contact or missing a beat. This was only the second time Nick had done this to him—deep-throated—and Corey could tell immediately that Nick's technique had improved in spades, so much so, that after just ten seconds, Corey tugged on Nick's hair to get his attention and squirmed away for fear of coming too soon.

"I want to make this last," he cautioned.

Nick backed off and sat up slightly. "Am I doing something wrong?"

Corey pulled him down for a kiss and whispered close to his lips. "Just the opposite, baby. You're doing everything right, that's why I had to slow you down."

"I'll make it last as long as you want," Nick murmured, placing a soft kiss on Corey's bottom lip.

Corey kissed Nick desperately, using plenty of tongue, and when Nick's rock hardness rubbed against his, he was ready to unload.

Corey pulled back to grab for the K-Y and condom on the nightstand.

"I don't know what I'm doing," Nick said, sounding nervous and unsure of himself when Corey laid the supplies on the bed.

"I'll help you," Corey coaxed, taking Nick's hand and placing the condom in it. "You do know what this is for, don't you?" he teased.

That got him a big smile.

"I think I can figure it out," Nick said, his tangled hair falling around his face when he looked down at his hand.

Despite Nick's noticeably trembling fingers, he had the package ripped open in two seconds. He slowly rolled the condom down on himself, grunting and tugging on the latex as if it were too small to fit and then finished with a snap. That simple act was the best X-rated show Corey had seen in a long time. He had to use all his willpower not to tackle Nick right then and there.

"Nice opening," Corey purred. "I can't wait until you get to the main event." Corey then squeezed lube on his own hand and slicked Nick's dick up good. Then he put a large glob on Nick's fingers, rolled on to his stomach, and lifted his hips up for the taking.

"I'm okay, go ahead," Corey said. "Please."

He relaxed as Nick's fingers, smooth and slippery, slid along his crack, and when Nick's dick hovered near his entrance, he braced himself. He was nervous, but this was the man he loved, and he trusted Nick. Even though Nick had never said those words to him, he felt that love when Nick looked into his eyes and by the way Nick caressed his skin.

Nick's warm hands softly massaged Corey's ass cheeks and then his touch became stronger, gripping, his fingers digging into Corey's skin, spreading him wider. After what seemed like an eternity of nudging and prodding, Nick's moan as he pressed in was exactly what Corey needed, slow and tentative at first, but Nick quickly picked up the pace with short, smooth strokes. Corey's breath hitched when Nick gave him several sharp thrusts.

Nick's lack of experience with men didn't have any bearing on his expertise with using that dick of his. All Corey could do was grunt, incapable of any rational thinking. What Nick was doing to him caused waves of electricity to surge through his ass, up his spine and then back down to his balls.

Corey tried to keep his hand off his dick, but he couldn't for long and soon he was shooting his load. His orgasm felt like a bolt of lightning had struck him, taking his breath away. Before his spasms finished, Nick gave one last deep thrust and dug his fingers into Corey's flesh, and from the husky, low moan from behind him, he knew Nick had sparks flying through him too.

They both collapsed on the mattress, Nick ending up slightly on top of Corey. Gasping for air, Corey felt like he'd run a marathon. Their lovemaking must have affected Nick the same way, considering how loud he was panting.

Corey finally had to struggle out from under his exhausted lover. He'd gotten a sound between a grunt and a sigh from Nick and then felt him sit up, taking care of the used condom.

When Corey had enough strength to turn over on his back, Nick promptly cuddled into his arms, and that's how they remained while Corey tried to get his heartbeat to slow back to normal.

This amazing feeling of contentment that had taken control of his mind and body must really be love, he thought, as he ran his hand over Nick's left cheek. In response, Nick snuggled his right one closer into Corey's shoulder.

"That was the best sex I've ever had," Nick mumbled.

Corey wondered if Nick was talking in his sleep because he sounded so groggy and was barely audible. He also wondered how deep Nick's feelings were for him. Was Nick capable of moving on to a new relationship without dealing with what he'd run from? Was he able to move forward with this new relationship, knowing that Nick hadn't dealt with his past? He'd been so worried about Katie getting hurt by Alan, but maybe the person he should be worrying about was himself.

He pulled Nick close and tried not to obsess. Monday was a long way off, and he intended to have a great weekend with Nick.

And, they'd be spending Thanksgiving together—with Nick meeting Uncle Ed.

Nick wasn't getting away from him if he had anything to say about it.

CHAPTER ELEVEN

TIME FLIES when you're having fun, Corey mused, while driving to work on the day before Thanksgiving. Nick had been busy painting at the gas station the past couple of days, so they hadn't seen much of each other, but tonight they'd be sharing a bed again, and he couldn't wait. He smiled thinking about them spending the holiday together.

Corey hadn't brought it up, but he knew the holiday wouldn't be easy for Nick. He had to wonder what the heck Nick's family thought about him just disappearing without a trace. They had to be worried sick. He didn't agree with how Nick had handled or was handling the whole situation but, so far, he hadn't pushed and had kept his opinions to himself—he sure didn't want to put a damper on what they were starting up between them. The weekend before had been perfect in all ways, and he wanted more. He almost felt guilty for being so happy.

Whenever he thought about how Katie had disappointed her dad by choosing to spend Thanksgiving with Alan, he felt bad. The negative vibes he had toward Alan worsened after what he'd seen on the video, leaving him troubled. And it wasn't just that, he didn't have a clue what to do about what he'd seen, or what it really meant, and he didn't dare tell Uncle Ed.

When he turned into the parking lot, the two police cars parked near the gym got his full attention.

What now?

He pulled into a spot right in front of the main entrance and quickly got out of the car. No policemen were in sight, so he assumed they were inside one of the nearby stores or were inside the gym. Sure enough, when he opened the front door, Katie and two cops were in the office.

"Good morning, officers," Corey said entering the room, looking up at the clock to see that it was only eight fifteen.

He recognized Officer Kelly from the other day, who quickly introduced Officer Matthews. The second officer seemed as serious as Officer Kelly and barely acknowledged his appearance. Corey took a second to look at Katie, who was clearly rattled. Having police at the gym twice in one week was pretty unsettling, so he understood totally how she felt.

She stared at him, her eyes wide with fright. "Pinocchio's Pizza was burglarized last night. I was just getting ready to check our security footage since I think it's close enough that we could have picked something up."

"If you have something we can use it would be extremely helpful," Officer Kelly said.

"The camera view doesn't reach over to their door, but it would depend on which direction the thief, or thieves came from. Did they get in through the front?" Corey asked.

"They sure did. They disarmed the security system before they entered, so the owner and staff weren't aware of anything until they arrived this morning," Officer Kelly said.

"Miss Knight has already given us a list of the members who were in here after Pinocchio's closing time, so we can question them," Officer Matthews added.

"Good," Corey said, nodding at Katie. "Why don't you take a breather and let me see what I can find," Corey told her.

From the look on her face, she seemed glad for a break and went out into the gym. Officer Matthews excused himself to go back to the restaurant, while Officer Kelly stayed.

Corey plunked himself down at the desk and gave his attention to the computer monitor, bringing up the menu and searching for the early morning hours.

"Here we are," he said to the officer.

Officer Kelly walked behind the desk and leaned over Corey's shoulder while Corey clicked past a few of the menu boxes. "I think they close at midnight?"

"Yes, that's correct. I take it you've eaten a few pizzas from there," Officer Kelly said.

Corey grinned, surprised by the officer's attempt to lighten the mood. "Yeah, quite a few. Best pizza in town if you ask me."

They began watching footage of the parking lot, beginning at midnight. Cars pulled out of the parking spaces and drove out of view, but none had entered the lot or parked. The shots were dark, and it was hard to make out detail, none of the frames showing the front of the restaurant. He and the officer kept searching the data feed, and in the box that was date stamped two fifteen a.m. a figure dressed in dark clothing walked briskly out of the shadows into the dim glow of the parking lot lights. He passed in and out of the frame in seconds.

"Let's look at that again," Officer Kelly said, focused on the monitor.

Corey ran it back and they watched a second time.

"Can you slow it down?" Officer Kelly asked.

Corey tapped a few keys to slow the video down, and along with the officer, he watched closely a couple more times, again noticing the dark-colored hoodie from the first viewing. The physique of the person was clearly male. He held his head down with his shoulders slouched and his hands in his pockets. The dark hood of the jacket covered his hair, and his face was not at all visible.

Officer Kelly scanned the paper in his hand. "I don't see anyone checking in here at two fifteen, and nothing else is open at that hour. By the looks of this guy, he's up to no good."

They watched the rest of the footage a while longer, and the hooded figure was the only person the camera picked up who seemed out of place, and suspicious.

"I'm going to the restaurant for a few minutes. I'll stop back and get a copy of this if you don't mind, before I head to the station," Officer Kelly said.

"Sure, no problem, I can burn it to a disk for you. Uh, do you think it's the same person who broke into the smoke shop?" Corey asked.

"We won't know that for a while yet," the officer answered and then he promptly left.

Corey was unable to get the image of the man on the video out of his mind. It could be anyone—the problem was there just wasn't enough light to make out anything specific about this person—he had an average build. Half the guys in town were built like that and probably owned dark-colored hoodies. Hell, even Nick's build could be called average and he had a black hoodie that he wore all the time.

Katie must have been watching for Officer Kelly to leave because he hadn't been gone a minute, when she came blazing into the office.

Corey gave a long, weary sigh as he started to copy the section of video the officer needed. The day sure wasn't going like he'd planned.

"I hope you didn't talk to Dean about this," he said, looking at the monitor that showed Dean putting his things into a cubby hole.

"He saw the police cars, so he already knew something's happened. Did you see anything on the video?"

Corey ran a hand over his face. "I'm making a copy for Officer Kelly."

"So, you did see someone," she exclaimed. "Let me see."

"I need to hurry. He's stopping back in a few minutes and wants to take this with him."

"Did you recognize who was on the video?" she asked.

"It wasn't lit very well, so no, we couldn't see the guy's face at all."

"But you think it's the crook?"

"I have no idea, Katie. I'm leaving that to the police."

"Was it just one person?"

"Who are you, Nancy Drew? Give it a rest. We have work to do." He gave her a pointed glare.

"Fine. I'll go stock the bathrooms, boss man," Katie groused. But when the phone rang, she snatched it up, so Corey mouthed the words, *I'll do the bathrooms, and this,* he held up the CD and set it on the desk, *is for Officer Kelly.*

On the way to the bathroom, he saw Dean on the treadmill and hoped to go unnoticed, but of course Dean promptly stopped and jumped off, catching up to him at the janitor's closet.

"I thought you had plans with your sister for the holiday," Corey said.

"You're not trying to get rid of me, are you?" Dean asked with a smug grin.

Corey didn't answer, just proceeded to get the supplies out of the closet.

"Actually, I'm leaving this afternoon, but I wanted to get a run in before I go. I hate Thanksgiving and all that fattening food, don't you?"

It didn't seem like Dean expected an answer because he went on without skipping a beat. "What do you make of all the crime around here all of a sudden?"

Corey headed for the first bathroom with his hands full of paper towels, soap, and toilet paper. "Can't say as I like it much."

"Here, let me carry some of this," Dean said, taking a few rolls of toilet paper. "Do you think it's someone from here? I mean, a member maybe?" he asked, staring intently as if he thought Corey held answers to the mystery.

"How should I know who it is?" Corey asked sharply.

"Don't get your panties in a bunch, babe," Dean scoffed. They began stocking the bathroom while Dean went on. "You were in the office talking with the police, so I—"

"I haven't a clue what's going on, but I highly doubt it's anyone we know. I think all of our members are aware that the surveillance shows part of the parking lot."

"You mean you picked something up on camera?" Dean asked, clearly eager to hear more.

"I didn't say that," Corey said, sorry he'd said as much as he had.

"But it sounded like—"

"I can't discuss this. The cops asked me not to," Corey said, even though that wasn't true.

Dean looked like he had something turning in that brain of his, and Corey didn't know why but it made him uneasy. He wished Dean would go back to the treadmill.

Instead, Dean pulled the bathroom door shut and stepped into Corey's personal space giving him an intense gaze. Corey took a step back, but Dean was right with him, grabbing his arm.

"What's the matter? No one can see us," Dean purred, leaning in for a kiss.

"Get the hell away from me before you end up with a black eye," Corey cautioned, drawing back disgustedly.

"Shit, you're no fun at all. Can't you take a joke?" Dean backed off toward the door. "Well, guess there's a treadmill with my name on it. Happy Thanksgiving," he muttered.

He didn't close the door on his way out.

~~*

At six o'clock, Nick arrived with his backpack slung over his shoulder. "Am I late?" he asked, entering the office.

Corey looked up in surprise from the computer. "Hey, you snuck up on me—did you get your painting all done at the gas station?"

"No, I thought I could get it done, but I'm not quite finished. I had so much prep work to do before I actually started painting that it's taking me quite a while. That bathroom is disgusting."

Corey laughed. "Most public bathrooms are gross."

"If I hadn't changed into clean clothes already, I'd ask you if we could stick around so I could do some more on the mural."

Corey almost started bitching about that, but then he saw the impish grin on his boyfriend's face, and he grinned too. "You almost had me going there for a second," he said, standing up and moving to stand close to Nick, loving the fact he was there.

"Well, I would like to get some more done on it, but I know how you feel about taking time off for the holiday and all."

"It'll be here when we get back," Corey said. "You're not in the habit of working on holidays, are you? I mean, back home."

As soon as the words left his mouth, he was sorry he'd asked, because Nick always looked sad at the mention of his family, and this time was no different. Corey wondered if he'd get a reply.

After a few seconds, Nick finally spoke. "No, I'd never have gotten away with that. We, me and Melissa, would spend Thanksgiving with my folks and Christmas with hers—all the traditional stuff going on."

Nick looked the same as he had that day at Sonic when they'd first talked about his family, like a lost little boy, his shoulders slumped, and hands jammed in his pockets.

"Well, good then, I'm glad to you know you're not a workaholic," Corey said, trying to sound upbeat. "Let me get the office shut down so we can leave."

Nick sat down in the chair by the desk looking deep in thought.

"Are you okay?"

Nick nodded absently.

The break-in was still on Corey's mind and he felt they needed a new topic of conversation. "Uh, when I got to work this morning, I found out the pizza place in the complex was burglarized." He waited for Nick's reaction.

Nick looked up with wide eyes. "Another break-in?"

"Yeah, that's what I said too. The police were here asking questions again. Not the way I like to start the day." Corey sighed turning off the computer.

"I wonder if it's the same person," Nick said.

"The cops wouldn't tell me anything. I guess they don't really know yet."

"I hope they catch whoever it is. So bizarre, to have two so close together."

"Yeah, no kidding, and so do I. It looks like the officers have a good handle on things, so it's probably only a matter of time before they catch the guy or guys. Seems pretty stupid to target the same area so close together, like you said."

"Do they have any clues yet?"

Corey got up from his chair and pushed it under the desk. "Not anything they're willing to share at this time. Why are we spending so much time talking about this when we could be starting our holiday? Come on, let's get out of here."

Nick stood up too. "Okay, sounds good to me."

Only four people were exercising when Corey and Nick stepped through the gym door. "I sure could have gotten a lot of painting done with so few in there," Nick observed with a playful smile.

Corey bumped him with his shoulder. "All work and no play makes Nick a dull boy." They both chuckled and headed for Corey's car.

On Thanksgiving morning, Corey finished his short conversation with Uncle Ed and hung up the phone. He couldn't help but notice the downcast look on Nick's handsome face as he sat at the kitchen table.

"You finished with breakfast? More coffee?" Corey asked.

"I'm good, thanks," Nick answered, a lot quieter than his usual self.

Corey put his hand over Nick's where it rested on the table. "I know I already suggested this last night, and you said no, but you could always call your family today. I'll bet they'd be happy to hear from you."

Nick looked Corey in the eye and said firmly, "I told you why I'm not going to do that, but thanks for caring."

After a few moments of quiet, Corey began clearing the table. "Sorry that all I had to offer you was cereal and toast. I'm not that great of a cook."

"The breakfast was perfect. Everything has been great, Corey." Nick stood up and helped clear their bowls, still looking like he wasn't present at all.

"There's plenty of chicken, and mac and cheese left from KFC if we're hungry tonight after we're back from the mission," Corey said as he arranged the dishes in the dishwasher. "That is if you don't mind leftovers," Corey added, looking at Nick hoping for a response.

Nick just stared at the floor and kicked at a spot with his bare foot and sighed.

"Earth to Nick!"

Nick leaned against the counter and folded his arms. "Hearing you talk to your uncle reminded me that it's been three weeks since I've seen my family, but there's nothing I can do about that. I've made my decision." He looked up at Corey. "I'll snap out of it. And don't worry, I won't ruin Thanksgiving for you and your uncle."

Corey pulled Nick into a hug. "I'm not worried about that."

"Well, I wasn't very good company last night either, was I."

Corey hugged him tighter and rocked them back and forth. "I had an awesome time... from dinner to snuggling with you on the couch watching TV, to bedtime and beyond." He pecked Nick on the cheek.

Nick hugged him back, and soon, the friendly supportive hug Corey had initiated progressed to a full-body press complete with groping and long, deep kisses, which brought back thoughts of the night before. Corey wasn't even thinking of backing off until Nick pulled away. Good thing he did, as it reminded Corey that he'd told Uncle Ed they'd be over to pick him up in fifteen minutes, and it had been ten already, and counting.

"Damn," Corey said, releasing his hold on Nick. "Yeah, I know, we've got to go. Better put your socks and shoes on."

"We'll pick back up where we left off later tonight," Nick said, winking.

With a groan, Corey stepped away and went to the closet for their jackets.

"I can sit in back," Ed said when he and Nick finished shaking hands.

Nick moved to get into the backseat. "I don't mind, sir. You go ahead and ride next to your nephew."

After a bit of small talk while Corey drove, and comments about how quiet the streets were on the holiday, Ed turned to Nick. "Corey tells me you're quite an artist."

Corey looked in the rear-view mirror and saw Nick's eyes light up. "Don't be shy, Nick. You know you're good." Then Corey turned to Ed and hoping to keep the conversation going in the direction it was, rather than anything more personal, he said, "Nick knows the name of every color of paint on the entire color wall display at the store."

Nick laughed. "Don't exaggerate."

"I think he chose the paint by the name of the color," Corey said.

"Is that so?" Uncle Ed asked curiously.

"Yeah, what's that color of green again, Nick?" Before Nick could answer, Corey snorted out a laugh. "Godzilla Green, wasn't it?"

"Very funny," Nick said in a deadpan tone.

"And the black paint—wasn't that something like Darth Vader Black?"

Ed smiled and chuckled.

"Don't mislead your uncle," Nick said.

"And how about the orange one? Something like Belly Button Orange—no, Navel Orange, that was it."

"Wrong again," Nick said, laughing along with Corey and Ed.

"Well, in any case, the colors he picked out really gave the gym a pick-me-up, and you should see the mural he's doing. On our way home, I'd like to stop and show you," Corey said to Ed.

"I'd like that," Ed said.

"I'd stop now, but I don't think we should take the time. I don't want to be late."

"I think you're right. We'd better get to the mission and get started," Ed said. He turned toward Nick again. "I guess you've met my daughter, Katie."

"Yes, sir. She's a hard worker."

"Yeah, I'm good at cracking the whip," Corey joked, hoping to change the subject from Katie and prevent his uncle from brooding.

Luckily, in less than a half a minute, they arrived at the mission. Corey didn't see any place to park in front, so he quickly made a U-turn and parallel parked across the street in the only parking spot that was left in the vicinity. The space was barely big enough for his Kia Soul to fit, but with some snazzy maneuvering he got the job done. He ventured a glance into the rear-view mirror and noticed the grin on Nick's face.

"Hold on to your hat, fellas," Ed exclaimed. "For God's sake, who taught you to drive?" he said good-naturedly.

"I learned from the best, Uncle Ed," Corey laughed.

The three of them got out of the car and walked across the street toward the steps of the mission.

As they approached the building, they were met with enticing aromas. Corey thought back to the last time he'd eaten a turkey dinner. The previous Thanksgiving he'd had the midday meal right here, and afterward, an evening meal with his uncle and Katie, who had cooked their turkey in Uncle Ed's kitchen. One whole year, and a lot had changed since then. Katie spending the day with Alan surely was on his uncle's mind, and what about Nick? He must have all kinds of memories for this holiday. And, would they get through the day without Ed hearing about Nick having stayed at the mission?

Instead of thinking about the past or things beyond his control, Corey needed to focus on giving the homeless and less fortunate a pleasant day. The three of them had decided to donate their time helping to make that happen, and here they were, ready to get started.

"It's a wonder we made it here in one piece," Ed quipped going through the door behind Corey and Nick.

"Thank God the angels of the mission were watching over us," Nick said as he turned and winked at Ed.

Twenty to thirty people, Corey guessed, milled about the room, and this was only the beginning of the crowd expected.

Nick patted him on the shoulder. "Be right back."

Corey watched Nick maneuver around a cluster of people, and once across the room, he stopped to speak to a couple with several kids huddled together. Corey assumed they were the people he'd mentioned inviting from the motel. He wondered if any of the people Nick had met when he'd stayed at the mission were still here, but it wasn't likely. Most were usually in and out of there pretty fast.

A cheery voice caught Corey's attention. "Well, hello there," Mrs. Franklin said loudly over the conversations in the crowded room.

"Happy Thanksgiving, ma'am," Corey said. "This is my uncle, Ed Knight. Uncle Ed, this is Mrs. Franklin, the program director here."

Corey noticed how Mrs. Franklin's eyes softened when she looked at Ed and shook his hand, and it sure caught his attention when she told his uncle to please call her Rita. She hadn't told Corey to use her first name. What really caught him by surprise was when his uncle smiled at her and insisted that she call him Ed. He looked from his uncle to Mrs. Franklin and suppressed a grin.

"Where's Nick?" Mrs. Franklin asked, just as he stepped up beside them. "Oh, there you are, young man," she said. "It's good to see you again."

Corey watched Uncle Ed for his reaction, but the fact that Mrs. Franklin had already met Nick before seemed to escape his notice. Obviously, Ed's mind was on other matters, so Corey breathed a sigh of relief.

"Follow me," Mrs. Franklin said. "And I'll get you all started in the kitchen."

The three of them, along with numerous other volunteers, stayed busy with a steady stream of people showing up for their free Thanksgiving dinner. With very little time for conversation about anything except the tasks at hand, Corey didn't have to worry about Ed asking Nick any awkward personal questions.

Despite the hard work, Corey enjoyed himself more than any other Thanksgiving in recent years. He loved watching Nick serve meals to the men, women, and children. His caring nature came through with every plate he served and every kind word and watching him made Corey's heart do flip-flops.

When it was time for their break, Corey followed Nick to the food line and listened amusedly as Nick instructed one of the other volunteers what to put on his plate.

"I'd like two slices of turkey, if that's okay, one dark and one light, and no gravy on it—uh, but I'll have extra gravy on my mashed potatoes." Nick must have sensed Corey staring at him because he turned and flashed one of his easygoing smiles.

Corey smiled back and held out his own plate to be filled. He accepted a little of everything, and when they found a place to sit, Corey eyed Nick's pumpkin pie.

"I see you wrangled an extra dollop of whip cream from the cute little volunteer who's been batting her eyes at you all day."

"You're just jealous I got more than you—and a bigger piece of pie." Nick chuckled, looking shy, but smug too.

They'd eaten about half their food when Corey saw Ed and Mrs. Franklin sit down together to eat. He nudged Nick's arm with his elbow and subtly glanced in their direction, making sure Nick knew who he was looking at. He leaned in whispering, "I'm blown away how my uncle hit it off with Mrs. Franklin. I noticed it the minute they met. Look, they're even eating together."

Nick was discreet and didn't stare, just smiled his approval. Corey wondered what Katie would say when she was told that her dad seemed quite attracted to Mrs. Franklin—Rita. The expression 'there's someone for everyone' seemed to be true for this family all of a sudden.

"Do you think he'll ask her out on a date?" Nick asked quietly.

The question took Corey by surprise because he'd never known of his uncle going out on a date before.

"Well, if he does, more power to him," Corey said softly.

On the way home, Corey pulled into the gym parking lot, glad for something else to keep Nick's mind off his family back home, and his uncle's mind off Katie.

"I'm looking forward to seeing how the gym looks with all the fancy colors, and I'm most interested in seeing the art," Uncle Ed said, getting out of the car.

"Let's have a quick look before going home. You're probably tired from the long day," Corey said, patting his uncle on the back.

"Well, not so much tired, I'm so full I can only waddle," Ed said.

Nick patted his own stomach. "I know what you mean."

The three of them trudged to the gym door, and Corey unlocked the main door, following Nick and Ed inside. A few members were scattered throughout the gym, but none that Corey knew by name.

"The place looks a lot brighter with the fresh paint," Ed said.

"I took pictures of it before and after, and I can't believe how much better it looks now," Corey said.

Once the three of them were standing at the mural wall, Uncle Ed let out a whistle. "Now this is really impressive."

"Didn't I tell you? He's a fantastic artist."

"Yeah, yeah, I'm a real Picasso," Nick said, a slight blush showing on his cheeks.

Corey put his arm around Nick, giving him a quick one-arm hug. "Don't be shy, it's the truth."

"The blending of the colors is fantastic," Ed said, stepping closer to get a better look. "The images really jump off the wall."

Nick's smile lit up his whole face.

After five minutes of admiring and talking about the new wall, the three of them headed toward the door to leave. Corey said 'Happy Thanksgiving' to the members they passed and then held the door open for Ed and Nick and locked it before he led the way to the car.

"I know I've always said I might come here to exercise sometime—well, I'm still thinking about it," Ed said.

Corey smiled. "You're welcome any time, you know that. I'll help you get started when you're ready." He opened the car door for Ed.

"Yeah, uh, Rita said she might be interested in a membership too," Ed said as he got in.

"Is that right?" Corey glanced at Nick, who had opened the back door, and they grinned at each other. Nick gave a thumbs-up before he got in.

"Well, that would be great Uncle Ed. You work too much. Some time spent in the gym would be good for you, so give it some thought and just do it."

Corey closed Ed's door and walked around the car and got into the driver's side, feeling content and satisfied with how well the day had turned out.

CHAPTER TWELVE

THE SOUND of raindrops echoed in the cramped space Corey called a laundry room. He'd washed the sheets he and Nick had made a mess of, and when he opened the dryer to transfer them, he found that Nick had forgotten the laundry he'd done on Friday morning before he'd left. Now Saturday morning, Corey hoped that sitting in a heap for twenty-four hours hadn't left them too wrinkled. He pulled out several T-shirts, numerous pairs of socks, a pile of boxers, a couple pair of sleep pants, and the last item he reached for was Nick's black hoodie.

Damn, I'll bet he'll be missing this, Corey thought. He held it up to his nose and sniffed while rubbing the soft fabric on his face. He missed Nick, had wanted him to stay the whole weekend and kick back and relax with him, but Nick was uneasy leaving his room empty for too long, and besides that, he still needed to finish painting at the gas station. On top of that, Katie had called and wanted Corey to meet at her dad's place this morning, so with the realities of life to deal with, he and Nick had gone their separate ways.

Folding Nick's clothes, Corey thought about the previous night when he'd been in the gym making sure that the disinfectant wipes and bathroom supplies weren't running low after the holiday. Thanks to Rhonda, who had been in earlier that day to check on things, nothing had needed to be restocked and the trash didn't need to be dumped. While he was there, only one member had come in. He'd known there wasn't much chance of Nick being there to paint, but that hadn't stopped him from being disappointed when he didn't see him when he walked in the door. Nick having another job was taking some getting used to.

There'd been another reason he'd gone to the gym the night before—to have another look at the footage that showed the hooded figure in the parking lot. He'd sat at the desk watching it over and over, trying to figure out if it was anyone he'd seen before. The whole thing had him unnerved.

After he stuffed the sheets into the dryer he was brought back to the present by the rumble of thunder and rain tapping on the tiny window above the dryer—the storm was getting stronger. He was glad that he didn't have to go in to work, but as he had the family meeting later in the morning he'd have to venture out in it soon, regardless.

Katie had been vague when she'd called on Friday asking him to be at her dad's place early Saturday morning. He wasn't sure what to expect, but he needed to get going or otherwise he'd be late.

Maybe afterward, he'd drive over to Nick's to deliver his laundry and to see if he wanted a ride to the gym to do some more painting. After eating so much on Thanksgiving Day his jeans were feeling a bit snug. He could sure use some time on the treadmill while Nick worked on the mural. Any time spent in the same place with Nick would be a great day, rain or shine.

"I sure didn't have to worry about being late," Corey said, looking at his watch after his second cup of coffee at Uncle Ed's kitchen table.

Ed looked at the clock on the stove. "That girl has gotten so inconsiderate since hooking up with that lamebrain. I have a customer waiting and I need to get going."

"Someone needs a plumber on Thanksgiving weekend?" Corey asked.

"Plumbing problems happen every day, and lucky for me, usually on weekends and holidays so I can charge more." Ed grinned, looking pleased with himself.

Corey smiled into his cup. "This coffee hits the spot. Takes the chill off, that's for sure."

"I didn't get a chance to tell you that I liked your friend," Ed said.

Corey looked up. "I'm glad. I like him too. We're getting to know each other a little better every day."

Corey took a drink of his coffee and said with a wink, "I like Mrs. Franklin too."

With a slight blush on his cheeks, Ed pushed back from the table and walked to the kitchen window and looked out. "Maybe Katie decided not to come out in the rain. If she was home in the garage apartment where she belongs instead of with that dimwit, she wouldn't have to drive across town in this miserable weather to get here to tell us whatever it is she has to share."

"Do you want me to give her a call?"

"No, we'll wait a little longer," Ed said impatiently, as he looked back at Corey.

"You have no idea what this is about?" Corey asked.

"I wish I did."

"You're not worried, are you?"

Before Corey got an answer, Ed glanced out the window again and then headed for the front door. "She's finally here."

Corey joined Ed and they watched out the living room window for Katie to get out of her car, struggling with her umbrella. When she finally reached the porch, Ed opened the door. She paused to shake raindrops off the umbrella before entering the living room.

"Sorry I'm late. Thanks for coming over," she said to Corey, giving him a hug. "How was Thanksgiving?" she asked her dad, giving him a kiss on the cheek.

"Let's get your wet coat off," Ed said as he helped Katie remove her blue trench coat, quickly hanging it to dry on the coatrack by the door.

"You want some coffee?" Corey asked.

"Sure, that would be good. I'm sorry I wasn't here to make the coffee since I was the one who invited you," she said, heading toward the kitchen with the men following.

"I had it made hours ago," Ed said, getting Katie a cup and filling it.

"Thanks, Dad," she said when he handed it over.

After they sat down around the table, Katie looked from her dad to Corey. "I guess you're both wondering why I asked you to meet me here."

Corey noticed how radiant she looked in her turtleneck sweater. Her cheeks nearly matched the bright pink color.

She took a big sip of coffee and then flashed a mile-wide smile. "I won't beat around the bush—I'm engaged."

She held out her hand to flash a sparkling pear-shaped diamond engagement ring. "Before Thanksgiving dinner, Alan asked me to marry him, and I said yes!" Her eyes danced, and her face beamed with pure joy.

Corey was completely stunned. So that would explain why she looked so vibrant—he sure hadn't seen this coming. He'd known how infatuated she was with Alan, but he hadn't known that Alan's feelings for her ran this deep. She was only twenty-two years old, and she wanted to get married—to a guy like Alan?

Chancing a glance at Uncle Ed, Corey knew without looking what his uncle's face would show—he was as white as a ghost, and his lips had thinned down to show how angry and hurt he was by this news. Corey couldn't ignore Katie's happy and hopeful look any longer.

"It's real pretty," he said, but that was all he could muster.

"Thank you," she said softly, giving her ring a twist on her finger. She then looked at her dad, who was staring at his folded hands on the table top and hadn't uttered a word.

Corey felt that was a blessing, but how long would his uncle's silence last? If Ed would lose his temper, it would not be a pretty sight.

The silence was endless after her announcement, the only sound was the hum of the refrigerator. Corey squirmed in his chair wanting to say more, but this wasn't his deal to make okay. He wanted to poke his uncle to get him to lose the look of grand disappointment he carried.

Katie fiddled with her necklace, then she ran her hand down her long braid, bringing it forward and then flipping it back in place. Her look of joy had been replaced by dejection. She wasn't making eye contact with either of them now and tears were ready to fall. She let out a deep breath and stood, leaving her cup of coffee barely touched.

"Well, I guess I'll be going," she said.

"I'll walk you out," Corey said. Ed was slow to stand, but he finally stood to follow them.

The three of them went into the living room, and Corey helped Katie on with her coat. Once out on the porch, Ed stepped close and hugged her. Corey could see that Ed's heart was breaking, but he admired the man for making an effort to try and support her.

Before her car had even backed out of the driveway, Ed started in, almost shouting.

"Jesus *Christ*, I can't believe this. She doesn't have the brains she was born with."

"I couldn't believe her news either. I had no idea they were even thinking along those lines. I was so shocked I didn't know what to say."

"I'm telling you, I had to bite my tongue."

"I figured as much," Corey said, patting Ed on the arm.

"Can you just see the two of them married? It would be a disaster. I'm glad her mother isn't here to see this. It's absurd is what it is. She doesn't know her head from a hole in the wall." Ed's jaw was clenched tight, and his neck and face were flushed.

"Let's go inside," Corey said, afraid his uncle was getting too worked up.

On the way through the door and into the living room, Ed's tirade continued. "What I'd like to know is where did that good-for-nothing loser get the money for a ring like that? I only took a quick look, but it must have cost a hefty sum from what I could tell."

"Yeah, it looked like an expensive ring, that's for sure," Corey agreed.

"He can't be making much at the cemetery, and I don't think he even works full-time."

"Let's hope it's a very long engagement and that she comes to her senses before it goes any further. And pray she doesn't turn up pregnant."

Ed gave him a horrified look and then reached for his cap on the end table by his recliner. "Well, I've gotta get going. I can't keep those folks waiting any longer."

"Yeah, well, I've got plans too, so I guess I'll see you later—are you sure you're okay?" Corey asked.

"I'll be okay once I get to work and get my mind off this stupidity."

"Try not to worry. I'm sure it'll all work out."

Driving past the dilapidated fence that surrounded part of the ramshackle motel where Nick was living, Corey finally put thoughts of his cousin on the back burner and directed his energy toward seeing Nick; at least he hoped he'd find him in his room. The hours had ticked by and not much of the morning remained though, so maybe Nick had already gone out. After all, what was there to do in his room without even a TV to watch? The rain had been falling fairly steadily though, so Corey hoped that might have kept him inside.

He drove around back and pulled up to the corner room. Seeing the curtain move suggested that his morning was about to get better and when the curtains parted, and his boyfriend's face peeked out, the sun may as well have come out as much as the sight of Nick boosted his spirits.

Corey got out of the car and grabbed the pillowcase carrying Nick's clean laundry and headed quickly to the door. The rain dampened his jacket and hood, but Nick swung the door open, so he got in without delay. Once inside, they shared a long kiss.

The sound of dripping water into the trash can didn't really set a romantic mood, although remembering back to when he'd been there a week and a half ago that hadn't stopped them, and it didn't this time either.

"Come here—get your wet jacket off and your clothes too," Nick ordered.

Corey liked his partner taking charge, so he did as he was told. He didn't stop until he had every last piece of clothing off. It almost seemed like he and Nick were racing to see who could get undressed first, because by the time Corey pulled his underwear off Nick was totally naked.

The next thing he knew, he was being tugged down onto Nick's unmade bed, and he settled in for some hot lovemaking. After all, it had been since Thanksgiving night that they had been together and having had Nick in bed on more than one occasion had him spoiled.

The thunder and rain on the roof created the perfect background to what was coming, despite the incessant dripping in the trash can. Nick's arms slid under Corey pulling him close. Corey wrapped his arms around Nick for an intense and passionate kiss.

Nick was first to break the kiss, pulling back and rubbing his finger over Corey's mouth. "I missed you," he whispered, his smile teasing.

"I could tell. Me too." Corey readjusted so he was more comfortable. "Sleeping alone last night wasn't my idea of fun." His heart was racing as he pulled Nick down for another hungry kiss. Nick responded with urgency, his hardness pressing on Corey's inner thigh.

Corey rolled them over so that he was on top, going straight for Nick's neck, trying not to suck too hard. The moans he got out of Nick were sweet music to his ears.

"We've gotta be quiet," Nick groaned. "Remember the walls." He trailed off as Corey went down on him and swirled his tongue around the top of his dick.

After they'd finished, Corey hoped they hadn't been too loud thrashing around on that old bed because, after all, Nick was the one who lived there and would have to deal with stares from other people if they'd heard anything.

Corey didn't want to move. Holding Nick and petting the soft strands of his hair made him feel so relaxed that he knew he could fall asleep with little trouble. Their relationship seemed so simple at this moment, and he didn't want to deal with the worries in his life. He just wanted to be.

After a few minutes, Nick shifted to reach something on the rickety nightstand, and suddenly music played from a clock radio. Corey listened trying to place the song, but couldn't, instead realizing the dripping from the ceiling had stopped, replaced by the deep, husky voice of a deejay announcing the next song.

"I didn't know you had a radio," he said lazily.

"I found it on one of my trips to the thrift shop on Third Street. A real steal," Nick answered, sitting up on the side of the bed, glancing down at himself and then over to Corey. "Guess we need to clean up. Wanna join me in the shower?" As soon as the words were out, Nick's small, weak smile and downward gaze told Corey that something was wrong.

"What is it?" Corey asked, moving to sit by Nick.

"Oh, nothing. Just that my shower's pretty rank. I try to clean it, but you'd never know by looking."

Corey put his arm around Nick. "It's okay, I understand. It doesn't bother me. Just as long as the water's hot."

Nick huffed out a breath as if he didn't quite believe him. "Well, after our shower, I can at least offer you some ice cream."

"Ice cream?" Corey asked, confused.

"I have a little refrigerator now, and it even has a freezer compartment, although it doesn't keep the ice cream too solid." He nodded toward the adjacent wall.

"Wow, that's nice," Corey said. "I didn't even see it when I came in."

"We were a little busy." Nick smiled shyly.

Corey smiled back. "And is that a microwave on the bureau?"

"Sure is. It's nice having a few creature comforts."

Corey stared at the small appliances and noted that they looked new, wondering where they'd come from—surely not from the thrift shop. Nick hadn't arrived in town with much—a pack over his shoulder—but then again, he had no idea how much money Nick had with him either. He cleared his throat. "Where'd all this come from?"

"A guy in the motel gave them to me."

"Gave them to you?"

"Yeah, uh, he was moving on and couldn't take them with him, so when he asked me if I wanted them, I jumped at the offer."

"Yeah, I guess you would. Why didn't he sell them and make some money?"

Nick looked offended by the question and seemed somewhat flustered. "What would make you ask that? How should I know? Maybe he didn't want to hassle with selling them, or maybe the guy wanted to pay it forward."

Corey nodded at Nick's sharp reply and let it go. He reached to the bottom of the bed and grabbed his socks, and after putting them on, he got off the bed and found his jacket and hung it over a chair to dry.

"I'll just wash up at the sink," Corey said and headed into the bathroom.

While cleaning himself up, Corey wondered what had made Nick so irritated—he'd never seen him pissy before. He guessed maybe it was because Nick wasn't the kind of man who liked to accept charity. That had to be it... and not what he kept pushing from his mind.

When he finished, Corey tossed the washcloth in the tub and opened the bathroom door, not sure of Nick's mood, but he needn't have worried, because Nick—dressed in a robe—seemed back to normal, flashing a smile when their eyes met. Corey saw a loaf of bread and sandwich supplies set out on top of the little refrigerator.

"I thought we were having ice cream," Corey said while pulling his shirt over his head.

"That's dessert. We need lunch first."

"I thought we already had dessert." Corey waggled his eyebrows suggestively as he pulled on his pants.

Nick hurried toward the bathroom, stopping to peck Corey on

the cheek on his way by. "Be right back. Go ahead and get started if you want."

Corey had two sandwiches partly made, but he realized he didn't know how Nick liked his. Thinking about how little he actually knew about Nick made him want to learn more, to know everything there was to know. He stared at the sandwiches and then felt silly, because who cared if he didn't know how much mustard to put on Nick's bread? He knew things about Nick that really mattered, like how he treated people, what was important to him, and how he made Corey feel. Those were the things that counted. Hell, in only three weeks, how could he know everything there was to know? It would all come in time.

Corey heard the water in the bathroom shut off—Nick hadn't bothered to close the door—and Corey chanced a glance into the little room just in time to see Nick drying off his upper half before putting on his blue fitness center T-shirt.

After the sandwiches were made, Corey, having put mustard and mayo on both, placed them on paper plates and then grabbed two bottles of water from the refrigerator. He sat down on the only chair in the room.

"Looks good," Nick said, taking his plate and sitting on the bed. "I love mayo and mustard together."

Corey smiled, pleased that he got it right, relieved that the tension between them had evaporated, and for that, he was grateful. "Not too bad, if I do say so myself."

"How'd the family meeting go?" Nick asked.

"Well, you won't believe what happened."

"Oh yeah? That bad, huh?"

"How'd you know it was bad?"

"I'm getting to know you pretty well. I can tell by the tone of your voice and by the furrow of your brow. What happened?" Nick took a swig of his water.

"It seems Cupid is running rampant. Katie told Uncle Ed and me that she and Alan got engaged on Thanksgiving."

"She's engaged to that muscle man?"

"Muscle head," Corey said, running his fingers through his hair.

"Wow. How'd your uncle take it?"

"Better than I expected, at least while Katie was there. He cannot stand Alan. When he first met the guy, Alan had the nerve to tell an off-color joke about plumbers, if you can believe that."

"Do you think she'll really marry him?"

"I hope not. I really can't picture it happening." Corey rubbed his temples and closed his eyes. "Thinking about it gives me a headache."

"How 'bout some ice cream to drown your sorrows?" Nick asked.

"Yeah, you did mention that. I've been wondering where it is." Corey blinked mischievously.

Nick left the bed. "Well, without further ado." He reached into the mini freezer and held up his prize. "Just big enough for a pint of *Ben & Jerry's Chocolate Fudge Brownie.*"

Corey stood and joined Nick on the bed. They sat thigh to thigh, sharing the pint with two plastic spoons. By the time they'd finished, the sun was shining through the small tears in the old, ratty curtains.

"Seems like the storm is over," Nick said, as he looked to the window and then back.

"I'm glad."

Nick gave Corey a cool kiss that tasted like chocolate indulgence. The kiss only lasted a moment, because it was interrupted by a commotion outside of loud garbled voices and car doors slamming, then a car alarm going off.

"Guess the crazies came out with the sun," Nick said with a sigh.

Corey couldn't tell if he was joking or being serious. He figured it was probably a little of both.

"Are there a lot of crazy goings-on around this place?" Corey asked.

"I try not to notice. And like I said before, there's some nice folks here too, so you take the good with the bad." Nick looked thoughtful and went on. "I feel sorry for the families who end up in a place like this."

Corey felt a pang in his chest and attempted to lighten the mood. "How about we head over to the gym. You can paint, and I can work off this meal on the treadmill." He patted his stomach.

Nick gave Corey's stomach a little rub. "You have great abs. You don't have any reason to work out, I don't see an ounce of fat on you," he said, and he sounded sincere.

Corey's face got hot, wondering if Nick could see his blush, but Nick rolled off the bed and went over to where the pillowcase of fresh laundry lay. He rummaged through the items inside and pulled out his black hoodie.

"I'll need this," he said, putting it on and zipping it up.

Corey had to make an effort to tear his eyes away. Nick probably wouldn't think anything of his staring, but every time he saw Nick's hoodie, he was reminded of the man in the video, and he wished he could get that out of his mind.

"Best take your jacket too, in case it starts raining again," Corey said, reaching for his own.

Before picking up his jacket, Nick turned to Corey. "I have an idea."

"What's that?"

"Well, just to prove to you I'm not a workaholic, how 'bout we go out someplace before the gym?"

"Out, like a date?" Corey liked the sound of that.

Nick smiled and closed the distance between them, taking Corey into his arms. "We could go to a movie," he whispered into Corey's ear.

"That's an offer I won't refuse," Corey whispered back.

"How long has it been since you've gone to a matinee?" Nick released his hold and grabbed his jacket.

"So long ago I can't even remember, how 'bout you?"

"Same for me—this is gonna be fun. I wonder what's playing."

"Who cares, just sitting next to you in a dark theater is the best part."

"I'm glad I thought of this."

Once outside, Nick gave the battered old door a hard pull. Surprised there was even a deadbolt, Corey watched Nick lock it up before they headed to the car.

When the lights dimmed in the theater, Nick swung the arm of the chair up and scooted closer to Corey.

"Now I know why you wanted to sit in the back row," Corey whispered.

"Isn't this more comfortable?" Nick asked in a low voice when their bodies were pressed together as close as was suitable for the time and place.

"Yeah, it is."

After watching the coming attractions for a few minutes, Corey offered the bag of popcorn to Nick who reached in for a handful. They nibbled popcorn and drank their Cokes and Corey felt a sense of peace and well-being. This was his idea of a great date.

Corey crumpled the bag up when the last kernel was gone and snuggled closer. Nick rested his arm on the back of Corey's chair.

When the movie ended, they stayed seated while the other moviegoers filed out before reluctantly getting up to leave.

Outside the theater, Corey was surprised how far the sun had set. "Seems late already," he said.

"Yeah, but spending some time together was nice."

"No argument from me. But... you're thinking of all the painting you could have done, am I right?"

Nick smiled. "You're getting good at reading me."

"Shall we head to the car?" Corey asked, taking a step in the direction of the parking garage, suddenly feeling young and free, not to mention horny.

Nick followed silently as they walked into the covered parking area. Corey could easily see the Kia across the mostly deserted lot. Glancing around, he pulled on Nick's arm. Nick turned and stared at him, obviously waiting for him to say something. Instead of speaking, he pulled Nick around a concrete pillar. He quickly unzipped his jacket and then did the same to Nick's, reaching inside, pulling him in tight so their upper and lower bodies lined up just right. The concrete was cold and hard on his back, but Nick's cuddly warm body made him forget fast. In fact, he forgot just about everything in this perfect span of moments—all except the man he had wrapped in his arms, the man he was kissing and who was kissing him back, the man he was absolutely crazy about and couldn't get enough of.

CHAPTER THIRTEEN

COREY LOOKED up from his notebook, watching Rhonda's progress as she arranged the Member of the Month photos and their corresponding write-ups on a piece of bright red poster paper spread out on the desk. He wondered how it could possibly take so long to do something he considered so simple.

"Let me know when you're ready to hang that up," he said.

"Just let me see if moving the pictures to the side looks better than on the top," she said, looking serious as she rearranged them again. "The pictures you took of the members turned out nice."

"Thanks, you got it how you want it yet?" he asked, wondering why he was so annoyed at what she was doing.

"Yeah, I like it this way. Now let me get the snowflakes on the corners and I'll be done."

"Snowflakes?"

"For December," she said as if he should already know the display needed them.

Corey smiled. Of course, there'd be snowflakes. She was a perfectionist, and he admired that about her, the same way he did about Nick and his art, which looked better and better each time he worked on it. The job would be done any day now, and the thought of Nick not coming in to paint left him with a hollow feeling inside.

He got up and stood over the desk to get a better look at what

Rhonda had put together. "It looks very"—he searched for the right word—"uh, festive, I guess."

"Thanks. And by the way, it's about time to bring the Christmas tree in so we can get it set up and decorated."

"Wow, yeah, I guess you're right. I hadn't really thought about that."

"I guess you've had a lot of family stuff going on, huh?" she said.

"You must mean Katie's engagement."

"She showed me her ring. I was shocked."

"I was too. I'm still having a hard time getting used to it." He tried not to sound too disapproving, but he figured that Rhonda knew how he felt.

"I wonder if Wes knows yet." She sounded as down about the situation as Corey felt.

"Well, he's coming in today, so he'll find out then I guess."

"It should be pretty slow in here until after the first of the year," she said.

"Yeah, in January, members who've let their workouts fall by the wayside will flood in after making New Year's resolutions, not to mention new members signing up."

"This is ready now," she said.

"Okay, I'll get it put up on the bulletin board."

Rhonda glanced through the open office door and out the front window. "Katie's back, so I'll be leaving. See you tomorrow."

Corey had just finished pushing in the last thumbtack when he sensed someone standing behind him. If he was lucky it would be Nick, but he didn't really expect him so early because he knew Nick had painted late the night before and, sure enough, luck wasn't with him.

"Back to the grindstone, huh?" Dean said in greeting.

"Hey, Dean," he said, not at all enthused.

"How was your holiday?"

"Fine, how about yours?" Corey fixed his eyes on the bulletin board even though there wasn't anything on it that needed his attention.

"Did anything significant happen?"

"What do you mean by significant?" Corey asked, feeling apprehensive.

"I heard about Katie's engagement ring. Weren't you gonna tell me?"

"Oh, that," he sighed. "Not really. It's her place to tell if she wants to."

"Yeah, well. I guess when I see her I'll have to offer my congratulations."

"Yeah, whatever. Uh, if there's nothing else, I've got work to do." Corey started to step away.

"Wait," Dean said, reaching for Corey's arm. "I wanted to show you my early Christmas present."

"I really have to get to work."

"It'll only take a minute. Come outside and I'll show you."

Corey sighed and decided to follow, resigned to the fact that he'd have to spend a few minutes humoring his ex. They stepped outside where a brand-new blue mountain bike stood chained to the bike rack.

"What do you think of that?"

"It's nice," Corey answered, impressed.

"Nice? Is that all you have to say about it?"

"Well... It *is* really nice. Where'd you get it?"

"Don't you remember all those times we used to say we were gonna get mountain bikes? Well, I followed through. Guess you still think they're too expensive."

Corey ran his hand over the handlebars and stepped back to get a better look. "It's a real beauty. You say it's a Christmas gift—to yourself?"

Dean seemed hesitant to answer, and when he finally did, he looked uncomfortable. "My sister and her husband gave it to me."

Corey searched Dean's face trying to figure out why he seemed different. He was used to Dean being all cocky and sure of himself, and right that moment Dean was neither. He really hoped Dean wasn't feeling bad that the two of them would never go riding together like they used to talk about.

"Well, I'm sure you'll get good use from it," Corey said and turned to go back inside. "I know it's something you've wanted for a long time." After a few steps he realized that he couldn't get rid of Dean, who had followed right on his heels.

"I've got something else to discuss with you," Dean said as they entered the front door.

Corey turned and met his former boyfriend's eyes. "Sounds serious. What's it about?"

"Can we go someplace private?"

"Someplace private?"

"Yeah, how does a cup of coffee at *Starbucks* sound?"

"What do you have to discuss that requires we go someplace else to talk? We can do that here."

Dean sighed heavily. "Okay then, we'll talk here. How 'bout downstairs if no one's there."

"All right, if you insist. Let's get this over with," Corey said under his breath.

There wasn't anyone in the downstairs space, so Dean motioned toward two chairs near the fitness balls. Corey sat down on one, as did Dean, and waited for him to say what was so important. He figured it was just another of Dean's games, so he didn't expect much.

Dean cleared his throat. "I've been curious about the sudden break-ins around here, concerned too, you know, so I did some digging. While I was at my sister's—you probably remember her husband's a cop—"

"He's not even in this county, Dean."

"That doesn't matter for what I needed him to help me with." Dean leaned in closer as if he had a big secret that he didn't want anyone else to hear. "I asked him to look up Nick Stewart."

"Nick? What the hell for?"

"Calm down."

But Corey was anything but calm. He sprang off the chair, fired up as hell, causing it to scrape the floor with a harsh sound. "Why are you doing this? You have no right."

Dean got to his feet too, trying to grab Corey's shoulder, but Corey shrugged him off. "You need to mind your own damn business and leave this to the cops. Your brother-in-law is not involved in this!"

"But, Corey, you've got to hear what I found out. Listen to me—"

"Why would you suspect Nick? You're just trying to make trouble—to cause trouble for us."

"No, I'm not. Corey, he's the most likely suspect. Nothing's ever happened around here, not until he came around."

"Forget it."

"Just listen. No one matching Nick Stewart's description showed up in the system. I'll bet he gave you a fake name. What does that say about him, huh?"

"That just means Nick doesn't have a police record. Of course, he's not going to show up in whatever database your brother-in-law looked in. He should have told you that unless he doesn't know what he's doing." Dean tried to grab him again, but Corey shook him off. "I'm not going to talk to you about this. The cops will handle it. Nick isn't responsible."

"There's something else too," Dean said, pinning Corey with his gaze. "Last night I was here working out and Nick was painting. Well, after I got done, I hung around outside waiting for him to leave so I could follow him."

"That's just great—hanging around in the dark is really smart, especially with what's been going on around here. You'll be the suspect if you're not careful."

"Don't try to change the subject. Let me tell you where your boyfriend's staying."

"I know where he stays," Corey said, fed up and running out of patience.

Dean's expression darkened. "You're an idiot. You've been over to that fleabag motel with him."

"That's none of your business."

"You're dumber than I thought you were. Why would you hire some transient to work here, in your precious gym... not to mention sleep with him."

Corey had to use every ounce of restraint not to grab Dean by his collar and yell into his face. He kept his voice low and looked straight into his eyes. "I'm not going to talk to you about Nick. It's none of your business where he lives or what his last name is. He isn't the person responsible for the break-ins. Got it?"

"Nick's up to no good, that I'm sure of. Why would you wanna hang with someone like him? A down-and-out vagrant who's going around burglarizing businesses, when you could be with me? You remember how it was between us, I know you do," Dean said, trying to touch Corey's face as he leaned in for a kiss.

Corey jerked away this time, but Dean just stepped closer, refusing to give up. But before Dean could make another move on him, Corey saw his eyes dart toward the top of the stairs. He turned to see where Dean's gaze was directed, and there on the top step stood Nick—his sweet, sensitive, kind, and beautiful Nick. His Nick, with sad but angry eyes.

Corey's heart ached seeing those brilliant, impossibly blue eyes look at him that way. Damn Dean anyway!

Nick turned and beat a hasty retreat. Corey took the steps two at a time trying to get to him—but what could he say? Obviously, Nick had heard at least part of the discussion, and Corey knew how it must have sounded, and looked.

Once Corey made it to the main floor, hoping like hell that Nick hadn't run out, he looked around desperately, scanning the cardio room and the weight room. He needed a chance to make things right. Relief washed over him when he saw him over at the mural wall opening a jar of acrylic paint.

Corey approached him cautiously. He didn't think Nick would make a scene by yelling or anything, but he really didn't know what to expect. He hadn't given Dean another thought, until now, and he hoped to hell that troublemaker would have better sense than to butt in where he didn't belong. If he did, he'd get his neck wrung.

He stepped close enough to speak without being overheard by any of the gym members, but far enough away not to crowd Nick as he began to paint. Corey was more than aware that he wouldn't be welcome in Nick's personal space right that second.

Before he could gather his thoughts, Nick, who remained focused on the half-painted green and blue figure in front of him, spoke up. His tone was cool and indignant.

"I'm not a quitter, so I intend to finish what I started. I'll be done with the mural today and the other two walls won't take long. After that, you can pay me what you owe me and then I'm outta here."

"Nick, let me explain."

"What's to explain? I heard your thoughts loud and clear," Nick said harshly.

"No, you didn't. If you're pissed off at what you think I said, you obviously heard Dean's thoughts, but not mine."

Nick finally looked at him, his eyes shooting daggers. "Oh, yeah, Dean. Now that's a story in itself."

"Yes, it is." Corey felt guilty as hell. Why hadn't he ever found the opportunity, or made it a priority, to tell Nick that Dean was his ex? Nick shouldn't have had to find out the way he just did.

Nick turned his head and went back to painting, letting out a heavy sigh and mumbling to himself, "I've gotta go downstairs and get the drop cloth."

"Look, we need to talk in private. There's stuff I want to say, and I can't do it here." Corey looked around uncomfortably, glad that no members were in the immediate vicinity, but he had to get Nick out of there, so they could talk—really talk—and the sooner the better.

"You'd better watch out—you'll ruin your reputation talking to a no-account vagrant."

"Nick, those were not my words. I would never say anything like that about you. That's *not* how *I* see you. Now, will you give me a chance to explain what you saw and heard?"

Nick took his attention away from his painting long enough to look Corey in the eye. "Fine. Where shall we meet?" he asked, and he didn't look near as resentful as a moment ago.

Corey gave Nick the smallest of smiles, hoping for one in return, but that didn't happen. "My place? When you're done here we can drive over." He waited a few beats for an answer, but none came. "You're not afraid of being alone with me, are you?" he asked, trying to coax a smile.

"Yes," Nick said, smiling slightly.

Corey patted Nick's shoulder. "Let me know when you're ready to leave."

He walked away, relieved, and stopped to talk to a couple of members on his way toward the office. He had no sooner said goodbye to them when Wes appeared, tools in hand.

"Hey, Wes," Corey said, always happy to see him.

"How was your holiday?" Wes asked.

"Great, how about yours?"

"Fine, but now I'm ready to get back to work."

"Good, we've got a few problems that need your expertise. I'll show you, so you can get started."

Before Wes got too far with the drive belt motor on one of the treadmills, Corey sighed loudly, his heart sinking, knowing he'd have to tackle the subject of Katie's engagement.

Wes looked up from his work. "Was there something else on your mind?"

"Yeah, well, there's something I need to tell you, although I don't really want to."

Wes put his pliers down and gave Corey his full attention. "Sounds serious. What is it?"

"Uh, well, I'll just get right to the point. On Thanksgiving, Katie and Alan got engaged."

Wes didn't say anything, just picked his pliers up and went back to what he'd been doing. Corey could see that he was trying to act like the news didn't bother him, but he'd seen the pain and confusion in Wes's eyes.

"I'm blown away that she wants to get married," Wes finally said, shaking his head.

"Me too. I thought the point of breaking up with you was to go out and have fun—not that you weren't fun, but you know what I mean. If she was looking for marriage material, you were it."

He could tell that Wes would rather not talk about it further, so he changed the subject, and after some small talk, Corey went into the office.

His defenses immediately went up when he found Dean and Katie together, especially when neither one of them said anything to him, or to each other, when he walked in. They stood there like statues, and the silence went on for several uncomfortable moments.

Corey looked from one to the other. "Don't let me interrupt." There was no missing Katie's unrelenting stare. "Looks like you have something to say, so go ahead, what has Dean been telling you?"

She didn't answer, so Corey looked at Dean. "I thought you were here to work out, not stand around in here gossiping."

Dean stiffened at the remark. "I don't gossip, I tell it like it is."

"Dean, maybe you should let me speak to Corey alone," Katie said, the muscles in her face tightening.

It seemed like Dean was more than eager to leave. Corey watched as he took a few fast-paced strides right out the door.

"I've had about enough of him for one day," Corey said.

Katie closed both office doors before she spoke. "He said he tried to talk to you downstairs and you didn't want to hear it."

"Damn right I didn't want to hear it. What has he been filling your head with?"

"Maybe you should sit down so we can talk," Katie said, as she sat down behind the desk.

"I don't need to sit to be able to talk," he said, but moved toward the other chair anyway and sat down. That's when he noticed the menu on the computer screen—the dates from the time of the second break-in.

"What the hell have the two of you been doing?" he asked, furious, but at the same time, dreading her answer.

"I'd wanted to look at the footage of the night of the pizza break-in, but I just hadn't gotten around to it until now."

"You mean until Dean put you up to it," he said, trying to keep his anger in check, grabbing a pencil and tapping the eraser end on the desk.

"Dean is worried about you—"

"Look, I know you like him, but he's not worried about me. All he wants to do is cause trouble."

"But he thinks there's a possibility that Nick could be responsible for the break-ins. And he told me Nick's a drifter and lives in that awful, rundown motel on Crown Street."

"He's new in town and trying to find work so he can get someplace better. Just because that's all he can afford right now doesn't mean he's a bad person, and he's not the one burglarizing the businesses. That's ridiculous, and Dean better keep his mouth shut—"

"But, Corey, Dean said he thinks Nick gave a false name, and we looked at the person walking in the parking lot and it *could* be Nick. He's even in a hoodie like he wears."

Corey's stomach lurched, and he felt physically ill. Hearing Dean accuse Nick was bad enough and now Katie too? But could he really blame them? After all, even he had allowed himself to wonder, even if just a little. He never truly believed it though. Hearing others accuse Nick was really pissing him off.

"It could be Nick? It could be a thousand other people in this town too. Hell, it could be Dean. Maybe he's trying to frame Nick."

"Now you're talking crazy, Cuz."

"Well, that makes two of us then. You're way out of line, and I don't want you talking like this. The cops will find out who the burglar is, and they don't need you and Dean pointing fingers at anyone."

"Okay, even if it's not Nick, I don't think you should be involved with a man like him."

Corey stood up and ran his hand through his hair. "That's not for you to say. Where Nick is staying has nothing to do with anything."

"What about Dean not finding anything about him when he did a search?"

"I'm not concerned about that, Katie. That means nothing. Only people with police records are in the system. Are you going to listen to me or Dean?"

"You're not objective where Nick is concerned," she said sternly. "I'll bet you didn't tell Dad that he doesn't have a normal home and a normal job. Dad wouldn't like it and—"

"A normal home and a normal job? What's that supposed to mean?" Corey wanted to throw something, but what good would it do? "And since when do you care what your dad likes and doesn't like?" Corey exclaimed. "Nick may live in a rundown motel room, but he's twice the man that Alan is!"

"You leave Alan out of this. We're talking about Nick, not Alan," she snapped, jumping to her feet.

"Don't you mean your fiancé," Corey said dryly.

Katie pursed her lips and the glare in her eyes wasn't a pretty sight. "Yes, my fiancé, and I know you don't approve, but at least he has roots here, has a steady job, and lives in a nice apartment."

"You mean working at a cemetery part time? Makes you wonder how he can afford that nice apartment."

"Don't even go there, Cuz."

Corey took in several deep breaths, trying to calm himself down. Between Dean and Katie badgering him, he was ready to lose it.

"And, do you know Alan well enough to know what he does when he's not working and not with you? How do we know *he's* not the one involved with the break-ins?"

Her face turned a deep shade of crimson as she stared Corey down with her dark, fiery eyes. She seemed as if she was about to say something more, but instead she turned away, sat back down and exited the surveillance program. When a loud knock cut through the palpable tension in the air, Corey jumped at the chance to open the door.

"Wes, what's up?" Corey asked, glad for the rescue, noticing Wes's flustered appearance.

"Sorry to interrupt." Wes looked to him then Katie and back to him. "But the toilet in the bathroom in the cardio room is plugged. Is there a plunger in the storage closet?"

"I'll take care of it, Wes. Thanks for letting me know," Corey said, grateful for a reason to leave.

He heard Wes ask Katie if she was all right before he hurried out of earshot.

Nick checked the time and wondered if he should stop painting for now because he just wasn't in the mood. He hadn't wanted to chance messing up the mural, as upset as he'd been, so he'd stopped and opened the can of Mango Tango paint and began on one of the other walls. He took a close look at the completed trim, and he'd done a good job even though he'd found himself glancing around the gym while he was painting, wondering if Dean would suddenly appear to give him a hard time.

He debated bringing out the roller and pan to continue. The drop cloth was spread out, the ladder was there, so he decided to go ahead and finish the wall. Work usually gave him a feeling of peace, but considering what he'd heard downstairs, he was anything but peaceful.

Why had he even agreed to go out with Corey to talk? He'd said he wanted to explain, and he knew he needed to give him that opportunity... he *wanted* to give him the opportunity, but he was just so pissed right now.

He couldn't believe that Dean and Corey used to be a couple... why hadn't Corey mentioned it? Everyone else in the place must know. He felt so stupid being kept in the dark. Would it have been so hard for Corey to have told him? He'd spilled his guts about Melissa, about David...

A couple members glanced his way. Must have been the banging of the ladder when he'd moved it. He needed to calm down and concentrate on what he was doing before he spilled the whole can of paint.

CHAPTER FOURTEEN

AFTER DRIVING a couple blocks with a sullen Nick sitting beside him, the lack of conversation between them added to the tension, and that had Corey tied up in knots. It wasn't every day that he had two of the most important people in his life mad at him and knowing full well that it was his own damn fault made him want to kick himself. If he had told Nick about Dean from the get-go maybe what went down today could have been avoided, at least that part of it. As for Katie, he wished he'd have kept his mouth shut about Alan, but she'd accused Nick too.

What a day.

The pained expression on Nick's face made it obvious he was not happy. He figured Nick probably regretted agreeing to this private time together—he wasn't surprised about the silent treatment, but he sure didn't like it. He missed Nick's smile and his easygoing disposition. With any luck, he'd see it again before the end of the day.

Corey let out a frustrated sigh. He just couldn't figure out where to start to get things back on track. Nick wasn't making it easy on him with his body pressed up against the passenger door and his head turned toward the side window.

"Looks like you want to jump out," Corey finally said.

Nick sat up straighter and repositioned himself in the seat. "I said we could talk, and I'm here," he said begrudgingly.

"I know I said we'd go to my place, but maybe it would be a better idea to stop and get something to eat first. Are you hungry?"

"I could eat something."

"Sonic?"

"As good a place as any, I guess."

The strained conversation wasn't helping the tightness in Corey's shoulders or the beginnings of a headache. He pulled in where they'd parked the other time they'd been there. They'd laughed a lot that day but had gotten into some serious conversation too, and Corey felt like that's exactly what they needed today.

"I'll pay for my lunch," Nick said, looking at the menu from his side of the car.

"No problem. Are you going to get ice cream for dessert?" Corey hoped his question would cut the tension that had settled in the car.

"I'll order some if I have any room left after I eat my burger," Nick said with a slight smile tugging at the corners of his mouth.

"You think we'll get someone on skates?"

"We did last time. She was a good sport when we teased her. Maybe this time we'll get a guy on skates."

"Are you looking for a new boyfriend?" Corey asked with a frustrated sigh.

"Well, if I was, I hear Dean's available."

Before Corey could respond, a male voice, sounding rushed and overworked, came through the loudspeaker asking for their order, so Corey gave it to him. After he finished, he looked at his blue-eyed, shaggy-haired friend and couldn't stand the downcast expression he saw.

"I'm really sorry I didn't tell you that I used to date Dean, but we broke up a long time before I met you and I just never got around to it. What we had is history. Besides that, I didn't think it was important. I wish I had mentioned it after this morning though. Can you forgive me?"

"How long did you date?"

"Oh, six months or thereabouts."

"Wow, six months. Who broke up with who?" Nick seemed uncomfortable with what he'd just asked and looked down into his lap. "Never mind, that's really none of my business."

"Yes, it is," Corey said. "*I* broke it off with Dean, and he still seems to think we should be together. He's jealous of you, Nick.

That's why he cornered me and started talking trash about you."

"Yeah, that."

Just then a pigtailed teenaged girl came gliding up on skates with their food. Nick handed over the bills for his part, and Corey added what he owed along with a tip. When the girl left, Nick tried to force more money into Corey's hand to cover his part of the tip, but Corey swatted it away.

"I hope that girl didn't think we were rude when we didn't talk to her," Nick said.

"She's busy, I don't think she cared."

"I hope you gave her a good tip."

Corey nodded that he did, and the conversation halted while they unwrapped their food and began eating. Having lunch here with Nick felt like old times, especially when they joked around watching the different servers skate by. Corey felt nervous and anxious, wondering what would happen when they finally started the serious talking.

When all they had left were their drinks, he took a chance and looked over at Nick.

"Uh, I was wondering if you accepted my apology... or not."

The question drew a strange response from Nick. He sat quietly with his head slightly turned in Corey's direction. His eyes were misty and then with a catch in his voice he said, "Apology accepted, and I'm sorry for overreacting. I know it was Dean saying those things about me—not you—but I sort of imagined that you felt that way too, you know?" He turned to look out the windshield then. "And it hurt me because..." After a short pause, he went on. "Because I've fallen in love with you, and I couldn't stand it if you thought of me that way."

Before Corey could say anything, Nick looked back at him. "You don't think I would steal from anyone, do you?"

Looking at the wide-eyed, innocent look on Nick's face—him waiting for Corey to say, 'of course not, I'd never think such a thing'—made Corey feel guilty as hell for allowing, even for a second, the thought that Nick could have been the man in the video. Wiping a tear from his eye, he wasn't sure if his tears were from how disappointed he was in himself for being such a fool, or happiness from hearing Nick's words. 'I've fallen in love with you' kept repeating in his head. He reached over and took Nick's hand, entwining their fingers. They stayed that way, with their hands joined for several quiet moments.

"Well, do you? Think I'd steal?"

Corey answered without hesitation, looking straight into Nick's eyes. "Would I have you working in the gym if I didn't trust you? Of course, I don't think you'd steal."

He then leaned his head back on the headrest and closed his eyes. His emotions were all over the place. The arguments with Dean and Katie weighed heavily on his mind, but he knew the only reason Dean had zeroed in on Nick as a suspect was because Corey was interested in him, and Dean wanted to make Nick look bad. What really bothered him was Katie coming down on Nick like she had, and the way she'd screwed up her face when she mentioned the motel on Crown Street. He didn't even want to think of how she'd look if she knew about the mission and how he'd actually met Nick.

"You falling to sleep?" Nick asked, squeezing Corey's hand and bringing him out of his thoughts.

"Are you kidding? I want ice cream," Corey said, turning his head so he could look at Nick.

"You're still hungry after what we just ate?"

"Sure, aren't you?"

"I guess I could eat a small sundae. Tell you what, I'll have one if you let me pay for yours too."

"Thought we were going Dutch."

"We did, but now I'm treating you."

"Well, okay, sounds good to me," Corey said.

Earlier that day Corey feared he'd never see that great smile of Nick's again, but there it was. He considered himself lucky and wondered if smoothing things over with Katie would be as easy.

"You look preoccupied," Nick said, giving Corey a worried glance as they let go of each other's hands. Nick reached into his pocket to pull out his wallet and turned his gaze back on Corey.

Corey smiled. "It's like you can read my mind sometimes."

"What are you thinking about?"

"Oh... Just that I had a... slight disagreement with Katie before we left the gym."

"Seems like it must have been more than slight if you're thinking about it now when you're supposed to be ordering our ice cream."

Corey snorted out a laugh and pushed the button to order. While they waited for their caramel sundaes, he noticed Nick staring at him and knew he should elaborate on the disagreement with Katie, but he'd need to choose his words carefully.

"About me and Katie," Corey started.

Nick turned in the seat to look at him, waiting intently.

"Dean had been in the office talking about the crime in the area and upsetting her."

"They were talking about me, weren't they?"

"No, it wasn't so much that."

"Did he repeat the stuff he'd said downstairs?"

"Yeah, some of it," Corey said resignedly. "Something you might not have overheard was that Dean snooped around to try to find a Nick Stewart matching your description."

The alarm in Nick's eyes made Corey sorry he'd brought that up, but he had to be honest.

"Damn, now your cousin knows things about me."

"That doesn't matter, Nick. Not in any way that counts." He exhaled and leaned back in his seat. "When we were talking, things got heated and one thing led to another—I said something that really pissed her off, something I really had no business saying."

"What?"

"I never told you my concerns about Alan other than he's rude and basically a loser, but some things have happened lately that make me really question what kind of stuff he's into."

"What do you mean?"

"I've seen him arguing with a couple of guys on separate occasions, and remember the night, or actually early in the morning, when you saw him go into the gym?"

That really seemed to pique Nick's interest. He sat up straighter. "Yeah."

"Well, I watched the footage of when that went down, and he and the guy who came in with him, Ted Faulkner, went downstairs and argued, and it looked like Alan tried to give Ted money, but Ted wouldn't take it. That seemed to make Ted even angrier, like maybe it wasn't near enough money or something. At least, that's the impression I got."

"You think Alan's into drugs maybe? Or gambling? Something along those lines?" Nick asked.

"Maybe so, and whatever it is, I'm really concerned for Katie."

"Did you tell her what you saw?"

"No, I'm not sure what to do. She isn't receptive to anything Uncle Ed or I have ever tried to tell her about Alan."

"Why'd she get so mad then?"

"Because I opened my big mouth and said that maybe Alan was the one committing the burglaries."

"I'll bet you said that because she said it was probably me," Nick said quietly.

Before Corey could answer, their sundaes were delivered by a young man on foot. Nick passed some bills to Corey, so he could pay.

The frosty, sweet treat helped Corey forget, at least for the moment, the unpleasantness of the day and the conversation he'd just had with Nick. In a way, he wished he'd have kept quiet about the whole Katie situation, but he knew that if he and Nick were to have a real relationship he couldn't keep secrets from him, so even though what he had told Nick was upsetting, it was the right thing to do.

There was no question how much Nick liked his sundae, seeing as how he licked the plastic spoon thoroughly with each bite as if missing even one smidgen of the ice cream and topping would be a sin.

"Here, have a bite of mine," Corey said, holding a spoonful toward Nick's mouth to entice him.

Nick chuckled and wrapped his lips around the spoon, eagerly devouring the whole offering. A small drip snuck down the corner of his mouth, and when his tongue darted out to quickly lap it up, Corey took a deep breath to compose himself. After Nick swallowed, he scooped a spoonful of his and offered it to Corey. They went on this way, sharing and giggling like kids until every last drop was gone.

Corey marveled at how something as simple as a little ice cream could steal the spotlight from all the drama and lift their moods so drastically. There was sure something great to say about having someone to share the good and bad times with.

"I guess we should head out. We've taken up this space for quite a while," Corey said.

"Do you plan to go back to work today?"

"Uh, I think I'll wait until tomorrow, or at least until after Katie leaves for the day."

"I might go back tonight and attack the last two walls."

"You worked late last night, so why not take tonight off—stay at my place," Corey said.

"I didn't bring anything with me."

"You can use my toothbrush and stuff. You don't need

anything."

"I'll come hang out for a while, but I really want to finish painting, so I'd best go on back to the motel afterward. I didn't have a chance to tell you—I have another job."

"You do? That's great." Corey cranked the engine and backed out.

"Yeah, I'll be painting decorative signs and banners for a kid's birthday party." Nick kind of snickered. "It may sound kinda weird, but it'll be fun, and a little bit challenging. I can really exercise my imagination."

Corey could tell how enthused Nick was by his big grin and the gleam in his eyes. He understood how a job like that would be a morale-booster compared to painting a gas station bathroom.

."How'd you stumble into that?" he asked.

"One of the gym members came up to me last evening asking if I ever did anything like that. We talked about what she had in mind, and she hired me."

"I'm happy for you. Maybe word-of-mouth will get you more jobs." Thinking about Nick branching out was bittersweet. He'd been spoiled having him all to himself, but this was good, and the way it should be.

"Yeah, back home that's how I got a lot of my jobs, so we'll see."

You know, you never told me exactly where back home is. You said you came from Oregon..."

"A little place called Hinkle," Nick answered. "Blink and you miss it, but there's some bigger towns close by."

Nick seemed quieter on the rest of the drive like he had something weighing on his mind. Today probably hadn't been the best time to bring up his hometown. He always looked sad when he thought about his past. And after all the crap that had gone down this morning, Corey wouldn't have expected him to just go on as if nothing had happened. He just hoped all the snooping Dean had done didn't have Nick spooked.

Corey pulled into the driveway of his house and parked. When they got out, it was an unusually nice day to sit outside on his new bench and, soon, there wouldn't be days like this—cool and crisp—so he walked on to the porch with Nick following. He stopped where the bench was nestled up next to the house, protected by the eaves.

"You want to sit out here for a while?"

"Sure, I guess," Nick answered, still appearing preoccupied.

They sat down and stretched out their legs, letting the December sun shine down on them. The yard looked rather dismal in Corey's opinion—winter had never been his favorite season.

"I've got to haul out the Christmas tree that's stored in my garage and take it over to the gym in the next day or so. Rhonda asked me about it this morning."

"Cool—you put up a tree in there, huh? How about one here in your house?"

"This will be my first Christmas here. I really hadn't thought that far ahead. Katie always puts one up in Uncle Ed's house. Not sure if we can expect that this year or not."

"Things are pretty different for me this year too," Nick said wistfully. "I didn't have room for a big tree in the house me and Melissa lived in, but my brother and I used to go out and cut a big one down for my parents' place. It's an old two-story house, been in the family for years."

Corey could only imagine how homesick Nick must feel, especially with the holidays coming. Wondering if Nick might want to talk about his family, he softly said, "Do you have other brothers and sisters, or is it just the two of you?"

"Just me and my brother. He's ten years older."

"Even with the age difference, having a brother must have been nice. I don't have any brothers or sisters, and I always felt like I missed out on something. Maybe that's why I'm so close to Katie."

"Yeah, it was nice having a big brother even though he was so much older. Even after he left home, he was around, and we did stuff together now and then." Nick hung his head and sighed.

"I'm going to decorate the outside of the house for the holiday," Corey announced suddenly. "Are you game to help me?"

Nick seemed startled out of his thoughts. "You said you hadn't even thought about decorating."

"Well, I just thought about it and I decided, but I'll need help." He stared at Nick, waiting for an answer and hoping he'd agree.

"Uh, well, maybe."

"And, you know what else I've just thought about?"

"What's... that?"

Corey touched Nick's hand, toying with his fingers. "Wouldn't it be nice if you moved in here with me?"

Nick froze with his mouth slightly open, looking totally surprised. Corey was just as surprised himself. He waited anxiously for Nick to say something and gave Nick's hand a little squeeze for encouragement.

Nick looked away and stared out into the yard or the street, Corey couldn't tell where. He just knew that Nick wasn't looking at him, which wasn't the reaction he'd expected.

"Well, what do you think?" Corey finally asked.

"Why are you asking me this now—today? Are you feeling guilty or something? That deal with Dean?"

Corey was momentarily speechless and couldn't quite tell if Nick sounded stunned or annoyed, so he tried to answer as honestly as he could.

"Uh, well, when we were having lunch, you told me you'd fallen in love with me, and you already know how I feel about you." He paused, hoping Nick would at least look at him, but he didn't turn his head in his direction. He didn't let that deter him, even though the vibes currently weren't encouraging. "So, anyway... I thought we had something special between us, and I've got this place that's big enough for the both of us." He paused again, but there still wasn't any response from Nick. "We get along great, at least I thought so."

When Nick took his hand away and tucked it under his thigh, Corey felt the loss of contact. At least Nick finally looked at him, but the lack of a smile and no warmth in his eyes made him feel tense and awkward.

"Now that your cousin knows where I'm staying, you want to get me into respectable digs before she tells your uncle, right?"

That threw Corey totally off his feet, and he didn't like Nick's statement one bit. "No, that doesn't have anything to do with it." Then he softened his tone and spoke from his heart. "I asked you because I love you and I thought we'd be good together."

"The timing seems weird," Nick said as he turned to look off down the street.

"Maybe it does, but what better time then, huh?"

He knew the timing sucked, and he probably should have thought it through before he asked, but he was head-over-heels in love. And maybe deep down inside he *did* wish Nick lived someplace better, but the reason wasn't all because of Katie and Ed. Nick deserved better than that dirty room with the leaking roof. Barely a month had passed since they'd met, but he had no qualms about sharing his home with Nick.

"It's not like I hadn't thought about it before today because I have. I guess talking about Christmas and family just made me wish we were together—really together, and today seemed like the right time to bring it up."

"Okay, sorry I got so worked up," Nick said, his lips set in a somber line, making Corey question the sincerity of his apology.

After a moment of silence, Nick let out a long breath and looked Corey straight in the eyes. "My life's a mess—I'm a mess. I can't drop my problems on you and screw up your life too."

"I'm walking in with my eyes open."

Nick leaned forward resting his elbows on his knees. "When I left home, I had no idea where I'd end up or what I'd do when I got there. No way did I ever think I'd find someone like you. Starting up a relationship is the last thing I should've done. That wasn't even on my radar." He looked exhausted all of a sudden—his face drawn as he lowered his head and looked down at his feet. "I can't even believe how fast this all happened. I'd been so far in the closet all my life—and now..." Nick seemed to be talking to himself as if he wasn't even aware that he was sitting right next to Corey. "Everything is snowballing out of control."

The hollow tone Corey heard had him troubled. "Please don't say this is the end of us," he whispered.

Staring at the ground, Nick went on. "Now that Dean and Katie suspect I'm using a fake name—I can't take any chances on my family finding out where I am. As long as no one knew who I was—"

"They don't know your last name, or even for sure that it isn't Stewart."

"It's probably only a matter of time before Dean finds out he's right about me using a fake last name."

"I don't see how he can, or why he would keep digging."

Nick looked at Corey, worry etched all over his face. "He went this far, and he even accused me of being the person doing the break-ins. What if he says something to the cops?"

"He won't. I'll make sure of that."

"How can you? You can't control him, and like you said yourself, he's jealous. Jealous people do awful things. Just think how he'd react if I moved in with you. This just isn't gonna work, Corey. I went to a hell of a lot of trouble to leave home without a trace, and I can't mess it up."

"Hiding from your family is more important than us? So, what if they find you? Being gay is not a crime," Corey said forcefully.

"I thought you understood! I told you what I did, about Melissa and everything."

"I know it was a bad scene—I know people got hurt, and I know you're afraid of what your family thinks, but you can't throw the rest of your life away. You can't always run and hide."

"I'm not you, Corey. I'm not strong like you are."

"You *can* be. I'll help you."

Nick stood up abruptly, and with narrowed eyes and a scowl on his face, stated, "I can't do what you want! I'm sorry—it's my fault for getting too close and hanging around too long. A guy like me has gotta keep moving."

Corey stood up as well, feeling paralyzed, and all he could do was watch the man who had become his best friend and lover rush across the driveway and out of his yard as if the fires of hell were burning his feet.

As he watched Nick race around the corner of the block, he struggled to breathe as he wiped tears from his face.

He prayed this wasn't the end.

At first, Nick pushed all thoughts out of his mind as he charged up the street, but after he'd gone a couple blocks, he slowed down and his steps became heavy on the pavement. He was mad, but he didn't really know who or what he was mad at. Himself—the whole world, maybe. Life and the people in it had left him tired and confused. Stuffing his hands further into his pockets, he put one foot in front of the other and couldn't believe how fast things could change from one minute to the next.

He'd thought he could make a life here, but now with everyone up in his business, how could that even be possible?

He kept on walking, to where he didn't know, but he kept going. Soon he was on Main Street and it was then that he started to think seriously about what he was going to do. The thought of skipping town and leaving the mural unfinished caused a hollow feeling in the pit of his stomach. He was so proud of that work, and what would Corey do? Paint over the wall as if the mural had never existed? Hire somebody else to finish?—Which would surely muddle it up as close to completion as it was...

Then there was the birthday job he'd told the gym member he'd do. He didn't want to disappoint her either. But, what the hell, he'd left a job undone back home too.

He'd reached the strip mall by then, but he sure wasn't going into the gym, so he walked through the parking lot and stopped for a few seconds at the trash enclosure, remembering that cold early morning when he'd sheltered under the tin overhang. Hard to believe, but he felt more lost and confused now than he had then. He walked on and headed around the sporting goods shop at the end of the row and on toward the open land that he'd limped across back in November. This path would take him down to the railroad.

As he got closer to the tracks, memories began flooding in—memories from his childhood and playing the dangerous game of chicken along the train tracks with his friends, his teenage years finding solace watching trains go by, and the guilt-ridden years with Melissa, those few times he played his own game of beating the train at the crossing.

Finally reaching the tracks, he walked on the rail for a short distance, but thinking better of it, he headed off to sit under a group of sad looking half-dead trees. He thought how ironic it would be to get arrested today for trespassing on the railroad track. He knew one thing for certain, and that was he'd be hitchhiking out of this town.

Hopping that train seemed like a lifetime ago. Sitting here able to see the tracks didn't give him that uplifting, hopeful feeling he'd always had when he was around anything train related. Actually, hopping a train must have gotten that out of his system. Days gone by.

Wouldn't it be nice if finally being with a man would have gotten that out of his system too? His life would be a lot less complicated, but, it was way too late for that now because being with Corey only made him want more, and anyway, he had accepted who he was, and going forward he couldn't see himself living his life any other way. He sure wished his future could include Corey, but that had slipped out of his grasp. He thought about David, wondering what had become of him, hoping Melissa hadn't made his life miserable after that fateful day.

A pair of ravens soaring overhead startled him out of his thoughts with their shrill call. He watched them until they disappeared from view, envying them so free in flight.

CHAPTER FIFTEEN

COREY FELT as if the bottom had dropped out of his stomach. He hadn't expected Nick to react like that, but given how the day had started for them, he shouldn't have been surprised. Watching Nick leave was agonizing, but he'd resisted the urge to go after him. He hoped that by giving him time to think things over, Nick would realize that he couldn't run away from his problems and that what they shared deserved a chance.

He pulled himself together enough to venture into his less-than-organized garage to look for the Christmas tree and trimmings for the gym—he really did need something else to focus on. After he found the boxes tucked behind boxes he hadn't yet unpacked he decided to dive back in and give the messy space some much-needed attention. By the time he'd finished three hours later he felt a sense of accomplishment. Even though his life might be spinning out of control, at least he had a clean garage with room to park his car.

Once he locked the garage door, Corey plopped down on his bench and sighed, telling himself Nick would never just skip town— he couldn't, despite the fact he'd already done that once before.

Sighing, he leaned forward and braced his elbows on his knees, letting his chin drop into his hands. Nick had committed to doing the art for that birthday party, and he would definitely finish the gym, so there'd be no way they wouldn't see each other again. Nick would have to at least collect the last of his pay for the gym work.

He sat for several more minutes and then decided to head inside the house. Checking the time when he walked into the living room, he noticed that it was almost time for Katie to leave work. He sure wanted to know if Nick was at the gym painting, so his options were to either drive over there and find out, using the excuse of dropping off the Christmas stuff, or he could just call Katie and ask.

Calling, or seeing her in person, wasn't something he looked forward to, but he'd have to do it sooner or later, so he picked up the phone that sat on the end table and dialed the gym.

It took several rings before Katie picked up, sounding out of breath, and it was obvious that she'd seen his name on the caller ID.

"Hi, Corey."

He hoped the fact she used his name rather than the nickname she usually used wasn't a bad sign. "Hey, sorry I never got back today."

After getting nothing in response, he guessed either she was too mad to talk to him, or she was waiting for him to say why he'd called.

"Anything happen there that I should know about?"

"No, everything's fine. Nothing out of the ordinary. What did you do today?"

Surprised that she seemed to want to make conversation, he went along with it. "I spent most of the afternoon straightening up my garage, and I found the Christmas decorations for the gym. I'll bring them in tomorrow."

"Sounds good," she said, sounding preoccupied. "Uh, you aren't going to believe this, but I found out that Dad is seeing someone."

"How do you know?"

"Because I called him today, to ask if he wanted to grab a bite to eat tonight at the corner diner, and he said he couldn't because he had a date! I nearly fainted."

"It must be Rita."

"You know about this?" Katie asked, the surprise in her voice evident.

"Well, at Thanksgiving, it seemed like he and the mission's program director, Rita Franklin, were enjoying each other's company."

"And you didn't tell me? Why not?" she scolded.

"I didn't really think anything would come of it."

"Well, it looks like something has. He even said he might bring this woman by here tomorrow and talk to you about them getting a membership. Can you just picture Dad exercising?" She burst out laughing.

The subject of his uncle's love life couldn't have come at a better time as far as he was concerned. Katie seemed absorbed by the news and that was fine by him—anything to help get them past the unpleasantness of the morning.

"Exercising would do him some good, and if he has someone who wants to do it with him, all the better."

"This lady, do you know much about her?"

"Like I said, she works at the mission. She seems very nice."

"What does she look like?"

"Oh, I don't know. Not too tall, not too short—not thin and not fat. Just normal looking, about your dad's age, I think. Maybe you'll see her tomorrow."

"Maybe I will. Look, it's almost time for me to go—so was there anything else you called about?"

Corey took a deep breath. The conversation was going so well with her that he hesitated, but he had to know. "Nick isn't painting by any chance, is he?"

"Yeah, he's here. He came in over an hour ago." Her tone turned cooler, but not too bad.

"Okay, well, maybe he'll finish up this evening."

"Do you want to talk to him?"

"No, don't disturb him. I just wondered."

"Okay then. Well, will I see *you* in the morning?"

"Yeah, I'll be in."

After he hung up, he sank down into the couch and closed his eyes. Damn, it sure would be nice to have Nick sitting there next to him. At least he'd been right about Nick not having left town, and the longer Nick hung around, the better his chances were of persuading his boyfriend to stay permanently, and for them to make a home together.

After washing his painting tools, Nick folded up the drop cloth and closed up the ladder for the last time and took both to the janitor's closet. As he walked back to where he'd just finished up his job, he took in all the work he'd done during the past three and a half weeks. He was going to miss this—not just the painting, but the gym itself, not to mention it's owner.

One person he sure wasn't going to miss was Dean, damn him. This was all his fault for sticking his nose into something that was none of his business, and not only that, but he'd told Katie stuff too. Nick had half-expected her to give him a hard time when he came in to paint this evening, but she'd just ignored him. She'd never really talked to him that much anyway, so maybe everything was normal. Things sure weren't normal for him though, not after the way he'd left Corey like he had.

At least he got the job done. He wouldn't have felt right about leaving town without finishing. He raked his fingers through his hair and blew out a breath. He'd remember this job for a very long time, and at that moment he wished he had a phone, so he could take a picture to remember it by. The mural had to be some of the best work he'd ever done.

Taking another long look at his masterpiece he sighed again, his heart aching. He hoped his initials in the lower left corner that he'd added at the end wouldn't be too sad a reminder for Corey. Maybe they'd serve as a constant source of annoyance to Dean, the troublemaker.

Well, he couldn't stand there all night, so he got his things together and headed for the door. As he walked out into the cool night, he wasn't in the mood for dinner. Maybe he'd stop at the convenience store and see if Mrs. Griego would be around and he could talk to her for a bit. He'd miss her, and her husband, when he moved on.

CHAPTER SIXTEEN

JUST AFTER eight the next morning, Corey was on his way to the gym but decided to stop at Donuts Galore. He figured a box of donuts to share with Katie as a peace-offering couldn't hurt, and he made sure to get extras of her favorite.

When he caught the red light in front of the Food Mart that was a block from the gym, he noticed several police cars parked in front of the store, and a couple officers standing on the sidewalk near the entrance. What had really attracted his attention was the yellow police tape encompassing an ATM to the right of the store's door. He was glad that this time the trouble wasn't in the strip mall that housed the gym, so he drove on past the scene when the light changed. But whatever the problem, it was too close for comfort, and his mind was still on what he'd just seen when he turned into the gym parking lot.

After getting out of his car, he realized that he'd gone without thinking about Nick for the past few minutes, but now thoughts of him flooded his mind full-force. Even though it had been less than twenty-four hours since he'd seen Nick he missed him, especially considering how they'd parted, and he wondered for the hundredth time when he'd see him again.

Once inside, he saw that Katie had the phone pressed to her ear and her back to the office door, so he stepped farther into the gym to check on Nick's progress with the painting. He wasn't surprised to see Nick had finished and it looked outstanding. Sighing, he felt a sense of loss now that there'd be no reason for Nick to come to the gym anymore. He had something else in mind—but that would hinge on convincing Nick he was safe staying in town.

He sure hoped Katie had moved on from the nonsense Dean had dumped on her yesterday concerning Nick. With any luck, her dad and Rita would take center stage, just like last evening during their phone conversation.

When he walked into the office, Katie wasn't on the phone anymore, and her eyes went right to the box in his hands.

"What's that?" she asked, her fingers waggling at the box, even though he figured she knew from the shape and from the smell of fresh pastries wafting in the air.

"I brought us some breakfast." He glanced at the full coffee pot and set the donuts on the desk. "Looks like the coffee's just brewed?"

Katie gave him a knowing smile. "Thank you, this is nice." She opened the lid and gave them the once-over. "Wow, so many. You shouldn't have."

"Those sprinkled ones are still your favorite, aren't they?"

"Yes, unfortunately." Her smile grew wider. "I suppose you expect me to eat them all? If I do, I'll gain five pounds." She sat down at the desk and promptly took a huge bite of the donut she had grabbed from the box.

"You can work the calories off decorating the tree," Corey said, taking the chair across from her.

"Right—I'll help Patty and Rhonda with it if you get it set into place."

"I'll bring it in after I eat."

He wished Nick would be around to help him with the tree, but that probably wasn't going to happen, unless Nick had second thoughts after their conversation from the day before or came in to get paid.

He tried not to let his face show his unhappiness when he reached for a buttermilk donut, placing it on a napkin in front of him. "On my way here, I noticed some activity at the Food Mart. Cop cars and police tape."

"Oh, my God. What's happened now? Why didn't you say something when you first came in?"

"I don't know. I was just glad they weren't here this time."

Katie got up and reached for the coffee pot, spilling some while filling Corey's cup. He grabbed a napkin and jumped to his feet to wipe it up, and when she over poured her own cup, he wiped that up too.

"Are you okay?" he asked.

"Yes, I'm fine, but just up the street—I wonder if it's the same person. Could you tell what happened?" She sat down with her coffee.

"No, not really." He sat down again too and took a sip from his cup. He was concerned that she seemed so distressed.

"I wonder if your dad and Mrs. Franklin will really come in today."

"Dad sounded like they would. I doubt that it's his idea though."

"Well, maybe she'll be good for him."

"That would be nice."

Her short answers led Corey to believe she was still preoccupied with the police activity, although she was more relaxed than a few moments ago.

He'd just put the last bite of donut in his mouth when he saw a pained look cross Katie's face and heard her mutter, *oh no*, while she stared behind him. He heard the door open before he looked to see Officer Kelly standing in the foyer.

Corey wiped his hands on a napkin and stood up. "Come in, Officer," he said through the open office door. "What can we do for you this morning?"

Officer Kelly entered, and they shook hands. Katie stood up as well, but she stayed behind the desk.

"There was an incident in the early morning hours at the ATM located near the Food Mart down the street," Officer Kelly said.

"What kind of an incident, and how can we help?"

"A woman was mugged as she withdrew money from the ATM."

"Is she okay?" Katie asked.

"She's pretty shaken up with cuts and scrapes, but they checked her over at the hospital and she'll be okay."

"That's good," Corey said. "Did she give a description of the attacker?"

"Yes, and that's why I'm here. I'd like a list of all your members and a list of the ones who were in here last night and in the early morning."

The grim look on Officer Kelly's face made Corey's stomach churn. "The painter you mentioned, the first time I was here, is he still in the picture?"

Before he could answer, Katie said in a small voice, "He just finished his work last evening."

"Will he be back?"

"He'll be in to collect his pay at some point," Corey interjected, afraid Katie would start to say too much.

"Good, add his name to the list if you don't mind, and anyone else who does business here who isn't an actual member."

"Sure—but why do you need the names?" Corey asked.

"In the description the victim gave, she stated that underneath the assailant's hoodie, he had on a New U Fitness Center T-shirt."

Corey felt the blood drain from his face. When he glanced at Katie, she looked as rattled as he felt. She gripped the desk and lowered herself into the chair as if standing was too much of an effort.

"Did the woman see the man's face?" Corey asked. He almost regretted asking as soon as the words left his mouth.

"We'll have a composite drawing by today or tomorrow," Officer Kelly said. "I'll be back later for the list, and you can add to that, any members who have purchased T-shirts if you happen to have that information."

"Sure thing."

Since their business was done, Corey walked Officer Kelly out, and when he returned to the office prepared to start compiling the list he saw that Katie already had the names up on the computer screen, the task under control.

"You can make a list of the other people he wants and add to this. Oh, and don't forget Wes and the cleaning crew," Katie said, her eyes never leaving the screen.

Corey stepped out into the foyer and sat down in a chair. He leaned back and stared up at the ceiling, crossing his arms over his chest. Knowing the cops thought someone from the gym had committed the ATM crime was a big cause for concern, but something else had him stressed out at the moment. He didn't know what to put for Nick's last name when he added it to Katie's list, and he wished he could speak to Nick about it. Since that wasn't possible, his only choice was to put down Stewart. Nick had trusted him where his real name was concerned, and he couldn't betray that.

Nick's last name was Stewart and that's all there was to it, even though he had a bad feeling about using the fake name.

Corey felt like he'd already been at work for the entire day, but the clock on the wall told him differently—it was barely eleven. The last thing he felt like doing was setting up the Christmas tree, but he figured that would help get their minds off the latest crime, so he went out to his car to get it. He set the boxes of decorations on the ground near the rear wheel and struggled to pull the tree box out of the back when from the corner of his eye, he saw Dean ride in on his new mountain bike.

Can this day get any worse?

With the tree box in hand, he realized he'd never get all the boxes inside in one trip, so when he heard Dean yell to wait a second, that he'd help, Corey did just that. Neither of them spoke while hauling the boxes in and depositing them in the foyer, Dean's silence surprising him—he didn't think Dean would have enough sense to let yesterday's topic drop. Now, he dreaded Dean getting wind of this new incident, but he knew it would only be a matter of time before he heard, especially when Katie didn't seem able to keep her mouth shut around him. And how would this affect business if the members found out about this most recent crime?

"What did we just haul in here anyway?" Dean asked, trying to open one of the taped boxes with his fingers.

"It's the Christmas decorations," Katie answered, standing in the doorway of the office, her hands on her hips.

"I should have guessed," Dean said, as he pulled off a long piece of tape.

Just then, Patty walked through the main door looking lively and cheerful. She stepped around the long tree box, stopping next to Katie. Her smile brightened up an otherwise dismal day. "It looks like I'm just in time to decorate," she said.

"Give me time to stand the tree up and then you can have at it," Corey said, giving her a smile he didn't really feel.

"I'll help you," Dean said, smiling at Corey like he'd saved the day.

"Don't you have an appointment?" Corey snapped, hoping Dean's client was due soon and he'd be rid of him.

"I'm running early. We can whip this puppy into shape in nothing flat."

"Okay, when you're done, we'll get started," Katie said, pulling

Patty by the arm into the office.

By the way Dean took charge, carefully lifting the tree sections out of the box and getting them laid out, it was obvious he knew what he was doing and that he enjoyed the task, like the holidays had put him in a festive mood, but Corey's mood sure wasn't festive, and Dean horning in was only making him cranky as all get-out. Still, he could use the help, so he didn't balk at the offer, and since Dean would have to leave for his session soon he hoped they could keep whatever conversation there might be on Christmas trees and holidays.

They adjusted the stand and assembled the sections to form the seven-foot tree. While they flared out the branches, Corey began to feel less tense—up until Nick walked in.

The last thing he wanted was for Nick to see him and Dean together, never mind that all they were doing was assembling a Christmas tree. The bad blood between Nick and Dean, and the way Corey and Nick had left things yesterday—this wasn't good. The three of them stood facing one another, and that had him wondering who was going to be the first to say something or be the first to throw a punch.

The icy blue stare that Nick gave Dean didn't surprise Corey because Nick had every reason to be pissed off at Dean. But when Nick reached out and pulled Corey into a possessive one-arm side hug, that surprised the hell out of him.

"How's it going?" Nick whispered near Corey's ear.

All Corey could do was look at him and smile. He wasn't sure what the heck was going on, one minute Nick was done and gone forever, and now he's all smiles and hugs. This one-eighty had his head spinning. Dean's glaring look spoke volumes about his dislike of Nick's actions, and Corey was glad of it. Dean probably couldn't believe that his butting in, trying to stir up trouble, hadn't done the trick in ending the relationship between him and Nick.

Dean shook his head like he was disgusted. "My client's here," he said abruptly as he stalked off.

Nick grinned at Corey, looking pleased with himself. "Was it something I said?"

Corey snickered, and Nick finally let go of him, looking at the tree, giving some branches a few adjustments.

"You got this thing up solid?" Nick asked, looking to the top of the tree.

"Uh, maybe it could use a few more tweaks," Corey said.

While they fiddled with it, Corey kept finding excuses to brush against his fine-looking man—hands and fingers, a bump of the shoulder, hip. He realized that for a while he'd put the problems of the cops, and Nick's last name out of his mind, but once the tree was finished and the distraction gone the situation came flooding back all too soon.

"The painting looks fantastic," Corey said, wanting to hold on to more pleasant topics for a little longer instead of having to talk about the problems weighing on his mind.

"Thanks, I'm happy with how it turned out," Nick answered, turning with a look of pride at the freshly painted walls he'd completed the night before, but when Nick's gaze shifted to the mural wall, that's when his face really lit up.

"I'll get your money when we're through here," Corey said, walking around the tree one last time making sure it was straight.

"Okay, and is there any chance you can get away to talk somewhere private?" Nick asked in a low tone, looking around to see who might be listening in on him.

Corey nodded, feeling elated but dreading having 'the talk' at the same time. "I'd like that, but I've got something to tell you, something important." But then Corey sighed loudly. "Crap."

"What's wrong?"

"I just remembered that my uncle and Mrs. Franklin are more than likely coming in today, and I need to stick around. We can leave after I've seen them, but what I need to talk about can't wait, so maybe when the girls come out to decorate the tree, we'll talk in the office."

"Yeah, that would be okay," Nick said.

"Great."

"So, are they actually going to sign up?"

"It looks that way, according to Katie." Corey reached into a box and pulled out an extension cord. "Let's see if this thing lights up."

Just as they plugged in the tree Rhonda walked in the front door, stopping to admire the multicolored lights before going into the office. Corey quickly adjusted the cord, so no one would trip on it, and then followed her inside as if he didn't have a care in the world, Nick right on his heels.

Knowing what Katie thought about Nick made it hard to act self-assured, but with Nick by his side he felt stronger, especially when Nick smiled at Katie in his laid-back kind of way, despite knowing Dean had shared information about him with her the day before.

"Go ahead and attack the tree and work your magic on it," Corey said to the girls as he headed toward the desk. "I'll cover the phones."

"Come on, ladies," Katie said, grabbing the step-stool from the far corner of the office. "I want you to get a picture when we're all done," she said to Corey before she led them out to where the tree stood waiting.

Once Rhonda, Katie, and Patty left, Corey shut both office doors and motioned for Nick to sit down, then took a seat himself behind the desk. Corey knew they needed to talk, but he wanted to stall as well because the thought of telling Nick what had gone down with the cops earlier had his stomach tied in knots, and having to ask about using his real last name had him on edge. So, to kill a few moments, he took his wallet out of his back pocket and counted out Nick's pay and laid it on the desk.

Nick reached for the stack of bills and stuffed them in his own pocket and pulled out his key chain and took the key fob off and set it on the desk where the money had just been. "Guess I won't be needing this anymore."

"Unless you want to start coming in to work-out, you won't. Since you hadn't taken me up on that offer while you were working here, how about now?" After a few silent moments, Corey huffed out a frustrated breath. "I guess that was a dumb question since you said you'd be leaving town soon."

Nick looked up and stared straight into Corey's eyes. "That's what I wanted to talk to you about."

"Oh, yeah? Did you change your mind, because yesterday you sure sounded pretty hell-bent on doing that."

"Yeah, well, I'm sorry about that. I... I did a lot of thinking after I left."

Nick hesitated so long Corey wondered if that was it, but he could tell by the way Nick was fidgeting he had more to say. He waited.

"You were right—that being gay isn't a crime." Nick readjusted himself on the chair and gave him a pitiful look.

"I'm glad you were listening."

"Yeah—anyway—I gave what you said a lot of thought. I hardly slept last night, and I *really* want to stay in town. I'm not gonna let Dean or anyone else run me off, and I doubt my... family is even looking for me."

Corey wanted to say something to him about that because he knew his family had to be sick with worry over his disappearance, but he bit his tongue and instead smiled, despite the tension that filled the room.

"I'm really glad you're staying." He took in a breath and blew it out, afraid what the answer would be to his question. "Can we keep on seeing each other?"

"That's what I want," Nick said, looking at Corey bashfully, a smile tugging at the corners of his mouth.

"Keep the fob, come in whenever you want and use the equipment."

"I can't really afford a membership."

"Like I said, you didn't exercise while you were painting, so you're entitled to come back if you want. How about one free month and we see what happens then?"

"I don't recall using the equipment was part of my payment."

"Are you sure? I'm sure we discussed that," Corey replied giving Nick a quick wink.

Nick reached for the key fob and put it back in his pocket. "You said you had something important to talk to me about. What is it?"

"Yeah, that." Corey's heart jumped up several notches, and he wiped his hands on his thighs. "Well, it's not good news like yours was."

Nick sat forward in the chair and clasped his hands on the desk. "What's wrong?"

"The cops were here this morning."

"Again? What the heck!"

"Yeah. Someone mugged a woman at the ATM near the Food Mart in the next complex." Corey stopped to gather his thoughts.

"Damn," Nick muttered. "Is she okay?"

"Yeah, she wasn't hurt seriously, but something like that shouldn't have happened, and it pisses me off."

"Why did the cops come here?"

"That's the bad part."

"Oh, no," Nick said with a look of apprehension on his face.

"Sorry, I don't mean to be an alarmist, but the officer said the woman saw a New U T-shirt under the mugger's hoodie, so it's a pretty safe bet the guy's a member here. That's why the officer came by—to get a list of members and to ask if we knew who had T-shirts.

Heck, most of the members have one."

"Yeah, not much to go on there, and every other person you see wears a hoodie, male and female."

"Especially this time of year—and with all the rain we've been getting."

"Is there a description of the guy?"

"They'll have a drawing later on."

"Wow."

"Which brings me to the next part," Corey said.

Nick didn't utter a word, he just stared at Corey and waited, a look of dread in his eyes.

"Officer Kelly asked us to include another list of people who come in and out, who aren't members, like the cleaning crew and... whoever else."

"Like me?" Nick asked.

"Yeah, like you. Officer Kelly knew from before that we had a painter in here, so he asked specifically for your name to be on the list."

"Well, that'll make Dean happy, I'll bet."

"Look, this is my dilemma and why I wanted to talk to you." Corey took in a deep breath, hating this. "I didn't know if you'd be okay with me giving out your real last name."

"Shit," Nick said, looking down and shaking his head.

"I didn't know if I'd see you before Officer Kelly came back, so I used Stewart, but I can change that if you give me the okay."

Nick looked deep in thought, just staring at the floor. Corey waited, but no words were coming from Nick.

"I really think the best way to go is to give your real last name. If we don't, and it comes out that you're not who you say you are, it's going to—"

"Make me look guilty," Nick said, still looking down.

"I didn't say that—but it'll make the cops ask questions and—"

"I know... I know you're right," Nick said. Then he finally made eye contact. "Use Sanders. It's... Yeah, go ahead and give him the name."

Corey breathed a sigh of relief and without saying anything else, he gave his attention to the computer, while Nick stood up and paced. After he corrected Nick's name on the list and hit the print button, someone rapped on the door.

"Yeah?" Corey said over the sound of the printer.

Katie cracked open the door and peeked in. "Sorry to

interrupt, but my dad and his friend just came in."

"Okay, be right with them," Corey said. He stood up and walked over to the door, pausing before reaching for the knob. "If you wait around, we can go somewhere when I'm done signing them up."

"Okay, I'll wait."

Nick wandered over to the vending machine, got himself a *Gatorade* and walked a few feet away and leaned against the wall before taking a swig. He wondered why the thing with his last name didn't have him more unsettled. Could be that all his thinking the night before had really done him some good, and maybe he was ready to live his life without looking over his shoulder.

All the gym sounds and the activity around him were comforting, and a peaceful feeling settled over him. He wondered what using the equipment would be like. There hadn't been a gym within miles of his hometown, so working out on fancy machines like this had never crossed his mind, although he could sure appreciate a man with toned biceps and pecs. He wondered if he'd look better if he committed to exercising on some of that equipment. Maybe Corey didn't think he had enough muscles and that's why he'd brought up the subject. Dean wasn't all that bulked up though, and Corey must have thought his body looked all right.

He'd noticed a few scrawny guys in there lifting weights—reminded him of himself back when he was a kid. In his late teens he'd finally put on a growth spurt, shot up six inches and put on twenty-five pounds. Elated was an understatement for how that had made him feel. He wouldn't have to go through life short, spindly, teased and picked on, but the downside was he started attracting girls, which brought a whole new set of problems. Seemed his whole life had been filled with difficulties of some sort, but finding this new town, new people, the gym—finally things were changing for good.

CHAPTER SEVENTEEN

COREY WOKE from a dream—a beautiful dream. He couldn't remember anything specific about it, just that the dream had filled him with such euphoria that he didn't want to let it go. But try as he might to drift back to that place, he was coming back to full consciousness.

Slowly he opened one eye, then the other and listened closely, wondering if the rain had stopped. He couldn't hear any hitting the roof or the window, but that might be due to the light snoring coming from the other side of the bed.

Nick—Nick in all his naked glory. He smiled, and stretched, remembering.

His dead-to-the-world guy hadn't come prepared to stay the night, but that didn't matter. He'd offered Nick pajamas, but Nick had told him he would rather sleep 'au naturel', and that was more than all right, so he'd slept that way too. Actually, sleep hadn't come until hours after they'd turned in, with the rain pouring down over their heads enhancing the romance and passion of it all. The temperature in the room had gotten a little cool toward morning, and they'd snuggled together for warmth—he remembered that. What he couldn't remember was when they had drifted to their own side of the bed.

Corey rubbed his eyes and tried to determine what time it was. He could see dark shadowy shapes in the room, so he guessed the time to be about six o'clock.

He was too lazy to turn and look at the bedside clock, so instead he turned his head toward Nick and watched him sleep, hoping his dreams were good ones and the bad ones from before would be few and far between.

Since no one had brought the composite drawing by yesterday, he figured they'd get a look at it sometime today and that made him nervous as hell, wondering if the face would be someone he recognized.

Between getting the Christmas tree trimmed and having Uncle Ed and Mrs. Franklin in the gym the day before, the afternoon had turned into a party of sorts. Mrs. Franklin, or Rita, as she asked to be called, had a great sense of humor and made everyone laugh, especially Uncle Ed, and that was great to see. Katie seemed to like her too, which was a relief, and what was even better—Katie had been friendly to Nick. Her concerns about him from the day before seemed to have evaporated. Corey hadn't even noticed Dean and assumed he'd left after his appointment. The only unpleasant part of the afternoon happened when Ed and Rita were just about to leave, and Officer Kelly came by to get the member's list. Of course, Uncle Ed wanted to know what was going on so he had to give Ed the rundown, but despite that, the day had turned out pretty good, and the night even better.

If only Nick hadn't reacted like he had the other day when he was invited to move in. He wanted to mention it again, but he didn't dare, not yet anyway.

Nick stirred, and Corey watched him come awake.

"Hi," Nick said, those eyes regarding him with a tenderness that melted his heart.

Corey leaned in for a soft kiss. "Good morning," he said afterward.

"What time is it?"

"Why, you got someplace you have to be?"

"Not this morning, but later on I have to start the birthday job I told you about."

"Right, and maybe after that we can meet here again." Corey ran his knuckles along Nick's jaw and they shared another tender kiss. "Are you coming to the gym with me? I thought you might want to look at the composite drawing when the officer brings it over."

"Yeah, sure. I wonder if they're going to question me about

anything."

"When they see that your description doesn't match the drawing, maybe not."

"How do you know what the drawing will look like?"

"I know it won't look like you."

"Well, they wanted you to put my name down, and you wanted to give my real last name."

"They don't know what you look like, but when they do..."

"I like your optimism."

Corey rested his head on Nick's chest, just listening to the beat of his heart.

"You going back to sleep?" Nick asked sleepily, giving Corey a squeeze.

"No, I think I'll go fix us some breakfast."

"Don't go to a lot of trouble."

"Nothing's too much trouble for you."

When Nick didn't respond, Corey levered himself up on his elbow and was captivated by the most dazzling smile he'd come to love, especially first thing in the morning. Even if the rain stuck around, and even with the uncertainty going on around the gym, Nick's sparkling eyes and killer smile almost made him forget.

Corey leaned in to whisper in Nick's ear. "I've got a great idea."

"Oh, yeah? Am I gonna like it?"

"I'd say there's a good chance you will," Corey murmured and then he lightly bit Nick's earlobe.

"Breakfast can wait," Nick said, covering Corey's body with his as he rolled over.

The unwelcome ring of the phone on the nightstand startled Corey and made Nick jump.

"Damn, probably a wrong number at this hour," Corey mumbled reaching to silence the shrill sound, but seeing the caller ID he paused before picking up the receiver. "It's Katie."

He sat up on the side of the bed and brought the phone up to his ear. "Katie, is something wrong?" he asked, trying to stay calm. He didn't get an answer, and all he could hear were muffled shaky breaths. "Have you been crying?"

He could tell she had when she struggled to form her words. "I... I just...called to say I... won't be in at my usual time. I know... you want someone there by eight."

"Tell me what's wrong."

"I'm f-f-fine, don't worry. I just wanted—" She took in a

stuttered breath. "—you to know not to expect me until later."

"Are you sick? Is your dad okay?"

"We're fine. I'll... see you later."

Corey held the dead receiver in his hand for a few seconds before turning to Nick. "I don't know what's wrong, but something has her upset."

Nick sat up and put his hand on Corey's shoulder. "You wanna go over and see her?"

"I'm tempted, but... who knows, maybe Alan's there or something. Best I don't walk in on that."

"You think maybe they had a fight?"

"If they did, and if she dumps him, it'll be cause for celebration. Come on, let's get dressed."

"The girls did a great job decorating. Gives the place a nice holiday feel," Nick said while pausing in front of the Christmas tree in the foyer of the gym.

"Yeah, between the tree and your paint job, it looks real good in here," Corey said over his shoulder while unlocking the office.

"A lot of people working out makes it look good in here too."

"I guess they haven't heard about the burglaries and robberies going on in the area."

"You've got good security, they won't stop coming, and I'm sure they'll catch whoever's responsible soon."

Once inside the office Corey turned on the computer, and before checking the answering machine he asked Nick to get a canister of water for the coffee maker. Nick had barely left when the front door opened and in walked a tall, serious-looking man in a dark suit. The briefcase he carried added to his look of authority. Corey went to the office door to greet him.

"Good morning, I'm Corey Preston." He held his hand out to shake.

"I'm Detective Munson. Good to meet you," he replied, giving Corey a firm handshake.

"I was expecting Officer Kelly."

"I'm taking over the case now," the detective said.

"Come in." Corey moved aside to let Detective Munson step into the office.

"I've brought by a composite sketch, such as it is. May I?" he asked, putting his briefcase on the desk before Corey could answer. "I'm afraid the witness couldn't recall much about the suspect. It's not her fault because, unfortunately, he had on a dark-colored knit watch cap that covered his hair and his whole forehead. With rather poor lighting, and the speed of the incident, her ability to help with a description was quite limited at best. About the only thing she seemed sure about was his eye color—dark brown—and the writing on his shirt." Detective Munson pulled out a sheet of paper from his briefcase and held it out to Corey.

As Corey studied it closely, Detective Munson went on. "She estimated his height at between five feet nine and six feet with a strong build. He didn't speak during the attack, so nothing to go on there."

Corey stared at the drawing wishing it was more detailed. He'd hoped, yet dreaded, that it would actually look like someone he recognized, but it didn't.

"Is this someone you might recognize?"

"Not at all. I'm sorry."

At least it was obvious that Nick wouldn't be implicated. With his long wavy hair, there'd be no way he could have hidden it under that knit cap, not unless he'd made sure to stuff it all underneath. And if the victim was sure about the eye color—they wouldn't be questioning him on that either, since Nick had blue eyes. The only thing they could question him on would be who he may have seen in the gym that night. Corey let out a breath, glad that he'd already checked the list, and no one he knew well, had been there.

"The witness is positive the man had on a T-shirt from here?" Corey asked.

"Yes, that was the first thing she mentioned," Detective Munson said. "We're still going over the list you provided, so I'll be back in touch soon. I just wanted to drop this sketch off today. I'll see myself out."

He turned and walked to the office door but then paused. "You might want to tack that up somewhere, so everyone can see it. Even if the face isn't recognizable, if the perpetrator sees it he might get nervous and do something to give himself away." The last statement Detective Munson uttered was, "Keep an eye open."

As soon as the detective had closed the main door, Nick appeared with the water canister and filled up the coffee maker, then looked in the brew basket, and pressed the ON button.

"A detective just brought the drawing," Corey said, indicating the sheet of paper on the desk.

Nick didn't pick it up but looked at it where it lay. "Could be a number of guys. None of the features really jump out, do they." His statement wasn't really a question. "If there was even just one defining characteristic it would help."

"Yeah, the face isn't very lifelike. The detective said the witness wasn't able to give much of a description, so the police artist didn't have a lot to work with. But, did you notice the height and weight in the description?"

Nick read the note next to the sketch. "Says five-nine to six feet, and one-eighty to two hundred pounds. That description fits a lot of the men in here."

Corey picked up the paper and in a low voice said, "Alan fits this description, and he has dark brown eyes."

"Did you say that to the cop?"

"No—it's not enough to go on. I'm just thinking out loud. This stays between us, all right?"

"Of course. You know, this description could even fit Dean."

"Or me for that matter." Corey barked out a small laugh. "I need coffee. This machine is getting slower and slower every damn day. You want some if it ever finishes?"

"Yeah, I could use a cup."

"I've got to check the bathrooms as soon as I have mine. I wish Katie was here."

"I'll help you."

"That's not the point, but thanks. I just hope she's okay."

"She'll be here soon. She takes this job seriously."

After Nick left, and Rhonda had clocked in and taken over in the office, Corey made the rounds, chatting with the weight trainers and the members leaving class. He'd held off calling Katie, even though he'd been tempted many times. He wondered if she'd have lunch before coming in. Maybe he could take her out if she hadn't and they could have a long talk. Damn, he sure wished he'd see her come through the door.

He hadn't put the sketch up yet and thinking about it again, no way would anyone recognize the man in the drawing—and seeing this mysterious person might just make the members nervous. But Detective Munson thought he should, so he decided to follow through.

Walking into the office to get the drawing, he overheard Rhonda talking on the phone, obviously a personal call, and he didn't have to hear much to realize she had Katie on the line. As tempted as he was to stay and listen, when Rhonda turned away and lowered her voice he could tell he wasn't welcome, so he took the picture and left. At least Katie was okay enough to be on the telephone—that was something.

He took his time tacking up the drawing, and when he got back Rhonda had hung up and was sitting there looking distracted and troubled.

"Did Katie say when she'd be here?" he asked. When she just stared at him, he added, "Uh, I didn't mean to listen in, but I could tell it was her on the phone."

"That's okay. She said she's on her way. Something's wrong though—she's very upset."

"Did she tell you anything? Anything at all?"

"Not much, but it's got something to do with Alan."

"Maybe they broke up?"

"I don't think so. But I think they're arguing."

"How do you know? Was he with her?"

"I don't know for sure, but I'd say no, because she made some remarks about him—uh, indirectly, like men are stupid immature jerks—stuff like that. I just let her blow off steam."

"I'm glad she has you to talk to," Corey said.

"She asked if the cops brought the composite sketch by. She wanted to know if it looked like anyone here."

"Yeah, well, we were anxious to see it. I wish the witness had been able to remember more detail."

"Yeah, it wasn't a very good drawing." Rhonda paused like she was thinking and then said, "That watch cap made me think of Ted Faulkner though. I've seen him wear one once in a while, more so now that it's gotten cold."

"You have?"

"Yeah, but I'm sure a lot of other guys have them too."

"Yeah," Corey said. "I've never really talked one-on-one with Ted other than to welcome him to the gym, have you?"

"No, I've always found him to be unfriendly and aloof. When I say hello to him, he just walks on past me."

Corey couldn't help but remember how Ted behaved on the video the night he and Alan went downstairs. Something else he remembered was that Ted had brown eyes and his height and weight matched the description on the sketch, but he didn't mention that to Rhonda.

"Why don't you have your lunch now, so that when Katie gets

here I can take her out if she hasn't eaten yet. Maybe I can calm her down."

"Good idea."

Corey felt better walking in the crisp, clean air from the Subway to the park with Katie by his side. He still didn't know what was bothering her, but he intended to find out, and she had agreed to lunch, so maybe, just maybe, it wouldn't be like pulling teeth to get it out of her.

"We should go out for lunch together more often, don't you think?" He glanced down trying to catch her eye.

She smiled slightly but didn't respond, just kicked at some clumps of fallen leaves.

"More rain's on the way, but it's sure nice out now, isn't it?" Corey said, trying to get some sort of conversation going. There sure hadn't been much on the drive to the Subway or in the restaurant, just Katie looking detached and uninterested, barely mumbling her choice of sandwich.

"Do you want shade or sun?" Corey asked, looking over the benches available near where they stood.

"The sun feels pretty nice, so let's take a bench in the sun," she said.

Corey was grateful that she seemed to have perked up, even just a little, and headed to the bench facing the skating park where a few boys were showing off on skateboards. He opened the bag and brought out their lunch, handing Katie hers.

"You know, I feel kind of bad for leaving the gym as soon as I got there to come here with you. I was already late."

"It's okay, I'm your boss, remember?" Corey snickered and bumped her shoulder with his.

She rolled her eyes and took a bite of her sandwich. For several minutes they ate without talking, letting the skateboarders entertain them.

"I wonder if they're playing hooky. They look like they belong in school."

"I was thinking the same thing," Katie answered and then with a profound look of sadness in her eyes she went on. "Some people just don't want to play by the rules."

The waver in her voice and her threatening tears, made Corey feel helpless, but then she took a deep breath and shook her head. "I feel really stupid."

"Why?"

"Please don't tell me I told you so," Katie said, her voice cracking with emotion.

Corey scooted closer and put his arm around her. "I promise I won't."

"It's just that I know you dislike Alan already, and if I tell you this..."

Corey tried not to press the panic button, but if Katie felt she had to tell him something about Alan, knowing full well how he already felt about the guy, it had to be something pretty serious.

"I want to help in any way I can. You can trust me."

"I know." Katie reached into her pocket pulling out a tissue to dab her eyes and wipe her nose. She held her hand out in front of her and stared at her engagement ring, turning her finger slightly to catch the light and make it sparkle. "I love my ring," she said sadly.

"What's going on, Katie?" he asked her softly.

"Alan asked me to give it back."

"What? He wants to break the engagement? You've only been engaged a week—what happened?"

Even though the thought of Katie being rid of Alan was a good thing in his mind, seeing her so devastated was not.

"No, he doesn't want to dump me—he still wants to be engaged," she said, but she looked more unhappy by the second.

"I'm not following you. Can you start at the beginning?" He gave her a little squeeze for encouragement.

"Alan has a gambling problem," she blurted out quickly. "I didn't know at first, even though I guess I should have." She sounded detached as if she was talking about someone else. But then in a sharp tone she went on. "Him and that creepy friend of his, Ted Faulkner. Ted's worse than Alan by a mile." Her shoulders slumped a little and she lowered her voice. "Anyway, there've been signs, but I tried to tell myself it wasn't that bad. Well, I really didn't think it was that bad, not until last night."

"So, that's how he was able to buy you this expensive ring. He must have had a windfall the day he bought it."

"Apparently."

"Weren't you curious how he could afford it?"

Katie looked at Corey with fresh tears in her eyes. "I should have been, but I was so happy I just ignored that nagging question."

"I'm afraid to ask why he wants it back."

"It's pretty ugly," Katie said with a sniffle. A tear rolled down her cheek.

"Tell me what you know."

"The only reason I know what I do is because I overheard him on the phone. When he saw me there he confessed—at least part of it."

"What do you mean, *part of it?*"

"He didn't tell me what's going down tonight, or other things, but he told me enough to make me sick."

"Has he got loan sharks after him?"

A loud sob escaped. She just couldn't hold it in any longer. Corey took her into his arms and let her cry. When she composed herself enough to talk, she took her ring off and put it in her purse.

"I'm going to give this to him, but I know it won't be enough to get him out of the trouble he's in."

"What's happening tonight?"

"I'm so scared for him, Corey." More tears ran down her face.

"Calm down and tell me," Corey said, even though he had a feeling he would wish he didn't know.

"I heard him say he'd meet someone at the cemetery tonight to pay them what he owes. Tonight, at midnight." She blew her nose and her whole body trembled. "I'm afraid they'll kill him when he shows up with just part of the money."

"Why did he tell them he'd meet them if he doesn't have it all?"

"He probably hopes to scrape more together by tonight."

"Yeah, out of an ATM—then maybe he'll have the full amount."

"You're saying you think he's the one who's been stealing, aren't you?"

"No, I'm not saying that... but it does seem like he has a reason to. And who knows, he might be committing more crimes than that."

"Well, I don't think it's him, especially at the ATM. He wouldn't attack a woman," she said, still obviously defending him.

"People do terrible things when they feel cornered. Let's hope not, but time will tell, I guess. In any case, he got himself into this, he'll have to get himself out."

Katie sat up straight on the bench. "I want to help him."

"I don't see how you can. It's his deal to clean up not yours."

"I know it's his problem, but we're engaged, so that makes it my problem too."

They were silent for a minute before Corey dared to speak his mind. "I hope you realize that Alan will only make your life miserable. You deserve so much more. When you give that ring back, you know what you need to do—tell him the engagement is off."

"I can't do that on top of what he's facing tonight. Maybe later—if he lives that long. I'm just so confused."

"I know you'll do the right thing," Corey said.

"Even if I move on, I still care so much for him, and I won't let anyone hurt him."

"It's out of your hands. Giving him the ring back is all you can do."

Katie turned to him, her eyes red and her face puffy from crying. "If I asked you to come to the cemetery with me tonight—just to make sure no one gets hurt—would you?"

"If you're this worried that something bad might happen, you should call the cops."

"No! No cops," Katie said adamantly.

"I don't see what we can do to help—in the dark—in a cemetery?" Corey couldn't help the rise in his voice. What in the world was she thinking?

"Well, if he gets beat up we could help him, couldn't we? Please," she begged, her fingernails digging into his arm.

Corey could see nothing good coming from this insane idea of hers. He didn't know what to say.

"If you won't come with me, I'll go alone," she said.

"You'll do no such thing."

Katie just stared at him, her eyes willing him to say yes. She must have caught his hesitation because she grabbed his hand, "Does that mean you're coming?"

Corey let out a heavy breath and closed his eyes. He didn't want to look at her, but he saw her anyway in his mind's eye. The sweet teenage girl who'd treated him like a brother when he'd come to town—the beautiful young woman who'd been right beside him sharing the load when he'd opened the gym, encouraging him every step of the way. She and her dad were the only family he had.

God, Uncle Ed will kill the both of us if he ever finds out.

He finally opened his eyes and looked at her. "We need more than just the two of us. Let me ask Nick to come." He could see her thinking it over. "Take it or leave it," he said.

"We've got a deal."

CHAPTER EIGHTEEN

ALAN'S CAR had been at the gym when Corey dropped Katie off—she was still determined to give him the ring back. Corey told her to call him if plans changed, otherwise he'd pick her up at her apartment at eleven fifteen that night and hopefully the plan they'd formulated while talking in the park would go off without a hitch. He couldn't believe he'd agreed to such an outlandish scheme, but he just couldn't let her go by herself.

He'd driven straight over to Nick's after saying goodbye to her. Sitting in the car across from the shabby, neglected motel Corey kept an eye out for Nick to return. He hadn't gotten an answer at Nick's door, which wasn't a surprise since it was still early. He figured Nick would be working on his project for most of the afternoon and knew Nick wanted to get some of his things before going back to the house, so waiting here seemed the best bet for catching up with him.

He wasn't totally comfortable pulled off the street in dirt, weeds, Land trash, not even a sidewalk, but it beat waiting in the parking space by the room, with people staring and probably wondering what he was doing there. Nick still not having a phone annoyed him, and once the mess with Katie, and the trouble going on near the gym, was over he intended on having a serious heart-to-heart talk with Nick about getting a phone, so they could communicate during the day. Corey rubbed his eyes and leaned his head back on the headrest. Maybe all this stress was making him irritable.

He took his phone out and punched speed dial number seven for the third time in the last hour. *Please pick up, man, I need you—Katie needs you.* When he finally heard that strong, deep voice on the other end of the line, he breathed a little easier.

"Wes, hey man, how's it going?"

"Good, but you don't usually call for small talk. Did something major break down at the gym?"

"No, that's not why I'm calling this time." Corey took a deep breath and gathered his courage, hoping he could make a good case for Wes to come along to the cemetery. "Look, I need a favor."

"I'll do it if I can. What do you need?"

He figured Wes still thought the call was about something at the gym, so he said, "I need a personal favor—well, Katie and I do." He felt bad asking because he really hated to ask for something that wasn't work-related.

"What's going on? What could Katie possibly need from me?"

At that point, Corey explained the situation, all the while keeping his eyes peeled for Nick. When he was finished, he tried to slow his breathing down and hoped for the best.

"I don't mean to insult you or Katie, but this plan sounds pretty hair-brained," Wes finally said.

"I know, I know, it's not the way I want to spend my night, but like I said, Katie is determined to go—with or without us. I can't let her go there alone."

"What about security? Isn't the place locked up at night? Wouldn't we be trespassing?"

"Katie says there's no security, and Alan will probably use his key to get in through the employee gate, so she figures we'll go that way too."

"She actually wants me to go?" Wes asked.

Corey heard the surprise in his voice, and he was so close to lying and saying yes, but he just couldn't go that far.

"No, but she didn't want Nick there either—only me—but I figure there's strength in numbers. Look, I don't want to go either, but I've got no choice. She's my cousin. I know I shouldn't ask you to do this—"

"I'll go with you, no problem."

The loud clang of a pot hitting the kitchen floor set Corey on edge, even more than he already was. "Damn, I'm clumsy tonight."

"Here, let me help," Nick said, picking it up.

"You've already done more than your share. You practically cooked the whole meal and loaded most of the dishes into the dishwasher."

"I don't mind. Let's set this pot down and go watch TV until Wes gets here."

"I don't think I can concentrate on anything."

"If you have a deck of cards, a game might help calm you down and pass the time."

"Yeah, I've got cards around someplace. What do you play?"

"My brother and I used to play gin rummy. Have you ever played?"

"Sure, my uncle taught me when I was a kid."

"Cool."

"Okay, let's give it a whirl. I'll be lucky to win even one hand though."

Corey searched and found a deck of cards in the catch-all drawer by the sink. They sat down at the kitchen table and each drew to see who would deal first. Nick won the draw, so he shuffled the cards and dealt ten each. Corey took the upcard on the discard pile and the game was on.

"I hope you know how much I appreciate you agreeing to go with me tonight," Corey said, as he arranged his hand.

"There's no place I'd rather be—other than snuggled in bed with you of course," Nick answered, taking his turn.

"I can't wait until we're back here and can do just that." Corey drew a card and discarded.

Nick smiled, picked from the stack and threw down the three of hearts.

"This has got to be the stupidest thing Katie has ever gotten me into. Maybe I shouldn't have involved you and Wes."

"I'm not complaining, and I'm sure Wes is glad for the chance to help Katie. He wouldn't have agreed to this if that wasn't the case."

"I hope there won't be a reason for us to come out of hiding, and we can all just leave with no one knowing we were creeping around a cemetery in the middle of the night," Corey said. His hand hovered over Nick's discard, then he snatched it up and arranged it in his hand.

"That'd be the best scenario—just hide and watch," Nick said, studying his cards before taking his turn.

"Well, as long as no one has a gun, we should be all right with four of us there, and we'll be there to pick up the pieces after the bad guys leave. That's all Katie expects us to do." Corey drew from the stock pile and then discarded.

"I hope we'll be able to find the meeting place. The cemetery must be pretty good sized."

"Katie thinks she knows where to go. She's been out there with Alan before."

"I'm surprised nobody guards the place at night," Nick said, drawing from the stock pile and discarding the ten of clubs.

"Well, I guess they figure locking the gates is enough."

"Yeah, it would be I guess, if not for a double-dealing employee."

"I hope the sky doesn't decide to open up about the time we get there."

"That'd be all we need."

With everything having been said about their late-night excursion, they settled into the game and played steadily until they heard the rumble of Wes's four-wheel drive coming up the driveway. They hurriedly threw on a couple more layers of clothes, and Corey stuffed his wallet, phone, and a small flashlight into the pocket of his jacket, grabbed his keys, and they stepped outside.

"Hey, Wes," Corey said, when Wes was just about to step up on to the porch, looking like he wished he wasn't there—his hands stuffed in his pockets, looking toward the ground and certainly not smiling.

"Hi, Wes," Nick said.

Finally, Wes looked up and mumbled something that passed for a greeting.

"Let's get going so we can get this over with," Corey said.

With no reply from Wes, Corey and Nick glanced at one another. "You're still on board, right?" Corey asked Wes.

"Yeah, yeah, sure. It's just that this has got to be the dumbest thing I've ever done, and I'm wondering why I ever agreed to it."

"You always were the voice of reason. Those are my sentiments exactly, but I couldn't tie Katie up, and that's what I'd have had to do to keep her from going out to the cemetery tonight—you know she'd have done it."

No one said anything, and Corey was at a loss as to what to do. He felt guilty as hell for making Wes, and Nick for that matter, a part of this mess.

"Look, if you want to get back in your truck and go home, that's cool. No hard feelings," Corey said.

Wes sighed loudly. "No, I'm here and I'm following through."

"All right then, we'd better get going."

Katie scooted into the back seat of Corey's Kia, sitting next to Wes with no hesitation, even though she'd scowled at Corey from where she'd been waiting by the garage when they'd pulled up. As she settled herself, Corey heard her acknowledge Wes. "I had no idea I'd see *you* tonight."

"Uh, I'm here to help if I'm needed. I hope you don't mind," Wes said.

"I'm sorry Corey felt the need to involve you. I'm sure you had other plans," she said, sounding annoyed.

Wes didn't answer, and Corey felt bad for putting him in this uncomfortable situation.

"Sorry, Nick," Katie said, leaning toward the front seat. "I didn't mean to ignore you. Thanks for coming."

"No problem."

"You're sure you want to go through with this? It might be dangerous," Wes said to Katie in a soft tone of voice.

Katie's reply was anything but soft. "Yes, I'm sure. If you want to back out, feel free to get the hell out of the car!"

Corey waited for Katie to apologize for snapping at Wes, but that wasn't happening.

"No one's getting out of the car," Corey said, taking charge of the situation. Then he glanced over his shoulder in Katie's direction. "I'm glad you wore black."

"Yeah, we all look like we're in the same club," Katie said, sounding calmer.

The fifteen-minute drive to Mountain View Cemetery was quiet except for the sound of the heater running. While driving on the winding two-lane road that was lined with bare oak trees, Corey got more apprehensive by the second and wondered how the others felt, but he didn't ask. He just wanted this night over as soon as possible.

They hadn't seen a single car on the country road, and when they were about a half mile from the cemetery entrance Corey slowed down.

"Where are we parking?" he asked Katie. Even though he'd

asked in a near whisper, she heard him.

"Go on past the main entrance. I'll show you where to park across from the employee entrance."

Corey did as he was told and then followed her directions to turn off the headlights and pull off on to a dirt road that was mostly overgrown with scrub brush. Slowly, he navigated the car on to a path branching off from the dirt road and parked behind a clump of bushes, killing the engine. The four of them wasted no time getting out and following Katie to the main road where she glanced left, then right, making sure she didn't see any cars.

"We'll have a bit of a walk," she said quietly.

"I thought you said if we parked here we'd be across from the employee entrance," Corey whispered.

"It's not right across, but pretty close. Try and hurry, so we're not out in the open for long. There'll be trees to walk behind when we get closer to the entrance."

"Hold up," Corey said. "Let me go first and then Nick, then you, and then Wes can bring up the rear."

All agreeing, they walked briskly in single file, their hoods pulled over their heads. Corey felt like they surely must look like shadow people and would scare the living daylights out of anyone who had the misfortune of crossing their path. With the moon nothing but a sliver, the darkness made it hard to even see where to walk without stumbling on rocks and the uneven shoulder of the road. Having Nick there gave him some comfort because if Nick had been successful in hopping a train he must be pretty good at this sort of thing. Maybe he should have asked him to lead the way.

Corey felt a little calmer once they reached the trees, even though their bare branches offered little concealment. Once at the cemetery gate, a small light on each side helped their ability to see, but he wasn't sure if that was a good or bad thing. The seven-foot chain link gate was padlocked, indicating that either they'd arrived before anyone else, or that Katie was wrong about the meeting place.

"How are we going to get in?" Corey asked, his breath coming out in puffs in the damp, cold night air.

"Climb?" Nick suggested.

"I don't want to climb this thing if we don't even know if we're in the right place," Corey complained.

"I'd bet money this is where they're meeting," Katie said.

"I don't like the idea of trespassing," Wes said. "But whatever we're gonna do, we'd best do it fast, because standing here isn't smart." Wes looked clearly worried and agitated. "Suppose they come driving up? It's almost twelve o'clock."

"Let's go then, who's first?" Nick asked, hooking his gloved hands together to boost someone up.

Corey gave a resigned sigh and stepped into Nick's hands, grabbing onto the chain link fence, struggling the rest of the way up and over.

Wes helped Katie over in the same manner, while Corey helped her down the other side and then Wes assisted Nick, who once on top of the gate, jumped down to the ground in one fluid motion. Despite feeling on edge, Corey couldn't help but notice and appreciate his man's fine form.

After all three were safely standing on the other side, Wes tackled the fence as the others had. Corey noticed Wes had on sneakers and realized he'd only ever seen him wear cowboy boots.

"Where to now?" Corey asked as soon as Wes's feet touched the ground. He looked at Katie for an answer.

Just then a few raindrops hit his face. He'd already surveyed the area and noticed a covered gazebo about fifty yards away and off the walkway, but lamp poles alongside the path, dim as they were, didn't make it a good choice to hide and wait.

"Damn, this is all we need," Wes said, pulling his hood tighter as the rain came down harder.

"Let's get over to the shed where they store the garden tools. We can wait there," Katie said, pointing to a shadowy structure that was about twenty-five yards across from where they stood and then farther up a small hill.

"You mean we won't have to walk among the graves?" Nick asked, his voice sounding as if he was telling a scary story.

"Let's just hope we don't end up in one," Wes said. His statement definitely carried no levity as they set out for the shed.

Corey was surprised when Katie wrapped her arms around one of Wes's like a sort of hug, and she even rested her head there for a moment. Then he heard her thank Wes for being out there with them and apologize for how she'd acted when she got into the car. She sounded sincere, and Corey noticed how Wes smiled and looked over the moon from Katie's attention.

He felt like patting himself on the back for coming up with the idea of asking Wes along. He looked at Nick, who smiled at him and gave him a thumbs-up.

Corey had tried to overlook the sporadic raindrops, but it was hard to ignore the larger drops coming down much steadier now. There was no ignoring the fact that they would soon be soaked if they didn't find shelter.

"We'd better get up to the shed fast," he suggested, and his three companions of the night readily agreed. They all turned and headed up the slope, the rain becoming more intense, the temperature feeling like it had dropped a good ten degrees since they'd left home. After a couple minutes of brisk walking, they reached their hiding place.

"They don't lock the door, so we can go inside," Katie said shivering, as she yanked on the handle. "I hope the rain lets up soon."

The door wouldn't budge, so Wes gave it a jerk. The resounding screech as the door was forced open a few inches on its rusty track had them all cringing.

"Damn, that's enough to raise the dead," Nick said as he looked toward the nearby graves, almost as if he expected to see ghosts rise from them. "This storage shed has definitely seen better days."

"We can't risk messing with a door that sounds like this. We'll just have to suck it up and stay out here. At least the wind isn't blowing too bad," Corey said.

They had hustled behind the structure, huddling for warmth, when headlights and the sound of a car motor startled them. Kneeling on the ground, with their hands shoved in their pockets and their hoods pulled tightly around their faces, they tried to be as small as possible. When Katie began trembling Wes pulled her closer and rubbed his hands over her back and arms.

Corey wished they'd stay still. He was tense and on edge, and he didn't want to take any chances on being seen. He watched as the car stopped at the gate, and Alan, the idiot—the reason they were all there freezing their asses off—got out and unlocked the padlock. He got back into his car and drove through the entrance, parking but not getting out.

The entire situation was making Corey more disgusted by the minute, but when Nick's strong, reassuring arms slipped around him and gave him a little squeeze he felt better. They stayed crouched and huddled for what seemed like an eternity, but in reality, it had only been about ten minutes.

"Hey, the rain's stopping," Nick whispered.

"Thank God," Katie said.

Wes checked his watch. "I wonder where the people are who Alan is supposed to be meeting. It's going on twelve-thirty."

The sound of Alan's car door slamming shut drew Corey's attention. "Well, he's finally showing his face."

They watched silently as Alan walked down the pathway, and when he got nearly as far as the gazebo he stopped and looked back at a car that had slowly come into view. The headlights went dark before passing through the gate.

"The show's about to begin," Nick said.

"Let's try to get a little closer," Wes said.

"One at a time—let's get over to that clump of shrubbery," Corey directed, indicating with a jerk of his head where he meant.

"Shit, it's so dark I can hardly see where to go. Excuse my French," Katie said.

"If you can't see well enough, stay here, because we can't risk using the flashlight," Corey said.

"I'll help her," Wes said.

"Just be careful—stay down," Corey said as he stooped down and crept carefully to the shrubs, keeping Alan in view as best as he could. Alan stood still, fixated on the car, which was slowly creeping to where he was standing.

Nick had joined him, sliding an arm around Corey's back as he came to a stop at his side. Just as the car door opened, and the headlights came on illuminating Alan; Wes and Katie rounded out the group. The four of them stayed as silent as the graves, eyes fixed on the scene down the hill.

The driver left the car, joined by another man from the passenger side, and the two of them created a menacing sight. Even though Alan was no lightweight, the two men towered over him and outweighed him by at least twenty-five pounds each, and there they stood not more than three feet from Katie's fiancé.

Alan stood, looking anything but intimidated with his chin held high, his chest puffed out, and his shoulders back. Hearing much of their conversation wasn't possible from the distance they were at—just a word here and there—so tone of voice and body language became the best clues for Corey to understand what was being said. It wasn't looking good.

After an exchange of words, Alan seemed to become less confident, rocking back and forth on his heels, his hands balled into fists. One of the men stepped forward, jabbing his finger on

Alan's chest, barking out orders. The only words Corey caught were, *money* and *now*. He couldn't see the other man's hands, but he had a feeling that they were ready to do some kind of harm. Whatever Alan had said must not have set well, because the other man got right up into Alan's face and grabbed hold of his neck, lifting him up on to his toes.

Corey could tell Katie was about to lose control by the amount of effort Wes was exerting to hold her still. He reached over and patted her shoulder as a tear ran down her face. He hoped like hell that Wes could hold her back and keep her quiet should she decide to try to intervene in some way. Nick looked worried too, probably thinking the same thing.

Corey shifted his attention back to the scene down the hill, watching as Alan reached into his pocket and brought out an envelope, holding it out to the man closest to him. The guy seemed reluctant to take what was offered, but he finally did and glanced at the contents. He handed it to the man who'd jabbed Alan in the chest. He looked into the envelope at what Corey assumed was cash. Whatever was inside, and whatever the amount, it obviously wasn't enough, because the guy holding the envelope slammed Alan in the face with his free hand so hard that Alan hit the ground.

"Oh, no," Katie murmured weakly while more tears fell. Wes gripped her tighter.

Alan tried to stand up, but before he could, the second man kicked him.

"Crap," Corey muttered.

"What should we do?" Nick asked, all the while both men bent over Alan punching and kicking, as Alan squirmed and twisted on the rain-soaked pavement.

Before Corey could answer, both men backed away, shouting obscenities and threats, as Alan lay there moaning. Corey heard one of the men yell something about 'Alan's grave needing tending to if he ever pulled that shit again.'

At least they didn't kill him while we just hunkered down here watching.

The men got into their car, and for a moment Corey held his breath hoping they weren't going to run over Alan. With a screeching of tires, they backed up and turned around, barely missing Alan, and then they sped through the cemetery gates.

"See," Katie sobbed, looking straight at Corey. "Alan didn't steal. All he had was the ring money." She buried her head in Wes's jacket and wept.

All Corey could think just then was that Alan was up to his eyeballs in trouble. Stealing or not, he had some serious issues he had to deal with.

Nick stood, and Corey did as well, while Wes helped Katie to her feet, handing her a red paisley kerchief that she wiped her tears with.

Corey took a couple steps away from the bushes, Nick following him. "We've got to go see what we can do for him. Katie, you have the first aid supplies in your coat pocket, don't you?" he asked in a loud whisper.

"Yes," Katie answered, still fighting tears.

"He'll probably need a ride to the hospital," Nick said.

Wes and Katie came up behind, Katie still sniffling, but getting herself under control. "He didn't deserve that. I feel so bad for him."

Before they took another step, out of the darkness near the gazebo two guys appeared and sprinted to where Alan lay.

"Where the heck did they come from?" Wes exclaimed while they all ducked down and huddled behind the shrubs again.

"My guess is they must have climbed the fence on the west side," Corey answered.

Katie peeked through a sparse area in the bushes. "That's Ted Faulkner, but I don't recognize the other one."

"Well, it looks like Alan has all the help he needs," Corey said, relieved they wouldn't have to get involved. "Let's see if we can get the heck out of here without drawing any attention."

"Well, hurry up, and if we're lucky, we'll get out the gate while they're still busy with Alan," Wes directed.

The walk out was faster than the walk in since the gate was open, and they set a quicker pace. No one said much on their fast trek back to the car other than an occasional 'watch your step and be careful'. Once safely inside the car, Corey had a difficult time getting the key into the ignition, because his hands were shaking so badly. The more he tried to hurry, the more his hand shook.

"What are you waiting for, let's get out of here," Wes said impatiently.

Corey finally got the key in the ignition and started it right away, giving the car the gas and getting them on to the main road in no time flat. All of a sudden Katie began crying uncontrollably. Corey glanced at Nick who looked into the back seat. "She'll be okay—Wes has her. Just drive," he said.

During the trip back to town, Corey thought about what Katie had said concerning the money, and maybe she was right about Alan not being the one responsible for the crimes.

But if not him, then who?

Rhonda's words came back to him. He wondered if she'd repeat what she'd said to him about Ted if the cops questioned her. Ted hadn't been wearing a watch cap tonight—maybe he'd seen the composite sketch on the bulletin board and thought better of it. Corey felt less shaky the farther they got from the cemetery, especially when Nick reached over and rubbed his shoulder. Katie's sobs and Nick's somber face made him feel helpless, even after Katie had calmed down and stopped crying. He also felt bad about leaving Alan in the shape he looked to be in, and he hoped Ted and the other loser that was with him knew what to do for the moron.

A light rain had resumed by the time they reached Corey's place. "You two want to come in for some coffee?" Corey asked as he put the car in park and shut off the engine.

"It's late, I'll just grab my truck and get Katie on home," Wes said. "You ready to go?" he asked her.

"Yeah, let's head out, I'm exhausted," she answered, her voice thick with tears. "I don't think I can take anymore tonight."

Once outside the car, the group hurried with hugs and handshakes before they got any wetter than they already were. From the porch, Corey and Nick watched Wes and Katie drive away into the night.

Inside the house, Corey took off his jacket and hoodie and Nick did the same.

"I don't know if I'll ever be warm again," Corey said, taking their wet jackets to the kitchen and hanging them over two chairs. "We'd better get out of our wet jeans," he said as he returned to the living room. He kicked his shoes off and began pulling his jeans off.

"You come right to the point, don't you," Nick teased.

With one leg part way out of his pants, Corey stopped so suddenly he nearly fell over. Nick saw the telltale pink in his cheeks, and he couldn't help but crack up and that set Corey off too.

Corey fell back onto the couch and pulled his jeans the rest of the way off. Nick, still chuckling, went into the bedroom and came back wearing sweatpants and handed Corey a pair.

"Thanks," Corey said, back to being serious.

Nick sat down on the couch, and for a few moments neither of them spoke. He reached for Corey's hand. "Are you okay?"

Corey squeezed Nick's hand and closed his eyes. "I think so."

"You look ready to pass out. You should head to bed."

"How about you? You must be tired too."

"Tonight wasn't as stressful for me, Katie being your cousin and all."

"I couldn't have done that without you," Corey whispered, laying his head on Nick's shoulder.

"You want me to make us some tea or coffee?" Nick asked, kissing the top of Corey's head.

Corey sat up and stretched. "No, I think I'll just go to bed, get under the warm covers, and thank my lucky stars it all turned out okay tonight."

"Sounds like a good idea. You go on ahead and I'll make sure the lights are out and the doors are locked."

Corey gave Nick a quick kiss and headed to the bedroom.

Nick watched Corey disappear down the hall and decided to make himself some tea to help him thaw out after losing Corey's warmth. He wouldn't have minded slipping under the sheets naked to warm up next to him, but he could tell his man needed time to unwind after their nerve-wracking evening.

Sitting at the kitchen table sipping his hot tea worked wonders to take the chill off. He tapped the little tag on the end of the tea bag with his finger. Chamomile. His mother used to drink tea, and he'd sometimes sit with her and drink a cup. She said Chamomile tea was good to have before bed. One time she'd snuck in a cup of green tea on him and he'd nearly spit it out it tasted so awful. She'd laughed. He wished he could keep thoughts like that out of his mind, because his new life was here with Corey, and he wasn't going to see her or anyone else in his family again. The choice was made, and he knew deep in his heart that he was better off now than he'd ever been back home. He finished his tea and put the cup into the dishwasher, heading to the bedroom to join his man.

CHAPTER NINETEEN

FOR THE second morning in a row, Corey sat on the edge of the bed holding the phone to his ear.

"Thanks for handling this, Rhonda," he said, ending the conversation. He turned the phone off and replaced the handset back in the base and turned to look at Nick, who hadn't made any attempt to rise.

Corey leaned over to give him a loud smack on the lips.

"What was that for?" Nick asked languidly.

"Nothing in particular—just everything—for being here." Corey's smile lasted only a brief moment and then he got serious. "Not to mention last night."

Nick stretched like a cat and then let out a big yawn. "Yeah, last night. No wonder we overslept."

"We overslept because of the fantastic sex we had when we woke up the first time," Corey said, his smile returning. He sure could get lost in the shit-eating grin he'd put on Nick's face, but unfortunately there wasn't any time to lounge around.

"We'd better hurry. Rhonda's there alone, and I have no idea when Katie will get in. And..."

"And, what?" Nick asked, sitting up.

"Rhonda said Detective Munson called a few minutes ago. He's going to stop by soon and wants to talk to me and anyone else who's around, including you."

"Me?"

"Rhonda said he asked if there was a way to contact you."

"Damn. I can't tell him anything. I didn't see a thing."

"I'm sure it's just routine. Rhonda said he wants to talk to her too. It's all informal, just there at the gym, so nothing to get worked up about. Maybe he just wants to make his presence known—you know, sort of like having the sketch up on the bulletin board to make the suspect nervous."

"Yeah, but who knows if the crook will even be around to see what's going on," Nick said, getting out of bed and picking up his clothes from the floor. "And, I wonder what the cops would say if they knew what the four of us did last night?"

Corey hung his head and rubbed his temples. "No one will find out. None of us is going to say anything about that, and you can bet Alan won't be advertising what happened either. Anyway, no one saw us."

"I didn't mean to upset you," Nick said, sitting down on the bed.

"It's okay, I'm not upset—not really, definitely not at you. I mean, we didn't do anything wrong—I guess. I'll bet you never had excitement like this back where you came from." He got up and stretched.

Nick chuckled. "Can't say as I did—well, up until I took the train outta there, and since then, my life has gotten a little crazy. Crazy in a good way though." Nick grinned widely up at him.

Corey noticed Nick looking around on the floor by the bed. "If you're missing your socks, I think I felt them under the sheet."

Nick reached under and came up with the pair. "Bet it'll be awhile before Alan lifts any weights at the gym."

"I really hope that what Katie saw last night was the final nail in the coffin for her relationship with Alan." Corey noticed the amused look on Nick's face and then realized why, and he snickered and shook his head. "No pun intended."

They shared a good laugh over that, and Corey threw a pillow at Nick.

Nick then retaliated, and a pillow fight ensued, ending with them both on the bed, Corey on top, breathing heavily, while Nick squirmed helplessly underneath him.

Corey really wished they had another hour because he could think of an awesome way to spend it. Those beautiful eyes of Nick's were spellbinding. He ran the back of his hand over Nick's cheek and then over his lips.

"I wish it could be like this every day," Corey whispered.

Nick didn't say anything, just stared up at him. The adoring look Corey saw made him feel on top of the world, but also confused, because what was stopping them from living together? Nick's comfort level apparently had shifted to where he wasn't scared for people to know his real last name, and he wasn't as uptight that someone from his past would cause some kind of trouble. Did he dare ask Nick again to move in?

"I hope you know you have an open invitation to move in here with me," Corey murmured. He kissed Nick softly. "Any time you want."

He didn't wait for an answer and promptly rolled off Nick and gathered up his clothes. He didn't want to belabor the subject, but he stopped before leaving the bedroom.

"I've been wanting to mention that I need some painting and other repairs done around here. I was hoping to make time this winter, and the work would go faster with two, especially with you being such a whizz at painting."

Corey tried to gauge Nick's reaction, he was so quiet and still, his face hidden in the dim light, that it was impossible to do so.

"Well, you think about it. Even if you don't want to move in, I know you'd do a great job. I'd pay you of course."

He left the room then, feeling good about putting the invitation out there again and, even better, that he hadn't gotten the same reaction as the first time he'd asked.

Nick sat up on the edge of the bed looking toward the half-open bedroom door. Corey was something else—so unwavering—so unafraid to ask for what he wants.

He got up and moved to the closet where he'd hung his clean shirt and jeans and took them off the hangers. Tossing them onto the bed as he walked over to the window, he looked out into the backyard, thinking that anyone would love living here. Corey's offer was hard to refuse, and he didn't want to turn him down, but he didn't want to be a dead weight either. Taking care of himself and making his own way was what he was used to doing. He'd done just that from an early age, and looking after Melissa, making sure she had a nice home, had been the only satisfying part of his marriage. Since leaving her, he hadn't done a very good job of providing for himself—living in that dump of a motel.

Corey had mentioned fixing the house up, and he could definitely help with that. He was sure Corey wasn't just inventing work for the sake of offering him something to do to pull his weight. The place, though nice, did need some sprucing up. A coat of paint, for one. He could see himself working on the walls and teasing Corey about the funny names of the paint colors.

The thought of moving in with Corey excited him and terrified him, but he loved him so much. Was this the right thing to do—the right time? If not now, then when?

He moved away from the window and picked up his clothes. After the meeting with the detective was over, he'd think about it some more.

CHAPTER TWENTY

ONCE THEY got to the gym and walked inside, Detective Munson was waiting in the foyer. The tree with its twinkling lights, candy canes, and elf ornaments, and the stern-faced detective didn't go together at all. He'd be so glad when the detective finished his interviews and left.

"This is Detective Munson, the gentleman I told you about," Corey said as he looked from the Christmas tree to Nick.

"Good to meet you," the detective said to Nick. "I understand you painted here the night of the incident at the ATM?"

"Yes, Sir, I was here."

"Is there somewhere I can talk privately with Mr. Sanders?" Detective Munson asked in that businesslike tone of his, directing his attention to Corey.

"Let me see if there's anyone downstairs." Corey hurried over to the stairs and looked down to the lower level.

Nick and the detective had followed, and when Corey turned around he said, "It's all clear. Go ahead on down. You'll see some chairs and a table in the back corner."

Once they were out of sight Corey took a few steps away, hating that Nick had to go through the questioning, but he didn't foresee any problems since Nick had said he hadn't noticed anything unusual that night. The questioning would probably be brief and that would be that.

"What do you need me to do, Rhonda?" Corey asked when he entered the office.

"I have everything under control right now."

"Good, that's what I like to hear." He plopped down in a chair. "Has Katie called?"

"No. Is she coming in today? Is she okay?"

"Yeah, she should be, and she's okay as far as I know."

Corey wondered if Katie had tried to check up on Alan. He guessed he was afraid to find out, so that's why he hadn't called her.

"I think Detective Munson wants to talk to her too."

"Did he say that?"

"No, but I think he wants to talk to all of us."

"Did he question you?"

"Yes, and he chatted with a couple members too. There wasn't much I could tell him."

"Uh, did you mention that the sketch made you think of Ted, because of the watch cap?"

"Yeah, I did say that. It was silly, I know, but I didn't really have anything else to share."

"What did he say?"

"He said that nothing was too small or insignificant, and that he was glad I said what was on my mind."

Corey saw Rhonda look beyond him out toward the front window, so he turned and saw Uncle Ed and Rita wearing workout clothes walking toward the Members' door.

"Well, Uncle Ed really means business. I'd better go help them get started."

Corey glanced toward the stairs on his way to greet Ed and Rita, but he didn't see any sign of Nick or Detective Munson yet.

"Good morning," Corey said, smiling at his uncle and Rita. They'd come at just the right time, he needed a distraction.

Rita looked as friendly and bubbly as ever, and judging from Uncle Ed's face, he felt in high spirits as well.

"So, you two are here to work out I see."

"We sure are," Rita said.

"Well, I'm here, but I'm not sure about using all this equipment," Ed said.

"Don't worry, you don't have to use it all. In fact, it's best to start slow. How do you feel about trying the exercise bikes?"

"That sounds good to me. How 'bout you, Ed?" Rita asked.

"I'll give it a try."

On the way to the row of bikes, Ed patted Corey on the back, and as if he had a secret to share, leaned in and just above a whisper said, "Wes's truck was parked at the house early this morning and it's still there. Guess he's in the apartment with Katie."

Corey raised his eyebrows and smiled, hoping that meant what he and his uncle wanted it to. "Well—I wonder what's going on." That was all he felt comfortable saying. What Ed didn't know wouldn't hurt him.

"I hope it means she gave the bozo the boot. I don't think it can mean anything else."

"I hope you're right," Corey said, putting an arm around Ed.

By then they'd caught up with Rita sitting on one of the bikes looking ready to get started.

"Look, Ed, we can watch TV while we exercise," she said, indicating the little TV attached to the bike.

Corey showed them how the bikes worked and the TV's too, and when they got underway he excused himself and walked over to the stairs, hoping Nick and Detective Munson would soon be up.

He caught himself pacing, so he made a concerted effort to calm down, breathing deeply as he walked to the vending machine to get two bottles of Gatorade. When the second bottle rolled out, he felt a hand on his back.

"Is that for me?" Nick asked in a smooth, warm voice.

"You're done? How'd it go?"

"I need a stiff drink." Nick took one of the bottles Corey held and twisted the top off.

"That bad, huh?" Corey asked, worried, as he watched Detective Munson leave out the front door.

"No, not really. It was okay, but... uh, I need to talk to you." Nick took a long drink. "In private," he added after swallowing.

"My uncle and Rita are here, and I need to show them some of the machines after they've had enough pedaling. Can it wait?"

"Guess it'll have to—yeah, it can wait, but I've gotta go work on that birthday job and I'd like to talk before I go."

"Did the detective give you a hard time about anything?"

"No, nothing like that, but it has to do with my talk with him— indirectly."

"Well, I don't think they're going to last too long on their first day." Corey nodded toward them. "I don't think I'll be tied up very long."

"Okay, I'll wait in the foyer."

When Corey walked back to the exercise bikes, Ed looked eager for an excuse to stop, but it seemed like Rita would have ridden longer if it wasn't for Ed wanting to move on and see the other equipment. Corey showed them several machines that he felt would be manageable for their fitness level, demonstrated each one and then watched both of them duplicate his moves as best they could. By the time they'd used three machines, Ed wiped his brow.

"I think we should leave now and pick up where we left off on our next visit. Is that okay with you, Rita?"

"Sure, that sounds like a good idea. We shouldn't overdo it on the first day."

Corey walked them to the foyer, and Ed stopped before going to the door. "I saw a man dressed in a suit leaving. Was he one of the investigators?"

Corey wished Ed wasn't so observant because he didn't want him worrying, but he answered honestly. "He was here talking with some of the staff and members, you know, just all part of the investigation."

"I hope they get it all sorted out soon," Ed said.

After that, Ed noticed Nick sitting in the corner by the tree and had a few words with him, with Rita joining in. Corey thought they'd never leave, and when they finally did, he looked at the clock, hoping there'd still be time to talk before Nick had to go to work.

"Do you want to go for a walk?" Corey asked.

"Sure."

After they'd stepped outside, Nick raised his face to the sky. "The sun feels good."

"Sure does, especially after standing in the rain last night."

"Have you heard from Katie?"

"No, but Uncle Ed said that Wes's truck was parked at the apartment this morning. I'll bet he was there all night."

"No kidding—I wonder what that means?"

"Uncle Ed thinks it means they're back together and that she's finished with Alan. Of course, he doesn't know anything about what happened last night, so who knows. Wes may have just stayed to calm her down."

When they got as far as the sidewalk on Main Street, a bright red Camaro passed by at such a high rate of speed they stopped in their tracks and watched it disappear into a side street.

"You know who that was, don't you?" Corey asked.

"No, who?"

"Ted."

"It was? Well, I guess that means he's not playing nursemaid to Alan. Or maybe he's on his way there now."

"Yeah, that's either good or bad. Alan could be in the hospital for all we know."

"Well, I hope not. I guess Katie will know unless Wes made her forget all about Alan." Nick snickered.

Corey came to a stop and looked at Nick, wishing he could read his mind. "You must have things you wanted to talk about other than my cousin's love life."

"Yeah." Nick jammed his hands in his pockets and stared down at his feet.

"What is it?" Corey asked, becoming concerned about what Nick was going to say.

"I won't beat around the bush." Nick kicked at a pebble and seemed fascinated by the crack in the sidewalk. "When the detective asked me my address I gave him yours." He looked into Corey's eyes. "Well, you did say..."

Corey knew he was grinning like a fool, but he didn't care—he was so damned happy. He wanted to grab Nick right then and there, give him a bear hug, and twirl them in a circle, but he controlled himself given where they were.

"So, you don't mind?" Nick asked, a hint of apprehension in his tone.

"It's what I've wanted for a while now."

"Yeah, well, I have too, even though I haven't acted like it." Nick's face took on a sober look. "I guess that day when I blew up at you and said the things I did about you not wanting your uncle to know where I lived—well, it was because I was the one who felt bad about where I was staying. You deserve a better man than me."

"You're the best man for me," Corey said, reaching for Nick's arm and giving it a brief squeeze. He felt a little guilty for ever allowing himself to worry about what his uncle, or anyone else, would think.

"Well, you said something about painting, and I thought if I could do that for my part of the mortgage payments and utility bills... and hopefully get other jobs after that, and I'll be able to pay—"

"Slow down, slow down," Corey said. "It all sounds great, and I'm excited and happy about this coming together."

"I hear a 'but' coming," Nick said, taking a deep breath.

"I just wondered why you didn't agree to my idea this morning. Why it took Detective Munson asking for your address for you to—"

"Yeah," Nick interrupted. "I won't lie to you—I got scared."

Corey noticed how the sun shining down on the strands of Nick's blond hair created a glow as if he were an angel with a halo, the breeze ruffling Nick's waves, making him look so young and vulnerable.

"Scared?"

"Nervous and scared—wondering what he'd think if I said I lived in that dump. He'd think I was some lowlife—someone untrustworthy—and maybe he'd start looking into my past. I just didn't want there to be any reason for him to start checking up on me."

"Okay, I get it and it's all right. I understand."

"I hope you do, 'cause I love you, and I do want to be with you."

The sincerity in Nick's eyes erased any doubts Corey may have had.

"I love you too, and I can't wait to move you in. Can we do it this evening after work?"

"I was hoping you'd say that."

Corey was so elated that he jogged the half block back to the gym after he and Nick went their separate ways. He couldn't wait to load up Nick's stuff and bring it to his house that evening. Seeing Wes's truck parked at the front door, though, forced him to put his personal business on the back burner and focus on Katie. He had to find out where her head was.

Inside, he found Wes leaning against the wall in the foyer holding a cup of coffee.

"Hey, Wes, is everything all right?" Wes's smile reminded Corey of the phrase, 'the cat that ate the canary.' "Are you feeling okay after our little outing last night?" Corey asked in a low voice.

Wes took a drink of coffee. "Oh, yeah, I'll live. How 'bout you and Nick?"

"Doing fine. It's all just a distant memory."

They shared a suppressed laugh and a knowing look.

"How's my cousin doing?" Corey asked.

Before Wes could answer, Katie popped out of the office looking none the worse for wear. In fact, she looked pretty darned good. Her hair looked beautiful, her makeup perfect, and the purple long-sleeved T-shirt and black yoga pants fit her like a glove. No one would ever guess what she'd been through the night before.

"I'm doing great, and sorry I'm late."

"You'll be even sorrier when you hear that your dad and Rita came in to exercise this morning and you missed it."

Katie giggled, and Wes looked amused. "Rhonda told me. I *am* sorry I missed them." Then she looked more serious and lowered her voice. "She also said the detective was here interviewing a few people."

"Yeah, he was, but he didn't stay long," Corey said, trying to downplay it.

"As long as he wasn't here to arrest us," Wes whispered in mock alarm. Katie punched him on the arm.

"Well, I'm gonna have to get on my way. Thanks for the coffee," Wes said, handing Katie the cup. "I'll see you later." He winked and pecked her on the cheek, and then stepped toward the door, but then stopped. He turned to look at Katie and then Corey. "Call me when something needs fixin'."

"Will do," Corey said.

When Wes was gone, Corey looked at Katie, hoping she wasn't going to make him drag the information out of her. She looked much like Wes had, as if concealing something private.

She said in a soft voice, "I hope Dad wasn't gossiping about me when he was in here."

"Your dad gossiping? I hardly think so."

"He didn't say anything at all about me?"

"I didn't say that—I just said he wasn't gossiping." Corey smiled, knowing full well that he was talking out of both sides of his mouth.

"Tell me what he said," Katie said firmly.

"Uh, he just noticed Wes's truck at your apartment and he was happy about it, that's all."

"That's all?"

"Oh, you know, he has it all worked out in his mind that you've broken up with Alan and are back with Wes. That's what he hopes happened, but of course he has no idea about last night and why Wes took you home and how upset you were, so I guess Wes probably stayed so you wouldn't be alone."

"You're babbling, Cuz—is that what you think happened?"

"Uh, I don't know, but I did notice the looks you and Wes were giving each other, and I saw him wink at you."

Katie smiled sweetly and shook her head, looking wistful all of a sudden. "It's kind of complicated."

"Maybe we can go somewhere more private, so we can talk," Corey said.

"But Rhonda is all alone."

"It's slow, she can handle it—come on, we'll go sit in my car."

Corey paused just long enough at the office door to tell Rhonda that they'd be back in a few minutes and they went outside to his car.

"Where's Nick?" Katie asked as she opened the passenger door.

"He's doing some artwork thing today," Corey said, settling into his seat.

"I assume he stayed with you last night after the adventure," she said, emphasizing the last word.

"Yeah, he did. And, uh, I may as well get it out there—I asked him to move in with me and he said yes." He chanced a look at Katie, not sure what reaction he'd see.

She gave him a contemplative gaze and didn't speak for a moment, but then she smiled faintly. "Well, I hope it works out for both of you—I really mean that."

"Thanks."

"Did you tell Dad?"

"No, not yet. Nick hadn't said yes until after I'd seen your dad, not that I would have told him then anyway."

"Dad'll be happy for you, don't worry. Nick's a good guy. The more time I spend with him, I can see that. Last night, coming with us to the cemetery, putting himself in that situation, shows me that you and the people you care about are important to him."

"You don't know how much that means to me," Corey said earnestly.

"You're a good judge of people, Cuz. I need to take lessons from you."

Corey covered her hand with his and asked softly, "Tell me what you're thinking about."

She blinked back tears. "I just feel so bad that I have to give up on me and Alan—I mean, I know in my head that I can't continue on with him, but it's just so disappointing and sad to give up on the dreams I had for us." A tear rolled down her cheek and she sniffed. "We were engaged."

"I'm sorry." Corey handed her a tissue he pulled out of a pocket pack in the center console.

"You're not sorry that Alan won't be a member of the family," she said, struggling to speak.

"You're right, I never did think he was the man for you—but you did, and I'm sorry you're hurt and upset by the whole situation."

"Well, I'm moving on, and the main reason isn't what you think." She blew her nose.

"What do I think?"

"You probably think that spending time with Wes made me fall for him again."

"Well?"

"I admit that I saw a different side of Wes last night. And I also admit that I've always found him attractive—who wouldn't. He has the most amazing hazel eyes I've ever seen, and he's just so damned sweet." She smiled and tried to wipe the smears under her eyes. "But that's not the point. He stepped out of his comfort zone to help me try to help Alan. Not many ex-boyfriends would do that."

"You're right."

"I haven't said thanks for getting him to come with us."

"You're welcome—now you were saying."

"Yeah, the reason I'm breaking it off with Alan..." Katie turned to Corey. "I called him this morning to find out how he was—to ask what happened last night, you know, with the ring and all that."

"Is he okay?"

"Who knows, he's such a liar, so really, who knows. He sounded okay—well, at least he could talk, but he didn't tell me the truth. He didn't say he was short on money or that he got beat up."

"It's obviously something he's not proud of," Corey said, surprising himself by coming to Alan's defense, even just a little.

"But relationships, at least any that I plan to have, will be based on trust and honesty. I already knew the score about his gambling debt, so why couldn't he tell me the truth about what happened last night? When he lied on top of everything else, that killed it for me."

She looked very sure of her decision, despite her tears, and Corey saw a strength in her he admired tremendously. Finally, she'd come to her senses where Alan was concerned, and not only that, Wes was back in the picture.

Could it be that he, and Katie, not to mention Uncle Ed, had all found love?

Maybe Nick's optimistic and lighthearted mood was helping to produce such excellent results on the birthday banner in front of him. He was pleased with the tints and shades he'd chosen for the butterfly design, and the brush lettering added just the right touch. He'd even gotten brave and done something he hadn't tried in ages—calligraphy—but today he'd felt emboldened, and the results made him glad he'd ventured into it again.

There were three banners and a couple of signs to do, and as well as the first banner was going, he'd get the majority done today. As he worked he was in happy place, despite turning his back on his past. He wasn't sure what had him in such a fantastic mood—a job he really loved, or his plans after he was done—to move in with Corey.

There were no lingering doubts from that morning—this was the right thing to do and the right time, and he couldn't wait to move his few possessions into Corey's house and begin a committed relationship with him. He just hoped that he'd be able to get more jobs because he needed to bring in money and pull his fair share of the weight.

Maybe word would get out now that he'd done a few jobs around town. Possibly some of the parents would notice the banners when they dropped their kids off at this party and ask who'd done them. Back home he'd gotten jobs when people had seen how well his banners at Melissa's granddad's retirement party had turned out.

Creating works of art—his all-time passion—and having a little money to buy more art supplies felt good. Ending up in this town had been a stroke of luck he hadn't ever counted on, and he wondered if he'd have been able to get back on his feet so fast if he'd ended up someplace else. He didn't even want to think about that because he'd found Corey here, who was everything to him now, and tonight he'd be moving into his house to start their future together.

He could hardly wait.

CHAPTER TWENTY-ONE

RELAXING ON the couch with his feet up on the footstool, Corey closed his eyes to reflect on the previous week. Each day had gone by in a whirl of activity, with getting Nick moved in and them setting up their household. Nick hadn't had much to bring with him, but Corey found out just how much *he* had, and making space in the closet, drawers, and bathroom turned into a bigger job than he'd imagined. While making space for Nick's things, Corey had decided to donate some of his old clothes to the mission, and in doing so he'd tried on just about every item of clothing he owned in order to separate them into stacks. Anything they couldn't use went out. Nick had made the chore fun on the day he'd helped. Corey had put on an old sweater that was a hand-me-down from Uncle Ed, and Nick had laughed so hard his eyes watered. He'd called Corey "grandpa," which made Corey break into fits of laughter as well. The most memorable part of Nick helping was when Corey had tried on old sleep pants. Nick got ideas, which had caused an intermission in the fashion show.

Sharing his home with another person took some getting used to, even though that other person was the man he loved. He had been living in his own space for a lot of years and having Nick there permanently now made him realize how set in his ways he'd become—he figured it would take a while to fall into a mutual routine. Nick had been married, in fact, was still—something they definitely needed to talk more about—so Nick seemed to easily settle in and go with the daily flow.

Corey hadn't really expected an adjustment period, after all, he'd been lonely and wanted someone to share his life with for a long time now. Even so, they were two individuals with different personalities each having their own way of doing things. But he had no doubt that he was strong enough to bend, and that he would learn to compromise and make this work.

The old saying 'you don't know a person until you live with them' proved to be true because Corey was learning so much about Nick in their first week together.

Like the way Nick pummeled his pillow before making the bed. The first time he'd heard and seen Nick do this, he had asked if Nick were trying to kill the poor pillow. Nick had looked at him as if he thought everyone beat on their pillows that way. And when Nick would bring in the day's mail from the mailbox—instead of putting it all in one pile, he'd make a stack for each category—bills, catalogs, ads, and junk mail. He especially loved when Nick ate grapes, tossing them up, one at a time, and catching them in his mouth. These were just mundane things, but fascinating just the same, and Corey drank in every little habit and quirk that came to light.

The aroma of homemade soup reached his nose, causing him to come back to the present, realizing that dinnertime was near. Nick had cooked a couple other times for them in the past week, and each time Corey had been pleasantly surprised. Nick's cooking far surpassed his, that was for sure.

"Hey," Nick said, coming into the living room. "Food's ready."

It was then that Corey noticed the layers Nick had on. He'd guess three—his undershirt, a turtleneck, and a sweatshirt, and he knew what he'd see glancing down—bare feet. Barefoot Nick, even when the rest of him indicated how cold he was. The first time he'd seen Nick walking around the house that way he'd asked about it, but Nick didn't really have much of an answer—it was just how it was. Corey had smiled and shaken his head.

Once in the kitchen, they each took a soup bowl to the stove and ladled the corn and bacon chowder into their bowls.

"This looks awesome and smells delicious," Corey said.

"Thanks, I think you'll like it. It's one of my favorites. My mom..." Nick paused, a quick look of pain passing over his face. "Used to make it all the time."

Corey smiled, pleased that Nick felt like he could share that with him. "You'll have to give me cooking lessons one of these days, show me more of your family recipes," Corey said as he sat down at the table.

Nick nodded. "Maybe I will. And just so you know, I like the things you cook."

"Well, you can't really call what I throw together cooking," Corey said, breaking crackers over his steaming bowl.

"Sure, I can. Here have one of these." Nick passed Corey a plate of hot muffins. "These are from a box, but I still consider mixing them up and throwing them into the oven cooking."

"Baking," Corey corrected.

Nick gave him a funny look and watched him take a bite. "How are they?"

"Very good—excellent in fact. I guess you're right, food doesn't have to be made from scratch to taste good." He blew on his spoonful of soup before tasting it. "This is to die for."

"Do you think we can start putting up decorations this weekend?" Nick asked after swallowing a spoonful of soup.

"Yeah, we'd better get that done before the rains come again. Katie already has Uncle Ed's place finished."

"The outside looked real nice when we drove by. I'm looking forward to seeing the inside," Nick said, putting a chunk of muffin in his mouth.

"Wes helped her, and if the tone of her voice was any indication, they had a lot of fun doing it."

Nick grinned and waggled his eyebrows at him.

Corey snorted. "I'm sure I don't want to know any more than that. We can go over anytime, if you want. Uncle Ed said we're always welcome, remember?"

"Yeah, you lucked out when they passed out uncles."

"He's your uncle now too—he said for you to call him Uncle Ed."

"I know—even after he found out I was, uh, kinda down on my luck when I first came to town and I stayed at the mission for a while."

"He knows what a good job they do there, getting folks back on their feet. Knowing that about you didn't make any difference to him."

"The fact he dates the program director probably didn't hurt when he formed his opinion."

Corey didn't know what to say to that. Maybe Rita did have something to do with how Ed had received that bit of information. She'd always seemed to have a soft spot for Nick. Whatever the reason, Corey was glad Ed hadn't seemed troubled by the knowledge that Nick had been homeless, and after getting to know Nick anyone could see he wasn't the type to try to take advantage of anyone.

Nick smiled and pulled off his sweatshirt. "The soup is making me too hot."

"You're hot all right," Corey said, waggling an eyebrow. "I guess we should have started decorating by now, but it's hard to take time away from the gym, and now that you've got that job painting scenery for the church youth group's Christmas play, you're on the go too."

"Yeah, and now that I've started working out, that takes time too—but Christmas isn't going to wait for us to catch up. It's coming in two weeks whether we're ready or not."

"You're right."

"And don't worry, I haven't forgotten about the painting you need done here. After New Year's that'll be my priority."

"It'll be both our priorities."

"At least things have been calm around the gym lately," Nick said, buttering another muffin.

"Yeah, but I wonder what's happening with the investigation. We haven't seen the detective since the day after he talked to you when he came back to question me, Katie and Patty." Corey soaked up the last of his soup with a half of a muffin.

"But at least nothing else around there has been broken into and no one's been robbed. I've seen some reports in the sheriff's log in the newspaper about break-ins in other parts of town though, and I can't help but wonder."

"You'd think if it was the same person, he'd have been caught by now," Corey said.

"I guess he's good at covering his tracks."

"Or lucky." They both stayed quiet for a few moments.

"How 'bout some gin rummy over dessert?" Nick suggested.

"You made dessert too?" Corey asked, surprised.

"Uh, I bought some cookies at a bake sale outside the grocery store," Nick said, grinning. "Hope you like Snicker Doodles."

"I know I like you," Corey said, leaning across the table to plant a big kiss on Nick's lips.

~~*

The next evening, after Corey and Nick had gotten the outdoor Christmas lights up, Uncle Ed stopped by while they were still out in the yard.

"You boys have done a wonderful job," Ed said, walking up the driveway and looking at the twinkling lights on the eves of the house.

"We got it done with just twelve strings," Corey said. "It won't be as bright as yours since you've got multicolored bulbs and we've just got blue and green twinkle lights."

"Wes said it took eighteen strings for my place," Ed said.

"See, we had it easy," Nick joked, bumping Corey with his shoulder.

"You never run out of energy, do you," Corey commented dryly.

"It must be the workouts at the gym. What do you think, Uncle Ed? Don't you find you've got more energy now that you're working out?" Nick asked, humor in his voice.

"I'm not sure about me, but I know Rita seems to."

"Hey, I work out too," Corey said, pretending to pout. "And anyway, I did most of the work."

Nick barked out a laugh. "We'll tackle the inside of the house tomorrow. You can do most of the work in there too."

"I guess I asked for that," Corey said.

"Keep him in line—he needs it," Ed said chuckling. "By the way, the holiday painting on the gym window looks real good. No doubt our artist here did it?" Ed said, patting Nick's back.

"Yeah, thanks, glad you like it." Nick smiled broadly.

"Well, you boys have fun," Ed said. "I was just on my way home and saw you out here, so thought I'd stop."

"Glad you did. Why don't you come in for some eggnog and Snicker Doodles, stick around for a while?"

"I'd like to, but I need to shower and get out of my work clothes. I'll take a rain check."

"Anytime," Corey said. "The lights will look even better when it gets dark out."

Watching Ed pull away in his work truck, Corey glanced at Nick who flashed him a dazzling smile. "I'd like to invite you out to dinner tonight," Nick said.

"Now that's an offer I can't refuse."

"Great—but about all I can afford is Pinocchio's Pizza. Is that okay with you?"

"Sounds perfect. I'm starving."

Once in the car and on their way, Corey tuned in a station playing Christmas carols. The songs and the car's heater made for a festive and cozy feeling. When they passed a uniquely decorated house Corey slowed down, so they could have a closer look and admire what they saw. Once on Main Street, the city's pine wreath pole decorations lit their way.

"I wonder how busy the gym is this evening," Corey said as they got nearer to Pinocchio's. "Sure not much traffic around here."

"Look at it this way, as long as you've got paying members, who cares how often they actually go. Saves wear and tear on the equipment too."

"That's one of the things I love about you—you always look on the bright side of everything," Corey said, turning his head toward his handsome man.

All of a sudden, the peaceful drive and conversation were shattered. Nick stiffened, abruptly sitting up straighter, his eyes widening in alarm. Corey slammed on the brakes and jerked his head back toward the street in front of them, bracing for a crash, but there wasn't anything of danger there, at least not in front of the car. A split second later Corey noticed what had startled Nick, and the scene was frightening. As he proceeded, he tried to make sense of what he was seeing in the shadows at the edge of the gym parking lot, but he knew deep down inside there was only one explanation.

"That's Dean, isn't it?" Nick asked urgently.

"Yes, that guy's stealing his bike, and it looks like Dean's had the crap beat out of him too," Corey exclaimed, screeching to a stop next to the curb, where he saw Dean laying on the ground. Nick had his seatbelt off in a flash, his door open, and his feet on the ground before Corey could get his hands off the steering wheel. The speed at which Nick reacted left Corey in awe, and scared to death for his safety because Nick was off running after the guy who'd just stolen Dean's mountain bike.

Nick could move, that was for sure, and the fact the assailant didn't seem to know how to shift the gears on this top-of-the-line bike helped. Nick caught up with him in less than thirty feet, took a flying leap and tackled the guy right off the bike.

Corey bolted from the car and reached them in time to help

Nick keep hold of the guy, who was squirming around violently on the ground. He wore a black knit ski mask with only his eyes showing, and despite the fact his head was thrashing back and forth, Corey noticed that they were dark brown. He had a mind to yank off the mask, but he thought maybe he'd best leave that to the cops, and anyway, all his strength and concentration was being used just keeping the man down.

"You son-of-a-bitch," Dean ranted when he staggered over to them. "Shit, at least my bike fell on grass," he mumbled. "I'm calling 911. I want this guy handcuffed, arrested and thrown in jail."

"Are you okay?" Corey asked Nick.

Breathlessly Nick answered, "Yeah, I think so. You better ask Dean how *he* is. He might need an ambulance."

Corey took notice of Dean's face then. It was puffy on one side, and there was the beginning of discoloration around his left eye.

After a few more seconds, the guy they'd been restraining had obviously worn himself out and he lay still, his chest heaving.

After Dean gave the address of their emergency and ended the call, he moved to stand over the attacker.

"What the hell did you think you were doing trying to steal my bike," he spit out, clearly pissed off and looking like he might fall over any minute. Dean looked down at Corey. "I started riding away from the gym and all of a sudden this S O B tackled me right off my bike. I should just—"

"Calm down, Dean," Corey cautioned. "Why don't you go sit down in my car."

"I'm not going anywhere. Who the hell is it anyway? Take that stupid ski mask off him so I can see."

The guy struggled in Corey and Nick's grip as Dean bent down, giving the ski mask a yank, only managing to pull it halfway off, catching the cap on the guy's nose. A loud moan of protest was uttered when Dean tugged it the rest of the way off. Corey recognized the face instantly, and he could tell that Nick did too. Dean's slack jaw and wide eyes said loud and clear that he definitely knew the man.

"Ted Faulkner, you ignorant motherfucker," Dean barked out.

Ted, looking like a raging bull, began to struggle again so Corey tightened his hold and bore down on him. Seconds later, the blare of a siren in the distance was a welcome relief, because he didn't know what might happen if Dean decided to take the law into his own hands.

A police car raced up alongside them and screeched to a halt next to the curb, just outside the parking lot. Two policemen hopped out of the car and ran quickly to them, a hand at their weapons. Instead of moving out of the way, Dean stepped in the cops' path and began telling them what had happened, repeating Ted's name several times, and pointing to the ground where he lay. The red and blue revolving lights flashing across his face cast an eerie light making him look even angrier. One of the officers asked Dean to step back, and he finally got control of himself and did what he was told.

Corey and Nick stood up and then stepped back too, and while Ted was handcuffed, all they could do was watch as the officers tended to their duties. Ted didn't fight, his head hanging in defeat.

While they waited for the police to finish up, Corey couldn't help but stare at Nick when the lights swept over his face. The blue from the revolving lights intensified the color of Nick's eyes. What had just gone down was sinking in, making him shudder to think how this could have ended. What if Ted had used a knife or a gun?

Once Ted was put into the backseat of the squad car and taken away, another cruiser drove up. Corey turned his attention to those officers as they exited their vehicle.

"Does anyone need an ambulance?" one of the newly arrived officers asked.

"Maybe you'd better get checked out," Corey said to Dean.

"No, I'm fine," Dean said.

"Your face is bleeding," Nick pointed out.

"I'll see a doctor later. I don't need an ambulance," Dean said adamantly, wiping his cheek with the back of his hand.

Corey noticed a few cars rubber-necking as they drove past. He hoped the capture of Ted would finally end the rash of crimes they'd been experiencing the last few weeks. In his mind, the obvious conclusion was that Ted Faulkner was responsible for all of it—he sure would like to hear what Detective Munson thought though.

After listening to each of them speak and taking down names and statements, the officer in charge thanked them, and he and his partner said goodnight and drove off, Ted most likely getting booked at the police station that very moment. Corey breathed a silent sigh of relief that the incident was finally over.

Dean lifted his bike upright and immediately started examining it. Seeing if the paint was scratched or any parts on the bike had been damaged was impossible in the dim light from the street lamp, but when Dean wheeled the bike back and forth, Corey didn't see any obvious problems.

With Dean occupied with his bike, Corey caught Nick's eye and mouthed the words, "Should we take him to the ER?"

Nick nodded his agreement.

"Come on, Dean, we've got to get you to the ER and have your face looked at. Do you hurt anyplace else?"

"I told you I was okay. I'll just wash my face when I get home."

"You really should see a doctor. Your eye isn't looking too good, and that way if you have any problems later on, you'll be covered. Are you sure you aren't hurt anywhere else?" Corey asked again.

"My shoulder is a little sore," Dean said reluctantly.

"All the more reason to go. Let's get your bike into my car and head over to the ER."

"I really don't think this is an emergency," Dean said.

"Then how about seeing a doctor at a walk-in clinic?"

Dean considered the suggestion for a few seconds. "You're not gonna take no for an answer, are you?"

"No," Corey said firmly.

"Okay, I'll go. But—" Dean looked at Nick. "I'll bet I'm interrupting a hot date. Where were you two heading, anyway? How'd you happen to come to the rescue?"

"We were on our way to grab a pizza," Corey said.

"Well, that was lucky for me." Dean looked at Nick again. "Thanks for stopping Ted like you did," he said, sounding like he had a hard time choking out the words.

"You're welcome," Nick said.

"And you did an awesome job too," Dean said to Corey.

Corey felt a little uncomfortable with the praise and with the whole situation. "Let's get your bike loaded up and get you to the clinic."

Two and a half hours later, Corey, along with his current boyfriend and ex-boyfriend were sitting at a table waiting for pizza. Of all the things he could have imagined ever happening, this wasn't one of them, but Nick had suggested inviting Dean while they had waited for him at the clinic, so here they were. At least they'd all agreed they deserved a beer because even on this cold night it hit the spot, and Corey took another long swig.

"I'm starving. I hope the pizza comes soon," Dean said, taking a drink from his own mug, wincing.

"Yeah, we were ready to eat hours ago," Corey said.

"Sorry about that," Dean said.

"We had a snack from a vending machine at the clinic," Nick said.

Nick seemed to be trying to make Dean feel better by telling him about the snack, and that sure surprised Corey since Dean had tried to make Nick look bad just the week before.

When the server set the extra-large pepperoni and mushroom pizza down in the middle of the table, all three of them dug in as if they hadn't eaten in a week. No one spoke until they'd each devoured a couple slices.

"Well, most likely Ted has been the one committing all the crimes in the area," Dean began.

"I'd say that's a pretty good conclusion," Corey agreed.

"What's up with the cops? They should have been able to figure that out by now. Damn, we're the ones who caught the creep. I wonder if there's a reward," Dean said, laughing.

They continued eating and then Dean looked at Nick. "Did anyone ever question you? That Munson guy spoke to me for about one minute. I don't think those cops investigated very well."

"We can't really say that, Dean. We don't know what they found out—what they knew or didn't know," Corey said.

"Ted was still out on the street. If they'd arrested him before tonight, I wouldn't have been put in the situation I was." Dean looked at Nick again.

"Ted's been pretty good, or lucky, at *not* getting caught," Nick said.

Dean blew air out his nose. "Well, did you talk with the cops?"

"Yeah, the detective asked me some questions."

"He asked a lot of people questions. He seemed to be doing a pretty thorough job," Corey said.

Nick took a drink of beer, cleared his throat and looked at Dean. "I wanna let you know that my last name is Sanders, not Stewart like I said when I first came here. I told the detective my real name in case you're wondering."

"You don't have to explain," Corey interjected.

"That's all I'm saying. It's none of Dean's business why I chose to give a false name at first."

"Well, excuse me," Dean huffed.

"Look, I'm not trying to be rude, here," Nick said.

"He knows that," Corey said, glaring at Dean.

Dean scowled and finished his last piece of pizza. After he swallowed he washed it down with more beer. "Since we're done here, can we get going?"

"Yeah, I think that's a good idea," Corey said. "You think you'll have to take time off at the gym?"

"Heck no, I'll improvise if I have to. So long as I don't scare anyone with my banged-up face. How do I look?" Dean smiled and held his chin up, proudly showing off his battle wounds and eight stitches along his hairline, first looking at Corey and then to Nick.

"You could say you're hiding a giant zit under that bandage," Corey joked.

"Or you've been to the dermatologist and had something burned off," Nick added.

"Okay, okay, I'm glad I could provide the entertainment for the evening for you two lovebirds, but now I'll just ask for a quick drive to my place and then I'll be out of your hair."

They all stood up, put on their jackets, and headed out.

Within ten minutes, they arrived at Dean's apartment, got him unloaded, and said goodnight. The two of them then watched as Dean wheeled the bike up to his building, and right before he turned the corner and disappeared, Dean turned around and gave a wave.

"Does Dean know I moved in?" Nick asked on the drive home.

"I didn't tell him, and I don't think Katie did either because I can't see him keeping quiet about that. He hasn't said a thing."

"Yeah, you might be right. Just that 'lovebirds' comment made me think maybe he knew."

"Well, it doesn't matter one way or the other." Corey stopped at a stop sign and continued on. "Uh, it was nice of you to let him come along to Pinocchio's. I know he's not your favorite person."

"Well, I know he's not your favorite person either—I am," Nick said, a hint of playfulness in his tone.

"You're right," Corey said, smiling. "Glad you're not scared away after all the craziness we've been through lately."

"Maybe life around the gym will settle down now that Ted's

been arrested," Nick said.

"I hope Detective Munson will be around tomorrow to fill us in on the whole situation."

Nick looked at the clock on the dash. "Don't you mean today? It's midnight already."

"Midnight—got to get you home then, before you turn into a pumpkin—or something like that."

They shared a laugh, and Corey made the turn on to the street leading to their home. When he pulled into the driveway, he kept the car running with the heater going and turned to Nick. He suddenly felt the way he had back at the crime scene when the realization had hit him just how much danger Nick had put himself in. Reaching for Nick's hand, he held it tightly.

"You know, you scared me to death back there when you took off after Dean's attacker."

Nick slid closer and used his free hand to gently touch Corey's cheek. "I'm sorry. I guess I wasn't thinking... it was all on instinct."

"Yeah, well, I didn't really have time to think either, while it was all going on anyway, but after..."

Corey shook his head and pulled Nick to him, hugging the guy who meant so much to him. He felt the love in Nick's heart when Nick pulled back and kissed him lightly on the lips, murmuring, "We've gotta stop all this cops and robbers stuff. We need to go inside, lock the door, and forget about this crazy night."

"That's the best idea I've heard in a while," Corey answered.

"We should go. I'm starting to overheat," Nick said.

"I like the sound of that." Corey shut the engine off. "I'm hot too."

"You sure are," Nick replied.

They quickly got out of the car and raced each other to the house. Once tucked away inside, they wasted no time getting into bed.

"Here, let me give you a massage," Corey said, tugging on Nick's shoulder wanting him to roll over onto his stomach.

"What? Why?" Nick asked but did what he was told.

"You might be sore from what you did tonight. The adrenalin rush and all." He ran his hands over Nick's back. "You do feel a little tense—relax while I work on you." He pulled Nick's top up and began tapping and kneading his back.

"Corey, I feel fine..."

"You'll feel better after this, believe me." In less than a minute, he had Nick peacefully grunting and moaning.

He leaned down and whispered close to Nick's ear, "You know who you reminded me of tonight?"

"No, who?" Nick said in little more than a murmur.

"Superman," Corey answered, and kissed the back of Nick's neck.

Nick snorted out a small laugh. "Get real, I'm far from Superman."

"You did an awesome job tonight."

"Thanks... all in a day's work." Nick trailed off and sighed.

Corey wondered if he was falling asleep because he'd gotten so quiet. "I can get your shoulders better if you take the shirt off," he said gently, blowing into Nick's ear.

Nick sat up and pulled his shirt off, tossing it aside, looking suddenly wide awake. He playfully pushed Corey onto his back against the sheets. The way Nick gazed into his eyes from above made his heart beat faster and the blood go straight to his dick. He smiled up at him. "Hey, what are you doing? I wasn't finished massaging you."

"I think you need a massage now. A full-body massage... starting here." Nick grabbed Corey's dick through his pajama bottoms causing his eyes to widen in surprise and his dick to stiffen even more. Nick grinned, his eyes twinkling. He leaned in and sucked on the base of Corey's neck, right above the collarbone, hard enough to leave a mark, his hand never leaving the prize he'd captured.

"What's gotten into you? Was the massage that good?" Corey giggled softly.

The next thing he knew, soft lips covered his, fiery and passionate. He accepted Nick's tongue greedily, his fingers tangling in Nick's hair. When they came up for air, Nick ran his tongue from Corey's neck down to his chest and below, farther and farther. Corey's breathing increased, his eyes lost focus, and soon he arched up off the bed grabbing handfuls of sheet, his last coherent thought being how much he loved this man of his.

CHAPTER TWENTY-TWO

THE NEXT day, with Ted's capture the night before put on the back burner, they went on with their Christmas plans.

"I'm glad you took the day off, and I came home early so we could do this. It's gonna look great," Nick said.

Corey took a step back from the seven-foot noble fir they'd bought at the Boy Scouts' Christmas tree lot that morning and looked to see if the lights they'd just strung were even. He should have known they'd be perfect with Nick directing the project, because when it came to art—dressing a tree fell into that category—Nick was a master. The way the blue lights twinkled reminded him of Nick's eyes.

"This tree already looks pretty, especially with the tree top we found in the bottom of the box."

"But wait 'till we get the garland and ornaments on. It'll really look awesome," Nick said excitedly.

"I can tell you've decorated a tree or two in your day, huh?"

Right away he knew that was the wrong thing to have said. Nick looked as if he'd had cold water thrown on him, and the sparkle that had been in his eyes a moment ago was replaced by a sad, gloomy look. Corey knew Nick missed his family more and more every day by the faraway gazes he sent to the horizons, the way his hands twitched when he was in the kitchen cooking up one of his mom's recipes. And there were more and more of them as the days neared Christmas.

Nick didn't answer, just readjusted the tree skirt, and Corey could tell the man was trying hard to hide his feelings. He wanted to say something—try to get Nick to face what had happened back home, but it was obvious Nick wasn't going to go there yet, and Corey didn't want to ruin their experience of decorating their first tree together, so he let it go one more time. Now wasn't the time to hit that topic.

Nick opened one of the cardboard boxes and pulled out yards of silver and gold garland. "This and then the ornaments," he said.

"I'll get a picture of it when it's all done," Corey said, as he lay his phone on the arm of the couch.

Just like with the lights, they worked together to place the garland just so and in no time they had the top third of the tree done.

"Let's make sure we have this right so far," Nick said, stopping to stand back and check their work.

With Nick giving the okay, they continued. When the garland was nearly complete, the doorbell rang.

"Go ahead, I've got this," Nick said.

"Has the mail come yet? Maybe it's the mailman."

Corey opened the door to find Katie on the other side. "Hey, what brings you by?" he asked, taking a step outside to wrap his arm around her for a hug while holding the door open for her to walk inside.

"So, this is why you aren't at work." Katie smiled, and Corey could tell the tree impressed her. "Hi, Nick. Is he making you do all the work?"

Nick laughed and straightened up, backing away from the tree. "This part's finished," he said to Corey. "Would you like some tea?" he asked, looking at Katie.

"Thanks, I'd love some if it's not too much trouble."

"Some for you too, Corey?"

"Sure, thanks. Do you need any help?"

"I've got it, you visit with Katie. Be right back."

When Nick left the room, Katie looked up at Corey. "I can't believe you guys. Here you are decorating a tree like nothing happened last night. When I heard what you two did, I was worried you'd gotten hurt and were too shaken up to come to work."

"How'd you hear?" he asked, helping her off with her coat. He tossed it on a chair in the corner of the living room.

"Thanks," Katie said as she moved to stare at the star on top of the tree. "Well, you might find this strange, but Alan and I are still on speaking terms, and he knew all about what went down with Ted—Don't look at me that way," she scolded, giving Corey a stern look. "Wes knows we talk and he's fine with that."

Corey raised his eyebrows but held his tongue. He moved over to the couch and patted the seat next to him. "Come sit down."

"Besides hearing from Alan, I was at work for only a short time this morning when that detective came in." Katie sat down.

That got Corey's attention, but before she could go on, Nick came with the tea. He set the tray on the coffee table and they began stirring sugar into their cups.

"Katie was just saying Detective Munson was at the gym this morning."

Corey waited for Katie to elaborate, and finally she spoke.

"He was hoping to speak with you, but since I didn't know what time you were coming in, he told me to pass along the information." Katie took a sip of her tea. "Evidently, he'd suspected Ted from almost the start. I didn't know, but Alan told me Ted has a record, so maybe that's why he was a suspect. Anyway, they didn't have enough evidence to warrant an arrest. Detective Munson has been working on putting a case together, and with what happened last night, well... after interrogating him, they've charged Ted with the robberies and the attack on the woman at the ATM, plus Ted implicated a guy from out of town, and I got the impression he'd be arrested soon too."

"Wow, that's great news," Nick said.

"Sure is," Corey agreed.

"I thought you'd be pleased. That's one of the reasons I came by instead of calling."

"What's the other reason?"

"Because I was worried about you, dummy," Katie said.

"Dean was the injured party, thanks to Ted pulling him off his bike and punching him."

"Ted sure must have been desperate to try stealing a bike with someone on it," Katie said.

"I agree. Uh, we took Dean to the clinic to get checked out."

Katie's eyes widened. "You did? Well, that was nice of you."

"And afterward we took him out for pizza," Nick said, grinning.

Katie looked from Nick to Corey, but before she had a chance to say anything, Corey spoke up. "You're not confused, are you? I mean, your association with Alan isn't exactly typical so—"

"It's okay, you don't have to explain. I guess Dean was okay if he ate pizza afterward."

"Yeah, he just had a few cuts, one that required stitches, some scrapes and a bruise or two. I think he was more upset about his bike than his injuries."

"Was it damaged?"

"It seemed all right when we wheeled it around, but I wouldn't doubt it has some scratches and dings after the way Ted and the bike hit the ground when Nick tackled him."

"He thinks the world of that bike. Are you sure both of you are okay?" Katie asked, looking intently at Corey.

"Don't worry, we're fine. Nick was a little sore, but he's better after a good night's sleep, right Nick?" He glanced at Nick, winking. "It's good to hear about Ted being charged."

"Yeah, nothing beats a good night's sleep," Nick said with a slight smirk aimed in Corey's direction. "And, it's a relief to know who was responsible for the crime, that's for sure. Would you like another cup of tea, Katie?"

"You're such a good host. But, no, I'd better get going seeing as how the boss is slacking off."

Corey laughed and got up to get Katie's coat. "Come back when you can stay longer," he said, walking her to the door.

"Drop by anytime and bring Wes too," Nick said, joining them at the door.

"Thanks, I'll do that," Katie said before she stepped out the door.

"I'll walk you to your car," Corey said.

Nick stood there a minute watching Corey and Katie walking down the driveway to her car parked on the street. Corey had said before that he wished he'd had a brother or sister, but from what Nick could see, they seemed more like brother and sister than just cousins.

His brother back in Oregon was never out of his mind, and he wondered how Richard was getting on and if he ever gave a thought to his baby brother who had disappeared.

He closed the door and went to pick up the teapot and cups. After putting everything on to the tray, he took another look at the tree and wondered if his family back home had one this year. He couldn't help thinking of them at times like this, as painful as it was.

At least one person wouldn't let his absence spoil things... Melissa. She'd been so hurt and angry when he'd last seen her that there was no doubt in his mind she was glad he wasn't around anymore.

As he placed the dirty cups in the dishwasher, he wondered what she'd done with his truck. Her dad was probably using it, but whatever she'd done was fine by him. She'd probably had a big sale on their lawn, after all, most of his stuff had been strewn all over the grass and bushes on that last day.

Restless, as he waited on Corey to come back inside, he walked back to the tree and reached out to touch a branch and then adjusted a section of garland. Last Christmas—his last with Melissa— he had given her a pretty heart-shaped necklace. He remembered her adoring smile when she'd unwrapped it and she'd even had tears in her eyes when she asked him to hook the chain around her neck. He'd been glad she'd liked the gift so much, but he'd felt like such a jerk, because he knew he was only leading her on giving her such a gift, trying to make everything all right—trying to convince himself, mostly, that things were wonderful between them.

He turned away from the tree, hating these depressing thoughts, and plopped down on the couch, his head cradled in his hands.

Guilt was eating him up.

CHAPTER TWENTY-THREE

A WEEK later, and four days left before Christmas Eve, Corey pulled into the driveway and could finally say he had his shopping finished. He'd always found picking out gifts difficult, and in fact, this year proved no different and was much harder since he now had a special someone to buy for. His special man deserved a special gift and, after much thought and a lot of searching, he felt confident that Nick would like what he'd selected, with the exception of maybe one.

Gathering the handles of the bags, he lifted them all out of the car and headed to the house. Once inside, he removed the wrapped gifts from the bags and placed them carefully underneath the tree before going to the kitchen to start dinner. No longer spending most of his time at work agreed with him. The house finally felt like a home.

An hour later, Corey had Italian sausage and rigatoni well on its way to baked perfection when Nick came home hollering, "What smells so good?"

Corey expected Nick to pop into the kitchen for a hello kiss, or at least to *say* hello, because Nick was always very complimentary and encouraging when it was Corey's night to cook. But when he had finished setting the table Nick still hadn't appeared so he went into the living room and looked at the tree and then out the window, wondering if Nick had gone outside for some reason.

When there was no sign of him there, he heard a noise and finally Nick came out of the bedroom wearing a smug look.

"Hey, what have you got cooking in the kitchen that smells so good?"

Corey snorted out a small laugh. "All I did was open the box and stick the tray into the oven. And I've got to say it's a good thing Katie, Rita, and Rita's daughter are cooking Christmas Eve dinner and we're invited."

Nick patted his stomach. "I'm not complaining about your cooking."

"Anyway, don't change the subject," Corey said, receiving a confused look from Nick.

"Don't look at me like that—you know what I mean."

"I do?" Nick asked, looking away.

"I knew it," Corey exclaimed.

"Knew what?" Nick asked, obviously flustered.

"You've been out shopping, and you hid something in the bedroom. It's for me, right?"

Nick threw up his hands and backed away. Corey was right on him, threatening to tickle the truth out of him. After they'd horsed around until they were out of breath and laughing uncontrollably, he flopped down on the couch with Nick right next to him. Times like this were his happiest—when Nick could let go as if he didn't have a care in the world. These times weren't near as often as he wished they were though, like the nights when Nick had one of his nightmares. And other times when he had caught Nick with a haunted faraway look—he was grieving.

"What are you thinking about?" Nick asked, still a little breathless from their roughhousing.

Corey felt the warmth of Nick's fingers gripping his and let out a huff of air, making an effort to snap out of his melancholy thoughts. He brought Nick's hand to his lips for a kiss.

"I'm thinking about throwing together the salad we're having with what's in the oven, so I can feed you." He patted Nick's stomach, stood up and headed for the kitchen.

Later that night, when they had crawled into bed under the handmade quilt they'd bought at the mission's Christmas fair, Corey hastily pulled off his pajamas and just about tore off Nick's in his rush for some skin on skin contact. He'd loved Nick's body from the first time they'd been together, and each time they made love he almost couldn't believe how lucky he was to have found this man. He slid his arms around Nick's back and pulled him close to kiss him, loving the feeling of stubble scraping like sandpaper against his face. There was no hurry here in their own bed, in the house they now shared, so he went slowly, Nick giving him control. Corey liked that from time to time, and Nick always seemed to sense when those times were needed. He tried with all his heart to show his man that he was loved—to soothe the pain he knew festered under the surface.

On Christmas Eve, after the last tray of food was placed on the dining table, Katie took her seat at the opposite end of the table from her dad, with Wes to her right. Rita sat down on Ed's left with her daughter, Jenny, next to her. Corey and Nick filled out the remaining seats on the right of Uncle Ed.

"The table looks great," Corey said, eyeing the evergreen and pinecone centerpiece with the red and white flowers. The red candles flickering in the middle of the setting gave the table a warm glow. Nick was always so thoughtful and had such good taste. He'd never have thought to bring such a nice addition to the table. There were a lot of things he could learn from Nick if he paid enough attention.

"The food looks even better," Wes said.

"Well, go ahead and start," Rita instructed, picking up the mashed potatoes and passing them to Jenny.

Ed took the serving fork and put some turkey on Rita's plate and then took a couple of slices for himself and passed the platter to Corey.

"These dishes are so pretty," Jenny said. "Are they a family heirloom?"

"Aren't they lovely and so festive?" Rita agreed. "We've never had a set just for Christmas."

"We've had these since I was six or seven years old," Katie said. "We don't always use them, but this year I thought something special was called for, so I got them out. A few years ago, I found the red goblets in an antique store and knew they'd go perfectly."

"I'm glad we're using them this year," Ed said. "Brings back some good memories from long ago when your mother was alive."

Corey gave Katie a smile, and then glanced at Nick who was piling a couple large slices of turkey on his plate. He took the gravy from Uncle Ed and ladled some on his turkey, but he knew Nick wouldn't want the gravy until he had his mashed potatoes on the plate.

"Leave room for pumpkin pie," Rita said after they all began to eat.

"I sure will. I'm looking forward to dessert," Wes said, and then he put a spoon full of candied yams in his mouth.

"Are you two fellas going to open your presents tonight or tomorrow, before we leave for the mission?" Ed asked.

"I think tomorrow, right, Nick?"

Nick nodded while chewing a bite of his dinner roll.

"We're opening ours tonight," Katie said, gazing at Wes affectionately.

"My family always opened presents on Christmas morning, but if she wants to open them tonight, that's fine with me." Wes smiled adoringly at Katie, and Corey almost eye-rolled they were that sweet with each other.

"If we exchange our gifts tonight we won't have to rush. There won't be a lot of time in the morning before we leave to help at the mission," Katie said.

"You boys will have to be up early," Rita said looking at Corey and Nick.

"We might be up all night waiting to catch a glimpse of Santa," Corey joked. He gave Nick a playful smile.

The evening was a success, from the meal to the company, and the easy and playful conversations they all had. Corey had high hopes that Christmas Day would be just as good, if not better than Christmas Eve.

The next morning, Corey plugged in the tree, the lights adding a feeling of warmth even though the furnace hadn't yet begun to give off enough heat to make the house comfortable. He pulled his robe tighter around himself and wished he'd have had more time to lounge in the warm bed with Nick. Wasn't Christmas morning a day to do as you pleased? But, that was a selfish thought, he mused. The folks at the mission deserved a good, hot Christmas meal, and someone to cook and serve it, and he and Nick had volunteered to help out. He knew Nick was looking forward to going, and he wanted to go as well, but one of the things he hoped to accomplish today would need some time, and with their busy day ahead, that might prove difficult.

He went to the kitchen, prepared to set up the coffee maker

and found that Nick had already put in the filter and coffee, so all he had to do was add the water and flip the switch. Living with someone who helped with the household chores came in handy. Then he noticed plates, cups, and utensils set out and remembered the cinnamon rolls they'd bought and planned to have that morning. Before he had time to think any further, Nick shuffled into the kitchen—barefoot—and Corey welcomed the strong arms that went around him, angling his head just right so that Nick's lips came together with his in a kiss that made his heart swell.

"This is the best Christmas I've ever had," Corey whispered when the kiss ended.

"How do you know? It's not over yet," Nick answered back.

"I just know."

Nick sighed happily and let him go. "Breakfast or presents first?"

"How about both at the same time?"

"Multitasking even on Christmas?" Nick laughed, giving up one of his dazzling smiles.

"We've got places to go, people to see, and things to do."

"You don't sound too excited about that," Nick answered, moving toward the coffee pot.

"I am. It's just that—" He started second-guessing himself about bringing up Nick's family, so he didn't finish his sentence.

"What?" Nick asked, grabbing two mugs and pouring the coffee.

"I like having you all to myself," Corey growled in Nick's ear as he moved to pick up his mug.

"I like that too, and we'll have time."

"I'm holding you to it." Corey grinned.

Nick shot him a devilish look but changed the subject. "I'll put the cinnamon rolls in the microwave and get some grapes and tangerines out of the fridge."

Fifteen minutes later the living room was warm and toasty, and the foil wrapped packages were sparkling under the tree just waiting to be opened.

Nick set his coffee and food on the coffee table and stood before the tree eyeing the gifts. "Shall we get started?"

"You're in a hurry, aren't you? Were you always this impatient on Christmas morning?" Corey asked, smiling at his man.

"Well, you said we'd eat and open at the same time."

"You're right, I did." Corey placed his breakfast next to Nick's.

"Why don't you start?"

"Okay, I will," Nick said, rubbing his palms together and then picking up a square box wrapped in Santa Claus paper. "This one's mine."

"Are you sure?" Corey took a seat on the couch.

"Oh, yeah, I noticed it before, and the tag says it's from you."

Nick sat down on the couch with the box on his lap. He reached for his coffee and took a drink, and then ate a bite of his cinnamon roll.

"Hey, what's the holdup? I'm waiting until you get one opened before I open one of mine."

"Oh, sorry, I didn't know the rules." Nick chuckled.

Corey ate a couple bites of his food while Nick tore off the paper and then slowly began to lift the lid off the box.

"There's nothing inside that's going to jump out at you," Corey said, amused.

"Are you trying to tell me you don't like the way I open a package?"

Corey leaned over and kissed Nick softly on the lips. "I love the way you open a package. I love everything about you."

"I love you too." Nick reached for Corey's hand and squeezed and then he peeked into the box.

"No way! Wow! This is so great." He lightly ran his fingers over the various painting supplies packed neatly inside the box.

"I hope these are things you can use. I wasn't totally sure, but I've watched you work and saw the stuff you have in the closet, and the salesgirl gave me some pointers. I hope she was right..."

Nick put two fingers over Corey's lips, and then replaced them with his own lips for a long, slow kiss. "You did a fantastic job. I love everything. Thank you."

"You're welcome." Corey smiled, giving Nick a quick kiss.

Nick placed the box of art supplies on the end table. "Okay, it's your turn now."

Corey popped a couple grapes in his mouth and Nick took one off his plate and tossed it in the air, catching it in his mouth. Corey giggled and went over to the tree and grabbed a gift from Nick. He shook the box as he returned to sit down again. "I wonder what this could be."

"Open it and find out."

"Now who's in a hurry to get to their next present?"

"That's not what I meant, take all the time you want."

Corey laughed and tore the paper off the box in two seconds flat. He threw the lid aside and pulled off the tissue paper to reveal a blue and gray warm-up suit. "Hey, this is just like the black and gray one I've got. Awesome! I love it." He checked the size. "My size too."

"I know you like the one you have, and I thought you'd like one in this color too."

"I do. It's a really useful gift, thanks." He kissed Nick once more. "This sure is fun."

"Yeah, and it's my turn again." Nick hustled over to the tree and came back with another gift from Corey, a box shaped like the one Corey had opened, only smaller.

"I wonder if this is something to wear."

"Did you open it earlier and replace the wrapping?"

"Me? No way. I'd never do that," Nick said, sitting down on the couch again.

"Okay, just checking."

"What about you?"

"What about me, what?"

"Did you unwrap and then rewrap presents back when you were a kid?"

"Well... maybe once."

Nick shook his head. "You were baaaaad."

Corey finished his last bite of cinnamon roll. "How old were you when you stopped believing in Santa Claus?"

Nick took a deep breath and stared off into space as if he was giving the question a lot of thought. "I'm not really sure, I mean, that was so long ago... maybe six?"

"That young?"

"Why, how old were you?"

"Oh, I don't know... probably eight or nine."

Nick gazed at him, his lips curling slightly at the corners.

"I lived a sheltered life, what can I say?" Corey said in his defense.

Nick chuckled. "With my brother being older, I probably grew up faster in that way."

"Maybe so."

"Well, back to the presents... Did I make a good guess about this being something to wear?"

"I'm not giving hints, that would spoil the surprise."

Nick shook the box and snickered as he ripped the wrapping paper off, and this time he flung the lid off the box, reaching under the tissue wrap to the contents. He pulled out a bright blue T-shirt with a Superman emblem on the front. Holding it up, he laughed. "I guess I'll be known as Superman forever now. Seems like that's my new nickname."

"Well, ever since I saw you take down Ted on the sidewalk in front of the gym, literally flying out of the car, and taking a flying leap..." Corey broke into a laugh. "I can't help it, you're Superman to me."

Nick took off his pajama top and pulled on the new T-shirt, stood up, smoothed out the wrinkles, and modeled it for Corey.

"How do I look?"

"Like Superman, let me get a picture."

After posing for the photo, Nick sat down. "Thank you, this was clever of you, really."

"Glad you think so. I knew you'd look super in it," Corey said with a wink.

"Open the other present I got you. I hope you like it."

"I'm sure I will," Corey said, walking over to the tree and returning to sit by Nick with a gift bag in his hands.

"I wonder what this could be?" He reached into the bag and felt around.

"Don't toy with it like a cat," Nick said.

"I feel something hard," Corey said, pulling out an insulated stainless-steel water bottle and holding it in front of him. "Nice. I can sure use this." He turned the bottle around in his hands to get a good look.

"I thought you'd get a lot of use out of this. You're always drinking water."

"You picked out great gifts. Thank you very much, baby." Corey pulled Nick to him, planting a long kiss on his lips.

When they pulled apart Nick smiled. "Wow, and we don't even have any mistletoe."

"I don't need that to get me in the mood for a kiss."

That got him a dreamy look from Nick, who brushed his fingers across Corey's cheek and whispered, "Thank you for my gifts too. They're great."

Corey grinned and tugged gently on Nick's hair. "Do you want any more to eat?"

"I could use more coffee, and maybe another cinnamon roll. This package opening burns a lot of calories."

"I agree, I need more to eat too, and then we'd better unwrap the other packages from Katie and the rest, so we can get ready to leave for the mission."

Between nibbling on breakfast, taking pictures, and listening to Christmas music on the radio, they had wrapping paper, ribbons, bows, boxes, and bags scattered all over the floor. The living room looked as if two children had done the unwrapping instead of two adult men, and it was quite a sight.

They began stacking their opened gifts under the tree, and there was quite the haul. Corey didn't rush getting the papers and bows picked up but realized he couldn't stall any longer—it was now or never—regarding Nick's last gift, which he'd hidden in the tree on a branch toward the back. He didn't think Nick had even noticed.

Corey cleared his throat. "Uh, looks like Santa brought you a present you didn't see."

"What? What are you talking about?" Nick moved closer, squinting into the tree, trying to see what drew Corey's intense gaze, and the bright green package caught his eye. "Santa?" He reached for the box. "Santa brought this?" he said, more to himself than to Corey, as if remembering some past Christmas from years gone by.

For a split second, Corey saw the small boy that Nick used to be, and he smiled.

"You might as well open it."

Nick made a big production of holding the package near his ear and giving the box a shake. "Why do I have a present from Santa and you don't?"

"Uh, because you were good on more days of the last year than I was?"

"Hardly," Nick said, his tone conveying the guilt inside. "I probably should have been damned to hell if Santa was going by who was good and who was bad."

"Hey, don't say something like that." Corey pulled him in for a tight hug.

"Sorry for being a downer," Nick said after they parted. He shook the box again turning it around in his hand and gave a forced smile. "Funny, the tag says this is from you."

"What? You're kidding," Corey said in mock surprise. He reached for the box and looked at the tag. "Hey, you're right. I must have forgotten about this one." He made an effort to laugh, but his nerves had kicked in, and he really didn't know how the gift would go over.

Nick tore the tape and paper off slowly, and when the box was revealed, he looked confused. "Is this what it looks like?"

"Before you say anything more, let me explain. It's just so damn hard to reach you when you're out... I just really want you to have a phone, so I got you one just like mine, and I added you... it's a family plan." He stopped to catch his breath.

"Corey, you know I don't want a phone—"

"I know, but I hoped that maybe the benefits of having one would outweigh the reasons you don't want one. And not only for the phone, but I know you can use the camera to take pictures of your art. You'll be able to show people what you've done." Neither of them spoke for several long seconds. "What do you say? Please take it."

Nick looked doubtful but thoughtful, and after a long pause, he finally answered. "I guess this present is from Santa to you too, huh?"

Then in true Nick fashion he said, "I'll pay my part of the plan. You really don't have to pay my way all over the place. I have money, and... I'm good for my share, no matter what it is."

"Oh, all right," Corey said. "You know, we get unlimited long distance."

"And your point?" Nick asked dryly.

Corey held up his hands in surrender. "Nothing, I was just informing you, is all. Now, it's about time we get showered and dressed, don't you think? We'll have to leave soon. There's some hungry folks out there."

Nick stepped into the shower and soaped up quickly, trying not to take too long. Corey getting ready in the other bathroom would save time. He smiled inwardly thinking about all the showers they'd taken together in one bathroom or the other, in fact, they'd had sex in almost every room of the house. Come to think of it, the laundry room was the only room left they hadn't made love in. He'd keep that in mind and rectify that at the next opportunity.

He squeezed shampoo into his hand and lathered up his hair, keeping his eyes closed tightly. When he was done he stood under the spray to rinse. A little conditioner and he'd be through. He turned the water down to a mist while he stepped aside to let the conditioner do its thing.

Leaning against the tiles he thought about the phone sitting under the Christmas tree. Corey's heart was in the right place but thinking about owning a phone and Corey telling him he could call long distance made him tense up. He stepped into the water again, and with his face toward the mist, he stood there trying to get the damn phone out of his mind. He knew what he should do with it—what he needed to do with it—but knowing and actually following through seemed like a monumental task.

When he was finished he stepped out of the shower and began drying himself off. Even if he didn't use the phone to call long distance, it would be good being able to call Corey and to take pictures of his work. He'd plug it in to charge before they left the house.

CHAPTER TWENTY-FOUR

FROM THE steps of the mission, a wonderful aroma wafted into the air that made Corey's mouth water. "Smells good already."

"Hey, the first order of business is feeding the less fortunate—you'll have to wait," Nick said, playfully scolding him.

"Wonder what's on the menu. I'd say turkey, stuffing, rolls—"

"Pies, there has to be pies," Nick added, giving the heavy door a strong pull.

"Smells even better now that we're inside," Corey said, stepping past Nick into the large hall where many people were mingling.

Nick closed the door, and Corey saw him scanning the room. "See anyone you recognize?"

"Not right off the bat."

"Uncle Ed, Katie and Wes are probably in the kitchen already."

Nick didn't answer, and Corey noticed something had caught his eye in one corner of the room. Quite a few people had gathered there, forming a line. The person at the head of the line had the telephone to his ear. Just then, one of the women waiting in line noticed Nick and called out a cheerful 'hello,' so Nick walked over to her. Corey stayed where he was and watched, figuring she must be someone he knew from the motel.

A minute later, Rita appeared by Corey's side. "Ed wondered if you'd gotten here yet," she said, patting Corey on the arm. "Good to have you. Where's Nick?"

As Corey motioned across the room, Rita saw him and smiled. "Good, you're both here."

"What's going on over there?" Corey asked.

"We're letting people make calls to home. Looks like it's a big hit."

"I'll say. That's a nice idea."

"I wasn't the one who came up with it. The supervisor did, but I agree that it's a good thing to do. Many of these people haven't spoken to their families in a long time, so what better day to do that than on Christmas?"

Corey watched Nick carry on a long conversation with the woman in the line who looked rather serious.

"Come to the dining room when you're ready," Rita said, as she headed that way and disappeared through the doorway.

Corey watched her go and then wandered around, taking time to speak to a few guests, wondering if he should get to work or wait for Nick. After spending a few minutes with an elderly woman who he'd seen on several occasions, Nick appeared to be ending his conversation, so he waited.

"Hey, sorry about that," Nick said upon returning. "Guess we need to start, huh."

"Not so fast. Who's the lady in the line?"

Nick grinned at him. "I met her at the motel. She used to do drugs, but she's clean now. She's pretty nervous because she's gonna call her family, and they basically disowned her and sent her on her way a year ago. She hasn't spoken to them since."

Corey searched Nick's eyes looking for something in his expression that would let him know if Nick might consider making a call of his own, but if he had made that decision, his face wasn't revealing a thing.

"Well, let's get into the dining room and see what we can do to help," Corey said.

For the next few hours all the volunteers stayed so busy there wasn't time to think of anything but passing out napkins and silverware, pouring hot cider, tea, and coffee, and putting the delicious food on plates.

So many people in need filtered in and out, and the sound of holiday cheer echoed throughout the old building. The seasonal decorations, and the carols playing from the sound system seemed to lift everyone's spirits—if the smiles on their faces were any indication. Corey's favorite part of the whole day was watching Nick interact with the less fortunate—he had a gift for relating with people. Corey could tell by the way Nick leaned in close to catch every word that he was genuinely interested in what they had to say.

Seeing Uncle Ed smiling and enjoying himself also made Corey happy. Despite the hard work, Ed looked like he was completely in the holiday spirit and, of course, Rita had a lot to do with that.

Before they took their break to eat, Corey noticed that Nick had walked to the other side of the dining room and was speaking with the woman who had been in line at the phone. He saw her smiling and Nick hugged her before returning to Corey's side.

While standing in the food line, Corey could tell that Nick must have worked up an appetite by the way he was eying the food. He got Nick's attention by brushing him with his shoulder. "Hey, your friend sure was smiling there a minute ago."

"Oh, yeah... she said her folks *cried* when they heard her voice, and said they were so proud of her and wanted her to call again."

"That's great. I'm glad for her."

"Yeah, me too."

Corey kept his voice low and leaned in. "You know, who's to say that wouldn't happen for you if you decided to call your own mother and father."

If Nick had a comment to make, he didn't get a chance, because one of the servers interrupted by filling his plate with big spoonsful of food. He just hoped Nick had heard what he'd said—really heard—and that what he'd said had made an impression.

Late in the afternoon, after the last plate had been served, Corey was dead on his feet and Nick looked that way too as they sat down at a table in the dining room across from Ed. Katie and Wes, on the other hand, looked like they still had energy to spare.

"Now that was a humbling experience," Katie said, sitting down next to her dad. Corey wondered if her smile was because she felt enriched and inspired by her good deed on this Christmas day, or if Wes by her side was more the reason. Whatever the case, he liked seeing her look happy and alive.

On the drive home, Nick didn't have much to say, and Corey wondered if he was thinking about calling his family when they got back to their home. He wanted to ask, but since he'd already mentioned it several times, he decided not to push. Nick had his own phone now, so if he wanted to call there was nothing stopping him.

When they walked through the front door, Nick plugged in the tree and flopped down on the couch while Corey went to the kitchen to make tea. When he returned with steaming mugs, Nick had turned on the TV to an old Christmas movie. Handing Nick a mug, Corey noticed the cell phone sitting on the table next to Nick.

"You really made this hot," Nick commented, carefully taking tiny sips.

"Sorry. I guess I didn't catch the kettle soon enough." Corey joined Nick on the sofa.

"That's okay. I can let it cool while I do something else."

"Oh, yeah? What's that?"

Nick met Corey's eyes. "I'm sure you have some idea."

Corey spoke slowly—hopefully. "Well, I could guess, but I might be wrong, so why don't you tell me?"

"I can tell by the way your face looks that you know. You look pleased with yourself." A reluctant smile tugged at the corners of Nick's mouth.

Corey snorted out a small laugh. "Is that so."

"You think you're pretty smart to have gotten me that phone, don't you?"

"Uh—well, I knew you could use one, so we can keep in touch throughout the day."

"Calling each other isn't long distance."

Corey acted confused. "Long distance?"

"Don't try to look innocent. You told me I could call long distance, and I know you meant my folks."

Corey sat up straighter and turned toward Nick. "Wouldn't that be a great present for them to hear from you on Christmas? For them to know that you're okay?"

"A real miracle." Nick sighed, leaning his head on the back of the sofa and looking toward the ceiling.

"Yeah—a Christmas miracle," Corey said, with enough enthusiasm for both of them.

Nick rolled his head in Corey's direction. "Just so you know—if this doesn't go well, and I don't think it will, I'll probably be pretty depressed. I wouldn't want to ruin your Christmas night."

Corey squeezed Nick's hand. "I'm here for you either way—no matter what happens."

Nick looked back up at the ceiling. "Damn, I don't know." He looked back at Corey. "That part of my life is over. I love what I've found here."

"But they're your parents, and they need to at least know you're okay. And your wife too, despite how things ended between the two of you. And, I know you miss them." Corey gave Nick's hand another squeeze. "Don't start second-guessing yourself. You know you want to call. It's the right thing to do. *You* know it's the right thing to do."

Nick pulled Corey's hand to his chest and pressed it over his heart. "My heart's pounding."

"It'll be okay—you'll see."

"I really don't think they'll wanna hear from me after what I'm sure Melissa told them."

"Well, at least they'll know you're all right and you'll know you tried. If they don't want to talk to you again, that's their choice. If they do, well... they'll have your number, and if Melissa wants to serve you with divorce papers, she'll be able to call too to get that started. You can then move on with a clear conscience."

"Everything you say makes sense." Nick just sat there not attempting to dial the phone.

"Is the phone charged? Do you remember their number?" Corey asked, reaching for the phone on the end table and trying to encourage him. "Oh, wait, I should give you some privacy." He started to get off the sofa.

Nick grabbed Corey's arm. "No, you can stay—I want you to."

Corey settled back into the cushion, and when Nick still hadn't made a move to make the call, he tried to lighten the mood.

"I hope the phone isn't too complicated for you. Do you want me to dial the number?" he asked, snickering and making like he was grabbing for the phone.

"Very funny," Nick said, pulling it away. He looked at the phone for a moment longer and then finally began to punch in the numbers.

Corey hoped Nick's parents were home because he didn't know if Nick would ever get up the nerve to try again if they didn't answer. He wondered what a son would say to his mother after disappearing without a trace seven weeks ago. Surely his mom would welcome the call no matter what Nick's ex had said about him, wouldn't she? Well, Nick must not think so since he'd been so adamant about not getting in touch. But being the parents of a man like Nick, Corey just knew their hearts must be broken not knowing what had become of him. Nick was such a sensitive man, Corey knew he must feel terrible to think of his mother worrying and wondering. And he obviously did, seeing that he'd finally dialed the number.

After a few rings, Corey heard a woman's voice faintly saying 'Hello?'

"Mom?" Nick said quietly.

Corey heard the woman speak, but he couldn't make out her words, so he concentrated on Nick, watching his facial expression and body language. Right away Nick's eyes filled with tears.

"Yeah, Mom, it's me."

As the tears rolled down Nick's face, Corey heard a loud sob through the phone.

"I called to wish you a Merry Christmas, and to ask how everybody is, and to say that I'm fine and not to worry about me," Nick choked out.

Corey put his arm around Nick and gave him a little squeeze. He strained to catch a few words from Nick's mom. Nick reached up with his free hand and held on to Corey's fingers tightly.

"I guess Melissa told you what happened?" Nick asked, untangling his fingers from Corey's and covering his eyes, as he leaned forward.

Corey rubbed Nick's back, wishing he could hear what Nick's mom was saying. All he could tell for certain was that she was still crying.

"So, you know what happened between us then?" Nick asked.

Corey definitely heard Nick's mom ask where he was.

"Mom, I'm safe and well. That's all I wanted to tell you for now. Maybe I can call again, and we can talk more later on."

Her voice became louder, and Corey could hear her begging Nick not to hang up. Nick stayed quiet, listening and wiping tears off his face.

"Mom, it was so good to talk with you. I have to go now, but I'll call again, I promise. Just don't you worry about me because I'm getting my life on track and doing real well."

Corey couldn't hear what was said back.

"Merry Christmas, Mom. I'm so sorry," Nick said as he ended the call. He choked out a sob and covered his face with both hands, and when he regained his composure, he dropped his hands. Corey handed him his tea.

Nick wiped his eyes with the sleeve of his free arm. "Did you spike this?"

"No, but I can if you want. Looks like you could use some fortification." Corey felt relieved that Nick could still joke around after such an emotional scene.

They both took a drink. "Maybe later. I need to sit with this right now."

"Are you okay? What did she say?"

"Well, she was glad I called. You were right to get me to do that."

"Does she know everything?"

"She said that Melissa had told her and Dad."

"See, she still wanted to talk to you. What happened didn't change how she feels about you."

"Don't get ahead of yourself. Sure, she was glad I'm alive, but I really don't know how she feels about the whole thing. She's had almost two months to let this sink in—who knows what she'd have said if I'd have been around right after, and I have no idea what my dad thinks."

"Well, you'll find out more the next time you call, and if she was mad and wanted to disown you she'd have just hung up when she heard your voice."

"You might be right," Nick said.

"You gave her a real good Christmas." Corey took Nick's hand and held it tight. "I'm happy that you made the effort to make contact with your family. Or at least your mom. I know that wasn't easy."

Nick let out a long sigh. "I'm glad I did it."

"That's what counts. Now, shall we relax for a while and watch this movie?"

Corey sank into the couch and stretched his legs out to rest on the coffee table. He placed a pillow in his lap and tugged on Nick's arm, wordlessly inviting him to lie down, and he went readily. As they settled into the movie, Corey wondered if the day's events would catch up to Nick and he'd end up falling asleep, but that didn't happen. They remained fixated on the screen, laughing throughout the entire movie.

"Shall I make us more tea? Or are you wanting something stronger?" Corey asked as the credits started to roll and Nick sat up. "We could watch another movie, or—"

Nick's eyes lit up and his slow smile did things to Corey's heart, and farther below too.

"I like that *or* part," Nick said. "I think I'll skip the drink.

You're all I want right now."

Corey let out a small chuckle and licked his lips, liking where the end of their Christmas was headed.

This Christmas had been one heck of a first together, and Corey looked forward to many more firsts to come with his guy.

EPILOGUE

EIGHT MONTHS *later...*

What an exciting way to spend an August weekend, Nick mused, his back to the warm midday sun as he waited on the platform. A glance at his watch told him the Amtrak train was due at any moment.

"Getting antsy?" Corey asked from beside him.

Nick wasn't sure if the butterflies in his stomach were from his good-looking partner standing next to him—Corey looked like a movie star in his new sunglasses, sandstone canvas shirt, and straight-leg jeans—or the anticipation of stepping on to a train as a paying passenger, with a specific destination.

"Actually, I'm hoping the train gets here soon, so I don't decide to turn tail and run," Nick grumbled, adjusting the duffle bag on his shoulder.

Corey patted him on the back. "I can't wait to see Oregon. This is an adventure, for both of us, it'll be fun, you'll see."

"Well, life *has* been an adventure, especially after I met you." He gave Corey a brief look and an affectionate smile, and then he turned to stare at the train tracks.

He was nervous, but why should he be? It was his brother, after all, who had invited him and Corey to Klamath Falls to visit, because he wanted to "see his little brother and the guy who had become so important to him." That's what Richard had said, and

Nick needed to make this happen—to forge a relationship with at least one member of his family.

The rumble, and the vibrations felt underfoot from the approaching train, interrupted his thoughts. The waiting passengers put their books, newspapers, and phones away as they crowded toward the edge of the platform, bumping past Nick, who had to make a concerted effort to remain by Corey's side. Another wave of excitement grew inside him, giving him chills. The gentle wind from the passing cars washed over him as the squeal of brakes brought the train to a halt in front of them.

Passengers engulfed them momentarily then disappeared behind them. Once the train was cleared for them to board, Nick and Corey scrambled up the steps and were instructed to find seats near the front half of the car.

"You take the window seat," Nick said. "You'll want a good view of the scenery since you've never been to Oregon before."

"Thanks." Corey pushed his duffle bag underneath his chair as did Nick, who then let out a deep sigh as he sat down next to Corey, ready for their five-hour ride.

"Comfortable?" Corey asked.

Nick leaned in close and said in a low voice, "Well, I'll tell you this—the seating arrangement feels a heck of a lot better than what I had when I rolled into town." He couldn't smile—sometimes he couldn't believe what he'd done last November, hopping that freight train to ditch a life he couldn't possibly live in anymore.

"Hey, you're a law-abiding, paying customer now. Don't think about what happened before," Corey whispered. "It's all good now."

"You're always trying to make me feel better, aren't you?"

"Am I succeeding?"

Nick took Corey's hand and held it for just a second. "Yes, you are."

"Let's get a selfie of us," Corey said, bringing out his phone.

When they were pressed close enough together, and Corey was satisfied with what he saw in the frame, he took the picture. After that, they didn't wait long before the engineer blew the whistle and the train began moving slowly out of the station.

"I guess there's no turning back now," Nick said, looking out the window along with Corey while the train jerked and clicked along the track.

Corey's hair smelled fresh and clean, and he leaned in closer and took a deep breath. What an irresistible, kind man he'd ended up with. He'd found Corey easy to look at from the first time he'd seen him—he'd liked the sound of his voice too. But what had really gotten his attention back on that rainy November morning was when Corey had come out of the gym holding that insulated mug of hot coffee for him to drink on the way to the mission. He'd known right then and there that this was a guy who truly cared about others, and he'd proved that over and over during the months that had followed.

A train attendant pulled his attention back to the present as she walked up the aisle checking tickets and posting end-of-line stubs above their heads. She also pointed out where the food and drink car was located.

"This is really fun," Corey said after she'd walked away.

"Sure is," Nick said. He couldn't help but remember how he'd felt on that cold fall evening crammed in the cubby hole of the freight train, with the wind blasting him in the face. It almost felt like a lifetime ago. So much had happened since he'd jumped off that train.

Corey turned his head to look out the window again. "Hey, you need to look out here. We're starting onto the bridge that takes us over the Sacramento River." Nick scooted closer to see. "This is beautiful," Corey said in awe, taking pictures through the window.

"You're beautiful," Nick whispered, as he leaned against Corey's back, hooking his chin on to Corey's shoulder.

When the train was traveling along at a good clip, Nick sat back in his seat and rested his head on the headrest. The gentle rocking motion started to feel quite soothing to him.

"You want anything to eat?" Corey asked, patting Nick's knee, pulling him out of his mental cocoon.

"No, I'm fine for now. I think I'll just close my eyes for a few minutes and take a rest. It's gonna be a long day."

"I think I'll watch the scenery go by or read for a while. When we make it to Lake Shasta, I want to take some more pictures," Corey said, reaching into his duffle bag for his book.

"Reading will pass some time," Nick said sleepily.

"Recline the seat. I'll get the blanket out of my bag if you want."

"I don't need a blanket, but I'll lean back for a while."

Nick fiddled with the seat until it was in a restful position for him. He actually thought he might be able to fall asleep despite his emotional unease and the rattling sound of the train. Sleep didn't come though, because too many thoughts were banging around in his brain.

He shouldn't have gotten his hopes up that his mom would accept Richard's invitation to join them in Klamath Falls. She'd said it was too long a distance to travel from Hinkle—of course she'd been to Richard's twice since he'd moved there, so that was a lame excuse. Obviously, she just wasn't ready to come face to face with the reality that her youngest son was gay, and maybe she never would be, and if she wasn't—like Corey had told him—he'd have to accept that.

He thought about last February when he'd felt comfortable enough to tell his mom where he was living. He hadn't told her how he'd gotten there, a detail he figured wasn't important, but one detail he couldn't leave out was his boyfriend. At the mention of Corey's name, his comfort level flew out the window because she'd abruptly changed the subject and did so every time he'd tried to bring it up after that.

Those phone conversations with his mom had been—strange—especially after she'd asked if he was ready to come home to Melissa. After he'd gotten over the shock of her question, he'd tried to tell her that part of his life was over, and he had reminded her again why he'd left town. He recalled how frustrated he'd gotten when she hadn't wanted to hear any of that and seemed as if she couldn't comprehend what he was saying.

The tone of her voice left little doubt how hurt and disappointed she was. Probably more than Melissa, who he'd only spoken to once on the phone, and that was when she'd told him he'd hear from her lawyer. He'd tried to apologize to her during the call, but she sure hadn't made it easy. He got choked up even now thinking about her asking him if he remembered the day a week before their wedding when they'd carved their initials in the old oak tree by the church. He hadn't been himself that day she'd said and, in hindsight, she knew exactly why. He too remembered that day, especially the jagged little heart with the arrow through it that he'd added next to their initials and how he thought by doing so that he'd somehow love her forever—that his secret shame would somehow disappear with the carving.

As he'd held the phone clutched in his hand, he'd heard her tears building up on the other end of the line when she'd asked why he couldn't have just told her he wanted to call off the wedding. He'd had no answer for her—all he had done was apologize again, but she barely acknowledged she'd even heard him. He'd told her he wouldn't contest the divorce and that seemed to be what she'd been most interested in. When he'd heard from her lawyer a few weeks later by papers delivered from a courier, he signed them without hesitation, but not without deep sadness as well for all the pain and embarrassment he'd caused her.

Reliving all this made him give up on sleeping so he opened his eyes to see that Corey had his book open. Corey was so excited about their first trip together, calling this a vacation, even though it would be only for a couple days at his brother's place. It had been Corey's idea to take the train rather than driving, even though the trip would take about twice as long as it would have by car due to the tracks meandering around and through the mountains. Nick smiled to himself at how Corey's face had lit up when they'd agreed on the idea, and that's when Corey had said he'd never ridden on a train before.

He closed his eyes again and tried to rest since he hadn't been getting much sleep in general and hadn't gotten more than a few hours the night before.

When Richard had first called him back in February, he'd been shocked. *Awkward* was the perfect word to describe how that conversation had gone, but Richard had tried, and afterward they'd talked every couple of weeks, and with some work from both of them, they'd slowly formed a relationship to the point where Richard had extended this invitation.

Adjusting himself to get more comfortable, his mind wandered to his dad. When he'd finally called home last Christmas, the old man's silence hadn't been a shock. Nick's heart had hardened from all the years he'd cried rivers wishing he could be the kind of son his father wanted, but of course that had been impossible and still was. These days his mom's continuing excuses for the way his dad acted toward him hurt far worse. Uncle Ed and Katie, along with Corey, were his family now, and after this visit with Richard maybe he'd have his brother as part of his family too.

Opening his eyes once again, because he was becoming more and more restless, he stared up at the ceiling. Heck, his folks had never known him—the person he really was. They had some kind of ideal in their heads about who he should be, and he was so not like his brother. And because of that, they never did pay much attention to him. Maybe because there'd been so many years between him and his brother, maybe because Richard was the perfect son from the beginning, not a mistake like his conception had been. He really didn't know, but he knew in his heart he never made it easy for them either. He hadn't felt loved or understood by them, so he acted out in weird ways, but from Ed and Katie there was love and acceptance and for that he was grateful. It was easy to be open and honest with them.

Living in California was great in every way he could think of. He'd been working steadily and at jobs he really enjoyed. Far from being merely a house painter, he'd found his niche as a muralist, having just finished his largest mural to date on the outside wall of the new high school that had gone up on the edge of town. If he could paint a mural on the train's ceiling he imagined painting a winding train track heading for a tunnel... they hadn't passed through any so far, but there were a few on this route. Black and white would be a good color scheme, he thought. His treasured DVD on train-hopping from his teens was filmed in black and white—no color to distract. As he shifted in his seat once again, he tried to think up some clever names for the black and white paint— maybe Ebony Slate, Carbon Copy, or Dark Shadows for black— Mirage White or Dream Cloud for white. Corey would laugh at these crazy names, especially at Dream Cloud. He so loved to make Corey laugh. But life wasn't black and white, or good and bad—even if some people saw it that way. There's a thousand shades of gray...

His muscles twitched, and he realized he'd drifted off. He rubbed at his face and wondered what he'd been thinking about. Oh yeah, his art. He was sure proud of the work he'd done for Corey at the gym—he'd given that job his all. Corey offering him work was about the nicest thing anyone had ever done for him. Having the gym to escape to, away from that dump of a motel, was what he'd lived for those days and weeks. It was what he'd needed to fill up his mind with something other than what a screw up he'd become. And there was the added benefit of getting to spend time with the gyms' owner—he'd sure fallen hard and fast for Corey Preston.

He'd also become friends with a few people at the gym, and what he'd found funnier than hell was that Dean had turned out to be one of them! Now that Dean had a special someone in his life he wasn't nearly as annoying as he had been, and the four of them went out together now and then and had a really nice time.

He was so deep in thought that when Corey touched his forearm he jumped.

"Hey, you seem miles away."

"Just... thinking, I guess." Nick put his seat in to an upright position and then stretched the kinks out of his muscles.

"I probably don't have to ask about what." Corey stuck his book into his bag and turned his attention Nick's way.

"I was thinking about all sorts of things... not just what it will be like to see Richard."

"Are you still nervous?"

Before Nick could answer, the train entered a tunnel and the scenery outside the window abruptly disappeared and the car went dark.

"Woah, I wonder how long this tunnel is," Corey said as he pressed his face to the window.

They were through it in a matter of a minute, and soon after emerging a beautiful view of Lake Shasta appeared. Nick looked over Corey's shoulder at the scene.

"What a sight!" Corey exclaimed as he took several pictures with his phone. "This is just gorgeous."

After looking out the window at the lake for several more minutes, Corey sat back and checked the shots he'd taken.

"Looks like you got some pretty ones," Nick said, looking on as Corey scrolled by each picture.

"Well, a few of them have a glare or are sort of blurry, but some turned out pretty good." Corey held the phone up and said, "I bet you think I'm silly taking all these pictures."

"No way. I think it's cute, and besides, they look good enough to remember the trip by."

"Yeah." Corey gave him a boyish grin. "You'll probably want to take pictures at Richard's place?"

That took Nick by surprise. He hadn't thought about using his camera there, or anywhere else for that matter, but maybe he would if the visit went well. He sure hoped Richard wouldn't be uncomfortable around him and Corey. Sure, he seemed to accept the situation over the phone, but when the brother and the boyfriend were staring him in the face, what then? Nick leaned back in his seat and let out a long sigh.

"You all right?" Corey asked, putting the phone in his shirt pocket.

"Yeah, I'm fine. My nerves are just kicking in again."

"It's natural to be nervous, but you wait and see, we're going to have a real good time. Your brother wouldn't have invited us if he didn't want us there."

"I'm sure you're right." Nick rolled his head to look at Corey. "You wanna have lunch now?"

"That sounds great. I hear they have pizza."

"Sounds like a winner."

Nick stood up, stretched, and headed down the aisle in search of food with Corey right on his heels.

"Feels good to walk a little. I'm taking a side trip to the bathroom," Corey said, as he headed down the stairs to the lower level of their car.

"That sounds like a good idea. I'm right behind you."

Once in the café car, they decided on pepperoni pizza and Cokes. "This isn't half bad," Corey said as they sat down with their food. "I don't know why I've never traveled by train before."

Nick saw right away what Corey had said had him looking uncomfortable, and he knew why. He forced a smile.

"Hey, don't feel bad—I love trains myself—maybe not quite as much as I used to, but yeah, they're a great way to travel, at least this time around. Maybe some time we can go on a longer trip, maybe all the way up to Seattle—stay in a sleeper car, the whole bit."

Corey waggled his eyebrows. "I like the sound of that."

"Good, we'll do it then." Nick took a bite of pizza, chewed and swallowed. "This is good, for train food."

"Yeah, I wasn't sure what to expect. It tastes fine." Corey washed down a mouthful of pizza with a drink of Coke. "Hey, let me get a picture of you." He wiped his hands on a napkin and took out his phone. "Hold up a slice."

Nick smiled, and after Corey got his picture, he put the phone down and took a huge bite of pizza.

"We'll be having supper with Richard this evening," Nick said, staring out the window at the scenery rushing by.

"I, for one, am looking forward to it."

Nick liked how carefree and confident Corey sounded—like nothing in the world could go wrong. This was all so new for himself—putting his newly founded life out there for his brother to see—the changed man he was. He pushed the rest of his pizza aside.

"Does Richard know how to cook as good as you do?"

"As good as me? Well, maybe not quite as good," Nick bragged. "Don't tell him I said that, though." He wiped his mouth with a napkin. "Our mom taught us both how to cook so we'd be able to fend for ourselves in case we didn't have wives. I guess she knew what she was doing since now both of us are divorced."

"Well, I'm reaping the benefits of how well she taught you," Corey said as he patted his stomach.

"Nut." Nick smiled and drank the last of his Coke. "I hope he's not gonna go to a lot of trouble. I told him not to."

"Don't worry about it. We can go out to eat most of the time." Corey finished his Coke too and scrunched up his napkins.

"You ready to head back to our seats, or do you want to stay in here a while longer?" Nick asked.

"Let's go back. The scenery is just too pretty to miss. It's nothing but a blur from here. You can sit by the window if you want."

"No, you go ahead and stay there. You'll want pictures of Mount Shasta. I can see well enough from my seat."

After settling in again, it wasn't long before Mt. Shasta came into view, so Corey got out his phone again and began taking more pictures. Nick loved seeing him enjoy himself so much.

Once the picture taking was done, Nick reclined once more and closed his eyes, telling himself that it didn't really matter what happened at Richard's because he had Corey and their life back home. That was more than he'd ever dreamed he'd have, especially last fall when the shit had hit the fan, and he had no idea where he'd end up and what would become of him. Lunch had made him sleepy, and he felt himself drifting off for real this time.

The next thing he knew Corey was gently shaking his shoulder. "Hey, it's time to wake up."

Nick opened his eyes to compassionate brown eyes, ones he'd come to love. For an instant, he was back sitting next to the dumpster looking at them for the first time—but this time he was warm and dry, not cold and wet to the bone as he had been then. Stretching, he noticed the travel blanket that covered him—the one Corey had packed. That brought a smile to his face, and then to Corey's too.

"You were sleeping so soundly, I wondered if you'd wake up by the time we crossed into Oregon," Corey said, softly chuckling.

"Damn, how long was I out for?"

"Over an hour."

"Wow." Nick raised his seat and sat up straight, taking off the blanket and folding it. Corey helped, and when they had a small square, he stuffed it into his duffle bag.

"So, we're getting close to Oregon then?"

"Yeah, it won't be long now. That's why I woke you."

Nick smoothed out his shirt and ran his fingers through his hair. "I'll bet I look rumpled."

"No, you look great. Do you want a drink of water?" Corey handed him half a bottle.

"I can't believe I slept that long." Nick took the water and drank most of it down. "I'm gonna make a quick trip to the bathroom."

After using the toilet, Nick washed his hands and wet his face with a splash of cold water, which did wonders to make him feel more alert. Not only did he feel more energized, he realized at that moment, his nervousness had turned to excitement. He really was excited to see Richard and to introduce him to Corey. He left the bathroom and headed back up the stairs and down the aisle back to his seat, where he found Corey looking as wide awake and ready to go as when they'd boarded the train.

"You feel better now?"

"Do I look better?"

"You always look good."

"Thanks," Nick said, winking as he sat down. He took a stick of gum that Corey offered and unwrapped it and put it in his mouth. They sat quietly for the last twenty minutes of the journey.

Nick wasn't sure how he felt about being back in Oregon again. Even though Klamath Falls was well over four hundred miles from his hometown, he had mixed emotions about being back in the state where he'd lived his whole life and had left so abruptly.

Just then, the conductor announced the arrival into Klamath Falls. Several passengers around them started to gather their belongings looking eager to be off, so Nick pulled his duffle bag out from under his chair and Corey did the same. As they waited the time seemed to drag. Nick kept glancing out the window expecting everything to be still, but the train kept moving along despite the banging and groaning sounds as the brakes were applied.

He wondered if Richard was as anxious and excited as he was. Surely, he was waiting for them, but what if he wasn't there? Maybe he had changed his mind and hadn't come. Nick didn't think of what that would mean for him, but more about how disappointed Corey would be. But that was stupid—of course Richard would be there.

He took some deep breaths to relax and then felt Corey's calming touch up and down his back. Of course, Corey had noticed his anxiety and was trying to help him through. Corey was always there for him, had been from that first day.

When the train finally came to a complete stop, they stood up, shouldered their bags, and stepped in line behind the other passengers who were making their way down the aisle to the stairs. Nick's heart was racing, and his fingers were hurting from gripping the strap of his duffle bag so tightly. He wiped perspiration from his forehead. When he got close enough to see the light coming in through the door he wasn't sure if he was anxious to leave the train, or if he wished the line would stop moving along. Corey's hand on his arm right then made him feel like half of his worries had lifted.

Nick stopped at the top of the steps and glanced at the people standing on the platform, but none of them was Richard.

From behind him, Corey took a deep breath. "Nice, fresh air. So far, I like Oregon."

Nick took in a breath as well and looked up at the bright blue sky with big, white billowy clouds.

"Do you see your brother?"

Nick looked back at the platform and then over near the station, and he finally saw Richard step from behind a small group of people.

"There he is," he said, motioning with his head in Richard's direction. "The guy in the black shirt."

"No kidding? He doesn't look a thing like you."

"We take after different sides of the family, and with him being ten years older than me there's never been much of a resemblance."

Just then, Richard looked toward the train and Nick could tell they'd been spotted when Richard's eyes brightened, and a huge smile spread across his face.

That look went a long way to reassure him that coming here was the right thing. He moved swiftly down the steps with Corey right behind.

They stopped a couple feet from one another and Richard didn't wait for introductions, he just grabbed Nick into a big hug saying, "I've sure missed you." And after he let him go he hugged Corey too. "Thanks for coming, Corey. And for taking care of my little brother."

Nick then made formal introductions, and after that, Richard grabbed Nick's bag and threw his free arm around his shoulder.

Corey got his phone out and promptly snapped a few pictures of the Sanders brothers who posed, smiling happily. "Just one more.

I want a close-up."

When Corey finished, Richard chuckled, and Corey did too. Nick snatched the phone from Corey's hand and looked at the pictures, wondering why the two of them looked like they were sharing a private joke. On the close-up picture, Richard had held up two fingers behind Nick's head.

"You let him ruin my picture?" Nick whined, acting like he was upset. "Thanks a lot, guys." He handed the phone back to Corey and pretended to pout.

"You look great, don't worry," Corey giggled.

"You two are probably hungry, hot, and tired, so come on and I'll feed you," Richard said. "I make a mean chili, Corey." He turned to Nick, "Did you tell him what a great cook I am?"

Corey barked out a laugh, and Nick shot him a look.

"I don't want you going to too much trouble, Richard."

"I didn't, just a little." Richard laughed, grabbing Nick by the neck and turning him toward the parking lot.

Nick walked between his brother and Corey feeling like he was as high as one of the clouds up above. He breathed in the fresh air and leaned toward Corey whispering, "The world is here for us, let's go discover it. Never underestimate the power of two."

About the Author

Born and raised in California, Leigh Vining has been creating stories in her head for as long as she can remember. Always drawn to male friendships, she believes that loving who you love should never be something to be ashamed of.

She and her husband are stray cat magnets and they share their home with a houseful of rescues. Leigh believes that cats are great companions for people who sit at their desks for long periods of time. A lap full of purring cat has kept her company many a night while agonizing over every typed word.

Her muse often goes into overdrive while working out at the gym. She finds that breaking up the day with physical activity is good for your muscles, including the creative ones.

Her favorite ways to relax are baking sweet desserts, taking long walks, and watching baseball on TV.

Follow her at leighvining56 on Instagram.

www.ingramcontent.com/pod-product-compliance
Lightning Source LLC
Chambersburg PA
CBHW071747190726
48292CB00003B/900